FALSE OATH

A NATE SHEPHERD NOVEL

MICHAEL STAGG

False Oath

A Nate Shepherd Novel

Copyright © 2021 Michael Stagg

All rights reserved.

All characters in this book are fictitious. Any resemblance to an actual person, living or dead, is purely coincidental.

For more information about Michael Stagg and his other books, go to michaelstagg.com

Want a free short story about Nate Shepherd's start as a new lawyer? Hint: It didn't go well.

Sign up for the Michael Stagg newsletter here or at https://michaelstagg.com/newsletter/

SNAP

1

They arrested Colt Daniels on the football field, right as his brother scored a touchdown. Colt was standing by the north end zone, pumping his fist into the air, when Detective Mitch Pearson grabbed that upraised fist, put it behind Colt's back, and cuffed him.

Colt's brother saw it happen. Tyler Daniels stopped in the end zone, dropped the ball, and stood there for a moment before his teammates mobbed him.

Our crowd was going crazy from the score. Nobody seemed to notice what was actually happening, which gave me a chance to hustle down the stairs and beat everyone out of the stands.

As I jogged along the fence, I caught a glimpse of my brother Tom on the sideline, flinging his head set and running down the field toward the boys. A second later, I saw Tyler push his way free of his teammates and run to the back corner of the end zone until two police officers blocked his way, separating him from his brother and keeping him corralled on the field. Then the Carrefour North crowd went quiet as Colt Daniels, brother of star quarterback Tyler Daniels, was escorted off the field in handcuffs.

I felt a flash of anger. A week before, Colt and Tyler Daniels had lost their father. I couldn't imagine what Colt was being arrested for now, but it wasn't right to do it here, not after what the two of them had been through.

Later, we would realize how much worse things could get.

2

My brother Tom was waiting for me outside the visitors' locker room. He was easy to spot, dressed in his black and red coaching gear and waving one hand over his head. As I jogged over, Tom turned to two assistant coaches and said something. The assistants nodded and hustled into the locker room with the team.

My older brother tapped his leg with a rolled-up play sheet. Tom Shepherd always had a jutting jaw and intense eyes, but right now he looked ready to chew glass.

"Pearson arrested him," he said.

"I saw. Did you hear what it was about?"

Tom shook his head. "I was keeping the kids back. Especially Tyler."

"I bet. Nothing at all?"

"I asked Pearson where he was taking Colt. He just said into custody." Tom chomped at his gum. "Figures Pearson would pull a stunt right as we take the lead."

I should explain that my brother is the head football coach for Carrefour North High School and so has a tendency to view everything through pigskin glasses. Although, to be fair to Tom in this particular case, the arresting officer Mitch Pearson had played for the other team, Carrefour South, back in the day and he did just arrest the brother of Tom's star player on the field during the game. Then Tom surprised me when he focused on a non-football issue and said, "Can you help Colt?"

"Of course."

"What those boys have been through," Tom shook his head, "it's not right, Nate."

"I'm on it."

And just that quickly, I could see Tom's attention for me was gone. He looked at the scoreboard, looked at me without really meeting my eyes, and I could almost hear the gears turning as he shifted back to the game. Honestly, I was amazed I'd kept his attention that long.

"The defensive end is giving the tight end a free release," I said. "Put him on the ground and he won't be able to get out into that drag route in time."

Tom gave me a tight smile, hit my shoulder with his rolled-up play sheet, and strode into the locker room.

I pushed through the throngs of fans seeking hot coffees and warm pretzels and headed to the parking lot.

I hustled off to the Carrefour police station.

CARREFOUR IS a small city that sits on the Michigan-Ohio border with the northern third of town in Michigan and the southern two-thirds in Ohio. This creates a rivalry in all of Carrefour's systems, ranging from politics to business to high school sports like the Carrefour North versus Carrefour South football game that had just been interrupted. Since the game was being played at South this year, that meant I was in Ohio and that law enforcement was handled by the Carrefour Ohio Police Department. And the Carrefour Ohio Police Department meant that I was dealing with the Chief Detective in Charge of Serious Crimes for Carrefour, Ohio, Mitch Pearson.

Pearson came out to see me right away. He was tall, blonde, and wore a suit that was tailored just a little too tight. He looked as happy to see me as I was to see him, which wasn't surprising given our history which I won't bore you with right now.

"What kind of a stunt was that?" I said.

He raised his pale eyebrows. "Nice to see you too, Shepherd. What do you mean?"

"In the middle of the football game? On the field?"

Pearson shrugged. "The arrest warrant came through our system. I knew where he was."

"And you couldn't wait until it was over?"

Pearson shook his head. "Not for something like this."

"What? Outstanding parking tickets? Minor in possession?"

Pearson didn't say anything. Instead, he handed me a piece of paper.

It was an arrest warrant issued by Ash County, Michigan for the murder of Brett Daniels. Colt's father.

"It didn't seem appropriate to wait," said Pearson.

"This has to be a joke," I said.

"Does it?"

I stared at the paper. "It doesn't make sense."

"Isn't Sheriff Dushane a friend of yours?"

"Yes," I said before I realized it.

"Then you should take it up with him. His office put the warrant into the system. I'm just the messenger."

I couldn't take my eyes off *murder of Brett Daniels*. I was having trouble wrapping my head around it, but it would never do to work things out standing there in front of Pearson, so I held the paper up. "May I?"

Pearson nodded. "Keep it."

"I need to see him."

Pearson stared. "Are you his lawyer?"

"Yes."

"He didn't ask for you."

"Really? The twenty-year-old kid didn't know exactly how to exercise his Miranda rights? I'm shocked."

"We read them to him."

I looked at the clock. "It's 9:52."

Pearson glanced over. "So?"

"So any information obtained after this moment while his lawyer is sitting in your lobby is going to get tossed."

Pearson smiled. "Does that really work out in the sticks?"

"It works everywhere."

Pearson stared a moment longer before he shrugged. "It'll be a little while before we finish processing him. Have a seat. I'll call you when we're done."

Pearson didn't wait to see if I did it before he turned and left.

I took my choice of seats among the pastel plastic chairs. Only one other seat was occupied, which I figured would change as this Friday night wore on. I knew it would be a little while before Pearson let me see Colt, so I pulled out my phone, scrolled through my numbers, and called Sheriff Warren Dushane.

"I take it you've heard," said Sheriff Dushane as he answered.

"It would be hard not to. They arrested Colt right on the field."

"On the field?"

"Technically, it was on the sideline. You know, where his brother was playing."

There was silence, then, "I didn't issue the warrant until six. I thought they'd pick him up at home. Who executed it?"

"Pearson."

"I suppose that explains it."

There was silence on both ends of the line before I said, "Are you the investigating officer?"

"My office. With help from others. Are you the lawyer?"

"For tonight anyway. Until we get to the bottom of this."

There was another pause before Sheriff Dushane said, "We have gotten to the bottom of this, Nate. That's why I issued a warrant."

"You and I just went down this road, Sheriff. Not more than a week ago."

"That doesn't change what happened here."

"Are you sure?"

"Nate, I coached the Daniels boys."

I heard what Sheriff Dushane said, and I heard what he wasn't saying—that he would never issue a warrant against one of the kids he'd coached unless he was damn sure that kid had done it. "You're saying Colt murdered his father?"

"I am."

"I guess I'll be talking to you in a few days."

"I'm sure you will." There was one more pause before Sheriff Dushane said, "Did we win?"

"North was up two at halftime. I had to leave before the game was over."

"That's something then. Good night, Nate."

We hung up.

The thing was, I knew Sheriff Dushane well enough to know how he'd approach this. He must have something, or more likely a lot of somethings, to hang on Colt for his dad's death.

I couldn't imagine what they were.

I pulled up Twitter and scrolled through a couple of accounts that were tweeting updates on the game. Colt's brother Tyler had thrown for two more touchdowns and North was up by nine with a quarter to play.

"Shepherd."

I looked up. Pearson stood in the doorway.

"The murderer will see you now."

3

Colt sprang to his feet as soon as I walked into the room. "Mr. Shepherd, what the hell? I told these assholes—"

I held up a hand. "Colt. Wait."

Colt looked confused, but he stopped. I turned to Pearson. "I'd like to talk to my client now."

Pearson smiled from where he stood, leaning on the open door. "Go ahead."

"Goodbye."

Pearson shrugged, reached in, and pulled the door shut.

I turned back to Colt. He looked confused, and I didn't blame him one bit. Colt was a little over six feet tall with a low brow and hair so thick that it added a couple of more inches. He had dark eyebrows and a strong jaw, and the harsh fluorescent light made his high cheekbones seem like gashes. He looked back and forth between me and the door. "Mr. Shepherd, what's going on?"

I pointed at the chair. He sat.

"First, call me Nate. Second, do you want to hire me as your lawyer?"

Colt scowled. "What do you mean?"

"I mean, do you want me to be your lawyer?"

"Do I need one?"

"Yes."

"I don't have much money."

I thought. "What you have is enough."

"Then yes."

"Good. They're accusing you of murder."

Colt jerked. "What?"

"They say you killed your dad."

I watched the emotions play over Colt's face. There was surprise and then confusion as that already low brow of his furrowed into a deep scowl. Then he cursed. I had to say for a twenty-year-old, he put together a pretty impressive string. When he stopped, there was genuine anger in his face as he said, "Even now he's screwing me."

"What do you mean?"

"What do you think I mean? I didn't kill him and he's done something that makes the sheriff think I have." He swore again. "We just buried the prick. Can't Tyler and I have even one second without him messing..." He took a deep breath, looked at the ceiling, and clenched his jaw. I gave him some time.

After a moment, Colt said, "How's Tyler?"

I shook my head. "I came right here."

"He can't let this distract him. The playoffs start next week."

"Colt, that's hardly a concern."

"It is for Tyler. And for me."

"Let Tyler worry about football. Our first concern is getting you out of here."

"He has to stay focused."

"So do you."

Colt looked unconvinced, but he nodded. "So what do we do?"

"First, you don't talk to anyone, ever, about this. No one in here, no officers, nobody."

Colt nodded. "Easy enough."

"And that means no one in your family. You don't talk to your mother or your brother or anyone else."

Colt cocked his head. "Why not?"

"Because none of that is protected. Anything you say to anyone else can be brought up in court."

"But I didn't do anything."

"That doesn't matter." I thought for a moment. "You were a good quarterback, right?"

Colt shrugged.

"You wouldn't tell the defense the play before the snap, would you?"

"Of course not."

"It's the same thing here except instead of a sack, you could give up a murder conviction. Don't talk."

Colt nodded. "Got it."

It seemed like he did, so I moved on. "Second, we're going to get you out of here, but it's going to take some time."

"Why? Can't I just pay some money or something?"

"You've been arrested in Ohio. You're going to stand trial in Michigan. They have to do something called extradition, which basically means that one state turns you over to the other. Since we're a border town, we're used to it, but it will take a couple of days to work through the process. Which brings me back to point number one—don't say anything while you're in here."

"Silence, got it. What happened to your eye?"

"My eye?"

Colt made a circle motion around one of his eyes. "You seem a little old to be getting into fights. No offense."

It had been a week, but the residual evidence of my discussion with Cade Brickson as to whether he should enter the house of Elias Timmons was still fading from black to green. "Sometimes these things come up, no matter how old you are."

Colt grinned. "Yes, they do."

"So last thing, I'm sorry for asking, but how did your dad die?"

Colt raised both eyebrows. "You don't know?"

"I don't."

"It was all over the news."

"I've been in trial. I haven't seen the news."

Colt shrugged. "Tyler found him at the back of our property. It was some kind of hunting accident. At least that's what they told us."

"They weren't sure?"

"It was...messy." Colt got a look on his face then, and I wasn't at all sure what it meant. "Apparently the coyotes had gotten to him."

There was a buzz at the door, and the guard walked in. "We have to get him locked in for the night."

I nodded and stood. "Remember what I said."

"You too," said Colt. "Tyler has other things to worry about."

I nodded, and the guard came in and took Colt by the arm. Colt yanked his arm away and walked out, angry.

I didn't blame him.

4

I was making my way out through the lobby of the police station when a woman leapt from a chair and said, "Nate Shepherd?"

The woman looked like she was in her mid-forties, although her blonde hair was long and styled like someone younger. She was wearing a Carrefour North Panthers jersey with a couple of hooded sweatshirts sticking out from underneath, along with gloves, jeans, and hiking boots. The jersey had a "9" on the front and I was pretty sure whose name was on the back.

"Mrs. Daniels?" I said.

"I'm Rhonda," she said. "But it's Mazur now. When can I see my son?"

I glanced over to where the duty officer was looking down at his computer screen as if he were diligently typing and not listening to anything at all. "Let's go outside."

"But I want to see—"

"We need to go outside, Rhonda."

"I am not going outside while my son—"

A man I hadn't noticed stepped forward. He was bundled in a black and red Carrefour North coat and wore a black stocking cap with a red panther on the front. I couldn't tell much about him under all the layers except that he sported a fierce red beard. "Rhonda," he said in a voice that was far deeper and raspier than one would expect. "We need to listen to him."

Rhonda Mazur looked over my shoulder toward the holding cells, then looked at me and at the man next to her. Finally, she said, "We're not leaving."

I nodded. "Not yet. We just need to talk where it's private."

She nodded and the three of us went out into the cold November night.

As the blast of cold air hit me, I realized I had never really warmed up from the game. I pulled out a North stocking cap of my own and pointed. "Are you in the parking lot?"

The man nodded. "The silver F150 over there."

I extended my hand. "Nate Shepherd. Lawyer."

He took it. "Rob Preston," the man's voice got even deeper. "Boyfriend."

"What about my son?" said Rhonda.

"Let's go over by your truck."

Rob and I started walking and Rhonda stayed put. "Someone needs to tell me what's going on!"

"I will. But I'm not going to do it in front of the police."

I didn't wait and, after hesitating, the two followed me to Rob's silver truck. When we got there, Rhonda crowded close enough for me to smell cigarette smoke and schnapps. "Coach Shepherd said that you would get things sorted out. What's going on?"

I looked at Rob. "Do you want Rob to be part of this discussion?"

"I can go back inside if you want," said Rob.

"Oh, stop it, you know I'm just gonna tell you everything anyway." She hit me with a mittened fist in the chest. "Spill, Shepherd."

"Your son has been arrested for murder."

Rhonda Mazur stared. She didn't blink, she didn't twitch, she stared. "What?"

"Colt's been accused of murdering your husband."

"Ex-husband," she said in a way that was clearly automatic. "But Brett had an accident."

"I've seen the warrant. They're arresting Colt for Brett's murder."

"But no one killed him!"

"The Ash County Sheriff thinks otherwise. Which means we're not getting Colt out tonight."

Rhonda Mazur wobbled for a moment and I leaned forward, afraid she was collapsing. She wasn't. She was gathering herself to explode.

"That miserable son of a bitch! Not enough to try and control everything while he was here, he's got to screw us all on his way out the door!"

"Rhonda, honey—" said Rob.

"—Don't 'Rhonda' me, Rob. We're finally free of that miserable POS and he still reaches out to ruin our son's life!"

Rob rubbed her back with one hand. "We can curse Brett later. Right now, we have to concentrate on helping Colt."

Her son's name seemed to cut through Rhonda's anger. "Can you get him out?"

"Not for a couple of days."

"Why so long?"

"He's been arrested in Ohio. There's a process to get him back to Michigan for trial. Once we do that, we can see about posting bond."

Rhonda looked from Rob to me. "A couple of days to get him back to Michigan? We're literally fifteen minutes from the line."

"Legal roads aren't measured in miles." That sounded like jerk lawyer talk as soon as I said it. I quickly followed with,

"There are some state jurisdiction things we have to work through."

"But you'll do it? Work through it?"

"I will. I need some information, though. When did your ex-husband die?"

"Last week. They found him on Friday night."

"Found him?"

"On his property. Out on M-339."

"Who found him?"

"Tyler."

"What had happened to him?"

"I don't know. I didn't really care. The boys told me that the sheriff told them that it was a hunting accident."

I did the math. "When was the funeral?"

"Yesterday."

"What were people saying at the funeral?"

Rhonda Mazur looked at me, her eyes intense. "I don't know. I didn't go."

"We did spend a lot of time with the boys though," said Rob. "They seemed to be having a tough time with it."

I thought about Colt's reaction when I had talked to him a little while ago. Grief hadn't seemed high on his list. "What kind of hunting accident?"

"It sounded like he had some trouble on his hunting platform or tree stand or whatever he uses and then collapsed on the way back to the house. I don't really know much more than that."

"Did they do an autopsy?"

Rhonda shook her head. "I didn't care how he died, Shepherd. I was just glad the bastard was out of my life." She looked back at Rob. "I need a smoke."

Rob nodded. "And we need to go check on Tyler."

Rhonda turned back to me. "There's no way Colt could've done it. Whatever 'it' is."

"I'll find out."

She grabbed my arm. "Do you mean it?"

"Yes."

"Then get after it."

"Sure. Right." I started to leave, then remembered and said, "How'd we do, by the way?"

Rhonda grinned. "Tyler had five touchdowns."

I nodded. "How about the team?"

Rob gave a thumbs up. "Won by twelve."

"Screw South!" yelled Rhonda at the streetlight.

There was nothing to argue with there, so I bumped Rhonda's offered fist, shook Rob's hand, and went back to my Jeep. I stomped a couple of times to get some circulation back and then hopped in and cranked the heater up.

I thought about heading home, then decided to go to my brother Tom's house instead.

5

Twenty minutes later, I was pulling into the driveway of a neat brick ranch house in an old neighborhood. By the time I reached the door, my sister-in-law Kate was opening it. "Nate, come in, come in."

"Hi Kate," I said, and gave her a hug. I had no sooner stepped into the living room than my youngest niece, Page, came barreling around the corner for a leg hug. "Uncle Nate!"

"Hey, troll," I said and picked her up. "What are you still doing up?"

"We had pizza!"

"Outstanding! Did you save me some?"

"No way!"

"Not even a little?"

She closed her eyes and shook her head hard enough to make her braids flare out like a mini-pizza-eating-helicopter.

I sighed. "I guess I'll just go to bed hungry then."

Page opened one eye. "Daddy might have some."

"Hmm. Should I check?"

She nodded.

I set her down. "I'll ask your mom if that's okay."

"Of course it's okay," said Page, and then she ran down the hall.

My sister-in-law smiled. "I shouldn't have said yes to the Pepsi."

I smiled back. "I'm sure she'll settle down in a couple of hours."

Kate's smile became strained. "Probably."

"Where are the rest of the kids?"

"Charlie's in bed, Taylor's doing a virtual something or other, and Reed," she looked at her phone, "has another half hour until curfew."

I shook my head. "I always forget that she's in high school already. She out and about?"

Kate nodded. "A bonfire. I worry."

"Don't. I'm sure she'll behave just like you did."

"Is that supposed to reassure me?"

"No. It's supposed to amuse me."

"Hope you enjoyed it." Kate's smile disappeared completely. "Did you see Colt?"

"I did."

"What was that all about? There were some terrible rumors going around the stands."

"Like what?"

"Like that it was related to his dad's death."

"It was."

Kate's eyes widened. "Really?"

"Really. Is Tommy around? I need to talk to him about it."

"Sure. He's in the garage breaking down game film."

"Would you mind joining us? I need as much info as you all have."

"Sure. Just give me a moment to get the kids settled. There's beer in the fridge."

"Thanks."

I walked through the living room to the kitchen, made a stop at the fridge, and walked out to the garage where my brother was hard at work.

When you're a schoolteacher, a high school football coach, and the father of four living in a one-story brick ranch house, you find workspace where you can. My brother Tom had turned his garage into a football viewing room. He'd mounted a big screen on the back wall over a long counter top that was stacked with equipment for watching games on every medium imaginable, from disc to drive to cloud. Tom was sitting at a long table in the middle of the garage with a computer and monitor on one side and two open, loose-leaf notebooks on the other, notebooks which looked just like the binders that filled the bookshelf on the far wall. I knew from experience that the table could be cleared and the equipment stowed so that the room could be converted for a group to watch the Spartans or the Lions or whoever was playing on Monday night because that was, you know, very important for research purposes.

Tom didn't look up when I entered. My older brother looked intent, which was pretty much a constant state with him. He was still in his North gear, the leaping red panther in stark relief on his black jacket. His blond hair was cut short enough that it was within a clipper attachment of a buzz. His face was lean and, even though he was almost forty, he looked like he could still run with his players, which wasn't a coincidence because it was true. He was clicking a mouse, making the game on the screen go back and forth as a ball dropped over the shoulder of a North defensive back into the arms of a South receiver for a touchdown.

"Were you in man coverage?" I said.

"Zone," said Tom. "The receiver never should have gotten behind him."

I waited. Tom clicked back and forth two more times

before he paused, made a note in his binder, and stopped. "Sorry," he said. "I have to get this graded by tomorrow morning."

I waved him off. "Congratulations."

Tom frowned. "We'll have to do better if we want to get past regionals. How's Colt?"

"He's been better."

"Did you find out what's going on?"

I nodded. "Let's wait for Kate though, I need to talk to you both."

Tom's eyes twitched to the screen, but he nodded.

"I won't take long," I said, knowing the clock that was counting down in Tom's head.

"No problem. "

He held out a pizza box and I wasn't too proud to take a couple of slices that sported a banana pepper topping. I took a bite and pulled off a stretch of cheese before I said, "The kids played hard."

Tom shrugged. "We let South get back in it in the second half."

"Ebbs and flows."

"We need more ebb. Less flow."

Kate came in then, which was just as well because that wasn't an argument I was going to win.

"Sorry," she said. "I really can't give Page Pepsi that late again." She sat on a chair by the wall. "So. Colt."

I nodded. "Colt's been arrested for murdering his father."

My sister-in-law Kate is about as placid a woman as I knew. Judging from the look on her face, though, if she hadn't been sitting, she would've plunked down into her chair. "You're kidding."

"I'm not."

"But we were all just at the funeral yesterday."

"I saw the warrant myself, Kate. It came from Sheriff Dushane."

Her eyes grew big. "He was at the funeral too!"

"He's known the boys for a long time," said Tom.

"Still," said Kate. "I'd expect better of Warren. We all know Colt couldn't have done that."

I looked at my brother. Where Kate seemed shocked, Tom seemed thoughtful. "You don't look surprised," I said.

"I am," said Tom.

"But?"

Tom appeared to think. "So Pearson wasn't just messing with my quarterback?"

I shook my head. "Dushane issued the warrant right before the game. He was planning on executing it later tonight, but Pearson saw it come over the wire." I took another bite of pizza and washed it down. "Colt didn't seem upset. About the charge I mean."

Tom nodded. "Colt is one of the toughest players I've ever had."

"It wasn't just that he was stoic. He seemed mad at his dad. So did his mom."

Tom raised an eyebrow. "You've seen Rhonda already?"

"At the jail. It seemed like she'd been drinking."

Tom pressed his lips together. "A bunch of the parents treat the high school game like a college tailgate. We've tried to stop it but..." He shrugged.

"She seemed almost as angry as Colt."

Kate nodded. "Their divorce wasn't pretty."

"How long ago was that?"

Tom thought. "I want to say Colt was a freshman or sophomore when it happened. Five years ago maybe."

"Colt seemed angrier than that."

"Brett was a little tough on the boys, but they still lived with him even though their mom left."

Kate had seemed to regain her usual calm, and she shook her head as she said, "Brett Daniels was an overbearing jerk, but those boys always did everything he asked. It doesn't make sense that Colt would kill him."

I grabbed another piece of pizza. "You know I've been preoccupied with the Archie Mack trial so I really don't know what's been going on. How did Brett Daniels die?"

"We don't know much," said Tom. "We traveled to Jackson to play Northwest that Friday night. Brett always made a point of meeting Tyler when he came off the field, but he didn't that night. Tyler looked around for a little while, but when Brett didn't show, he went into the locker room and we left. Brett wasn't at the high school when the bus got back either. From what I hear, Tyler went home and found Brett's body out back."

Kate shook her head. "I heard Tyler called the ambulance, but Brett was long dead. The casket was closed. One of the moms heard that something got to the body."

"What do you mean?" I asked.

"She said that the body had been chewed on enough that an open casket wasn't going to happen." Kate looked at Tom. "But you know Marilyn."

Tom nodded.

"I keep hearing it was a hunting accident," I said. "Do you have any idea what it was?"

Kate and Tom looked at each other before both shook their heads. "All we heard is that his body was found somewhere between his hunting stand and his house," said Kate.

I thought. "Where was Colt in all this?"

Kate shook her head. "I really don't know. But those two boys seemed pretty broken up after the funeral. It's no easy thing to bury your father."

Tommy and I each reached out at the same time and

knocked on the wooden table. Tommy's knock turned into a finger drum and he glanced at his video screen with the picture of the ball dropping into the receiver's arms. I stood. "I'm sorry, I'll let you go."

"No, I appreciate you looking after Colt," said Tom.

"When do you hear who you have in the first round?"

"Sunday afternoon."

"I'll keep an eye out."

Tom's eyes were back on the screen before I'd taken two steps. Kate walked me to the front door.

"I just don't think he could've done it, Nate."

"We'll see, Kate. I'm concerned. Sheriff Dushane wouldn't bring charges without good reason."

"You've beaten him before though, haven't you?"

"I'm never against Sheriff Dushane, Kate. And the last case I had that he was involved in was very different. Sorry to be here so late."

"Don't be. I'll be up until Reed gets home. The company was a nice distraction."

"When is she due?"

"Ten minutes ago.

"I think I'll get out of here before I catch any shrapnel."

Kate smiled. "Don't worry. My strikes are very precise."

"Yikes. Thanks, Kate."

She gave me a quick hug, and I walked out to my car.

I had learned as much as I was going to tonight. But one thing struck me about everyone I'd spoken to.

More people were mad at Brett Daniels than sad.

6

It was late when I got home and dark in the house and, if I wasn't completely used to it yet, at least I wasn't looking around for someone who wasn't there. The game had been long and, despite my brother's pizza, I was hungry in the way you are when you've been outside in the cold for a long time and gone to jail after. I scrounged around the fridge and then the freezer before deciding that frozen pizza was as good a follow-up to leftover pizza as anything.

I threw the pizza in the oven without waiting for it to preheat because, honestly, who has time for that. While it cooked, I checked my phone for recaps of the game. It turned out that Tyler's five touchdowns looked as good as they'd sounded and they were even better for having come against our rival South. One of the articles, from the *Carrefour Courier* I believe, already ranked the game as one of the greatest in the history of the North-South rivalry.

I pulled the pizza out when the thin crust was crisp and brown and proceeded to burn the roof of my mouth on scalding hot cheese because I wasn't about to wait. I finished the article, picked up the pizza on its convenient cardboard circle, and made my way back to my office.

It used to be our office, Sarah and me, which we used at night and on the weekends when one of us had to work. It still had a two-desk setup that I found I couldn't quite get myself to change even though it would have made sense. The progress, though, was that I realized I was putting it off and actually took a little comfort in it so I guess that was something.

I set my pizza on my desk and had a few bites. I started to open my work tablet, then thought better of it and decided to wait and start fresh in the morning. As I sat back and chewed, I looked at the collection of pictures on the one wall we could each see from our desks. There were shots of Sarah with her sisters, me with my brothers, and some of all of us together.

I'd rearranged them since Sarah had died so that now my two favorites were in the middle. The one on the left showed Sarah, her right arm extended above the volleyball net, hair flying behind her, as she smashed the ball that streaked in a white blur toward the floor. The one on the right showed our whole family on the turf at Ford Field—Kate, my younger brother Mark and his wife Izzy, me, and all my nieces and nephews surrounding my mom and my dad and Tom. It had been taken last year, when Tom's team had made it all the way to the finals at Ford Field. Their state runner-up finish was the farthest any Carrefour North football team had ever gone in the playoffs and it was one of those rare photos that had my whole family in it so my mom had framed it and given it to all of us for Christmas.

She couldn't understand why Tom hated that picture so much.

I finished my pizza, touched Sarah's picture on the way out, and went to bed.

7

I slept a little later the next day because it was Saturday and by God you have to stand for something. I ran, showered, then sat down with an egg wrap in front of my tablet because it was time to find out what everyone else knew about Brett Daniels' death.

I went to the news articles first. The death of the star quarterback's father had made all the local papers and television channels. They didn't tell me much more than what I had learned last night, though; just that Brett Daniels, father of Tyler "TD" Daniels, had died in an apparent hunting accident and that it was not clear whether TD would play the next week in the rivalry game against South.

I went to social media next. The official channels first—the Carrefour North football Twitter account, the *Carrefour Courier*, the *Ash County Torch*, and from there to the accounts of family and friends, which led me down one rabbit hole after another of speculation and theories on Brett Daniels' death.

That was how I found @AlexisFury.

The avatar was striking. It was a sketch of a woman, red and white, with wild hair that writhed like snakes. The eyes were solid white and the face angular, angry, and compelling. I'm not even sure what trail of breadcrumbs and hashtags led me to the account. But once I was there, I discovered that she had plenty to say about Brett Daniels.

The posts that I was interested in had started the week before.

> *A boy's father is dead. All anyone cares about is whether he's going to play football. #perspective*
> *Is the body cold? Who cares, it's almost kick-off. #pantherpride*
> *Suck up that grief and get out there. #wherearetheadults*
> *Five touchdowns, no fumbles, no father. #priorities.*
> *Honor your father by winning the game. #loss #suckitup*

There were more like that in the week leading up to the game, a surprising number of them really, but they seemed to be coming farther and farther apart until yesterday, when at noon, @AlexisFury tweeted:

> *What kind of monster kills his own father? #evil*

She posted a picture of Colt with it. Then nothing. From her anyway.

The team-related Twitter accounts had blown up shortly after 8:30 p.m. last night, which had been right around halftime. Literally thousands of people had seen the arrest and one account after another posted cell phone pictures of Colt being led off the field by Pearson.

The tenor of the comments, at first anyway, ran along team lines. Fans of South tweeted mockery and scorn, wondering when the rest of the North team would be arrested. Fans of North tweeted that South couldn't even win when they cheated by having one of their alumni try to mess with North's best player.

Most guessed that it was related to some sort of college transgression that had caught up with Colt while he was back home visiting. No one except Alexis Fury had put it together yet, and she didn't appear to have much of a following among the locals. I knew that wouldn't last.

It was time to start digging into the source material. First, that meant another call to Sheriff Dushane.

I was half surprised when he picked up. "Nate," he said without waiting, "I'm not talking about it."

"From everything I've heard, it was a hunting accident."

"People hear a lot of things," Sheriff Dushane said.

"But murder? His own dad?"

"He wouldn't be the first, Nate. You know that."

"He doesn't seem like the type."

"A lot of them don't. Are you on this case for good now?"

"Yes."

"I thought you might be, with Tommy and all."

"North football looks after each other. You know that."

I heard the pause before Sheriff Dushane said, "Not fair and you know it."

He was right, of course. "Sorry. So what happened?"

"I've handed it over to the prosecutor, Nate. You're going to have to talk to her."

"Her?"

"Tiffany Erin."

"Not T. Marvin Stritch?"

"He's recused himself."

"Is Erin from his office?"

"No. They're bringing her in from Jackson."

"Already?"

"When a popular football player's brother kills his father—"

"Allegedly kills his father."

"—Kills his father, it has a way of getting people's attention."

"You're really not going to tell me anything?"

"I'll send you Erin's contact info." There was a pause, and then Sheriff Dushane said, "Tell Tommy we're pulling for him next week."

"He knows. Talk to you later."

We hung up. I didn't know this Tiffany Erin that Sheriff Dushane was talking about. The chief prosecutor for Ash County was a guy named T. Marvin Stritch who I had just tried a case against. I was curious to know why he had recused himself from taking the case; the cynical lawyer in me thought that an astute politician might decide that prosecuting the brother of the most talented football player Ash County had seen in a generation wasn't the best way to campaign for re-election. Ash County wasn't the biggest district so my second cynical guess was that, rather than hand the case off to a less experienced attorney in his office who could use that high profile experience to run against him someday, T. Marvin had decided to bring in a more experienced prosecutor from outside the jurisdiction who, conveniently, would be no threat to his re-election.

Jackson was a bigger city and a prosecutor coming from there would certainly have experience with murder trials. My guess was that Tiffany Erin wasn't going to be available over the weekend so I would have to put off contacting her until Monday. In the meantime though, I still wanted more information, so I decided to drive out to the Daniels' property and take a look. I called Rhonda, got the address and directions, and headed out.

M-339 was a Michigan highway that marked the western border of the Carrefour North school district. It was a quiet country road, both because there wasn't much out there and because it wasn't a way one took to get somewhere else.

I missed the green address marker for their house the first time. It was bent toward the ditch, as if someone had hit it when they missed the driveway, and I had to circle back around from the other direction after I realized I'd gone too far. I turned onto a two-track drive—two stripes of gravel with a strip of grass in between—and drove in.

It was November so most of the leaves were gone and the green undergrowth of the Michigan summer had vanished, giving me a clear view of the house as I pulled in. It was one and a half stories with cedar siding in need of stain and a hard-slanting green metal roof. There was a used brick walkway that ended in a concrete step to a green front door. Three yew bushes, evenly spaced, were planted on either side of the door, not in beds of mulch but in the grass of the front yard.

The two-track ended in front of a detached garage that looked like it was part barn and had a green roof that matched the house. A black F150 pickup of middling age with a full, eight-foot bed and a built-in toolbox sat in the drive.

I parked my Jeep out of the way and got out. I walked toward the truck, saw no one was in it, and changed direction toward the house. A path worn in the grass led from the drive to a concrete landing in back so I followed that up to the white storm door.

No one seemed to be home, which wasn't a surprise since Tyler was at practice, Colt was in jail, and Brett was dead. I peered through the storm window and the panes of glass on the inner door. I saw a small dining area and a kitchen with a once-white linoleum floor yellowed with age and three wooden chairs sitting around a brown kitchen table.

Nothing and no one stirred inside so I turned toward the backyard. Actually, backyard is what people in subdivisions say; it conjures images of fences and flower beds and maybe a swing set or a pool. No, I should say that I turned toward the back of the Daniels' property.

There was an old red picnic table on the left sitting next to a storm cellar door that indicated a Michigan basement. The same worn dirt path that led to the drive also branched off to a door in the side of the garage/barn. As I looked around, I saw that a couple of acres had been cleared in a big rectangle, bordered by woods on all three sides. The rough grass had been mown down after it had grown tall enough to go to seed so that there was still a layer of now-yellow stalks scattered throughout.

A large willow tree grew off to the left, about halfway back. A tire hung from its lower branches. Unlike a swing though, this tire was secured to the branch with one rope and anchored to the ground with two more ropes driven into the ground with tent spikes. On the right, a few dozen yards past the barn, was a stack of hay bales with a target attached to the front. After the single willow tree and the hay bale, the cleared property ran all the way back until it transitioned into light woods.

Just in front of that tree line, a yellow stripe flickered in the breeze. I realized it was police tape held up by thin wire posts.

Like what you'd use to mark a body with.

8

It was cold but not bitterly so as I zipped up my coat and headed toward the back of the cleared section of the Daniels' property. I took a quick detour to the stack of hay bales to look at the target attached to them. There were a series of concise holes impressively bunched in the center circles. Judging from the bare patch of ground by the barn that was thirty yards away from the target, someone was a good shot.

I kept walking back to the police tape. It had been wound around thin metal rods that were jammed into the earth to form a circle about twenty feet across.

I couldn't remember if it had rained that week, but it must have because I didn't see much inside the tape. No pressed down grass, no bloodstains, no scraps, although I did notice that there weren't as many dead grass stalks in there. I assumed that meant the tape was still there to mark an area rather than to preserve evidence. I took a few pictures with my phone, primarily to get a sense of distances from here to the house and to the treeline. Then I walked into the woods.

It would have been harder to find my way in summer but the leaves were all down, giving me a clear view for quite a ways. I wasn't sure where I was going but a trail of little yellow flags, like the kind utility workers use to mark underground lines, marked the way. I followed them.

The flags led me through the woods, maybe a hundred yards or so, until I came to what looked like a hunter's field. Some hunters will plant corn or alfalfa or some other specialty crop to attract deer and this had that look to me, although I didn't know my stalks enough to identify the remnants of what were sticking up.

I followed the flags across the field to another treeline that formed the northeast corner. I was still some yards away when I saw the tree stand. No, not a tree stand; it was more of a platform really. It looked like Brett Daniels had sunk six posts into the ground near a tree, framed it, then built a small platform on top with deck boards. It was all treated wood but not stained or painted. A wooden ladder was built onto one side and all of it—the posts, the decking, the ladder—was a worn, weathered gray that matched the bark of the tree they were built against. I walked around to the ladder side.

There was dried brown blood on the rungs.

The flags ended at the ladder and there was no police tape here, which confirmed my thought that the tape in the yard was to mark the spot where Colt's dad had been found rather than prevent access to it. The sheriff's office must have already taken everything they needed here and figured the platform wasn't going anywhere. So, I climbed up.

I'm not going to lie—I grabbed the outside of the side rails and stepped around the blood on the rungs. Even though it was dried and more of a stain than a glop, it was still blood and still disconcerting to pass. I climbed the ten feet up to the platform and, as I stood up, noticed that it didn't rock an inch.

The platform was about six feet by eight with perfectly square corners at the edges and a half circle cut out on the middle of one side for the trunk. It would fit one person easily and two comfortably while three would be too many. Like the posts, the decking was a worn, weathered gray. Except, of course, for the scattered spots of brown dried blood.

There was one spot that was bigger than the others, right in the middle, that looked big enough that some must have run between the deck planks. I couldn't tell now just how much volume there had been, but it wasn't hard to recreate part of the story—Brett Daniels had been injured here and had been trying to make it back to his house when he succumbed to his wound.

Or, if it was murder, someone might have finished the job.

I pulled my eyes away from the bloodstains and looked around from my vantage on the stand. From here Brett would have had a clear shot in about a 150-degree radius to the field and more limited but still viable shots into the woods behind the platform depending upon where the deer or coyote was in relation to the trees. I stood there and turned slowly around, looking, then I took out my phone and recorded the same thing. After that, I took a number of pictures. I noticed the tree branches didn't start for another ten or so feet up, giving plenty of clearance if someone wanted to move a bow or gun around, and I took a few more pictures to help me remember what I'd seen.

I took a last look at the bloodstains on the deck and climbed back down the ladder. I walked around underneath the stand but, like the ground closer to the house, I didn't see more bloodstains or anything else of note on the ground underneath.

I thought about the route as I walked back. It didn't seem like too long a walk to the platform, but it also didn't seem like a distance someone who was critically injured could make. Brett Daniels had, and then he had died.

How though? Had he cut himself by accident? Had someone attacked him? And if it was clear someone had attacked him, why wasn't that known right away? Why had Sheriff Dushane taken a week to arrest Colt? From everything I'd heard so far, the family and everyone else had thought it was a hunting accident, not an attack.

Nothing on the walk back made the answer any clearer.

∽

I WASN'T GOING to be able to get any information from official sources until Monday, so I decided to go home. I made it back to my house that afternoon in time to watch the rest of the Michigan State game and, during the commercials, hopped onto social media to see if anyone was posting about Colt or the murder.

One of the local channels managed to get a quote from T. Marvin Stritch commenting on how this was a very serious crime and that, due to a conflict in his office, he would be bringing in a visiting prosecutor from out of county. Interestingly, he didn't mention Tiffany Erin's name.

There were more stories about Colt's arrest with more cell phone footage of him being arrested at the game. By now, his mug shot was available and people had plastered it all over the posts I was wading through. Not a great development but unavoidable.

From what I could see, no one online knew how Brett Daniels had been killed, although at least one animal-rights person posted a story that proved, scientifically and without doubt, that coyotes were not a danger to humans.

I continued to scroll until I came once again to the red and white sketched avatar of Alexis Fury. This time she wasn't commenting. Instead, she retweeted one story after another about Colt's arrest. Local news stations, cell phone videos, and even links to articles in those antiquated things called newspapers. All mentioned the arrests, all mentioned a warrant for murder, but none had a description of the killing.

Her most recent post played a cell phone video on a ten second loop of Pearson cuffing Colt next to the end zone. In the background, Tyler was jumping in celebration. He'd been celebrating the touchdown, of course, but on the video it looked like he was cheering the arrest. "When Justice Comes," was her comment above the clip. The likes and retweets were increasing like a rolling odometer as I watched.

When I stopped scrolling, I found that I had missed the end of the State game but the Spartans had won so all was well.

9

On Monday morning, I went to the office a little early so that I had time to check on things before going to Colt's extradition hearing. If you're looking for it, my office is in a professional services building in the suburbs of the Ohio side of Carrefour. It's made of steel and glass and is one of those well-kept, functional buildings you can find in the low-rise sprawl of most cities. It housed doctors and accountants and lawyers and my office was on the third floor in a small suite that my associate Daniel Reddy and I called home.

Danny wasn't there yet, which meant that I really was early. I turned on the lights, made the coffee, and brushed up on the rules for the extradition hearing. Extradition is the process where someone who is arrested in one state is delivered to the state where he will stand trial. It had been some years since I'd handled that as a Carrefour prosecutor, so I took a quick look to refresh myself. As I recalled, Carrefour had a specialized local process for handling it. Since the Ohio-Michigan line ran right through town, it was in everyone's best interests to have a streamlined system for delivering someone from one side to the other; it was normally handled here without much fuss.

I was packing up to go when Danny arrived. Danny was tall, thin, and always moving a little faster than his nervous system could keep up with. He was taking off his overcoat when he noticed the lights, the coffee, and, lastly, me.

He froze. "This can't be good."

"Good to see you too, Danny."

"You made coffee."

"You're welcome."

"So you've been here for a while."

"Never too late to get a jump on the day."

"I take it we have a new case?"

"We do."

"Please tell me it's a nice shareholder dispute for control of a small but profitable corporation."

"Certainly. It's a nice shareholder dispute for control of a small but profitable corporation."

Danny set down his laptop case and hung up his coat. "What is it really?"

"Remember how you said you wanted to get away from handling murder cases?"

"I do."

"I'm certain that will happen in the not-too-distant future."

Danny smiled for a second until what I'd said registered. Then the smile left, he picked up his case, and went into his office.

"If it's any consolation, we're not getting paid much for this one, so really, it's more like charity work, which you love."

Danny turned back. "A murder case *and* we're not getting paid?"

"I'm sure we'll get paid something. I'm a business genius."

Danny nodded, went to his desk, and docked his laptop. He looked at me, opened his mouth, closed it, then looked down.

"What?"

Danny didn't make eye contact with me as he said, "I wasn't kidding, Nate. I don't want to be a criminal lawyer."

"I understand. We're going to branch out. It's just that this was one of my brother's players. Well, a former player, but it meant a lot to him."

Danny looked up. "The Colt Daniels case?"

"Yes."

"You sure know how to pick 'em."

"I think I said this before, but they seem to pick me. Us."

"Right. *Us*."

I detected a note that I normally didn't hear from Danny. "Hey, are you okay?"

"I am. And you can count on me. But we need to talk about this. I don't want to spend my life representing murderers."

"Good. Because we've been representing the unjustly accused."

"I mean it, Nate."

"I know. Let's talk when this one is done."

"We're going to."

"I know. That's why I said it."

"Okay. What do you need me to do?"

"Find out what you can about Tiffany Erin. She's a prosecutor out of Jackson who's going to be handling the case. And see if there have been any pleadings filed in Ash County yet. I've seen the warrant, but I don't know anything else."

"Got it."

"I'm going over now for an expedited extradition hearing."

"What?"

"I'll explain when I get back."

Danny nodded, and I left.

As I went out to my Jeep, I digested Danny's words. I was surprised that he had reacted so strongly. He'd mentioned that he wasn't happy with the kinds of cases we were handling, but he'd never put it so bluntly. I wasn't that thrilled about it either, but sometimes you just have to take what comes to you. Of course, in this case, what was coming to us was no money, but sometimes you do make exceptions. Regardless, I was going to have to deal with this and come up with a plan, or judging from what I just saw, there was a good chance I was going to lose Danny.

The plan would have to come after the case, though. For now, I had to get to my hearing.

~

JUDGE ANNE GALLON tilted her head down so she could look over her clear frame glasses. "Well, Mr. Shepherd," she said from the bench. "This is an unexpected pleasure. But I didn't see any Vikings on the docket today."

Judge Gallon had sharp features and a sharper wit, and I was pretty sure the glasses were just a device to soften both. It had been more than a year since I'd been in her court to represent a man, who was indeed very Viking-like, against an accusation of murder. We had served together in the prosecutor's office years ago, and I still joined her and her husband for dinner or a drink here and there, although it had been a while.

"Nothing so dramatic today, Your Honor," I said. "Just a midnight express hearing." That was the term we'd used back in the prosecutor's office since extradition between the Ohio and Michigan sides of Carrefour could usually be handled in a day.

"I didn't see an extradition case today," she said. "Which one is that, Stacy?"

"That would be the Daniels case, Your Honor," said Stacy Cannon, the court's bailiff.

Judge Gallon shuffled through a stack of papers before extracting one. "Colton Daniels?"

"That's the one, Your Honor," I said.

Judge Gallon scanned it before she lifted an eyebrow and looked up. "Murder?"

"So I've been told."

"Is this the football player's brother?"

"Yes."

Judge Gallon shook her head. "I see you decided to take up a quiet, small town practice, Mr. Shepherd."

"Yes, Your Honor."

"Do you want the typical terms for midnight express?"

"We admit identity, then he's transferred to Ash County and bonded out over there?"

"Yes."

"Do they still do the pickups daily?"

"He should be up there tonight and have a bond hearing tomorrow."

"Even for serious charges?"

"Especially for serious charges. We don't want those lingering."

"Then yes, that's what we'll be seeking."

"All right. Is he here, Stacy?"

"On his way, Judge."

An attorney from the prosecutor's office showed up then. He was young, harried, and preoccupied with balancing an armful of brown folders that represented a morning's worth of hearings of all kinds. It being both Monday morning and a routine hearing, he was probably the newest lawyer in the office.

As the prosecutor set up, three Carrefour officers led a group of seven prisoners into the courtroom, half in orange jumpsuits and the other half in their street clothes. Colt was in the middle. His hands were cuffed in front of him and his thick hair was spiking up a bit, but he looked okay other than being a little more disheveled than he had been Friday night. He saw me and started to speak. I raised a hand and mouthed, "Wait." He nodded and waited, but I could see that he was on edge.

"All right, let's get things going then," said Judge Gallon. "The first is in the matter of Colton Daniels." I walked up to the defense counsel table as an officer pulled Colt out of the line and brought him over.

"What's going on, Nate?" he said.

"We're having a hearing to transfer you up to Ash County. Once you're there, we can arrange bond and get you out."

"Why can't I get out now?"

"Because we need to get you to Michigan first. Then a Michigan judge will issue the terms of your release. We'll have this hearing this morning, you'll be transferred to Michigan, and then we can get you a bond hearing tomorrow."

Colt scowled. "Another night in jail?"

"Just the one. Then we'll be able to ask for bond to get you out."

Colt took a deep breath, then nodded. "You're the boss. Let's do what we need to do."

Judge Gallon had been giving us a moment to speak. When I looked up and nodded, she started the extradition hearing. Essentially, the arrest warrant from Michigan was presented for Colton Daniels. She asked Colt if he was indeed Colton Daniels. He agreed that he was. She then asked if he was willing to waive the extradition process and present himself for transfer to Michigan. I nodded to Colt, and he said that he was willing to waive it.

"Mr. Daniels," Judge Gallon said, "under the Uniform Transfer Act, the State of Michigan has up to fourteen days to come and get you. I will tell you that because we are a border town, we have an expedited process here that should have you picked up by the end of the day. Either way, by waiving extradition, you are waiving your right to contest your identity and will not be permitted to post bond until after you are transferred. Do you understand and waive those rights?"

Colt looked at me. I nodded. "Yes, ma'am," he said.

"Very well." After repeating his admissions for the record, Judge Gallon ordered Colt to be held for transfer until he was delivered into the custody of the appropriate Michigan official. Then she called the next case.

Colt and I stepped back from the defense counsel table.

"What happens next?" he said.

"Just sit tight. They should pick you up late today. In the meantime, I'll get to work on your bond."

Colt did not look at all certain about what was going on. I didn't blame him.

"And remember," I said. "Do *not* talk to anyone. No inmates, no guards, nobody. No one is your friend, and no one is looking out for you in there, do you understand?"

Colt set his jaw. "Got it."

"You okay?"

He ground his teeth and nodded. "I'm fine. I just want out."

"This is the first step toward doing that."

The officer took Colt and put him back in the jury box with the other prisoners. I picked up my copy of the order from Stacy, nodded to Judge Gallon, who nodded back, and left the courtroom.

It was time to find out just what Colt was accused of.

10

My first step was to talk to the prosecutor. I called T. Marvin Stritch directly and was told that he was in court but that if I wanted to leave a message, he'd try to get back to me as soon as possible. I called the general number, and a receptionist told me the same thing. When I asked if Tiffany Erin had set up an office yet, the receptionist asked who that was. When I explained that she was an incoming special prosecutor, the receptionist assured me that she didn't know anything about that and that the only people currently working there were T. Marvin Stritch and his two deputy prosecutors, neither of whom were named Tiffany Erin. However, she would be happy to inquire and, if I would like to leave my name and number, and if this Ms. Erin did, indeed, at some point, arrive at their office, she would most certainly make sure that my message was one of the first things that she received. I thanked her, left my name and number, and hung up.

I thought about contacting the coroner since the autopsy wasn't confidential, but I wasn't sure yet who was on this case. The Ohio side of Carrefour was big enough to support a full-time coroner, but Ash County, Michigan was not. Instead, it entered into arrangements for part-time coverage through local hospitals and other larger counties, and it would take a little legwork to find out who was being used in this case.

Still, I had an uneasy feeling. This wasn't like a case involving a car accident or a beating, or even a heart attack, where I, at least generally, knew from the outset what had happened. I felt like I was in the dark in need of a light, so I took the step I often did when I ran into a dead end. I called Olivia Brickson.

"Shep," she said. "There's nothing you can say to me on the phone that you couldn't say to me here in person at the gym."

Olivia was the person I turned to whenever I needed an investigation done. She also owned a gym with her brother, Cade.

"I'm not going to be in until tomorrow and I'm working the background on a new case now."

"Are you suggesting you don't need to work out today?"

She was also, by all accounts, a maniac.

"Just suggesting that I needed to prioritize, Liv."

"You certainly do."

There was no winning that argument so I didn't try. I just waited until she said, "Fine. Since I'm not having much success with your conscience, how can I help as your investigator?"

I told her about how I'd been retained to defend Colt Daniels on the charge of killing his father, Brett. "But as of right now, all I can get out of people is that there was a hunting accident. I can't get any details."

"What about from the client?"

"Since he says he didn't do it, he can't tell me anything about it. He thought it was a hunting accident, too. And that coyotes might've been involved."

"Of course they were. What about the prosecutor?"

"The prosecutor's from out of town and unreachable so far. I have a bad feeling that I'm falling behind already."

"Got it. What are you looking for?"

"Let's start with basics on the deceased Brett Daniels and our client Colt. You'll see a lot of articles about the youngest brother as well, Tyler. He's North's quarterback."

Olivia chuckled. "Quarterbacks. Your favorite."

"I'm hoping he's young enough that the syndrome hasn't set in yet. If you have any connections with the Sheriff's office in Ash County or anyone who might've been involved in the investigation, that would help a lot."

"Doesn't Sheriff Dushane fish with your dad every weekend?"

"Pretty near. But I've already gone to that well, and he's not saying anything."

"Okay. I'll do it. I assume you want it yesterday?"

"If you can't get it the day before."

"Great. I expect to see you tomorrow."

"You will."

We hung up. I decided I'd made it as far down those avenues as I could and headed back to the office to see what Danny had turned up.

～

"It's never simple with you, is it?" Danny said.

"I'm exceedingly simple, Danny. Ask anyone."

"Not you. *With* you. As in, I tell you I don't want to do murder cases and you bring in four in a row."

"To be fair, one was attempted murder."

Danny ignored me. "And if it isn't enough for you to bring in your fourth consecutive murder case, you've decided to do it going against her."

If Danny were not so nice, the look he gave me would have been one of disgust. Being who he was, though, it was more a combination of concern and frustration. I picked up the clip of papers he'd slid across the table and said, "What's this?"

"That is the bio of Tiffany Erin I pulled off the Jackson County website."

"Okay."

Danny stared at me.

"Geez, what Danny, is she one of the X-Men or something?"

"No, but she's just as unusual for a prosecutor around here."

"Explain."

"Let me give you the highlights. Columbia undergrad. Stanford Law School. Federal clerkship in Philadelphia."

"So she's a terrible student who hates travel."

"From Philadelphia, she went to Chicago to work in the prosecutor's office where she quickly rose through the ranks and was handling serious crimes within a year and a half."

"Good for Chicago."

"Do you know what Chicago has a lot of?"

"Deep-dish pizza? Annoying Bears fans?"

"Yes. Also murders."

"I see. Is there a link?"

He ignored me and tapped the file. "She handled the Whittlerun case."

"Is that supposed to mean something?"

"It did in Chicago because it was all over the news and after that she spent the next five years trying nothing but homicide cases."

"That's a lot."

"It is. Then she moved back home, which is apparently 'in the Jackson area,' and has been working for the Jackson County prosecutor's office ever since. Now Jackson has murders and homicides but nothing like Chicago and certainly not enough to keep someone like Tiffany Erin busy, so guess what she does?"

I was beginning to see where this was going. "She hires out to surrounding counties as a special prosecutor for big murder cases?"

"Exactly. Care to guess how many times she's done that?"

"More than ten?"

"More than twenty."

"Anything else? Great-granddaughter of Clarence Darrow? Heir to Daniel Webster?"

"Who?"

"Never mind. So she knows what she's doing. Most of them do."

Danny shook his head. "Not like this."

"None of this matters to Colt. We still have to get him out and get an acquittal."

"If we can."

"See now, that's just negative thinking."

"No, we're just back to my original premise that you really know how to pick them."

"And you were worried that the practice of law would be boring."

"Boring would be nice."

"Probably. But not yet. Anything in the pleadings?"

"Nothing significant. They're generic pleadings to support the arrest warrant but no specific allegations about what happened."

"About what they *claimed* happened."

"Of course. There wasn't any of that." Danny flapped the papers in his hand. "So what did happen?"

I shook my head. "I don't know yet. At this point, all we have is that Brett Daniels went out hunting on Thursday night, that something happened at some stage in his hunting stand because there's blood there, that he was found Friday night outside his house by Tyler and his dog, and that coyotes were involved."

"Was Colt there that day?"

"I don't know. We haven't had time to talk in depth yet."

"We really don't know how he died?"

"We really don't. Newspaper articles and the obituary all say hunting accident. That's consistent with what Colt, Tyler, and my brother all said was the story up until the funeral just a day before Colt was arrested."

Danny nodded. "Seems like the first order of business is to find out the cause of death."

"That's the second order of business. The first is to get Colt transferred and out on bond."

"You handle that while I find the coroner's report?"

I smiled. "See, you're a natural."

Danny didn't smile. "No, Nate. I'm not."

I kept smiling anyway and the two of us got to work.

BLOCK

11

When you go to trial, you have to push everything else aside and limit your involvement in other things to triage until the trial's over. That's especially true in a small office like mine. Danny and I were only a little more than a week removed from a big one so there were still all sorts of small fires that had been pushed to the back burner that were now smoldering to the front. I spent the rest of the day at the office putting those fires out, or at least dampening them to a level where they wouldn't engulf us.

I finally felt like I was getting a handle on things when Rhonda Mazur called at a little after five o'clock and said, "What is my son still doing in jail?"

The cigarette gravel in her voice was even more pronounced over the phone.

"Rhonda, he was never going to get out today. The Michigan officers were just going to pick him up today so that we can start the bond process tomor—"

"—That's my point, Shepherd. He's still in the Ohio jail."

"He is?"

"That's why I'm calling!"

"Let me find out what's going on and call you back."

She hung up without saying another word.

It took me two internet searches and three calls, but eventually I reached the officer in charge of prisoner custody and transfers at the Carrefour jail.

"This is Greg Lin," he said.

"Greg, this is Nate Shepherd. I'm an attorney here in town and I'm calling to check on the status of a client."

"Sure, go ahead."

"Colt Daniels. Excuse me, Colton Daniels."

"The quarterback's brother, right?"

"That's the one."

I heard the clack of keys before Greg Lin said, "Yes, sir, he's here. Is there anything else?"

"Yes. He was supposed to go out on the midnight express this afternoon."

"Ahh," said Officer Lin. Another series of clicks. "It looks like there was no pickup today or tonight, sir."

"Isn't there a pickup every night?"

"Apparently not. Is there anything else I can help you with, sir?"

"What time is the normal express pickup?"

"It usually happens at 2:30. Anything else?"

"No, that's it. Thanks for your help, Greg."

"Yes, sir," he said and hung up.

I knew there was normally a pickup every day, or at least every day that there was someone in custody—that was the whole point of the express arrangement—so this was unusual but likely a paperwork mix-up.

I picked up the phone and called Rhonda. I explained that the Michigan officers hadn't come to get Colt and that it would be another day. She wasn't having any of it and started cursing. I let her run it out a ways until she lost some momentum and then said, "Rhonda, Colt has been accused of murder. There are going to be an awful lot of things that seem unfair or don't go exactly how we plan. This is the least of them. We need to be ready for a long haul."

"But they can't just leave him in there—"

"Rhonda, they can. And Colt needs you to hang tight."

There was silence on the other end and I heard a sharp inhale followed by a pause and an exhale. "Right," she said. "I will. But you need to keep on this."

"Of course. Thanks for letting me know. I'll check on the pickup myself tomorrow."

"Okay." She hung up.

I thought it was probably just a coincidence, but I made some calls to Ash County anyway. I called the jail and I called the switchboard and I got a live person twice, but each time when I was sent to transfers and prisoner status, I got a voicemail telling me what the administration's normal office hours were—which, of course, was not right now.

I felt like a Roomba caught in a corner, just bouncing around against the woodwork going nowhere. I decided that I had done all the damage I could do at the office and left for the Brickhouse.

∼

IN THE NORTHERN section of Carrefour where the town ends and the woods begin lies an abandoned spur of railroad track and two old brick buildings that date back to when the trains ran. We won't talk about the first building because it houses the best barbecue in the area and, since I wasn't going there right then, describing it would just depress me. It was enough that the smell of hickory smoke was wafting across the parking lot as I walked to the other brick building in the complex, an old warehouse now known as the Brickhouse.

The Brickhouse had been converted into a gym by its owners, Cade and Olivia Brickson. Olivia was normally there at this hour and, since this was also where she kept her office for doing her investigations, I figured I'd kill two birds with one stone.

"Look at this," said Olivia as I walked in. "Either his conscience got to him or he wants something."

"Obviously, I was overwhelmed by the desire to better myself."

"He definitely wants something," she said to the air.

I smiled and walked over to the counter. Olivia was in her typical workout gear of a red tank top and black yoga pants and her spiked white hair swooped down in front of the half-mirrored glasses that she always wore. She made a point of taking my membership card, swiping it, then shaking her head and saying, "You really need to get more for your money, Shep."

"Yeah? Maybe there are one of those 'no lunk' chains opening nearby."

"You're out of luck. They ban punks, too." She handed me back my card, extending an arm that was covered in a tattooed sleeve from elbow and wrist.

"Did you have any luck with the Daniels' death?"

"It's barely been an afternoon, Shep."

"Right. And?"

"I did."

"What did you hear?"

"One of the guys in my morning class has a cousin who... never mind. I had a connection to a rescue squad driver and a deputy."

"And?"

"The rescue squad driver was on the call that Friday night.

They went out there thinking they might be rendering aid, but it turned into a recovery run pretty quickly."

"Yeah? What was he willing to say?"

"That the coyotes had done a pretty thorough job."

"What does that mean?"

"That there wasn't much of an abdominal cavity left. Or I should say it was all abdominal cavity and no abdomen."

"Yikes."

"Right. That's what got him talking about it. One of the guys on the call was a newbie who apparently corrupted part of the crime scene with vomit."

"Okay. What about the deputy?"

"He was more ambiguous. All he would say was that he had heard that the forensics group had gone back a few times and searched a broader area than where Brett Daniels had been found."

"Did he say what they were looking for?"

"He didn't know or wouldn't say. But he left the impression that they were looking for a weapon."

"Did he say what kind?"

"No, he wasn't really comfortable talking about it. I had to play on our history a little bit."

I raised an eyebrow. "History?"

"He seems to think we dated for a little while."

I chuckled and decided I couldn't really top the nuance of that comment. "All right, keep digging if you can. I'm going to catch a lift."

She smirked. "I see the eye still hasn't faded all the way."

"You should see the other guy."

"I have. And I've concluded you're both morons."

I shrugged. "Probably. So remember that the next time before you charge out after a murderer in a parking lot."

Olivia's eyebrows rose over her glasses. "You're trying to put this on me?"

"Cade wasn't going to beat Professor Timmons to death because *I* was hurt. 'Bye."

There was no winning an argument with Olivia—you had to abandon it when you were ahead so I went on back to the locker room to change, preoccupied with coyotes and searches.

12

It was three o'clock the next afternoon when I hung up with Officer Gregory Lin of the Carrefour jail. The Michigan officers for the midnight express hadn't come again. Colt was still in Ohio.

I was becoming irritated. And worried.

I dialed the Michigan numbers from the day before. Once again, I was shunted to voicemail. I left a message with my name and Colt's name and asked when he'd been scheduled for pick up.

When I was done, I made another call to T. Marvin Stritch. This time he answered. "Hi Nate," he said. "I was just about to call you back."

"Thanks, T. Marvin. Getting back to the routine?"

"I wish. Going right from one case to the next. Speaking of which, I thought we had everything wrapped up on the Archibald Mack case?"

Archibald Mack was the attempted murder trial that T. Marvin and I had just finished. "We do. I'm calling on a new case."

"Oh? Which one?"

"The Colton Daniels case."

"Ah."

"And I remembered what you'd said when we started the Mack case, that you believed in open disclosure, which I appreciated by the way, and I thought I would call you directly to find out what this Daniels case is about."

"I see." There was a pause. "I'm actually not involved in that one, Nate. I've brought in a special prosecutor since I have a conflict."

"That's what I understand, and I'm not asking for any specific action on the case, I'm just asking what the case is about and finding out when I can get some disclosures."

"I'm sorry, Nate, but you know if I have a conflict, I can't be involved at all so I have not looked at any of the materials in detail."

"But you've looked at it some. You have to know what the general allegations are."

"Well, sure. The general allegation is murder."

"But why? How?"

"Those details are being handled by the special prosecutor, Nate. You're going to have to deal with her."

"That's Tiffany Erin?"

"Yes, it is."

"Do you have her contact info?"

"I do." He gave it to me.

"Will she have the same philosophy as you about disclosure?"

Another pause. "Ms. Erin will handle the case as she sees fit."

T. Marvin and I get along fine, but there were never any warm fuzzies between us. There certainly weren't any now.

I was about to hang up when I thought of the other angle. "Is your office involved in the midnight express extradition agreement?"

"You mean the Agreement for the Transfer and Extradition of Prisoners between Ash County, Michigan and Carrefour, Ohio of 1986?"

"That's the one."

"It is."

"It's still in place, isn't it?"

"Yes."

"Is there anything that's currently causing a delay in its execution?"

A pause. "Not from me."

"I see. From anyone else?"

"Not that I know of."

"All right. Thanks T. Marvin."

"Goodbye, Nate."

I hung up and called Tiffany Erin's cell phone. It went straight to voicemail. "You've reached the Chief Prosecutor for Jackson County. Please leave a message."

I don't know that I'd ever heard a voicemail greeting of someone identifying themselves by their position instead of their name, but I suppose I had never called the President of the United States or the Last Starfighter either. I left her a message that I was calling about the Colton Daniels case and then hung up.

Carrefour isn't small, but it's not big either—it's one of those places where, even though it's a good size, the lawyers and the officials treat each other pretty well, knowing that what goes around comes around. This case was beginning to feel a little different.

Having hit another dead end for information, I thought about other avenues.

Then I decided to go to football practice.

It got dark by 5:30 at that time of year so I knew my brother Tom would be pushing the kids pretty hard, running a precise, intense practice while there was still daylight. I didn't want to be a distraction, so I stayed in my Jeep, watching from the parking lot that butted up against the practice field. The Carrefour North team was running plays on the goal line, the offense in their red practice jerseys against the defense in their blacks. Tyler was easy to pick out because he was the quarterback and because he was taller than everyone except two of the linemen. I saw him hand the ball to a running back, who then dove into the middle of the line and, judging from the jumping around of the black jerseys afterward, stopped short. Tyler took the offense right back to the line and did the same thing again, only to the other side. The defense pushed the line back and stopped him. Tyler hurried the offense back to the line and did the same thing a third time, handing the ball to the running back who dove into the middle and was sandwiched by three defenders.

As the defenders cheered, I saw Tyler, hunched over, running around the line in the opposite direction before he crossed the goal line all by himself and held the football up in the air. I looked back at the line and saw the running back gleefully raise both hands and wiggle them to show they were empty. The red jerseys jumped and collectively crowed while the black jerseys gathered themselves and took off for a lap around the field accompanied by clapping and cheers from their offensive teammates.

I saw Tom standing in the middle of the field behind the offense, his arms crossed. His look was stern but then I saw him turn and say something to the offensive players, who started laughing and cheering. Tom smiled then walked forward to slap the hand of each defender as he finished his lap. Then he gathered all the players around him and had them take a knee. I got out of the Jeep and leaned against the hood as Tom talked about effort and focus and heart, about how great teams play complementary football, how great teams lift up their teammates, and how great teams play together as hard as they can on every play.

Although it was a little hard to hear, I knew exactly what he was saying. It's not that it was a rote speech; it's just that when you grow up with the same father and play on the same teams with the same coaches as someone, you get a sense of how that person's mind works. For me to know what Tom was saying in a certain situation, I usually just figured out what I would say and then ratcheted up the intensity by one hundred. I smiled as Tom brought the kids in, they chanted "Panthers" on three, and then cleared the field.

I wasn't the only one watching practice. Other cars, maybe twenty or so, lined the border between the pavement and the grass as parents and friends watched from a distance. I went to most of Tom's games so a lot of the parents looked familiar to me. High schoolers being high schoolers though, none of the boys stopped to talk to their parents. Instead, the players stayed in their own groups and headed into the school.

Tyler was in the middle of one group that was an even mix of black and red jerseys. The players were jawing pretty good and one black jersey made a motion of knocking down a pass. Tyler shook his head, mimed a soft throwing motion, then waved his fingers like falling rain. The boys laughed.

As Tyler's group crossed the border from grass to asphalt, their cleats began to clack. Parents waved and called their sons' names and a few of the boys even waved back. I heard "Tyler!" and "TD!" a number of times, and it seemed as if Tyler nodded or waved in response to each one.

As Tyler and the players crossed the parking lot, they passed another cluster of cars. I noticed Rhonda Mazur's boyfriend,

Rob Preston, standing next to his old silver F150 pickup, distinguishable even at this distance by his fierce red beard. He was talking to a man leaning on the hood of a black Audi and, if you know southeast Michigan, you know that doesn't always play well. The man looked like he was in his late thirties, had an expensive haircut, and wore a collared shirt under a navy peacoat with black leather gloves. I thought the guy looked a little over-dressed for the North parking lot until I realized I was standing there in my suit and overcoat so you can probably file that observation under "descriptions of pots by kettles."

Rob waved at Tyler and the man nodded. Tyler waved in their general direction but didn't stop walking. After Tyler passed, the man shook Rob's hand, got in his Audi, and drove away.

"Did you catch the last series?" Tom said.

I started a little at his voice behind me, then said, "I did. The safety bit on the dive fake."

Tom shook his head. "I keep telling him to follow his keys, but he always wants to track the ball. Or where he thinks the ball is."

I nodded. "To be fair, Tyler hid the ball pretty well."

Tom grinned. "It *was* a nice play. What brings you here?"

"Do you have a second?"

Tom looked at his ever-present watch, which in case you're wondering, is set to Lombardi time so that he's always fifteen minutes early. "Not much more," he said. "We have to watch film yet."

"I'm having trouble getting information on Colt's case. I need more background."

That got Tom's attention. "How can I help?"

"What can you tell me about the Daniels boys and their dad?"

"Like what?"

"Like anything."

Tom had a laminated play sheet with the practice schedule in his hand. He rolled it into a tube and began to tap his thigh. He thrust his jaw to one side before he said, "Brett was pretty strict with the boys."

"Strict how?"

"He made sure they were at every workout, every practice. Always had them doing extra. He put them through some maniacal workouts in the summer from the time they were in grade school."

"Too much?"

"Hard to say that when he did it right along with them. Brett was always focused on making them, both of them, great quarterbacks. He was relentless about it."

"So a helicopter dad?"

Tom shook his head. "Not really. He never came to me and complained about playing time or play calls. Instead, if one of them had a bad game, he would light into them, telling them they had to do better, be better. Not in a public or embarrassing way but in the car or at home or somewhere else."

"If it was in private, how did you know about it?"

"At first, I didn't. Later, it was because I had to undo some of it."

"What do you mean?"

"Both boys are tough as nails. But there's a fine line in a great athlete between trying to get better and being afraid to make a mistake. I had to work with both of them to quit overthinking and let it fly."

I nodded. "Was he abusive?"

"Not how you're thinking. I don't think he ever hurt those boys, not that I saw anyway. Instead, it was things like taking the car or making them study film or things like that."

"Where was Rhonda in all this?"

Tom cocked his head. "You've met her, right?"

I nodded. "A couple of times."

"Then you might guess that their personalities clashed a bit."

"It seems like they both stayed involved though?"

Tom nodded. "They both came to everything. She still lives close-by." He tapped his leg with the schedule and looked toward the locker room.

Tom had given me a little flavor for the situation and I could see that he was getting antsy. "Thanks, Tommy. I'll keep following up. This helps though."

"Colt's a good kid, Nate. There's no way he did it. Whatever 'it' is."

I nodded. "Go get 'em Friday night if I don't see you before then."

"You'll be there, right?"

"Of course. I'll bring Mom and Dad."

"Great. Thanks."

With that Tom followed his team into the school. I thought about talking with Rob Preston to give him an update, but his old silver pickup was already gone so I climbed into my Jeep and drove home for the evening.

13

At exactly three o'clock the next day, I called Officer Greg Lin who advised me that yes sir, Colton Daniels was still at the Ohio facility, no sir, the midnight express had not picked anyone up that day, and, if that's all sir, I have a new resident to process. I thanked him, hung up, and went to see Judge Gallon.

Her court was not in session so I went in. Her bailiff, Stacy Cannon, was sitting at her desk. Stacy had pure white hair and just about as sweet a disposition as you'd find in a courthouse. She smiled as I came through the gate and said, "Good afternoon, Mr. Shepherd. You don't have anything scheduled this afternoon, do you?"

"No, Stacy, I don't. Does the judge have time to see me?"

"She's in, but she's working through a few things. Are you on business or just visiting?"

"A little bit of both but mostly business."

"Let me check for you then."

Stacy disappeared back into the judge's chambers and I heard a faint murmur before she emerged and said, "Please come on back, Mr. Shepherd."

I pushed through the swinging gate and entered the chambers of Judge Anne Gallon.

It had been a while since I'd been in there, but it looked the same. There was a neat stack of files on one table and an open folder on her desk with what looked like a couple of motions and related materials. It was exactly the sort of working space I'd expect of her—neat, efficient, and crisp—with a couple of mementos like the Carrefour Club Sporting Clays Trophy and the Nutcracker's Order of Mother Gingers, both of which indicated there was a little more under the surface of the all-business judge than you'd expect.

Judge Gallon smiled. "This is a nice surprise, Nate. Why don't we get the business out of the way so we can get to the bull-shitting."

"Is the midnight express still operating?"

She scowled. "You were just here three days ago for one of those, weren't you?"

"I was. I'm here on the same one. My client is still sitting in Ohio."

Her scowl deepened. "That's unusual."

"My recollection from when we were in the prosecutor's office is that it was a same day transfer, or the next at the latest."

"And that's how it's continued. Otherwise, Carrefour would be an unholy mess of people committing crimes and crossing the street to get away."

"That's how I remembered it."

Judge Gallon thought. "Your client's been accused of murder, hasn't he?"

"He has."

"So there's no guarantee he'll get out on bond once he's transferred."

"No. But we'd like to get to that decision point as soon as possible."

"I understand. Hang on a second." Judge Gallon picked up her phone and dialed. "I'll talk to Martin and see if there's a problem."

"Martin?"

"Martin LaPlante. The administrative judge up there."

She raised her hand then and said, "Martin, it's Anne. Good and you? Calling on the midnight express...Yes. Has there been a problem on your end?...I have a defendant that I put the transfer order on three days ago and he's still sitting down here....Murder....Right, that's why it has my attention, too. It's high profile....The Daniels boy....No, his brother."

Judge Gallon was quiet for a minute, listening and nodding. "I agree...No, with a case like this I figured the bond should be handled from your end...No, I know you would do the same... Will I see you and Bev at the holiday party next month?...Excellent. Talk to you there...Thanks Martin. Bye."

She hung up. "He wasn't aware of it, there's no reason for a delay from his end, and he's not happy that a man accused of murder has been sitting here for three days."

"So he didn't know the reason for the delay?"

"No. And I don't envy the person who caused it; Martin prides himself on the efficiency of his court."

She looked at me over those glasses she didn't need. "So how have you been?"

"Good thanks."

"I mean with everything."

Judge Gallon knew me from when I first started seeing Sarah, so I answered, "I'm fine, Anne."

"Did the Braggi trial make it better or worse?"

"Worse then better, I think."

She pursed her lips. "I didn't think you were going to do criminal defense work when you went out on your own."

I shrugged. "I didn't either but that's how the cases have been falling lately."

Judge Gallon and I had worked together for a good number of years so we spent the next fifteen or so minutes catching up. When Sarah was alive, we'd gone out with Anne and her husband a number of times but since Sarah had passed, we hadn't seen each other nearly as much. It was good to talk to her.

Eventually, I stood, thanked her for her help, and promised that this time we really would get together soon at Barry's for a drink.

I left her office, waved at Stacy on the way out, and headed over to the jail.

~

I CALLED AHEAD to make sure I could see him and found they had already put Colt in a small interview room when I arrived.

"Mr. Shepherd, what's going on?" he said as soon as I walked in. "You said I'd be out of here three days ago!"

Colt looked ragged and I wasn't surprised. Since he had always been on the verge of being transferred out, it looked like he hadn't been given a chance to change or shower since he'd been there. Add to that being in jail and being accused of killing your father, and it's bound to wear a guy down.

"There's been a delay," I said. "I think I have it fixed though. You should be getting moved tonight or tomorrow."

"Then I can get out?"

"Then we can have a hearing to find out if you can get out."

I went through the extradition and transfer process with him one more time. By the end, he seemed to understand because he shifted gears and said, "What about my case?"

"That's the other thing I want to talk to you about. I haven't been able to get much information about your dad or how he died. And we're early enough in the case that the prosecutor doesn't have to give me details yet. So I need everything you can tell me about what happened leading up to his death and what you heard about how he died."

Colt ran his hand through his unruly hair, which only made it stick up more. "You know I go to school at Grand Valley?"

"I heard."

"So I came home to see Tyler play before the playoffs started."

"What day?"

"Thursday. I was going to blow off class Friday."

"Did you stay with Tyler and your dad?"

Colt nodded. "Yeah."

"Did you see him? Your dad?"

"Yeah."

"How was he?"

Colt shrugged and looked away. "Dad was dad."

"I don't know what that means, Colt."

"He was focused on Tyler and the game."

"How so?"

"He had Tyler watching film and studying coverages."

"Do you help with that?"

"Only if Tyler asks. He's pretty good at it now."

"So did anything unusual happen Thursday night?"

Colt thought. "Dad was working a little late, so we missed him at dinner. We talked briefly after he got home."

"What does he—did he—do?"

"He was a drywaller."

"Did your dad say what he was going to do later that night?"

Colt nodded. "Yeah. He said he was going out to the stand."

"Did he do that often?"

"He did. Especially in the fall."

"I didn't think you were allowed to hunt after sunset."

Colt shrugged. "Coyotes you can. Dad thought it was more of a challenge."

"So did you see him that night?"

"After he went out?"

"Yes."

"No. Tyler and I each went to our rooms, did schoolwork and went to bed."

"What about during the night? Did you see anything, hear anything?"

Colt shook his head. "Nothing. But I was working on a project most of the time."

"What about the next morning?"

"Tyler and I were both up early. He went to school. I realized I'd forgotten to hand in a paper before I left and had to run all the way back to Grand Valley to turn it in so I was on the road by eight."

"You couldn't email it?"

"This professor's always a hard ass about it."

"Did you see your dad when you left?"

"No. But I didn't think anything of it. I figured he was at work."

I remembered the black truck from my visit. "Wasn't his truck still there?"

Colt's face twitched. "Oh, yeah. I guess I thought he was still sleeping."

"So what did you do Friday?"

"I drove back to school, made my appearance with my prof and turned in my paper, and drove back in time to make it to the game."

"Grand Valley is about three hours away, right?"

"More or less depending on traffic."

"We know your dad wasn't at the game."

"Right. I sat with Mom and Rob."

"Then Tyler found him Friday night?"

"Actually, Chet did, Tyler's lab. Chet found Dad, Tyler found Chet, then all this started."

"Where were you?"

"Meeting up with some friends since I was in town. Tyler called me. I told him to call the rescue squad and that I was on the way." Colt shook his head. "I didn't know how bad it was."

"Did you see your dad's body?"

Colt shook his head. "By the time I got there, the rescue squad and the police were there so they wouldn't let us near him." Colt made a face. "Tyler said Dad was chewed up pretty bad."

"Did the police tell you anything?"

"No."

"Did they interview you?"

He nodded. "Tyler and me both."

"What did you tell them?"

"The same thing I'm telling you."

I thought for a moment. This was all good background, but it didn't really help me figure out what had happened. All it established was that, if the killing happened on Thursday night, Colt was there without much of an alibi since he and Tyler were in their own rooms. I decided to try another angle.

"I was out at your dad's house. There was a tire swing and a target out back."

Colt nodded. "They're both targets. One for throwing and one for shooting."

"Did you do both?"

"All three of us did. My dad had us throwing balls through that tire from the time we could stand. I suppose the same is true for that straw bale."

"What did you shoot?"

"A bow mostly."

There was a knock at the door and a guard walked in. "Transfer orders are in," he said. "Time to go."

Colt looked at me. "Where?"

"To Michigan. We should have your bond hearing tomorrow."

"Will I be getting out?"

"We're going to try, but it depends on what the judge does with your bond. This is progress though. I'll talk to you tomorrow."

"When?"

"Just as soon as we can get the bond hearing scheduled."

"Let's go," said the guard.

Colt and I stood and I nodded to him as he left.

I thought as I made my way back to the parking lot. I had more information for sure, but I still didn't know how Brett Daniels had died, or even exactly when. And I certainly didn't see the basis for Colt being accused of murder.

But I knew it was coming.

14

Judge LaPlante set the bond hearing for 8:30 a.m. the next morning. That was when I first met Tiffany Erin.

I had tried to speak with her before the hearing, but she hadn't returned my calls. I was standing in the courtroom before the hearing started, answering Rhonda Mazur's questions about the bond process, when Tiffany Erin walked in and, by the time I could break free, the bailiff had entered the courtroom and I had to hurry to the counsel table to take my place.

Tiffany Erin stood at the prosecutor's table, pulling an iPad out of a patterned, black briefcase. She was tall, with sharp features and a strong jaw that were accentuated by short blond hair that was cut above her ears. She wore a tailored blue suit and heels that were higher than you normally saw with lawyers. I looked over to make eye contact and nod hello, but once she had her iPad set up, she crossed her arms in front of her and looked at the bench.

Before I could walk over to introduce myself, the bailiff said, "All rise for the Honorable Martin LaPlante."

Judge LaPlante entered. I had not met him before. He looked

to be in his late fifties, on the spare side, with dark eyes and a quick stride. He was bald with a black fringe of hair that was beginning to show sprinkles of gray at the sideburns. He nodded to the bailiff, said, "Thank you, Patricia," and sat.

After a momentary shuffle of paper, he said, "We're here this morning on the matter of State versus Colton Daniels to set bond for the defendant. Mr. Daniels is appearing via video from the Ash County jail. Good morning, Mr. Daniels. Can you hear me?"

Colt's face appeared on the video screen that sat off to the side, next to the jury box. "Yes, sir."

"I'm going to speak to the attorneys now and I would ask that you remain there and silent. Do you understand?"

"I do, sir."

"Very well. Could the attorneys please identify themselves for the record?"

"Tiffany Erin for the state, Your Honor." Her voice was a little deeper than I expected.

"Nate Shepherd for Mr. Daniels, Your Honor."

"Very good. Are the two of you ready to discuss bond?"

"Yes, Your Honor," we both said.

"Ms. Erin?"

"Your Honor, the State recommends that Mr. Daniels be held in custody until the time of trial without bond."

Judge LaPlante turned to me. "Mr. Shepherd?"

There was only one response to a demand like that from the prosecution. "Your Honor, we submit that Mr. Daniels should be released on his own recognizance without bond prior to trial."

Judge LaPlante pressed his lips together and set down his pen. "Ms. Erin, I realize that you are a special prosecutor coming from Jackson and so have not practiced in this court. I further realize that this hearing was scheduled on short notice because of an unexplained delay in processing Mr. Daniels. However, we have standard bond amounts here that are customary for the Court to impose unless one of the parties provides us with a reason to deviate from it. Do you have a reason for the Court to deviate from its standard practice?"

"Your Honor, this foul crime, the murder of a father by a son, shows a depth of moral depravity and violent intent that makes the defendant an imminent danger to the community."

Judge LaPlante's head twitched from side to side. "Save your arguments for the jury, Ms. Erin. Can you demonstrate any of the enumerated aggravating factors to increase or deny bond?"

Tiffany Erin raised her chin and said, "We would cite the Court to factor (b)(2) a crime demonstrating extreme violence, (b)(3) moral depravity, and (b)(7) risk of further violence."

Judge LaPlante turned to me. "Mr. Shepherd, I know you do not practice here often either. Are there any of the enumerated mitigating factors that you believe should influence the Court's decision on bond?"

"Actually, Your Honor I just tried—"

Judge LaPlante raised his hand. "I'm very aware that you just tried a case here, Mr. Shepherd. I'm also aware that it was your first one in our court, which is why I said you don't come up here often. Do you have any factors for me to consider?"

"Your Honor, I can't speak to the alleged nature of the crime that Ms. Erin cites because, to date, the prosecution has not provided us with any information describing the manner in which they claim Brett Daniels was killed. That information is not otherwise available to the family because it has been their understanding that Mr. Daniels died from a hunting accident. For that reason, we'd ask the Court to disregard the prosecution's request to increase bond. We would further ask that bond be lowered from the standard amount because my client is a twenty-year-old college student with no priors and no history of violent conduct that would pose a threat to the community, which falls under mitigating factors (c)(4) and (6)."

Judge LaPlante turned back to Tiffany Erin. "Ms. Erin, would you care to elaborate on the nature of the alleged crime?"

"That more detailed filing is not due yet, Your Honor, so the prosecution will wait to disclose that information until it is required to do so under the Court's schedule."

"Very well," said Judge LaPlante. "The Court hereby sets bond in the standard amount of $500,000 and sets the terms of release in accordance with the Court's standard monitoring protocol. Is there anything else?"

"Your Honor, the prosecution moves that this be a cash bond."

Judge LaPlante shook his head. "That motion is denied as the prosecution has not demonstrated any aggravating factors to warrant it. The defendant must produce ten percent as in any other standard bond arrangement."

"And when will the prosecution provide its Brady disclosures?" I said.

Judge LaPlante's eyes bore in. "Counsel, this is a bond hearing. Case discovery and disclosures will be governed by our standard order, which will be issued in due course."

Judge LaPlante stared at both of us and he seemed more irritated than angry. "We expect counsel to know our procedures and work together to follow them. This is not Jackson or Carrefour—it's Ash County. I expect you both to conduct yourselves accordingly if you're going to practice here."

"Yes, Your Honor," I said. Tiffany Erin nodded.

Judge LaPlante turned back to the screen. "Mr. Daniels, I have set the terms of your bond. Your attorney and a bond agent will be down shortly to discuss it with you."

Colt looked at the camera. He clearly didn't have any idea what was going on, but he managed to stutter out a "Yes, sir."

"That's all, counsel. Patricia, please call the next case."

The attorneys for the next case came through the gate and switched places with us. As I held the gate open for them, I caught Tiffany Erin's eye as she passed, which she met coolly as she kept on walking toward the courtroom door. Rhonda Mazur came up to me, but I asked her to wait a moment and followed Tiffany Erin out.

"Tiffany," I said as I caught her. "Do you have a moment to talk?"

She turned back to me. Her eyes were a startlingly light blue-green and surprisingly hard. "I'm sorry, Nate, I don't. This hearing was last minute so I have to get back to Jackson. We'll talk soon."

Then she turned and walked away.

"What did all that mean?" said Rhonda from my elbow.

I recovered from the abruptness of Tiffany Erin's departure and turned back to Rhonda. "It means that Colt can be released once you've pledged fifty thousand dollars and security for four hundred and fifty thousand more."

Rhonda's face panicked. "I don't have that kind of money."

"I've got someone for you to talk to. People sometimes have more resources than they think. He's good at figuring this out."

"He can't find money I don't have."

"That's all right, we'll go over to the jail and I'll introduce you to Cade Brickson."

Which is what we did.

∼

CADE CALLED me later that afternoon. "I don't think they're going to be able to afford it," he said.

Cade was Olivia Brickson's brother. He owned the gym with her and also ran a bail bond business. Since I'd gone out on my own, I'd directed clients with bail needs to him and he had usually been pretty creative about figuring out how to post it.

"Really? They don't have any property to pledge?"

"Not enough really. I might be willing to be a little short on the collateral if I think they're a good risk, but they can't come up with the cash either. And I'm not going to front that. They have to have skin in the game or he'll jump."

"I get it. They can't get a loan?"

"Not right away. They're looking at cash advances and crowd funding, but I think it's going to take a little time."

"During which Colt is still in jail."

"That's why I'm telling you."

"Okay. Thanks for letting me know."

"No problem. How's your face?"

"Better than your leg. You'll let me know if they post?"

"Yep. But I'm not optimistic."

"Got it. Thanks."

After we hung up, I stared at my phone for a moment. Then, against my better judgment, I hit the blue button with the little white bird to see what people were tweeting about the case, and by people, I meant @AlexisFury.

There was the avatar—the sketch of the screaming face, the wild red hair writhing like snakes, and the accusing finger, pointing. She'd retweeted an article with the headline "Bond Set for Man Accused of Killing Father." Then she tweeted a clip of a young Ricky Schroeder begging the Champ to wake up. Then she followed it with footage that looked like cell phone video of Colt walking into the Ash County jail the previous night.

I changed screens and called Olivia. "Hey, Liv. Two questions."

"Shoot."

"How hard is it to get a Twitter account shut down?"

"Are they threatening violence against anyone?"

"No."

"Are they lying?"

I thought. "They're probably expressing an opinion."

"Then it's damn near impossible."

"How about figuring out who someone actually is?"

"You'll never find out from the company. The best you might be able to do is piece together clues from what that person says or where the material comes from. People make burner accounts all the time though."

"Okay. I'm going to send you one. You don't have to spend too much time on it, just see if there are any clues on who this person might be."

"Why do we suddenly care about this mystery person?"

"Because she's poisoning my jury pool."

"Or he. What's the name?"

"@AlexisFury."

"Oh. Don't bother."

Olivia would normally research anything so that surprised me. "Why?"

"It's an aggregator account."

"You know it?"

"I've come across it before. Anyone anywhere can send it video or a post and the account culls through it all to find the stuff that's getting the most traction and reposts it. The @AlexisFury account likes crime in general and murder in particular. I've come across it in some of my other investigations."

"I don't remember you mentioning it."

She chuckled. "You're not my only client, Shep."

"Ah. Right."

"I will do background on your people tonight though. I'll let you know as soon as I have something."

"Thanks."

We hung up. Normally when I got a case, we started digging into the evidence right away. This was different. This time there were obstacles to even getting the basic facts.

I was pretty sure, based on the arrest, that it wasn't going to get any easier once I had them.

15

I was at the office the next morning when I received two calls. At the time, I thought that one was bad and one was good.

The first one was from Olivia.

"What's up, Liv?" I said.

"Do you want the bad news or the bad news?" she said.

"Let's go with the bad news."

"It looks like Colt and his father didn't get along."

"How so?"

"Colt and his father got into a fight at Borderlands."

Borderlands was a local bar and grill that everyone went to on the north side of, well, the border, especially after football games. "By fight, you mean argument?"

"By fight, I mean punches thrown and a broken video game screen that cost $3,332.86 to fix."

"That seems awfully precise."

"Police reports are like that."

"Was anyone arrested?"

"No. It looks like they decided that it was family dispute and let it go."

"Any information on how it started?"

"No. According to the report, both of them threw hands."

"I suppose that's something."

"But it was Brett who put the top of Colt's head through the video game screen."

I couldn't decide right then if that part made it better or worse. "Any other joy you'd like to sprinkle on my morning?"

"Other than the sound of my voice? No."

"Thanks, Liv. Keep digging?"

"Of course. Make sure you get down here this week."

We hung up. I was still digesting the fact that there was a witnessed, violent altercation between my client and the victim when my phone buzzed again. Cade.

"What's going on, Cade?"

"Colt Daniels posted bond this morning."

I blinked. "The whole fifty thousand?"

"He wouldn't be out otherwise."

"How in the world did they come up with that?"

"Nate, we've had this discussion before."

"I know you didn't ask but did they mention anything?"

"No."

"When does he get out?"

"I should have him out of there by eleven. You're going to have to reinforce with his mother why he can't stay with her."

"Right...Why can't he stay with her?"

"She lives in Ohio. He has to stay in state."

"Got it. Where is he going to stay?"

"His dad's place. Technically, he owns it along with his brother. For now anyway."

"Thanks for the optimism."

"No charge."

"Driving privileges?"

"No. Home restrictions."

"All right. Have Rhonda take him home and I'll visit later today."

"Got it. Talk to you."

It's easy when you're practicing law and dealing with big companies to lose track of money, to forget the scale of what actual money is to actual people. Opening my own law practice a couple of years ago had recalibrated my understanding closer to what it had been when I grew up.

Fifty thousand dollars was a lot of money. People can't just come up with that, let alone on short notice. Colt's mom had. I filed that away in the "things to keep an eye on" category.

Figuring out that mystery wasn't going to keep Colt out of jail, but the story Olivia had just told me might contribute to putting him in it. So I checked the clock, decided it was close enough to lunchtime to get away with it, and went to Borderlands.

～

EVERY TOWN HAS a place like it, a place that's as much restaurant as bar, a place that serves burgers and wings and poppers and beer in a bucket, with plenty of TVs for a big game, plenty of space at the bar for a few friends on the way home from work, and plenty of four-top tables that can be pushed together to accommodate an extended family for grandma's birthday in an atmosphere where small grandchildren could make a fuss and not be noticed.

On the north side of Carrefour, that place was Borderlands. And the owner of Borderlands was Kenny Kaminski.

I was a little early for lunch, but a young woman in a Lions jersey said the grill would be running in just ten minutes if I wanted to grab a seat now and wait. I passed on her offer of a Borderlands Bomber since grapefruit juice and an indeterminate number of rum shots seemed excessive for 10:50 on a Tuesday morning. Instead, I ordered water and a club sandwich and asked if Kenny Kaminski would be willing to come out and see Nate Shepherd for a minute.

The young woman nodded, said she'd check, and left. As I waited, I looked at the walls and I had to say that Kenny knew his clientele. All around the room there was the memorabilia you'd expect in southern Michigan—two framed tickets from Game 5 of the '84 World Series, a game-worn jersey of Barry Sanders, and a picture of the Red Wings' Darren McCarty putting it on the Avalanche's Claude Lemieux who definitely, indisputably, had it coming to him.

Interspersed through all that pro memorabilia though lay Kenny's real genius—his cultivation of a connection to the Carrefour community. There were pictures of the state championship girls' volleyball teams from 1996 and 2012, of the wrestling teams from 1984, 1999, and 2003, and the state runner-up baseball and football teams from 2015 and 2018. Besides the team photos, there were eye-catching action shots scattered about—a couple of tables over, a high school Cade Brickson was captured launching a two hundred eighty-five pound man over his head onto the mat as if it were nothing at all. And, just above my booth, was one of my brother Tom pumping his fist and screaming on the sideline after his football team beat South for the third year in a row.

"I was there that night, you know," said a voice. "We were down fourteen going into the fourth but your brother never flinched; he kept running the ball even though time was ticking down because he knew those city boys were tired."

I smiled. "The two-point conversion was still a risk."

"Bah," said Kenny Kaminski. "Not when the other team's linemen can't even stand up anymore. Easy money." Kenny Kaminski held out his hand. "How are you doing, Nate?"

Kenny Kaminski was in his late forties and looked like he ate at his restaurant a lot. His face was a little red and his cheeks were a little full, and it's likely that the picture of him by the door in his North football uniform was taken right around the last time he ran a lap. But Kenny was enthusiastic, he was everywhere in the community, and he was about as ardent a supporter for the Panthers as you were going to find.

"You're a little far out today, aren't you?" he said. "I don't usually see you during the week."

"I am. Do you have a minute to talk?"

"Of course." Kenny sat right down. "What's going on?"

"You know Colt was arrested last week?"

"Know? That's all anyone's talking about. Just like those O-holes to pull a stunt like that, trying to get in our boys' heads."

Some people on the north side of the border had taken to calling those on the south side "O-holes" and the name had stuck. I'm not endorsing it, I'm just telling you what he said.

"I'm representing Colt," I said.

"Good! I'm glad to hear he's got one of us in his corner. What do you know? There're all sorts of rumors."

I usually play things pretty close when I'm talking to someone about a case, but everyone knew Colt was accused of killing his dad, or soon would, so my best bet to get help here was to tell Kenny myself. "They're accusing Colt of killing his dad."

Kenny stared at me, then said, "That's about the dumbest thing I've ever heard."

"I agree."

"You need anything, anything at all for that boy, you let me know, okay?"

"Sure. Thanks, Kenny. "

"I mean it. You tell me."

"I will. Right now, I'm following up on a story I just heard."

"I do hear a lot of stories."

"This one actually happened here."

Kenny looked confused. "What's that?"

"The fight between Colt and his dad."

Kenny's face fell. "Ah, yeah, that. Well, they did have a little scuffle, but what boy hasn't scrapped a bit with his pop now and then?"

I didn't say that most boys aren't accused of murdering their pops. Instead, I said, "When was it exactly?"

"Oh, must have been a year, year and a half ago, maybe."

"What happened?"

"I don't know as I could say exactly."

"What could you say generally?"

Kenny's face flushed a little more. "Generally, Colt and Brett were here for dinner one night and then they got into an argument that got a little aggressive."

"Where were they sitting?"

"Right over there." He pointed to a table at the far end of the restaurant near a Galaga video game and one of those clear glass cubes with a claw where you can spend your life savings trying to win a stuffed animal.

"Who was with them?"

"Tyler for sure. Maybe Rhonda and Rob were too, but I'm not for sure on that."

"Did you see any of it?"

"I didn't see how it started. By the time I heard the commotion, the two of them were tumbling around over there."

"What did you see exactly?"

Kenny stared at me. "Why do you need to know, Nate?"

"Because I think the prosecution knows about it or is going to find out, and if I'm going to help Colt, I need to know what they know so that I can deal with it."

Kenny thought before he nodded and said, "Brett had Colt in

a headlock." He smiled and pointed at the picture of Cade a couple of booths down. "Not with the head and arm like Cade Brickson used to throw but just both arms around his head, squeezing, calm as could be. Colt was behind him like, trying to push Brett face first into the wall so Brett, he pivots at the same time Colt is driving forward and Colt's head winds up smashing right into that Galaga screen over there. I ran over to break it up, but the broken glass seemed to stop them both faster than a bucket of cold water. I remember Tyler being here because he grabbed Colt and I grabbed Brett and we hustled them off in different directions. Colt had a couple of cuts on his forehead that were bleeding pretty good so Colt and Tyler went in back with one of the girls to get a towel on them and I stayed with Brett while one of my boys swept up the broken glass."

"Were there other people here?"

"Some. We weren't full, but there were a few tables. I offered most of them discounts for the disturbance, but I don't think anyone took me up on it. I think they thought that was about as exciting a night as there'd been in a while."

"The police came?"

Kenny scowled. "Yeah, that was unfortunate. One of the girls called as soon as the fight started." He appeared to catch himself and raised both hands, "Which is fine, I understand, I want them to feel safe and certainly, if I'm not here, that's the best course. She didn't know that it was just a family squabble." He shook his head. "But the police came and took statements so, there you go."

"Did they arrest anyone?"

"Not that I recollect. Although Colt was Brett's son, he wasn't a minor anymore so I don't think they looked at it as an abuse situation. When they sorted it all out, I think they thought that Colt might have started the physical part even though he's the one who got hurt. I think they got a promise that Colt would stay with his mom that night so that they wouldn't be in the same house and let things cool off." Kenny shrugged. "I knew the deputy pretty well from the Sheriff's Shuffle Invitational and the Coat Drive. I think he came to understand that this was just some boys letting off some steam and no one needed to be arrested over it."

"Was Brett hurt?"

"No, not at all."

"So he was able to handle Colt?"

Kenny laughed. "Yeah, Brett was able to handle Colt."

"Why is that funny?"

"Did you ever meet Brett?"

"No."

"Colt would have needed more seasoning before he gave Brett any trouble."

"I see." I looked at the Galaga machine. "Is that the same game?"

"It is. I only had to replace the screen."

"Was that on the police report?"

Kenny looked embarrassed. "I'm afraid it had to be so I could turn it in to insurance. That wound up causing more trouble for the two of them so I had to tell the police that I didn't want to press charges for property damage either."

"And did insurance pay for it?"

"No, no it didn't. It was within my deductible so I never made the claim."

"Who paid for it?"

"Brett did. That's the way he was. Even if Colt started it, he wasn't going to let a friend take care of that."

"You were friends with Brett?"

"Just about as good friends as you could be." He smiled. "Or as Brett would allow."

"How much was it? The damage?"

"I'd say three thousand, give or take."

My waitress came with my club sandwich and Kenny stood. "I'll let you eat. If you need anything for Colt, you just call me."

"Thanks, Kenny."

"And tell that brother of yours that we're planning on going to Ford Field to see him win it all this year."

"I will."

Before I finished, Kenny was off to the next table where he greeted a man who had apparently not been to Borderlands in a month of Sundays.

Kenny's story had me concerned. Sure, Colt was the one who'd gotten pounded by Brett but that was almost worse.

Revenge is a powerful motivator. Any good prosecutor will tell you that.

16

I made a quick call to Cade on the way back to the office. He told me that he had Colt processed and out and that they were on their way to Brett's house for a meeting with the electronic monitoring unit. I thanked him and told him I'd stop by at the end of the day.

I could hear Danny talking when I came in. He couldn't see me because he was in his office.

"I know that, Jenny, but it's not what Nate planned on doing either...I know that...Yes, I liked doing business cases, but you've got to develop a reputation before people give them to you...No, Nate feels the same way...That's not fair, Jenny. He's been through a lot and has always taken care of us...I'm sorry, Jenny, but this really isn't the time. We can talk about it tonight if you want."

There was a silence that I assumed was listening. I'm ashamed to say that I stood there quietly and listened, too.

"Sure, I can talk to him about it...I'm going to help him with this case though...Jen, he's just a kid. He's barely twenty...No, he's *accused* of killing his father...Of course I sound like a lawyer, that's what I went to law school for...Just because they're calling him that doesn't make it so...Jenny, you know that's not true of Nate and it's not true of me either."

I decided I shouldn't hear any more of this conversation so I reopened the front door and kicked the bottom a couple of times before banging it shut.

There was a quieter, "I've got to go...Normal time tonight...Love you, too."

I bumped around a couple more times for good measure and then stuck my head into Danny's office. "Hey. How's it going?"

"Good. How did the bond hearing go?" No trace of the conflict from a moment before showed on Danny's face.

I wasn't sure whether to feel proud or guilty.

I told Danny about Colt posting bond unexpectedly, about Olivia discovering the fight between Colt and Brett, and my visit to Borderlands to talk to Kenny Kaminski about it.

Danny understood right away. "That's not good."

"No, it's not."

"Want me to get on a motion to keep out prior acts?"

"Just put it on the list for now. We'll have to address it but not until closer to trial. What else are you working on?"

"Little fires everywhere. You?"

"Same. Keep working on whatever else you're doing this afternoon. I have to go out to the Daniels' house around four."

"Sure. Want me to go with you?"

"No. This'll just be a quick visit. You ought to take off early if you can."

Danny looked up. "Who are you and what have you done with Nate Shepherd?"

"We're coming off one trial and are on our way into another. You have to take advantage of the gaps when you can."

He looked at the pile of papers on his desk.

I shrugged. "Up to you if you can manage it."

I went back to my office and went out of my way not to hear

the murmur of the phone conversation in the next room. I looked at my own phone and realized that I hadn't had the reflexive urge to call home and check in for a while. That lack hit me harder than I would've expected so I decided it was time to get to work.

∽

AT THE APPOINTED HOUR, I drove out M-339 to Brett Daniels' metal-roofed house. As I pulled in the two-track drive, I saw that a couple more vehicles had joined Brett's black F150—a green Jeep Patriot and a blue base model Dodge Ram pickup. Both were old and the blue pickup had pronounced streaks of rust along the bottom of each door. I figured from the "Panther Mom 9" sticker that the Patriot was Rhonda's, meaning the truck must be Colt's. Sure enough, as I turned off my car, Rhonda came out the back of the house and opened the Patriot's hatch.

"Go on in, Shepherd," she said as I climbed out. "I've just got one more trip."

"Can I carry something?"

"Ain't that like a lawyer to offer help when the work's done." She smiled when she said it to dull the sting of truth. "I'll be right in."

I followed the worn path to the back landing and opened the white metal storm door that led to the kitchen. It looked how I remembered, yellowed linoleum, brown wooden table, although now I was close enough to see the worn spots on the table's varnish from years of plates and elbows. The air was a little stale and the smell of cigarette smoke hung in the air.

Colt was unpacking a couple of bags of groceries. His thick hair was still wet and spiky, I presumed from showering after a few days without.

He looked up. "Hi, Mr. Shepherd."

"Please. Nate. Do you need help?"

"No, I'm almost done thanks." He put a gallon of milk and two dozen eggs in the fridge and slid a stack of frozen pizzas into the freezer. "Restocking the essentials," he said as he put all the plastic bags into one and stuck them in a drawer. "You can never have enough dog poop bags."

I smiled. "You never miss 'em 'til they're gone."

Rhonda returned then, carrying a large plastic laundry basket in both hands. I moved to take it for her and got a raspy growl in return. "We're not paying you to unpack laundry, Shepherd. You talk to Colt. I'll take care of this."

"Just put it on my bed, Mom. I'll put it away."

"What about Tyler's?"

"Same thing."

Rhonda shook her head. "I don't know how you boys go through so many clothes."

Colt smiled. "I wore one set for five days, Mom. What do you want?"

Rhonda's look fell, and she went down the short hallway into one of the bedrooms.

"How are you doing?" I said.

Colt shrugged as he unpacked some hamburger and spaghetti sauce. "Okay. Do I have to wear this ankle monitor the whole time?"

"What did they tell you?"

"That I do."

"Well, there's your answer."

"How long?"

"Through trial."

"But that's going to be months from now, right?"

"It is."

"And I'm not supposed to leave?"

"That's right."

"What about school?"

"You're not going to be allowed to go back for now. You'll need to arrange to do everything you can remotely."

"But that's not fair. We've already paid for this semester!"

I didn't tell him that if he actually murdered his father, no one in the system would care that he lost his pre-paid tuition. Instead, I said, "That's just the way it works."

Rhonda emerged with an empty laundry basket. "I'm going to have a smoke and then I'll make you and Tyler dinner."

"When is he getting here?" said Colt.

"About twenty minutes. He texted." She set the basket on the old wood table and went out the back kitchen door.

"I'm going to talk to your mom for a minute, Colt."

"Have at it. I'm going to drink a Coke and not be in jail."

I joined Rhonda out back. The concrete pad wasn't much more than six feet wide so she had walked down by the picnic table. She was wearing a dark blue felt coat with a gray wool scarf pulled tight around her neck and her long blonde hair spilled down the back over both. She looked over her shoulder as I came out the door then took a deep draw and blew the smoke up into the air in the opposite direction.

She smiled, deepening the lines at the side of her eyes, and held up the cigarette. "I try to keep it outside, what with raising a couple of athletes and all."

I smiled and shrugged. "I'd say you deserve one after today."

She took another pull and blew it up into the air. "After this week." She shook her head. "I must've gone through a pack and a half a day while he was in there."

"Well, he's out for now. So you were able to post bond with Cade?"

She watched the smoke rise. "Yep. We had more resources than we realized."

"Colt understands that if he violates the terms, you lose the money and he goes back in jail?"

She tossed the butt on the frozen ground, crunched it with her boot, and lit another. "He knows."

"I hear your house is across the state line. That means he can't go there either."

"He's not going anywhere." She took a draw, squinted one eye, and pointed at me with two fingers and a glowing ember. "And it's your job to make sure it stays that way."

"It is. What can you tell me about the fight between Colt and his dad at the Borderlands?"

Rhonda didn't flinch. She took a draw, blew it out, and said, "Nothing. I wasn't there."

"Kenny Kaminski thought you were."

She took a draw, blew it out, and said, "Kenny Kaminski is wrong."

"What did you hear then?"

"I heard that mean old ass-bag put my son's head through a video game screen."

"Was it true?"

"It's true. Colt had stitches and Brett was after me for half the money to fix the video game."

"What did you tell him?"

"I told him go bend himself and that he should think about that the next time he used his son's head as a hammer.

"Did you think about pressing charges?"

"I'm not going to get much child support for my youngest boy if his father is in jail now will I?"

"I suppose not. Any other fights between the two of them?"

"No. There wasn't much future in that."

"Why?"

Rhonda stared straight back into the woods and pointed. "Shepherd, my husband hunted coyotes at night with a crossbow. For fun. If I need to explain it to you, then I should probably find another lawyer for my son."

She had a point.

There was a flash of headlights and the sound of an engine from the drive. "That'll be Tyler." Rhonda crushed the butt, picked them both up, then climbed the concrete stair and went back inside. I followed.

As I walked into the kitchen, a yellow lab blew through the side door and charged its barking, jumping, tail-wagging way first to Rhonda and then to Colt, who grabbed him under the ears and started scratching. The tail wagged more, slamming against a table leg so hard that I thought for a moment it might move. Then Chet—of course, it was Chet—broke loose and made his merry way over to me. Chet sized me up, then sat, so I ruffled the fur behind his head then scratched him right behind the jaw as Chet closed his eyes in apparent agreement that he was, in fact, a very good boy. That lasted for a second before he shot straight to the back door and scratched. I looked a question at Colt, who said, "Let him out. He won't go anywhere."

I opened the door and Chet bolted outside.

It was impossible not to chuckle at his enthusiasm so I did and turned back to find a young man entering the kitchen from the front of the house. He was tall, maybe six foot five, and had that wide but thin frame that showed he still had some filling out to do. As tall as he was, his hands and feet still seemed a little big for his body. The young man had blonde hair that was short and uniform in a way that meant it had been shaved clean off in the not-too-distant past and was a few weeks into growing back. He was wearing a black varsity jacket with red leather sleeves and had a large gym bag thrown over his shoulder. It was no mystery who he was, but the black and red varsity jacket with "TD" embroidered on the left chest solved it anyway.

"Sorry about that," Tyler said and tapped the gym bag. "He took off before I could grab him."

"He's fine," I said. "I'm Nate, Tyler."

He strode right up, looked me in the eye, and shook my hand. "I remember you from your brother's football camps."

"I'm going to make spaghetti," said Rhonda with a clatter of pans.

"Nice to see you again, Mr. Shepherd," said Tyler. "I'm going to dump this stuff in my room, Mom."

"I put your laundry in there too," said Rhonda. "I wasn't sure where you wanted it so it's on the bed."

"That's fine." Tyler nodded to me and walked out.

Colt looked back to me. "What else do you need, Mr....Nate?"

As Rhonda pulled hamburger out of the fridge and pasta out of a cupboard, I realized that Colt had just gotten home after five nights in jail and that this trial wasn't going to be for months. "I need you to get some rest and a big helping of that spaghetti your mom's making. There will be plenty of time for us to talk at the end of the week. What's your number?"

He told me. I texted him. "Here's mine. Call me anytime, especially if you have a question about whether you can do something."

"Sure."

"Now this next part is going to be really hard, but I need you all to promise not to talk about the case."

Rhonda looked at me over the pot. "Why the hell not?"

"Because the prosecutor can put you on the stand to testify against your son. Either of you can call me anytime if you need to talk about something with the case."

Rhonda looked skeptical but Colt said, "Got it."

Right then, Chet scratched at the back door and Tyler returned to the kitchen. As I opened the door, Chet went straight to a bowl and started nosing it around the room because it was empty.

"I bet you're thirsty after all that yelling," said Tyler. He picked up the bowl, which was bone dry, and went over to the sink and filled it. He set it back down in its place and went to the pantry and pulled out a bag of dog food. It was crinkled and ragged and when he turned it over in the bowl, food dust and seven nuggets clanked out. "No dog food?"

"I didn't have time to shop," said Colt. "Jail, remember?"

Tyler looked at him. "Right. Sorry. I forgot to stop."

Colt gave Chet a scratch, who was more than willing to stand there for it. "I can watch him when you get some after dinner."

Tyler nodded, apparently irritated he'd forgotten.

The three of them were obviously settling in and it was time for me to get going. "I'll leave you all to it. Colt, I'll call you in the next couple of days."

"Sounds good, Nate. Thanks."

"Bye, Shepherd," said Rhonda. Tyler waved goodbye and patted his dog.

I climbed into my Jeep to head home. As I left, it occurred to me that the three of them were acting like a family, that there wasn't an undercurrent of anger or hate or hurt. In other words, neither Rhonda nor Tyler acted like they thought Colt had killed his father.

Or they didn't care.

17

Danny was waiting for me when I arrived at the office the next day. "Two things before you get going."

I looked over his shoulder. "How about coffee so I can get going?"

He followed me to the coffee machine and, as I grabbed a thermocup that read "Panther Pride Golf Outing," said, "I ran down the coroner in the Daniels case."

"Oh, good. Who is it?"

"Warren Archuleta."

"I don't know that I've heard of him."

"I don't know that you would have. It looks like he covers three counties, including Ash, which don't have enough activity to justify a full-time coroner. Seems like he contracts with law enforcement and the bigger hospitals on a case-by-case basis."

I poured then snapped the lid on the coffee cup. "Nice work. Did you reach out to him for the autopsy?"

"I did. He said the results were still pending so he couldn't release it."

"Did he say when?"

"Six to eight weeks."

"That's bullshit."

"Why?"

"The autopsy's done. He examined the body within a couple of days. And he already knows the cause of death because we've got a murder charge. Even if he made tissue slides, those would be done by now, too."

"What's he talking about then?"

"The only thing that takes another six to eight weeks are the toxicology results and we know those aren't going to alter the cause of death because they've already filed charges." I took a sip. "Unless the local coyotes have taken to drugging people of course."

"What's going on then?"

"I'd say we're getting stonewalled."

"Is that unusual?"

"It is for around here. Wait a minute, let me guess, is Dr. Archuleta based out of Jackson?"

"How did you...oh, right, got it."

"Exactly. Do a Lexis search of the times Archuleta has been named as an expert. My guess is that our Jackson-based coroner has appeared in some cases involving a prosecutor out of Jackson who specializes in murder cases."

"So we aren't going to get that autopsy until they absolutely have to give it to us."

I nodded. "Which isn't for a few weeks yet."

Danny looked worried. "We need it sooner."

"We do."

"How do we get it?"

"I have an idea, but I think I want to run it by an expert first."

"Really? Who?"

"Cyn Bardor."

I couldn't swear to it, but as Danny shifted his weight back and forth, he might, *might*, have started to sweat just a little bit at the temple.

"She's in Minnesota," he said. "How can she help?"

"To get the information we need, we're going to have to light a fire under the prosecutor and her experts. I'd like Cyn's opinion on whether we can control it."

"When are you going to call her?"

"Right now."

"I'll be in my office if you need me." He stumbled a little as he turned to go.

I smiled. Even from six hundred miles away, Cyn had that effect on Danny. I didn't blame him.

∼

CYN BARDOR WAS a paralegal with the firm of Friedlander & Skald out of Minneapolis, Minnesota. I'd worked with her on the Braggi case, the first murder trial I had handled once I went out to practice on my own. Cyn was the most practical, sharp, efficient person I've ever worked with and had an eye for strategy and case management that far exceeded that of most attorneys.

Although she never admitted to it, she had manipulated the media coverage around the Braggi trial with involvement that was so subtle I hadn't even realized it was going on. For what I was considering, I couldn't think of anyone whose opinion I would value more. I called the number in my phone I hadn't used in more than a year.

"Nathan. This is a pleasant surprise." Her voice didn't sound the least bit surprised.

"Hi, Cyn. Is it cold up there in Minneapolis?"

"It is. But I'm in Louisiana at the moment so it's hot."

"Really? What's in Louisiana?"

"A trial."

"So nowhere on the Mississippi is safe from you?"

"You know how it is, Nathan, we go where we're needed. Speaking of which?"

I'm not kidding, I could practically see her unblinking green eyes waiting for me to get to the point.

"Right. I'm considering a strategy I wanted to run by you. Do you have a moment?"

"Of course."

I told her about the case, about the dynamics, and about the fact that the prosecution was running out to a head start while I spun my wheels trying to get the bare facts. "So I was considering—"

"Going public in righteous outrage that the prosecution has charged a young man with his father's murder and won't even come forward with the most basic evidence."

I mean it was the reason I called her in the first place. But, man.

"Exactly."

"I agree that's the best way to prompt some movement."

"But I'm concerned that if I light that fire, I can't control it."

"You can't. Once you give it oxygen, you can't control how high it burns."

"What if I make it worse?"

"Then you need to be prepared with fuel to shift the fire in a new direction."

I didn't know if I had that, so I said, "What do you see as the biggest downside?"

"That the autopsy conclusively shows that your client did it and you've invited the prosecution to stick it squarely into your...case."

"That was my concern."

"But you mentioned this prosecutor is experienced?"

"Very."

"Then if that were true, she already would have done it."

"Like the police and prosecutor did in the Braggi case?"

"Exactly like that. She would have announced the findings when she filed the charges and ridden the banner headlines all the way to trial. So what's more likely?"

I thought. "That the autopsy is inconclusive or that it establishes the cause of death but not that my client did it."

"And you need *that* information as soon as possible so that you can start crafting your defense."

It seemed pretty simple when she said it. "Thank you, Cyn. This helps a lot. Sorry to bother you."

"Don't apologize, Nathan. We all need to bounce these things off someone. I'm glad you thought of me."

"It wasn't a hard choice. What you did in Braggi's case was pretty subtle."

"I don't know what you mean."

There was a pause then, before she said, "Are you well?"

"I am."

"Good," and it sounded as if she meant it. "It was good to hear from you. Don't wait so long next time."

"I won't. And if your traveling road show ever makes it out this way again be sure to stop by."

"You can count on it. Goodbye, Nathan."

"Goodbye, Cyn. And thanks."

"Of course."

As soon as we hung up, I picked up my phone to light some fires. Then I thought about everything that Cyn had said, about making sure that there was only fuel for the fire to burn in one direction, and I decided that there was one more thing I needed to do before I struck the match.

I had to go to Jackson.

18

I only had to sit in the lobby of the Jackson Municipal Building for ten minutes, which surprised me given that Tiffany Erin had gone out of her way to avoid speaking with me so far. All things considered, it really wasn't long at all before she came out, asked if someone had offered me coffee, and guided me back to her office.

It was nicer than I expected for a county prosecutor, more like a private firm from the 1990s with furniture of polished dark wood, shelves with leather-bound books that were more for show than research, and a couple of nicely framed, classic-looking paintings. I did a double take as I realized one of them was of a man being pursued by a group, his hands covering his ears.

"It's a Bouguereau," Tiffany Erin said. "A print of course."

"Ah."

"Do you know realism?"

"Not really."

She pressed her lips together and took a seat in a large leather chair. The light in the room seemed a little low, which somehow made her pale eyes brighter, which I was coming to believe she absolutely knew. She didn't smile, but she was polite as she said, "I have a hearing in a few minutes, Nate, but since you drove all this way, I wanted to at least touch base with you."

"Thanks. I appreciate that."

"You can call me anytime, you know."

"I have, but I haven't been able to reach you."

Tiffany Erin gave me a neutral nod that could just as easily have indicated that I was calling the wrong number as that she was ducking my calls. "So what can I do for you?"

"I'd like you to tell me why you charged my client with murder."

She nodded. "Because your client killed his father."

"How?"

"I don't have to produce that yet, Nate."

"I understand that. I'm asking you anyway."

"I look forward to giving you all of that information in accordance with the Court's deadlines."

"I'm not asking for your theory of the case, Tiffany. I'm asking for basic information like how Mr. Daniels died."

Tiffany Erin nodded. "I can assure you that we will have that all pulled together by the time the Court says it needs to be disclosed."

"Why aren't you letting Dr. Archuleta release the autopsy?"

She didn't blink. "It's my understanding that the autopsy is not complete yet."

"You know that the physical exam and the slides are finished."

"That's not what I said. I said that it's my understanding that the autopsy is not yet complete."

"How can you bring a murder charge if you don't know how Brett Daniels died?"

"Who says I don't know how Brett Daniels died?"

"You just said the autopsy wasn't complete."

"That's right."

Tiffany Erin didn't feel the need to say anything else. She just sat there and stared at me with those disconcerting eyes until I said, "You have to disclose that you know."

"Of course, I do. By the Court's deadline. I haven't missed any deadlines, have I, Nate?"

"No."

"Well, I appreciate you coming all the way out here although it wasn't necessary to make a special trip since you'll have everything by the time the Court says you should. Still, it's not a wasted trip since it's always nice to meet with opposing counsel and perhaps address a disconnect I find when I take a case in a smaller community."

"Sure."

Tiffany Erin didn't lean forward and she didn't fold her hands and she didn't even change the tone of her voice. She just gave me a sea-green stare as she said, "Your client murdered his father. Not some random person or an enemy or even a friend. His own father. I feel no duty to help you prepare his defense."

I shrugged. "I thought your job was to serve justice."

"Convicting killers serves justice. Particularly when their own family isn't even safe from them." She raised one finger. "I know it can be different in small communities, particularly with the old boys' club. But I am not part of that community and I am not a part of that club."

I was certainly a part of my community. I was not a part of any club but no comment from me was going to convince Tiffany Erin otherwise, so I just nodded and said, "I see."

"You can rest assured that I will scrupulously follow all of the rules and will give you every single thing to which you are entitled at the time you are entitled to receive it."

"I appreciate that," I said and stood. "And I appreciate your time. Thanks." I extended my hand.

Tiffany Erin immediately stood and took it. Her grip was strong and she looked me right in the eyes as she said, "I look forward to seeing you in court."

I smiled. "You, too."

I left. And on the way home from Jackson, I pulled out my phone to light some fires.

I called Danny first.

"What's up, Nate?"

"When did our discovery go out in the Daniels case?"

"Monday. As soon as you told me about it."

"Usual topics?"

"Let me make sure." I heard the clicking of his keyboard. "Looks like. Names and addresses of lay and expert witnesses, recorded statements of any witnesses, expert resumes and reports, criminal records, and a description and opportunity to inspect any physical evidence. Then exculpatory information or evidence, any police reports and interrogation records, and any statements by the defendant."

"So if that went out last Monday, they still have two-and-a-half weeks to get it to us?"

"Right. Unless they give us what they have like T. Marvin did."

"They're not going to."

"Really?"

"I just spoke to Tiffany Erin. She's not giving us anything until she has to."

"So what do we do?"

"We're going to start doing media interviews to see if we can turn up the heat on their production."

"Is that wise?"

"I'm not sure."

"What did Cyn say?"

"She wasn't expressly against it."

"You can't possibly think that reassures me."

"It shouldn't. Thanks, Danny. I'll be back in a couple of hours."

It took me a few minutes to find the next number since I was using the hands-free feature and it had been a while since I'd contacted him, but eventually I was able to call Ted Ringel of the *Ash County Torch*.

"Ted, it's Nate Shepherd."

"Well, that's a twist. I'm normally chasing you down."

"Thought I'd save you the trouble. Have you been running anything on the Brett Daniels case?"

"Uhm, let's see, is that the story about the brother of the best quarterback to come out of the county in twenty years being accused of murdering his father?"

"That's the one."

"We've mentioned it."

"I have a comment for you."

"On the record?"

"Yes."

I heard a pause of surprise or maybe he was just getting a recorder ready. "Go ahead."

"Colt Daniels recently lost his father. While he was still grieving, the prosecutor of Ash County decided to charge Colt in relation to his father's death. However, they have refused to provide us or the public with any evidence to support this charge. Despite our repeated requests, they won't even release the autopsy so that the public, and our office, knows what Mr. Daniels died of."

"Wait, Nate, you don't know how Brett Daniels died?"

"We haven't been given that information, Ted. The prosecutor's office is refusing to produce the autopsy. They may say toxicology is pending but the physical exam is long since done."

"The family doesn't know?"

"They were under the impression that it was a hunting accident."

"How did they hear that?"

"Law enforcement. Speaking of which, the prosecution's stonewalling on this is even worse when you consider the public spectacle they made of my client's arrest. If they're going to make a public scene and try to poison the jury pool, they should be ready to back it up."

"That doesn't sound like T. Marvin's style."

"It's not. Ash County has brought in a prosecutor from out of town. The bottom line, Ted, is that Colt is still grieving the loss of his father. We look forward to proving Colt's innocence at trial, but in the meantime, we hope that the prosecution starts representing the people of this county by providing its citizens with the most basic information they used to reach their charging decision."

I heard a click and a scrawl. "Is it true that the coyotes had gotten to him by the time he was found?"

"That's what I've been told. I haven't been able to see the autopsy to confirm it."

"That's pretty unusual, isn't it?"

"From my perspective, it sure is."

"Okay. I'm going to do some checking and make some calls, but we'll definitely run with this."

"When?"

"As soon as I can confirm details and give the prosecutor a chance to comment. Who is it if it's not T. Marvin?"

"Tiffany Erin out of Jackson."

"No kidding?" He chuckled. "Good luck."

"You know her?"

"Only by reputation. Which it looks like you're getting acquainted with."

"Best guess on when you think it'll run?"

False Oath

"Not tonight. Probably tomorrow."

"All right. Thanks. Call me if you need to confirm any other details."

Ted chuckled again. "It sounds like you don't have any. That's why you called me."

I smiled. "There's a reason you're a reporter."

"There certainly is. Thanks for calling me."

"Take care, Ted."

I made one more call, this time to a television reporter in Carrefour, and told her the same thing. Like Ted, she wanted to confirm the details and would probably run with it by the 11:30 show or the early morning. She was sure that her sports department would want to get a quote on it from the football angle, too. I thanked her and hung up.

I took a deep breath and just concentrated on the drive for a while.

I had done it. I had called attention to us and invited the prosecutor to tell us what she had. At the very least, I hoped that this would make her cough up the autopsy. And if we reached a portion of the jury pool with our side, so much the better.

Hopefully, I hadn't made things worse.

19

The next day was Friday and I kept half an eye on the media as I worked. The *Torch* and the TV station ran stories with my quotes and struck the tone I'd hoped for, questioning the basis for the prosecutor's case. But as the minutes turned into hours, and the hours passed to the end of the day, there was no response from the prosecutor's office. So, when the clock struck five, I turned off my computer and did what everyone on the Michigan side of Carrefour was doing—I went to the football game.

This was the first week of the playoffs and Tom's team was undefeated so it was a home game. I changed into some Carrefour North Panthers gear, bundled up, and headed over to the high school campus.

The Carrefour North Stadium is built into a hill so that you walk down into the stands instead of up. That grassy hill continues around the north end of the stadium so that people can sit on the hillside, on blankets or chairs or the grass itself, and watch the game from there. It was normally a little less crowded on the hill and, after Tommy's first year of coaching, we learned that it's not a bad idea for the coach's family to sit a ways off from the three thousand other coaches sitting in the stands.

I made my way around the walkway at the top of the stadium over to the hillside where I saw that my two sisters-in-law and my parents had claimed our usual spot.

Tom's wife Kate was there, sporting a black coat and a red hat, sitting with her son Charlie and daughter, Page, on a blanket. My sister-in-law Izzy had thrown a blanket down next to Kate and was sitting with two of her sons, James and Joe, and my mom. My brother Mark stood behind the blankets next to my dad, who was defiantly hatless so that his stark white hair stood out like a beacon.

I realize that the family roll call can be just as complicated at a football game as it is at a barbecue so, if it's been a while since you've seen them, my oldest brother Tom, the coach, is married to Kate and they have three daughters and a son, Reed, Taylor, Page, and Charlie. My younger brother Mark is married to Izzy and they have three "J" boys—Justin, James, and Joe. I was the last one to arrive, so I hugged my mom and my dad, said hi to my brother and sisters-in-law and held Charlie and Joe down with one hand each and tickled them with the claw of doom.

The boys laughed and kicked and said, "Not the claw!" until the claw was appeased. Charlie was still giving a good-natured four-year-old chortle when I said, "Where are the other trolls?"

Izzy pointed at the stands. "Reed is in the high school student section and Justin and Taylor have discovered there's a junior high section."

"When did they get that old?"

"I know, right?"

"How old does that make you?"

She smiled sweetly. "Far, far younger than you'll be when you're in my position."

"Evil woman."

"Speaking of which, you didn't answer my text about game night tomorrow."

"I have not. The guest list seemed a little limited."

Izzy smiled. "It's an eight-player game."

"And targeted."

"We didn't assign partners. You can be paired with anyone you want."

"Six of the eight people are married."

"You don't say? I suppose that does make it easier to pick teams."

"I'm afraid I'm busy tomorrow, Izzy."

"How could you possibly be busy on Saturday?"

"A new case has me scrambling a bit."

Izzy shook her head. "You know one of these days people are going to stop getting murdered around here and you're going to have to actually go out."

I held my hands out. "I look forward to the day."

"Hmph," she said and looked back at the field.

I took a step back to stand with my dad and Mark.

"How is Marshall supposed to be this year, Dad?"

My dad didn't take his eyes off the last of the warm-ups. "They have a running back that's big but slow. I think they ran over a few teams. Shouldn't be too much of a problem if our boys follow their assignments."

I hadn't seen any of them during the week so we chatted and caught up on the kids. They were nice enough not to ask me about Colt's case, which I appreciated.

The game finally started and Dad was right—Marshall's running back was huge but he was slow. North was able to put a lot of helmets on him to stop him, and it didn't seem like Marshall was able to change to anything else. Tyler threw for two touchdowns and ran for another right as the first half ended.

"I'm going to get some coffee," I said. "Anybody else want to come?"

"I'll go, Uncle Nate!" said James.

"Me too!" said Joe.

I took assorted orders for coffees, pops, and pretzels, swept Joe up onto my shoulders, and headed up the hill with James.

James was bundled against the cold and he wore a black stocking cap with a leaping red panther emblazoned on the front. We were walking up the hill to the pathway so our steps were uneven anyway, but I could see that James was limping a little, so I slowed down even though my nephew Joe was bouncing up and down on my shoulders and slapping me on the back saying, "Giddy up!"

"How's school, James?"

"Lunch is good. Math stinks."

"Sounds about right. Don't tell your mom though."

"Heck no."

We made it up to the flat concrete path and James walked noticeably easier but still limped. I remembered that he'd stopped playing basketball for now and had picked up something else. "How's wrestling going?"

He smiled. "We learned a chicken-in-the-basket this week!"

I laughed at the kids' name for a wrestling move. "Yeah? How did it taste?"

"You don't taste it! You pin with it!"

"Oh, oh. You had me confused."

"Dad says that happens to you all the time when work gets busy," said James.

I smiled. "He does, does he?"

"Yep. Are you busy?"

"Not so busy that I can't put my chicken in a basket."

Joe giggled as I flipped him off my shoulders, trundled him up into a cradle, then flipped him back onto my shoulders.

I stopped as we came to the concession stand and took a place in a line that was about twelve people deep. James was telling me the difference between a single leg and a double leg takedown while Joe was antsily wobbling from side-to-side on my shoulders when I felt a touch at my elbow. I turned to see the fierce red beard of Rob Preston.

"Hi, Nate," he said.

"Hey, Rob. Tyler's playing well."

Rob's teeth gleamed through the beard. "Rhonda's fit to burst. I was telling her these guys aren't that good, but she won't listen."

I smiled. "You can only play who they put in front of you, right?"

"Got that right. Any message for me to give Rhonda? She'll badger the living hell out of me once I tell her I saw you."

I glanced significantly at the people all around us. "Nothing new, Rob."

He didn't get the hint. "So no information about what happened? About how he died?"

"Not yet. Tell Rhonda the best thing you all can do right now is keep Colt company and keep his spirits up. We have a long road ahead of us."

Rob nodded, making his beard bob. He grinned up at Joe and rubbed James' cap. "So who are these little football players?"

James dropped his head.

I put my hand on his shoulder. "These are couple of wrestlers, my nephews Joe and James. They just learned how to put the...chicken-in-the-biscuit?"

"Chicken-in-the-basket!" they both said.

Rob Preston's grin broadened. "All right! Did you learn an arm bar yet?"

"Not yet," said James, which led to an animated discussion about how to pin someone that I was glad to see James join.

When we finally made it to the front of the line, I popped Joe off my shoulders so that he could do his part carrying a couple of bottles of pop. Joe took his two Sprites, and I grabbed a carrier of coffees, and James cradled a wax paper packet of soft pretzels. It took me long enough to organize with my two minions that, by the time I was done, Rob had bought his three coffees and joined us as we walked back toward the hill.

We were just about to split up when a man in a navy peacoat and blonde hair that was not messed in the slightest even though it was the second half of a football game in November came striding up and said, "Rob, I told you I'd get that."

"No bother." Rob shrugged and handed the man a coffee. Rob started to point at me around his coffee cup when Joe said, "Uncle Nate! These are heavy!" His arms, weighed down by two sixteen-ounce bottles of pop, sank toward the ground.

I smiled. "Sorry, excuse me, guys. Good to see you, Rob."

"Sure, Nate," said Rob. "Talk to you soon."

"You bet."

With that, Rob and his friend split off toward the stands while James and Joe and I went down the hill carrying our shipment of pop, coffee, and pretzels. You'd think we'd delivered gold, frankincense, and myrrh from all the fuss but, to be fair, the little trolls were pretty charming. The boys sat, the adults sipped, and we watched Tyler Daniels lead Tom's team to a 49–12 win.

20

Sometimes you get exactly what you wish for. Sometimes it's magnificent. And sometimes you wonder just what the hell you were thinking.

On Saturday, Tiffany Erin went public with her case. She didn't do it by half measures.

I first learned that something was breaking on Twitter. I had taken to checking the @AlexisFury account every day and, while I didn't necessarily think that looking at a virtual, writhing-haired lady first thing in the morning was the best life choice, I wanted to be aware of rumors the potential jury pool might be hearing. @AlexisFury kicked off that day by linking to an article about Tyler leading North to a playoff win and then re-tweeting seven posts of people wondering how Tyler could be allowed to play when his brother had been arrested for his father's murder. Then, the account tweeted out that "word was" that "big news" coming today on the Daniels murder, followed immediately by a tweet that simply said "Tiffany Erin" with the watching eyes emoji.

I hopped on the website for the *Ash County Torch* where Ted Ringel had posted that Tiffany Erin would give a press conference at noon that day about the Colt Daniels prosecution, followed by helpful instructions on how to get the live feed on the *Torch* website and Facebook Live.

I checked my work email to see if Tiffany Erin had sent me her disclosures or reached out to let me know what was going on. She had not, which really wasn't a surprise. Her disclosures weren't due for another couple of weeks yet, and she had made it pretty clear that she wasn't going to do anything until she had to.

I shot texts to Danny and Olivia letting them know about the press conference just in case they'd missed the posts. I started to text Colt, thought better of it, then called so I could warn him it was coming.

Colt already knew. Apparently, his social media accounts were blowing up with mentions and notifications and whatnot as people talked about the press conference and tagged him. I told him it was best to stay off his accounts for now and that, under no circumstances, should he reply to, retweet, or like anything. He said he wouldn't, but I wondered.

I decided I had enough time to go run. I would tell you that I used that time to clear my head, regroup, and come up with a strategy for defending Colt but that would be a lie because I still didn't know what I was defending. So instead I just ran and put my head somewhere else for about forty-five minutes. Then I showered up, made a sandwich and some soup (it was November, after all), and sat down at the table to watch the press conference on my tablet.

Tiffany Erin came on promptly at noon. I couldn't tell where she was, but there was a lectern with an American flag on one side and the state flag of Michigan on the other. She wore a blue suit with a white shirt and her short blonde hair was styled tight to the sides and up on top. Her pale eyes pierced straight through the camera as she said, "Good afternoon. For those of you I haven't met, I'm Tiffany Erin, special prosecutor for Ash County in the case of the State of Michigan versus Colton Daniels. Let me say at the outset that this press conference is unusual for me. I believe that justice is an important, deliberative process that takes place in the courtroom and not in the media. Although some attention is inevitable in cases involving allegations of murder, I prefer to describe the crime in the courtroom rather than in blizzards of bite-sized statements. Our Constitution is more than two hundred and eighty characters."

She paused and if there were any chuckles, they didn't make it over the feed. She continued, "However, because of the nature of this case and the family involved, there has been a great deal of speculation, along with inflammatory opinions, that there has not been sufficient explanation for charges that are so serious. As a result, the purpose of this press conference is to outline the nature of the charges against Colton Daniels and our reason for bringing them."

Tiffany Erin paused again, and it was clear that she was not at all uncomfortable talking to the press. She waited a little longer to be sure she had everyone's attention, then said, "Two weeks ago, Brett Daniels was killed while hunting on his own property. He was on a night hunt when he was shot in the leg by a crossbow. This crossbow."

She pulled a crossbow out from behind the lectern and held it up. "It's rare to find a murder weapon with a name engraved on it." She flipped the crossbow around so that the butt of the stock was visible. The camera obligingly zoomed in. "Colt" was engraved right on the stock.

Tiffany Erin set the crossbow aside as she said, "Brett Daniels was shot in the leg. From our investigation of the scene, he bled severely and was only able to make it a couple of hundred yards before he collapsed. Mr. Daniels died alone, of blood loss, behind his home."

Tiffany Erin clenched her jaw for a moment before she said, "Mr. Daniels tracked a significant amount of blood from his hunting stand to the place where he died. This blood attracted coyotes so that, by the time Mr. Daniels was found, coyotes had consumed significant portions of his body."

"Because of the coyote activity, the cause of death was not immediately apparent. That is why it was initially reported as a hunting accident. However, through the outstanding work of Tri-County coroner Dr. Warren Archuleta, we discovered that an arrow wound had caused Mr. Daniels' death. With that knowledge, further investigation of the site revealed Colt Daniels' crossbow and the arrow used to kill his father. We also garnered additional evidence that placed Colt Daniels at the scene of the crime and established a motive for his actions, all of which we will present to a jury in due course."

Tiffany Erin straightened papers on the lectern. "Our office does not bring a charge of murder lightly. We are very aware of the consequences of such a charge, particularly when it is brought against a family member. I am not going to try our case for you now. However, I will simply state that we understand exactly what we have charged Colt Daniels with and have evidence to support all of it. The killing of Brett Daniels was a monstrous crime. We intend to bring the person who committed that crime to justice. Thank you."

Tiffany Erin picked up the crossbow without answering questions and left the room. A moment later, the screen went blank as the feed stopped.

I sat there absorbing what I'd just heard and seen. It didn't sound good when she laid it all out like that, but then again, it never did. They had a murder weapon, a motive, and—if they were to be believed—evidence of Colt at the site.

And I finally had an idea what the case was about.

It was time to get to work.

∾

When I arrived at the Daniels' house, the side door to the barn was open. I parked behind Brett Daniels' black F150 and got out of the car. When I was halfway to the barn, Chet came tearing out through the barn's open side-door and bounded over to me with a tail-wagging bark full of glee. I gave him a scratch under both ears before he turned and sprinted back inside.

The barn was about a story and a half high with a concrete floor and bare bulbs hanging from the ceiling. It was big enough to hold a truck and a tractor, or maybe two trucks. Right now, though, it was empty. Except for Colt.

Colt was standing at the near wall, staring. He didn't look at me as I entered and took a place beside him. There were four racks on the wall. The one on the far left held three composite longbows, each one resting horizontally on pegs in a neat vertical line.

After the bow rack were three brackets that each looked like a capital "I." There was a single peg in the middle of the top and ten holes in the board that ran along the bottom. A crossbow hung by its cocking stirrup from the first bracket and ten arrows filled the ten holes, point down. The third bracket, the one at the far right, held another crossbow and ten arrows.

The second crossbow rack, the one in the middle, was empty. There was no crossbow hanging from the hook, no arrows in the holes.

Colt just stood there, staring at the empty rack.

I waited, but he still didn't move. "Colt?"

When Colt finally turned to me, I saw anger and disgust on his face as he said, "I didn't realize it was gone."

DIVE

21

A little less than three weeks later, we finally received the State's disclosures from Tiffany Erin. Buried among them was the autopsy report.

I went immediately to the cause of death. "Exsanguination due to laceration of the femoral artery secondary to puncture wound in the right thigh. Co-morbid findings–postmortem examination limited by animal consumption of subject."

I flipped to the section of the report where the coroner documented the wound. He described a puncture that went clean through the right thigh, cutting the femoral artery, the main artery in the leg. The coroner listed the measurements of the laceration, but those weren't necessary to know that, with him being almost a quarter of a mile from his house at night, Brett Daniels hadn't stood a chance.

Much as I liked to start my day with tales of exsanguination and coyote-consumption, I set the autopsy report aside and spent the rest of the morning scrolling through witness statements, investigative notes, and findings. Then I grabbed my tablet and went to meet with Danny.

He was set up in our conference room, computer out, a few

brown files sitting off to one side. "How far did you get?" I said as I sat down.

"The file's all scanned into the system. I glanced over some witness statements and part of the investigator's findings but haven't studied anything yet. You?"

"Same. Along with the autopsy. Which witnesses?"

"The family. Colt, Tyler, Rhonda. Rob. And Kaminski. Did you know about the fight?"

"I did. It looks like Kenny gave the same story to the police that he gave me. Why don't we compare notes and then we'll start dividing this up."

Danny nodded, slid a legal pad closer, and grabbed a pen, as I said, "So according to both boys, on Thursday night, Colt and Tyler eat dinner together at the house. Brett comes home late from work, they all speak briefly, then the boys go to their rooms to do schoolwork, and Brett decides to walk a quarter of a mile to a platform in the woods to hunt coyotes."

Danny nodded. "Doesn't everybody do that on Thursday night?"

"I usually wait 'til the weekend. That's the last time either of the boys sees Brett."

"That's what they told the sheriff, yes."

"We'll nail down the times, but Tyler told the sheriff that he got up for school Friday morning around 6:45, didn't see his dad, and left."

"Right. And Colt says he worked on his report most of the night, slept, then left around eight Friday morning to head back to Grand Valley to turn it in."

"Right. And he didn't see Brett either."

We each thought for a moment before Danny said, "Brett's truck had to have been in the driveway though, right?"

"That is where they found it."

"So they had to think he was around somewhere."

I shrugged. "I'm getting the impression that Brett Daniels wasn't the kind of guy you disturb. And if one had a paper and the other had to get to school, I'm not surprised they didn't check in. The big thing for me is that everything in the boys' statements was consistent with what they've told me."

"Small favors." Danny ticked off something on his notepad. "I didn't get a chance to read Mrs. Daniels' statement yet."

"It's Mazur."

"Right, right. Anything there?"

"Other than cursing Brett Daniels for bending them all on the way out the door—that's a direct quote, by the way—she said she hadn't seen him since the previous game and even that was too recent for her liking."

Danny scribbled away. "So when Tyler gets home after the game Friday night, he discovers the body and calls Colt and the police."

"Right. So that leads us to the investigation report."

Danny set down his pen and hit his touchpad a few times before scrolling through his screens. "It was clear right away that Brett was dead—"

"Scattered entrails will do that."

"—so the investigating deputy speaks to Colt, who tells the deputy about his dad's hunting and the hunting platform. So, a couple of deputies go back there, and they find the blood, but it's too dark to do too much so they come back on Saturday morning and do the usual, pictures of where they found the body, of the platform, and everything else."

Danny turned his laptop around and showed me a couple of pictures of the stand. I nodded. "That's consistent with what I saw—the bloodstains on the platform and the ladder were pretty obvious."

Danny turned it back around, tapped, and said, "It seems like the circumstances made them think hunting accident."

I nodded. "That's consistent with what everyone was being told at first."

Danny was scrolling down. "But then it looks like they come back on Tuesday afternoon and search again. Why? What changed?"

I thought. "If I had to guess, I'd say that the preliminary findings came back on the autopsy. They found out about the leg wound."

Danny nodded. "Makes sense. Then they searched the area around the platform and eventually found the arrow."

I shook my head. "I've been bow hunting. It's hard enough to find an arrow when you know where you shot it. How in the world did they find this one after the fact?"

"No idea. But they did, and apparently it matches the set in Colt's rack in the barn."

"That seems thin, doesn't it? There's no ballistics to match an arrow to a crossbow."

Danny shrugged. "But the arrow was the one that was missing. And here we are."

I stared at my notes. "Okay, I'll take the autopsy and cause of death. I think we're probably going to need to hire a pathologist of our own. I'll take the crossbow evidence too since that's going to tie-in to cause of death."

"What are you thinking?"

"I'm not sure yet. Mostly, I'll check to see if what they're saying makes sense. Why don't you start with the family's witness statements. It doesn't sound like they have too much direct knowledge of what happened, but we're going to need background on this all the same."

"Rob Preston, too?"

I nodded. "Start with two areas—what they know about the night it happened and what they know about potential motive. That fight between Colt and Brett at Borderlands doesn't seem like enough, but it might be an indication that more was going on."

"Got it." Danny kept scribbling. "Anything else?"

"I think that gives us plenty to get started. Once we have a sense of where we're going, we can regroup."

"So you can make sure you have the stuff that is the most fun and the least work?"

"I'm hurt, Danny. Deeply hurt."

He smiled. "That's not an answer."

"So young. So cynical."

"Still not answered."

"To the quick, Danny. You cut me to the quick."

He sighed. "I'll get started."

I saluted as he left.

∽

I DON'T KNOW about you but, for me, the worst part of any project is before you get started. The last two-and-a-half weeks had been nothing but waiting, knowing that Tiffany Erin was sitting on the case, working it up, but not yet obliged to hand over any of her evidence to us. I found the thought of what I might need to be doing more nerve racking than actually doing it and I was relieved to get started.

I had read more autopsies than I cared to remember, but that's no substitute for an expert pair of eyes. I wanted to know exactly how Brett Daniels died and needed help interpreting all of the little things in the autopsy to make sure I didn't miss anything. So the first thing I did when I was back in my office was pick up the phone and call Ray Gerchuk.

Ray Gerchuk was the coroner on the other side of the state line in Carrefour, Ohio. He was as objective and honest as you would hope a government official would be, and I knew he would tell me exactly what was going on if I was lucky enough to retain him. He was also an old friend of my father's, which meant that I had his number and that he picked up the phone when I called.

"Well, it's too cold to have the boat in and it's too warm for your dad's lake to be frozen, so either you guys want to go to Florida on a fishing trip or you're going to hit me with more work."

"Hi, Ray. I'm afraid I don't have any plane tickets."

"Pity. I was halfway out the door. What can I do for you? Don't tell me I'm involved in one of your cases again?"

"Only if you want to be."

"What does that mean?"

"Are you allowed to review cases privately?"

"Not for cases pending in Ohio. They don't want local coroners testifying against each other."

"What about cases in other states?"

"I'd be allowed to do that. Don't know if I would though. What's involved?"

"You know the case involving Tyler Daniels' dad?"

"Yeah. I was at the game. That arrest seemed a little heavy-handed."

"I just got the autopsy on Brett Daniels. I need an expert to check the work."

"Looking at it is no problem but would you need me to testify?"

"I really wouldn't know until after I hear what you found. If you just agree with the State's autopsy then no, there wouldn't be any purpose in calling you."

"And if I don't agree?"

"Then I would definitely want to call you."

There was a pause. "Who's on the other side?"

"The examiner?"

"Yes."

"Warren Archuleta."

Ray Gerchuk snickered. "I'll do it."

"Really?" I had thought I was going to have to play the family-friend card.

"To go up against Warren? I might not even charge you. I mean, you know, I will, but I would consider it."

"What do you have against Archuleta?"

"Besides the fact that he's a pompous, condescending prick?"

"Yes."

"Nothing. He's a good doctor. But you definitely need someone to take a second look."

"I'll send the materials over to you then."

"Does that include tissue slides?"

"No, just the report and photos. You can tell me what else to ask for after you take a look."

"Perfect."

We hung up.

I sent the materials to Dr. Gerchuk and then decided on the next thing. It was time to learn more about crossbows.

22

"When did you start using one of these?" I said.

My brother Mark handed me the crossbow. "I don't anymore. Remember when I tore my shoulder at work?"

I nodded.

"I couldn't draw a bow for a season so I used this instead. Not the same, but it gets the job done. Have you used one before?"

"No." I hefted it. "Weighs about the same as a shotgun?"

Mark nodded. "Do you want to shoot it?"

"Of course."

Now, as I tell you that Mark had a foam deer target with a hay bale backstop set up in his yard so that I could shoot his crossbow, you may be thinking, "Good Lord, does everyone in Michigan have portable targets and projectile weapons?" The answer, of course, is no, but, well...it's also not hard to find a friend that does. Or a brother.

The crossbow had the length of a short rifle with a stock, trigger, and guard at the back end. At the front end, it had a double bow mechanism and pulleys that stuck out like the arms of a "T." A U-shaped piece of metal stuck out from the very end.

Mark tapped the metal U with one finger. "This is the

cocking stirrup. Set it on the ground and stick your foot in." When I did, he handed me a string with a handle on each end and two plastic hooks in the middle. "Put the hooks on the bowstring and pull it back with the handles."

I did and cocked the crossbow easily.

"Once the string's loaded, keep your fingers clear of the release area. Now take this arrow and slide it with the odd colored feather face down in the groove until it's nocked on the string."

The concept was no different than a bow, so I put the sole white feather down into the groove and nocked the arrow.

Mark pointed at the target. "The scope is sighted in for 30 yards so you can put it square on."

"Is that about its range?"

"You can shoot farther, but the drop becomes hard to account for."

I brought the crossbow to my shoulder and Mark was right, the weight of it felt about the same as a shotgun, but the bow mechanism was spread out over a greater area so that it was easier to rock from side-to-side.

As I sighted in, Mark said, "Make sure your forward hand stays on the grip handle there. If you hold it higher, there's a good chance the string'll take the tip of your thumb off."

That would put a damper on things. I did what he said, put the crosshairs on the target, exhaled, and squeezed.

It was an interesting sensation. It felt like holding a gun, but there was no kick. And the sound was a little louder than shooting a bow but far less than firing a gun.

"You're in the yellow," said Mark. "Not bad. Another?"

"Yep."

"Do it."

I went through the whole process again, cocking, nocking, and shooting. It was a little smoother this time, but the arrow ended up in the same place. I handed the crossbow back to him. "Definitely more of a process than shooting a bow."

"Not really. It's more in advance, but at the time you shoot, it's less because you've already drawn. The biggest pain is that if you're hunting in a tree stand, you have to come down to cock it again after you take a shot."

"I suppose that's why he hunted from a platform."

"Who?"

"Brett Daniels. He had a hunting platform that looked wide enough so that he could stand there and re-cock his crossbow from up there."

"Huh." One of the great things about my brother is that he doesn't care about my cases at all. Instead, he said, "Talk to Tommy this week?"

"No. You?"

"Yesterday." Mark smiled. "He was wound up."

"Yeah?"

"Yeah. He was trying to come up with some convoluted scheme to contain Central's quarterback."

"Seems appropriate. It *is* the state semi-finals."

Mark shrugged. "I told him that anyone can see his defense is faster than their offense so run a base set and let the boys play."

I smiled. "How'd he take that?"

Mark grinned. "About how you'd expect."

Mark was, by far, the best athlete of the three of us. He also had a higher than normal not-give-a-shit gene and was about as laid-back a guy as you could find so his solution to things was usually to suggest just winging it. This drove my hyper-competitive, uber-prepared older brother crazy, to my younger brother's unfettered delight.

I shook my head. "I'm glad the law bores you."

"Why?"

"Never mind."

We walked down to the target and I pulled the arrows out of the foam deer. "The field point punches a pretty clean hole."

Mark held up an arrow. It had a smooth pointed cylinder at the end with no barbs or blades sticking out to the side. "If I used a broadhead, it would tear the target apart in just a few shots."

"You wouldn't hunt with a field point, would you?"

"Only small game."

"Coyote or deer?"

"Broadhead all the way."

"And the crossbow's powerful enough to take something that size down?"

"Easily."

I knew that if the crossbow could drop a deer, it could drop a man. At that point in the case, though, I couldn't conceive of what it would take for a son to shoot one at his father.

23

It was late in the day when I left Mark's house so I called Danny to make sure everything was under control at the office. He said he was about to head out, then asked, "So what did you learn about crossbows?"

"That you don't shoot them on the spur of the moment."

"Is that important?"

"I'm not sure. I think so. It certainly speaks to premeditation."

"Yeah?"

"There's too much cranking and cocking first. How about you?"

"I've been going through the witness statements like you said. I started with Rob Preston, thinking the current boyfriend and ex-husband might have a history."

"And?"

"They do, but it's pretty mild."

"What?"

"There are a couple of accounts of them arguing after football games."

"Fights?"

"No. A vigorous exchange of ideas."

"What about?"

"Don't know for sure. So, it seemed like an interesting angle, but according to his statement, it looks like he has an alibi."

"What's that?"

"On Thursday night, a bunch of the parents get together and make the food for a team meal the next day. Looks like there were about a dozen of them that night."

I remembered that Tom had a meal for the team each Friday so the kids didn't have to go home after school. "Where did they make it, at the high school?"

"Yep. In the cafeteria."

"So a dozen parents saw where Rob was that night."

"More or less."

"For how long?"

"They got done about eight."

"And after?"

"They went to Borderlands with some other parents and had a meal and drinks until a little after midnight."

"And after that?"

"They both went home and slept until about six, then they each went to work and then from work went straight to the game. It was enough that the police seemed to lose interest in them pretty quickly."

"I wonder when the time of death was though."

"Let me check my notes. Oh, here it is—that's Nate's job."

"Fine. I'll do everything. You about done for the night?"

"I am."

"Give Jenny my best."

Danny hesitated, then said, "I will."

I hung up and thought about my next steps. Then I took a left turn and drove over to the Borderlands.

False Oath

∾

I WAS surprised at the number of cars in the parking lot on a Monday night until I remembered Monday night football and realized it made some sense after all. It's easy to get buried in your own little work-tunnel and forget that people actually enjoy going out to watch a game with their friends during the week.

Borderlands was packed. The hostess had just left with a group of six to guide them toward the back when Kenny Kaminski came up to take her place and slid a stack of laminated menus into the hostess stand. He broke into a grin when he saw me. "Nate, Nate, come in," he said and gave me a handshake and a half hug. "Nice to see you. I'm out of tables right now, but I can seat you at the bar if you like. The service is just as fast."

I waved it off. "I had wanted to talk to you real quick, but I had no idea it was such a busy night. I'll just put a 'to go' order in."

He straightened and his air of distraction vanished. "Talk to me? About what? Is it about Colt?"

I nodded. "But it can wait. I'll catch up with you later in the week."

Kenny motioned to the hostess as she came back and pointed out where two families should be seated. Then he tapped me on the arm and indicated the door. As I went back outside, Kenny ducked in another door, grabbed a heavy canvas jacket, then joined me. Kenny's breath steamed as he shrugged awkwardly to get the bulky coat settled around his waist before he zipped it and said, "So what do you need? What's going on?"

"I just wanted to follow up on a couple of reports."

"Sure. What?"

"Apparently, Rob Preston and Brett didn't get along?"

"No, they sure didn't," said Kenny. "But I suppose that's to be expected."

"Because of Rhonda?"

Kenny looked surprised, then chuckled. "No. Rhonda's her own woman and the two of them were smart enough to know it."

"Then what?"

"They differed some on the boys."

I was lost. "What do you mean?"

"Rob and Brett didn't agree about the best way to handle them."

"Did they fight about it at football games?"

"Fight is way too strong. They argued."

"About what?"

Kenny shoved his hands deeper into his pockets and shifted his hands around. "Brett could be pretty critical about the boys' play. Rob liked to accentuate the positive, as they say. They drove each other nuts."

"Were Rob and Rhonda here the night Brett was killed?"

Kenny nodded. "The Sheriff asked me the same thing. They were here with a bunch of the football parents that night."

"Do you know when?"

"I couldn't say. They got here a little later than the others as I recall, but they were all here 'til close, which would have been about one on a Thursday."

A group of eight walked out and Kenny thanked each adult by name, then welcomed a family of four that was just walking in before he said, "I'm sorry, Nate, but I need to get back in there."

"No, no, it's my fault, Kenny. I should've called."

"Order at the bar before you go. I'll make sure it comes out first."

"No need, Kenny, thanks."

Kenny had a hand on the door when his face brightened. "Wait, what am I thinking, we're in the state semis!"

I smiled. "It's pretty amazing."

"Two years in a row! You're going, right?"

"You bet."

"After we win Friday, we'll be open for the team and families for a late meal so make sure you get back here."

"I'll try."

"That Central quarterback is shifty, but I know your brother'll have our boys all schemed up to stop him."

"I'm certain he's figuring it out as we speak."

"I'm sure of that," said Kenny. "Hey, how about a Diablo Chicken sandwich and fries? I always have them ready to go."

"No, really—"

"Coming right up. Give me two shakes."

I relented. "Thanks."

"I'll put it in for you. Go Panthers!"

I followed Kenny back in as he struggled out of his heavy coat, dumped it back in the side room, and vanished behind the bar into the kitchen. I waited with a group of six and a family of five and thought about how long the drive was from Brett Daniels' house to here.

It wasn't more than five minutes later that the hostess came out looking for Nate Shepherd and made me the happy recipient of a bag that smelled of sharp sauce and french fries. I thanked her and headed home, thinking of crossbows and car rides.

24

I've mentioned before that I don't have an assistant. In these days of automated voice answering and electronic filing, it's easier to get by without one than it used to be. The fact was, when I had started out on my own, I couldn't afford it. Now that I could afford it, I was still hesitant to take on the additional overhead. Danny disagreed with my analysis, which wasn't surprising since he usually got stuck with any task that an assistant would normally do.

One of the disadvantages of not having an assistant, though, is that there is no one to run interference for you when something unexpected happens. That's exactly what confronted me on Tuesday morning when I found a woman standing outside my locked office door.

She had long black hair, olive skin, and a cleft in her strong chin. She wore a black overcoat, held a black leather folio in front of her in both hands, and her dark eyes locked on me the moment I emerged from the stairs onto the third floor.

When she didn't move, I said, "Can I help you?"

She tilted her head at my office door. "Are you Nate Shepherd?"

"I am."

"Then yes." And she didn't say anything more.

I nodded, jingled through the keys to the right one, and unlocked the door. "If you'll give me just a minute to open up, I'll be right with you."

The woman didn't say anything. Instead, she stared, unblinking. Honestly, it reminded me of a cat surveying a morsel without indicating whether it would pounce or walk away.

"Would you like some coffee?"

"No, thank you."

Heretic. I flipped on the light and held open the door for her. She entered. I gestured to the large conference room as I walked over and turned on that light too. "You're welcome to wait in here. Are you sure I can't get you some water or coffee?"

"I'm sure. Thank you."

Then she walked by me and sat, placing her folio on the table right in front of her without opening it.

I bustled around the office, turning on more lights, starting coffee, and powering up my computer. I felt bad about making her wait, but my computer needed to wake up and so did I. Once I was logged in and my coffee cup was filled, I grabbed a legal pad and headed into the conference room.

The woman hadn't moved. Instead, she watched me with that intent gaze as I sat down, straightened my legal pad, and picked up my pen. She didn't say anything.

"I'm sorry, have we met?" I said.

"We have not. My name is Meg Dira. I'm with the State Attorney General's office."

That got my attention. "Okay."

She slid a card across the table. It read "Megan Dira, Office of the State Attorney General of Michigan, Public Integrity Unit."

As I sat there, I couldn't think of anything that would put me at cross purposes with the State Attorney General's office, let alone something called the Public Integrity Unit. A clear conscience didn't prevent a slight stomach knot from forming at having its representative show up unannounced in my office.

"I'm sorry Meg, are we on a case together?"

"No."

"Then how can I help you?"

"We think that one of your clients may have information related to an investigation of ours."

"Who's that?"

"Colton Daniels. We'd like to speak to him."

"We?"

"Me. On behalf of the State of Michigan."

"I'm sorry, Meg. But if you're here and you know about Colt, then you know that he has been accused of murder."

"I do."

"Then you must know that I'm not going to let him talk to any law enforcement officer right now, whether it be the Sheriff or the prosecutor or the Attorney General."

Megan Dira straightened her folio. "My investigation has nothing to do with the crime your client has been accused of committing."

I smiled and shrugged. "Still."

We sat there for a moment and I decided that she didn't have to be the only one who played the silent card.

Finally, she said, "We're investigating certain public institutions in the state."

"I see."

"We believe that your client may have information related to that investigation."

"Okay."

Silence again.

"We could subpoena that information from him. But we would prefer not to as we would prefer not to let the actual targets of our investigation know where we are headed."

"I appreciate that, Meg. But I would prefer not to commit malpractice."

Megan Dira's eyes narrowed. I waited. Then her expression lightened and she said, "Could you ask him a question?"

"No promises."

"Please ask if he or his family have had any dealings with Steve Mathison."

"Who is Steve Mathison?"

"That will be clear if they've had any dealings with him."

"What kind of dealings?"

"Any."

"That's a little broad, Meg."

"It seems to me that is a very specific question, Nate."

"It would help if I knew what sort of dealings we were talking about."

"If your client or his family have, they will know."

I supposed they would. "Why do you want to know?"

"I told you, because it's relevant to one of our investigations."

We had now gone from "an investigation" to "one of her investigations." I was getting a very bad feeling about this and had no desire to go further without knowing what was going on.

"Like I said, Meg, my client is not going to be talking to anyone until this trial is over. I'm sure you can appreciate that."

"I understand the tactic. I don't appreciate it."

"Well, there you go." I stood.

Megan Dira did too. "Please ask. Your client is not a target."

"I don't see how I can do that right now."

"We'll likely hold off on a subpoena for a little while. We will not hold off forever."

"I understand. But like I said, I don't see us changing our position until after the trial."

Megan Dira picked up her unopened black folio and walked to the door. I opened it and started to say goodbye, but she never turned back.

I stared at the closed door, sorting through what had just happened. It re-opened a moment later, to reveal not Megan Dira but Danny.

He stopped when he saw me. "Hello?"

"It's part of our new greeting program. I think Walmart is onto something."

"Fantastic. What's going on?"

"I am not at all sure."

25

Danny, of course, didn't have any more of an idea what the State Attorney General was doing nosing around our case than I did. I left him to go through more witness statements and gave Colt a call.

"Hi, Nate," he said. "Has something happened with my case?"

"No. Well, not with the murder case, but I just had an unexpected visit from a lawyer with the State Attorney General's office this morning."

"The who?"

"The State Attorney General. They're the lawyers for Michigan for other kinds of matters."

"Great, are they coming after me, too?"

I could hear the edge in Colt's voice. I didn't blame him. "They don't have anything to do with the murder case. This woman was from the Public Integrity Office."

"What does that have to do with me?"

"I'm not sure. She was asking whether you had anything to do with a guy named Steve Mathison."

There was quiet on the other end for a moment before Colt said, "That name doesn't ring a bell."

"Nothing at all?"

"Not that I can think of. I can text Mom and Tyler though—"

"No! Don't communicate with anyone about anything that might remotely be related to your case."

"But if they know something—"

"Then it's best that I talk to them to find out. You really don't know anything about this Mathison guy?"

"Wolf's hand, Nate, I don't."

I thought I'd misheard him. "What did you just say?"

"I said, 'I don't.'"

"No, before that."

"I said his name doesn't ring a bell."

It sunk in then. I knew exactly what he had said. And I knew that he would deny saying it. I left it for the moment and focused on the more important thing. "Colt, I can't stress this enough—don't talk to or text anyone about any of this. Do you understand?"

"Got it, got it. Stay in the bubble under house arrest, don't do anything, and go crazy."

"Better for you to go crazy than to say something that gets you convicted. I know this is hard, but you need to sit tight."

"For how long?"

"For a few months."

"Months?!"

"Yes."

"Nate, I'm going bat-shit here."

"I understand, Colt, but you have to sit tight."

"I'll try. But it's not easy."

"I know. And—"

"Stay off social media too, I know, I know."

"Good."

We hung up. I called Rhonda Mazur next.

"Calling to tell me my son's free, Shepherd?" she said.

"No, we're still getting ready for trial. It'll be a while yet."

I could hear the disappointment in her voice as she said, "What do you want then?"

"Do you know a guy named Steve Mathison?"

"Why do you care?"

"Because I got a visit from the State Attorney General's office this morning asking about him."

"Hang on a second." I heard some rustling and then the distinctive rasping click-click-click of a cigarette lighter. There was an inhale and then an exhale and then she said, "I don't know any Steve Matthews."

"No, Mathison."

"I don't know him either. It seems to me that you should be working on my son's case and not bothering his mother with B.S."

"Rhonda, having the State Attorney General show up at my office at 7:30 in the morning isn't B.S."

"He was there?"

"She was. An attorney named Megan Dira."

An exhale. "Haven't heard of her either."

"Rhonda, if there's something else going on, I don't want to get surprised with it in the middle of Colt's trial."

"There's nothing going on that could possibly show that my son had anything to do with killing his father. And that's really all that you should be worrying about."

I hadn't planned on talking to Rhonda about the night of the murder but as long as I had her on the phone and she was already irritated with me...

"Rhonda, did you make the team meal at the high school on the Thursday night Brett was killed?"

"You mean the night Brett died in an accident? Yes."

"Rob too?"

"He'd been working doubles and we hadn't seen each other in a while so he offered to join me. Which was very sweet."

"What did you do after the meal?"

"We went to Borderlands with some other parents. And I'm not sure I like your tone."

I ignored her. "Did you go straight over?"

"No, we stopped home first to...to drop some things off."

"How long did that take?"

"As long as it took. What's your problem?"

"No problem. Just trying to figure out where everyone was when that night. Did Rob ever argue with Brett?"

"You bet your ass he did, and I did too."

"About what?"

"About Brett being such a prick to Tyler and Colt."

"Rob got involved in that?"

"Not at first. But Rob's a good man and he doesn't like seeing my boys mistreated. Now I know lawyers don't have to worry about things like clocking out for breaks, but you've just taken all of mine with these stupid questions. Call me when you have something that actually has to do with Colt's case."

She hung up. I stared at my phone. If push came to shove and I had to give Megan Dira an answer, I had one "I don't know any Steve Mathison" from Colt and one "I don't know him and mind your own business" from Rhonda so I could technically say that I had not heard of any connection between the Daniels and Steve Mathison. I knew though that Megan wouldn't be asking me unless there probably was one, so I wasn't going to respond to that question and, if I did, I would have to be very careful with how I phrased my answer.

I didn't like this bumbling around in the dark; it felt like I'd been one step behind this whole case. So I made one more call to help catch up.

"What's up, Shep?" said Olivia Brickson.

"I had an interesting visit this morning."

"It certainly wasn't to the gym."

"I'm coming tonight."

"Lies."

"Truth."

"What was the visit?"

I told her about Megan Dira waiting for me at the office and what she had wanted.

"That's odd," said Olivia. "And she didn't spill at all?"

"Not even a little. I could use some research."

"On Dira? No problem."

"And on the Public Integrity Unit. I'm not sure that I've heard of it. Just a thumbnail on what they're involved in and if you can see any pattern to the type of cases Megan Dira handles."

"Sure. Seems like we should look at Mathison too."

"You read my mind."

"Do you have anything else on him? Seems like a pretty common name."

"That's it. Although I assume that he's located around here somewhere."

"Not necessarily. The whole world's just a click away now."

"Fair enough."

"Anything else?"

"That's all."

"I'll have what you need tonight or tomorrow."

"Perfect. Thanks."

After I hung up, I decided I wanted to have my next conversation in person, so I said goodbye to Danny and left.

∼

Although I went to the high school regularly for events, they were usually at the football field or in the gym so it had been a while since I'd been to my brother's office. As a science teacher, Tom spent most of his day in the classroom, but as the head football coach, he also had an office right next to the weight room. And by office, I meant a cinderblock room painted beige, a battered desk, and shelves stuffed with new books and old films.

I knew he had a free seventh hour and figured that, in the week that his team was going to play in the state semi-finals, I'd be able to find him in that office studying film and planning practice.

I was partially right. He was in his office, but rather than watching film, he was diagramming plays in a notebook the same way I'd seen him do it since high school.

Tom glanced up then did a double take. "Nate? What do you want?"

I never took the things Tom said during football season as rude; his mind was just so preoccupied that conversational courtesy and filters were the first things to go. I just considered the essence of his question and assumed he was coming from a good place.

I pointed at the notebook. "What are you running this week?"

He tapped the page with his pencil. "I'm not sure. Our strong safety hurt his shoulder last week so I'm trying to figure out how to protect his substitute."

"There's no hiding place on a football field, you know that."

"I do. But our safety had range that made up for a lot so I'm trying to figure out a way to keep his replacement from having to do anything extra. In the limited time I have."

Remember. Coming from a good place. "Right. I won't take

long." I sat. Tom half-looked at me, but he didn't lift his pencil from the playbook.

"Are your players taking the War Oath?"

Tom didn't blink. "Of course not."

"Are you sure?"

Tom scowled and set his pencil down. "Yes, I'm sure. Things aren't the way they were twenty years ago, Nate. That would be viewed as hazing. It *is* hazing. I'd lose my job."

I nodded. "Good."

Tom's eyes narrowed. "Why do you ask?"

"Someone said something to me recently. It only made sense if that person knew the War Oath. Do people talk about it at all?"

"Not around me. At home or alumni..." he shrugged.

"When did it stop?"

"After I graduated but before I came back here to teach. Who said what to you?"

"I can't say."

His jaw clenched. "Then thank you for this vague and unhelpful warning. What did you come out here for?"

"I came out here because if it's true, and it's going on without you knowing, I didn't want you to lose your job."

"Warning delivered. I'll look into it." He gestured his book. "Do you mind?"

"Of course not."

I was just about out the door when he said, "A recent player?"

I looked at him, paused, then shrugged.

He was able to glare at me for almost a second, but his pencil was scratching on the paper before I was out the door.

∽

A SHORT TIME LATER, I pulled my gym bag out of the backseat of my Jeep and walked into the Brickhouse. Olivia Brickson was waiting for me behind the front desk.

Her half-mirrored glasses turned on me as I entered with a blast of cold air. She was sweating like she'd just finished a class and she smiled as she pulled on a track coat and said, "He appears. I was just about to put you on the 'shirked and shrank' list."

"Don't give up on me, Coach."

"I wasn't giving up, I was just thinking that it would be a shame for you to miss since you're finally getting in less loathsome shape since your last trial."

"Less loathsome has always been one of my life goals. Did you find anything?"

"I did. I'll give you the folders after you lift."

"How about the highlights?"

"The Public Integrity Unit investigates government corruption in any Michigan governmental entity. It seems that most of its effort has been focused on state contractors."

"I've never really heard of it."

"I get the sense that it's just getting started."

"And Megan Dira?"

"She was one of the first appointees to the unit. It looks like she found a kickback scheme to overcharge for the construction of dorms at a university and brought down a city councilwoman who was using zoning variances like her own personal piggy bank."

"What in the world could that have to do with Colt and his family?"

"That's why they pay you the big bucks."

I obviously wasn't earning them because I had absolutely no idea. "How about this Steve Mathison?"

Olivia ran a hand through her bleached white hair and

shrugged. "I can tell you that there are at least fifty Steve Mathisons in the tri-state area that can help you with anything from dog grooming to pediatrics to a review of the very latest death metal band to come over from Sweden."

"So nothing?"

She shook her head. "And that's just nearby. I stopped."

"Got it. You said the folders are in your office?"

She nodded. "On my desk. Just grab them on the way out."

"Thanks."

"At least an hour and a half from now."

"I was thinking about an hour from now."

"I don't think they'll be ready then."

"You just said they were on your desk."

"They will be. An hour and a half from now."

I sighed.

"You'll thank me."

"I doubt it."

I didn't.

26

One thing about being a lawyer, you never know where the little bomb is going to come from that blows up your whole day. It can be in an innocuously titled email, a casual voicemail, or the innocent footnote of an opponent's brief that reveals an overlooked fact that stands your whole case on its head. You're just skipping along, innocently opening, listening, or reading, when you realize that you have to drop everything you had planned and defuse the bomb or repair the damage.

On Wednesday morning, that little bomb came in the form of a supplemental witness list from Tiffany Erin.

We file witness lists all the time and update them as the case goes along. Sometimes they're lists of fact witnesses, people who saw or heard something related to the case. It's pretty common to add to those as the case progresses when the parties discover new people with information about the case.

Sometimes, though, the witnesses are experts, and those lists are another matter entirely. An expert brings a level of weight to certain opinions that you usually have to respond to and the disclosure of a new expert immediately raises the concern that you've missed something.

Tiffany Erin's Supplemental Witness List contained two new experts.

The first expert was Samson Ezekiel Wald, a Michigan DNR officer (that's the Department of Natural Resources). According to the list, DNR Officer Wald was going to discuss Michigan hunting rules, as well as coyote activity and markings. That was a bit of a surprise, but I wasn't overly concerned about it.

The second new expert, though, was psychiatrist Diane Liester. Dr. Liester was going to talk about the trauma of abuse, the resentment it builds, and the violent manner in which an abused person can lash out, particularly when that abuse was carried out by a parent or loved one.

Her report was attached.

I flipped to it immediately.

Dr. Liester had access to some information that I did not. She noted the fight between Colt and his dad at the Borderlands when Brett had put Colt's head through the video game screen. More than that though, she referenced two other incidents, one in high school and one in college, when Colt had gotten into fights at parties. Not scuffles, but full-fledged brawls. She also noted Colt's history of ejections from three football games and a suspension from school for "an aggressive disagreement" with a teacher and came to the conclusion that Colt had an oppositional defiance disorder with a tendency toward violence that would support the proposition that he was capable of killing his father.

Leaving the science of it aside, this kind of conclusion wouldn't be admissible at trial in a hundred years. The prosecution can't use other bad acts to show that the defendant committed the one he was being accused of and she certainly couldn't use a psychiatrist's opinion to show that Colt was predisposed to commit the crime, especially since I wasn't putting Colt's sanity in question.

No, this was a pure tactical move, designed to make me burn man-hours and resources before the trial to get this witness tossed. Normally, a prosecutor didn't have the time or money to waste on tactics like this. Apparently, Tiffany Erin was different.

I walked over to Danny's office. "Did you see it?" I said.

"She can't do this!" Danny flapped one hand at the screen. "She knows none of this is...She just can't file..." He turned to me. "It's just not right!"

"I agree. We need to respond to this right away. Put together a *Daubert* motion to strike it."

Danny switched screens and started typing. "Got it. Want me to add a 'prior acts' section?"

"Please."

"Should we move for sanctions?"

I thought. "Draft it but don't file it. We have a pretrial coming up at the end of the week. I'll see which way the judge is leaning first."

"Done. What about the DNR guy?"

"That seems more fact-based. If he's just going to talk about coyotes or what the hunting rules were at the time, I don't see a basis to object. It shouldn't hurt us."

Danny smiled. "We never see how it hurts us until it's too late."

"That's what makes it fun."

Danny tapped the screen. "Do we need to retain a psychiatrist, too?"

"Let's see what the judge does first. We've got time."

"On it." Danny was typing before I left his office.

Danny might be reluctant to participate in these murder trials but the fact was, once he was in, he did a great job. He was diligent, he was smart, and he wasn't the least bit afraid of hard work. As I left him, his keyboard clacked for justice.

These expert issues made me think of the one that I had

retained. I gave him a call and he said that he did in fact have time to see me so I hopped in my Jeep and drove over to see our expert coroner, Dr. Ray Gerchuk.

∽

DR. GERCHUK'S office was right in Carrefour so it didn't take me long to get there. I texted him that I was in his lobby and not two minutes later, Ray Gerchuk walked out.

Ray Gerchuk defied every stereotype of a forensic pathologist. He was tall, walked straight, and his skin was always slightly tanned as if he'd been somewhere warm just two weeks before. He was in his early sixties and, if you looked closely, you could see that his blonde hair was turning white around the edges. Oh, and he smiled all the time.

He was doing that now. "You never get the normal ones, do you?" he said as he extended his hand.

I shook it. "Apparently not. I'm just glad we're on the same side with this one."

"Come on now, Nate. I've told you a dozen times there are no 'sides' in pathology. The body just is."

"I think you might be alone in that philosophy, Ray."

"There are a few of us scattered about here and there. Come on back."

Ray Gerchuk led me down an antiseptic smelling hallway, past a row of steel doors to his office at the end. The office defied the stereotype too—it had a row of windows on one side and a picture of the Big House, the University of Michigan football stadium, up on the wall that I tried not to hold against him.

Dr. Gerchuk took a seat behind his desk. As I grabbed one of his vinyl and metal chairs, he shook his head and smiled. "There's a lot to unpack with this one."

"What are you thinking?"

"You know I'm at a bit of a disadvantage since I'm not looking at the body itself. I'm just interpreting Archuleta's findings in his report and the slides. And the pictures, of course."

"Right."

"Have you looked at them?"

"The pictures? Briefly."

"They're pretty horrible. So I'd bet that you're going to be seeing an awful lot of them at trial."

"You would know."

In my first murder trial after I went out on my own, Dr. Gerchuk had testified for an entire morning about his gruesome findings from an autopsy he'd performed.

Dr. Gerchuk shrugged. "I don't ask the questions, I just answer them. Did you eat today?"

"Not much."

He grinned. "Good. They don't clean the floors until Friday. Come here." He waved me over, then tilted his screen so that I could see. "Ready?"

"Sure."

The first picture was of a naked man lying on a steel table but you could hardly tell it was a man. I had a brief impression of a mop of blondish-brown hair and a clean-shaven face, but what drew my attention was that his abdomen was gone. And when I say gone, I mean that when I looked where his belly should be, I saw spine and the back of his ribs. I blinked, a lot, then forced myself to look closer.

Dr. Gerchuk gave me a chance to settle in, then said, "See these narrow, pointed marks along here?" He indicated lines along the lower ribs.

I nodded.

"Those are teeth marks. You can see that the skin is shredded here all along the bottom of the rib margin. You can see that whatever got to him didn't leave any of the organs behind."

"Is that usual?"

"Let's say it's not unusual for a body found in the wild."

"Carrefour is hardly 'the wild.'"

Dr. Gerchuk nodded. "Then let's say it's not unusual for a body that's been scavenged by wild animals. And coyotes are that. We don't see this much in Michigan because we're not as remote, but it happens more often out west. When bodies are found in the wilderness, the viscera are the first things to go."

I found myself inspecting the body closer. "I would've thought that they went for the thighs and butt first."

"Now you're thinking like a human and not an opportunistic carnivore. Two reasons that's not true. First, the soft underbelly is exactly that—it's easier to get to and there's more nutrition in the organs. Second, these particular legs had a protective coating on them."

I raised an eyebrow.

"The blue jeans."

I saw what he meant. Brett Daniels was wearing jeans and, although they were torn in places, they were mostly intact.

"That brings us to the interesting part," Dr. Gerchuk said. He clicked several times until an image of Brett Daniels' right leg filled the screen. "I really can't blame the Sheriff's department for thinking it was a hunting accident at first. When you find someone with no organs, it's pretty easy to assume that's why they're dead. But Archuleta was reasonably careful in his examination and that's why he found this."

Dr. Gerchuk split the screen so that it showed the front and back of Brett Daniels' leg. There was a hole in each picture and the jeans around them were dark with blood.

"So the wound came first?"

"It did. He was pretty well exsanguinated. The extremities would have looked different if he'd been suffocated or killed by the coyotes. Archuleta's exam showed a lacerated femoral artery."

"And that would have killed him?"

"He would have bled out in less than ten minutes. The coyotes came after."

I stared at the hole in Brett Daniels' leg. "They're saying it was a crossbow arrow."

Dr. Gerchuk frowned. "This definitely wasn't done by a broadhead. There'd be way more damage."

"No, they recovered the arrow. It was a field point."

Dr. Gerchuk thought. "That could be true then. What makes them say it was an arrow?"

"The exam. And they found one at the scene."

Dr. Gerchuk tapped the screen. "I can tell you that the wound is consistent with a crossbow arrow, but I can't say it's a fact. I understand we don't have the body anymore?"

I shook my head. "It's been cremated."

"So, I can't do my own tests, but I'll double check Archuleta's findings to make sure he didn't make any mistakes."

"Is he good?"

"Very. But he's under the impression that his excrement has no odor so he sometimes makes assumptions that he shouldn't."

"Is there anything else I can get you that would help?"

"Description of the specs on the crossbow and an arrow that's the same as the one that was used. I don't need the actual arrow necessarily, but if you can get me one that's the same size and brand, it would help."

"Done. Anything else?"

"If Archuleta kept any tissue samples, I want to look at those."

"You got it." I stood. "Thanks for your help."

"Of course."

As we shook hands Dr. Gerchuk said, "How do things look for Tom's team this weekend?"

"We've never beaten Jackson Central in the playoffs, but I think Tom feels like we have the horsepower to do it this year. Especially with the way Tyler's throwing the ball around."

Dr. Gerchuk shook his head. "This really is a tragedy. This should be the best fall of Tyler's life and instead..." He trailed away and gestured at the screen.

"I know. It's terrible. You going?"

"Going to watch the live stream. Couldn't convince my wife to sit in Jackson Municipal Stadium in November to watch a bunch of kids she doesn't know."

"We'll miss you."

"Tell your dad I said 'hi.'"

"Sure will."

"Get me the slides when you can."

I nodded and left.

I was lost in thought as I made my way back to my Jeep. My head was still back with the pictures and the story Tiffany Erin was going to tell about a dying man who was eaten by coyotes.

As I climbed into the car, my phone buzzed. It was a text from Olivia.

It said:

You need to check @AlexisFury.

27

There is a saying that the Internet is undefeated. It means that no matter how clever you think you are or how brilliant the point you think you've made is, one person is no match for the boundless well of the creativity of tens of thousands of people and, if you chose to fight that fight, you will soon find yourself buried in a string of hilariously pointed memes, gifs, and men in hot dog suits.

That principle usually applies when someone posts something they think is clever. It also comes into play, though, when someone is accused of a heinous act, when a virtual swarm of ridicule, scorn, and hate can bury the accused by blunt force with the sheer weight of rebuke and rejection from around the world in a matter of minutes.

@AlexisFury had primed the pump against Colt for weeks. Someone, somewhere must have been checking the filings in our case every day because in the two-and-a-half hours since Dr. Liester's report had been filed, @AlexisFury had posted it to her followers, who were now flinging its contents back through the ether at Colt.

I scrolled through five or six screens worth before I stopped.

It was enough. There were cries for justice and calls for action and implications of violence just muted enough to get past the platform's filters. It was enough to stagger a man. I wasn't at all sure what it would do to a twenty-year-old, but I knew what it was doing to my jury pool as I watched the likes, retweets, and comments increase like a rolling odometer.

I texted my thanks to Olivia, then texted Colt and told him to stay off social media, which I realize is like telling somebody not to yawn. I texted Danny and told him to finish the motion to strike Dr. Liester's report before he left for the day, which was not remotely fair to him but had to be done. Then I found the number for Patricia Weathers, the criminal bailiff of Judge Martin LaPlante, and called.

I asked if we could have a conference with the Judge. Ms. Weathers said we were already set for a pretrial on Friday. I told her that was too far away. She said the Judge was booked all day tomorrow. I asked if we could have a conference call today. She said that he was at a seminar and so wasn't available. I asked if there were any possible way for us to have a call in the morning. She said only if there was an emergency. I said this was exactly that. She asked if I'd contacted opposing counsel yet. I had to admit that I had not. She started to use that as a reason not to schedule the call so I pointed out that this call was due in part to opposing counsel's conduct so we couldn't be expected to agree on a call to discuss it.

Patricia Weathers sighed and asked if I was sure. I said I was. She asked if I realized what I was asking in a tone that clearly suggested it would be my ass if it was unwarranted. I said I did. I also said that I could be there in person at whatever time the Court required. She said that tomorrow was the Judge's motion hearing day and that she could squeeze me in at the end of the first session. I said I'd be there. She said she would give Ms. Erin the option of attending by phone. I agreed that was the fair thing to do. She said to be there at 8:30 and hung up.

I texted Danny and told him to write faster. He loves that.

∼

At eight o'clock the next morning, I was sitting in Judge LaPlante's courtroom. Patricia Weathers, the court reporter, and a sheriff's deputy came in and out at different times over the next half hour and, eventually, the attorneys who were scheduled for motion hearings started filtering in as well. At eight twenty-eight, more or less, Tiffany Erin walked in. She didn't look at me, but she knew exactly where I was because it was the one spot in the room that she didn't look.

A couple of minutes later, Patricia Weathers stuck her head out of the Judge's chambers and said, "If you want to come in Mr. Shepherd, we can contact Ms. Erin."

Tiffany Erin stood up. "I'm here, Patricia."

Patricia Weathers nodded as if that's exactly what she expected then said, "Then please come back."

We walked through the gate and behind the bench to the door that led to Judge LaPlante's office. It was, like so many, decorated with pictures of family, plaques, and framed degrees, but I didn't have time to take it in before Judge LaPlante said, "Why are we here, Mr. Shepherd?"

I sat down in front of the judge's desk. Tiffany Erin stayed standing.

"Your Honor, the prosecutor filed a supplemental witness disclosure naming a psychiatric expert yesterday."

Judge LaPlante had dark eyes, scowl lines, and an ability to use both of those to convey displeasure. "That's an emergency?"

"No, Your Honor. She also provided a report from that expert."

Judge LaPlante sat back in his chair. "I'm surprised you didn't pull the fire alarm."

"Judge, the report is filled with a description of other incidents that have nothing to do with this case—including an inadmissible encounter between my client and his father—and a pseudo-psychiatric opinion that has no business being a part of this trial."

Judge LaPlante shifted in a way that directly conveyed his impatience. "So file a motion to strike."

"We have, Your Honor. This morning."

"Then why are we having this conversation in chambers instead of at a hearing on your motion three weeks from now after the prosecutor has a chance to respond?"

"Because Your Honor, the report was attached to the witness disclosure and filed with the clerk, making it a public record. People watching the filings have already taken the report and plastered it all over the Internet."

For the first time, I had Judge LaPlante's attention. He shifted his focus to Tiffany Erin. "You attached the report to the witness disclosure?"

Tiffany Erin raised her chin. "I did."

"Why would you do that?"

She held her hands out. "I practice in a lot of courts, Your Honor. That's often required."

"Not in this one, Ms. Erin. All that was required was for you to disclose the witness and provide the report to counsel directly."

"My apologies, Your Honor," she said.

Judge LaPlante turned back to me. "Still, this seems well short of an emergency, Mr. Shepherd."

"Are you on Twitter, Your Honor?"

There was the faintest twinkle in Judge LaPlante's eyes. "Are you implying that I'm old, Mr. Shepherd?"

I smiled. "No, Your Honor. I'm asking because it's relevant to what I have to say."

"I am. But only to get Tigers' scores."

"Your Honor, the report—which again, contains things that we believe would never be admitted at trial—has been liked and retweeted more than seven thousand eight hundred times. Since yesterday."

"What?!"

"Here," I said and handed him my phone with the @Alexis-Fury account up. "You see that it indicates—"

"I said I'm on Twitter, Mr. Shepherd. I understand how likes and retweets work."

Judge LaPlante stared and scrolled down. As he did, his bald brow furrowed. "Ms. Erin?" he finally said.

Tiffany Erin shrugged again. "Your Honor, we didn't provide that material to anyone. All we did was file our pleading with the Court."

"You *inappropriately* filed a portion of your pleading with the Court."

"I did, Your Honor, for which I certainly apologize. But we can't help what other people do with public filings."

"No. But you can make sure you do your job properly."

"Again, Your Honor, I apologize. But the State can't help it if the horrific nature of the defendant's reprehensible act garners attention." Tiffany Erin had now apologized three times. She didn't look the least bit sorry.

Judge LaPlante tore his gaze away from my phone. "Save your closing for the jury, Ms. Erin."

"Yes, Your Honor."

"Here's what's going to happen," said Judge LaPlante as he handed me back my phone. "I am going to issue a gag order in this case although I don't believe that would have altered what happened here. Neither of you will talk to the press or anyone else who disseminates on social media about this case. Do you understand?"

"Yes, Your Honor," we both said.

"Neither of you will directly or indirectly provide materials to people to publish on social media. Is that clear?"

"Yes, Your Honor."

"You will review our local rules and file only those things which are required. Anyone who puts anything into the public record that shouldn't be there will be subject to sanctions. This is your warning. Is that understood?"

"It is, Your Honor," said Tiffany Erin.

"Mr. Shepherd, we will rule on your motion to strike this particular expert in accordance with our typical motion deadlines. Ms. Erin, you have fourteen days to respond. We will have a hearing after that."

"I understand, Your Honor," I said. "But the posts are poisoning the jury pool."

"Those posts, as you know Mr. Shepherd, are from all over the country and perhaps the world. We don't know how many, if any, are from our pool."

I thought. "The report itself should not be part of the record, Your Honor. Can that be stricken from the filings anyway?"

"Yes. I'll have the clerk remove it today."

"But, Your Honor—" said Tiffany Erin.

Judge LaPlante turned to her. "I believe you've already admitted the filing was a mistake, Ms. Erin. Are you objecting to correcting it?"

She didn't bat an eye. "No, Your Honor."

Judge LaPlante looked back and forth between us. "Ms. Erin is correct that this sort of case garners attention. You of all people should know that, Mr. Shepherd. I'm choosing to look at this as an inadvertent complication in this case. I will not view any other inappropriate filings or unauthorized postings in the same way. By either of you. Is that understood?"

"Yes, Your Honor."

"Very well. It's a pleasure to see you both, but now I have a motion day I'm late for. You're dismissed."

"Thank you, Your Honor," we said and left.

The two of us walked back through the courtroom, past the waiting attorneys, and into the hall.

"That was out of line," I said quietly.

"So is murdering your father," she said and left.

28

Danny was waiting for me when I got back. "How'd it go?"

I told him what Judge LaPlante had said. "So hang on to the motion for sanctions, the judge won't grant it. Oh, and this is going to shock you, we're under a gag order again."

"Whatever will I tweet about?"

I smiled. "Exactly."

Danny's own smile faded. "What about the jury pool? All these posts have to be affecting it."

"I got the impression the judge was sympathetic but that he didn't think there was anything he could do other than issue the gag order. Which I suppose there isn't. Social media reaches everywhere. It's not like we can change venue."

"Isn't there a place in West Virginia or Virginia where they don't allow electronic devices because of satellites or telescopes or something?"

"I don't know. They won't return my texts."

"You know, Nate, that was almost funny."

"I almost thank you."

"What do we do next?"

"Dr. Liester is covered. Why don't you see what you can find out about this DNR officer, Samson Wald."

"Put together a little research file?"

"Please. Thanks."

I'd gone straight to Court that morning so when I went back to my office and checked my email for the first time that day, I found an email from Megan Dira that was sent at 6:59 a.m. that morning. The subject line was "Mathison contacts."

The message simply said:

Dear Mr. Shepherd,

　Please advise if Colt Daniels or his family have had any dealings with Steve Mathison.

　Thank you.
　Megan Dira
　Assistant Attorney General
　Public Integrity Unit

I thought, then replied:

Good morning Ms. Dira,

　Thank you for your second request for information regarding Mr. Mathison. As was the case before, you have not provided me with any information regarding who Steve Mathison is or what the case is about which led to your request. As a result, as I mentioned before in our conversation in my office, I will not be providing information or testimony from my client to Michigan law enforcement officials while charges are pending against him. This will also serve as written confirmation that I represent Mr. Daniels and that any attempts to contact him should be directed to me.

　Please don't hesitate to contact me if you wish to discuss this further.

　Thanks.

Nate Shepherd

I thought about hitting send and then decided that getting a day's leeway would be better so I changed good morning to good afternoon and scheduled it to be sent at the end of the day. Yes, sometimes my life is just that exciting.

I spent the next two days reading autopsy reports and witness statements and crossbow specs to prepare for trial. But I really didn't get any new information about the case until the Friday night of the state semi-final football game in Jackson.

~

WITHINGTON COMMUNITY STADIUM in Jackson is a huge concrete edifice built in the 1920s. It's been retrofitted over the years, from lights to Astroturf to Real Turf. It's a large stadium for a high school game, seating almost ten thousand and was the "neutral" site selected for the Carrefour North vs. Jackson Central high school state semi-final playoff game.

I met my family in the parking lot for a pregame tailgate. High school tailgates, at least up our way, are not quite the same as one for a college or pro game since most high schools are alcohol-free zones. My experience was that parental compliance was about fifty-fifty, but at least those who were drinking kept it low-key and hid it in a thermos or insulated cups.

The Shepherd clan was playing it straight and we had bottles of water and cans of pop and a few Arnold Palmers for those of an iced tea and lemonade persuasion. My sisters-in-law had brought subs and pinwheel sandwiches, my mom had made cookies and hot chocolate for the kids, and I'd bought a bunch of crunchy, salty things in bags. My nieces Reed and Taylor and their cousin Justin had already scattered to wherever cool high school and junior high kids went while the younger ones—Page, James, Joe, and Charlie—all tumbled around the cars trying to inhale football-shaped, frosted sugar cookies while avoiding passing cars.

Kate, Tom's wife, didn't eat anything. She stomped her feet to warm up and kept looking over her shoulder at the game clock, which was visible from outside the stadium.

I walked up next to her. "Still another forty-five minutes," I said.

"I see that."

"Sure you don't want some sandwich?"

She shook her head. "I already ate."

I didn't believe her. "How's Tommy been this week?"

"Spitting nails."

"So normal?"

"Exactly." She smiled. "I think he was actually more wound up than when he played."

I nodded. "You get just as jacked up when you're coaching, but there's nowhere for the energy to go."

"Do you get that way with cases?"

"Not exactly. It's a little different."

"How so?"

I smiled. "You don't get to tackle anybody for starters."

"Then what's the fun in that?" Kate's expression was entirely serious.

Her expression changed as she leapt and grabbed four-year-old Charlie by the hood, pulling him back from a car that was idling down the row of the parking lot. Charlie gave a squealing laugh, wriggled free, and ran toward his grandma with a mouthful of sugar cookie as Kate left in pursuit of the frosting-faced miscreant.

I was standing in the wake of the Charlie-hurricane when my niece Page walked up holding a football, my nephew James right behind her. "Throw with us, Uncle Nate?"

Page and James were bundled up in North jerseys with red hooded sweatshirts underneath and black North stocking caps. Only a heartless fiend would be able to resist that invitation and, since I was oft accused of being heartless but had not quite risen to the level of a fiend, I took the ball from them and we ran around the front of the cars to a grassy area and formed a triangle.

"TD Daniels back pass," said James as he limped back two steps and threw a ball that made it all the way to me.

"Touchdown!" I said as I caught it and held the ball over my head. Then I tossed it to Page, who broke into a touchdown dance and spiked the ball.

"Go Panthers!" screamed a shrill voice. "Screw Central!"

I turned to see Rhonda Mazur standing right behind me. She sported a Panther cap like the kids and a "9" jersey over her black down coat. She wore knit mittens and had somehow managed to thread a cigarette through one while she held a thermal-topped cup in the other. She grinned when I saw her, leaned back, and gave a general "Woo-hoo!"

Rob Preston was next to her, his red beard jutting out from under his own black cap.

I smiled. "Hey, Rhonda, Rob."

"We're going to whip some Central butt, am I right?" said Rhonda.

It doesn't do to equivocate and talk about "doing your best" in a situation like that. "You bet," I said.

"Damn right!" said Rhonda and took a drink from her cup. She glanced at my niece and nephew who were a little wide-eyed. "Whoops. Don't swear, kids. It's a bad freaking habit."

James nodded as Page raised a fist and said, "Whip Central butt!"

I ignored Kate's head whipping around at the sound of her

daughter's voice and the word "butt" as Rhonda grinned and let another, "Woo-hoo! Thatta girl!"

Rob smiled, looked up at the stadium clock, and nudged her. "C'mon Rhonda, I want to see warm-ups."

"That's right," she said and took a drag on the mitten-held cigarette. "Gotta see that boy chuck the rock!"

"See you, Nate," said Rob.

"Screw Central!" Rhonda said in farewell.

"Screw Central!" said Page.

"Page!" said Kate from the van.

I smiled, put a finger to my lips to Page, then tossed her the ball. As she threw it to James, I watched Rhonda and Rob's meandering journey to the stadium with Rhonda stopping to "Woo-hoo" at every vehicle flying a Carrefour North flag.

Page came a little closer. "Is that TD's mom?"

"It is."

"Then that's why she's happy." And there was really no arguing with that.

We had just re-formed our passing triangle when I heard Rhonda's voice from two rows down. "Stevie M! Did you come all this way to see my boy whip Central?!"

I didn't hear the response, but I did turn quickly enough to see who she was talking to—a man in his mid-thirties with a navy peacoat and neatly trimmed blonde hair unencumbered by any hat that would hide its glory. The man leaned in and hugged Rhonda, who kept her cup and cigarette out to the side, then shook Rob's hand while slapping his back.

In this context, I remembered seeing the man when I'd run into Rob at halftime of a game a couple weeks earlier. My nephew Joe had wanted to go before I could be introduced.

Apparently, to Stevie M.

I saw the three of them talk for a little while before Rob pointed to the stadium. Stevie M. nodded, and Rhonda leaned back and yelled, "Screw Central!" Then the three of them walked toward the stadium.

I saw that the stadium clock was down to thirty minutes and everyone agreed it was time to pack up. We loaded everything back into our cars, every adult grabbed a kid's hand whether they wanted it or not, and we headed in.

On the way, we passed the black Audi that Stevie M. had gotten out of. It had an Illinois plate. I took a quick picture and followed my family in.

North won by the way, 29–28, when Tyler "TD" Daniels threw a beautiful 42-yard pass that dropped right into the receiver's hands in the back of the end zone with 32 seconds left.

My brother was taking Carrefour North back to the state finals. Tyler was leading the way.

29

I wasn't much for big celebrations at the time, and I wasn't really part of the booster group for this particular North football team, but when your brother leads his team to the state finals for the second year in a row, then exceptions needed to be made so I went with the rest of my family, and most of the parents, to Borderlands after the game.

Kenny Kaminski met every last person at the door like it was a receiving line at a wedding. He stood there in his bulky canvas coat holding open the door, shaking hands, and giving hugs and offering praise to every single parent about the contribution their son had made to the great history of Carrefour football.

Now, I'd known who Kenny was before all this had started, but I really didn't know him very well. That didn't stop him from wrapping me in a big hug and saying, "Your brother is amazing."

I had to agree. I also began to understand why Borderlands was always full.

I found my way inside and over to a long table set up for my family. As I squeezed into a chair by the wall, I could see the only reason I had a seat was because of the little placard that said "Coach" in the middle.

The place was raucous and, since we had never been able to beat Jackson Central in the playoffs before, even my mom and dad didn't mind the racket. It was mostly parents and fans and assistant coaches. None of the players were there, both because it wasn't cool to be hanging out with your parents after the biggest victory in school history but also because, according to Kate, they were all at a bonfire at Amy Winthrop's house with strict orders to be on time for practice tomorrow morning at 7 a.m.

Mark poured from a pitcher and we were putting in an order for snacks when what could only be described as a ruckus arose that soon organized itself into a chant of "Coach! Coach! Coach! Coach! Coach!"

My older brother Tom walked in and I clapped and cheered with all the rest. He looked embarrassed, but he smiled and he shook every hand and bumped every fist and slapped every high-five on the way over to our table. He kissed Kate and he hugged his girls and picked Charlie up in one arm. I looked over and saw that my mom was misty and my dad was beaming like a hickory lantern. Mark whistled and I clapped and, well, you get the idea. Football means a lot to our family.

And Tom means more.

After a moment, Tom raised one hand and the noise dropped a few decibels. There was a chorus of "Shush"es and eventually the only noise was the ting of silverware and the clank of bottles.

When it was quiet enough to be heard he said, "Your kids are amazing."

The place broke out in cheers.

"Now let's go win state!" came a voice from the back. And the place erupted.

Tom grinned and raised a fist to even greater cheers before he gave Charlie back to Kate and took the Styrofoam container of food she had ordered for him. He made his way around the table, thanking us and making his apologies that he had to leave. He gave me a quick hug.

"Great job, man," I said.

"Sorry, gotta go watch film."

"I know. Go get 'em."

"Thanks for coming, Nate."

My brother is a driven coach who is always focused on the next game. Still, on that evening, he just about floated out of the room.

My family and I felt the same way. I relished the elation of the win and the accomplishment of Tom's team for about half an hour.

Until the call came.

∼

I HAD FOUGHT my way to the bathroom and was just coming out when my phone buzzed. I didn't recognize the number. I put my phone up to my ear and plugged the other one. "Hello?"

"Mr. Shepherd?"

I was having trouble hearing. "Hello?"

"Mr. Shepherd, it's Tyler." I couldn't hear what he said next.

The bathrooms were right by the front door so I ducked outside. "Say again, Tyler?"

"Colt's destroying my dad's truck."

"What?!"

"He's taking a bat to it."

"Why?"

"He said dad's going to send him to jail."

"Can you stop him?"

"I don't think that's the best idea right now."

"I'm on my way. Did you call your mom?"

"I tried. She won't answer."

"I'm at Borderlands with her. I'll grab her. See if you can get him to stop but just stay clear if you can't."

"Done."

"We'll be there in fifteen minutes."

We both hung up without saying goodbye.

When I went back inside, it was like one of those nightmares where you can only move in slow motion. I pushed my way over to the other side of the restaurant where Rob and Rhonda were sitting at a booth with another couple whose son was apparently number thirty-seven.

"There he is!" yelled Rhonda. "Another Shepherd. Screw Edwardsburg!"

Rhonda had apparently found out our next opponent. Fortunately, Rob was on the outside of the booth. I leaned down next to his ear and said, "Something's wrong with Colt. Meet me at Brett's house."

As I pulled back his eyes were wide. "Is he hurt?"

"I don't think so. I'm going." Then I turned and left.

As I pushed my way to the door, I heard Rhonda say, "What the hell is an Eddie?!"

A moment later, I opened the door to the cold night, sprinted to my Jeep, and headed for M-339.

I called my brother Mark first, told him there was an emergency, and asked him to pay my bill. After a couple of obligatory charity jokes, he agreed and said he would make excuses to Mom and Dad for me. Fortunately, Mark had a supreme ability to not give a shit about anything that wasn't squarely his concern, so he didn't ask for more detail.

I flew down the road until I hit M-339 then shot north and west.

I have friends who grew up in cities and they can never get over how dark Michigan roads are at night. Even people who live on the Ohio side of Carrefour come up north and, once they get out of town, are completely spooked by the lack of streetlights. M-339 was just like that; it was unlit and was lined with ditches deeper than your car and trees that stretched branches over the road like darker fingers of night. When, like that night, there was no moon, the road was utterly dark with the only light being what you brought to it.

I out-drove my headlights the whole way.

FAKE

30

I almost missed the turnoff to their two-track, but I had been out there enough by then that I caught the slanted green and white street number sign, slammed on the brakes, and took the hard left into the rough drive.

As I pulled in, I saw Tyler's battered red Silverado parked behind Colt's rusted blue Dodge Ram. Or I should say, battered and rusted is how I would have described the two trucks yesterday. Compared to the black F150 next to them, the boys' old trucks were sparkling floor models.

My headlights lit glass fragments all over the ground, along with the remnants of a couple of side-view mirrors. As I climbed out, I saw that the F150's taillights and rear window were gone and, if I wasn't mistaken, I was looking right through the cab without a windshield on the other side. There were dents everywhere, big, small, and a few exceptionally wide.

I was walking closer when I heard a crash from the barn and barking. The door was open, pouring light out into the yard. I ran inside.

Tyler stood in the center of the concrete floor, arms crossed.

Chet was at his knee. There was a splintering noise and Chet barked once before Tyler said, "You better not smash my shit."

I followed Tyler's gaze to the near wall. Colt stood there, panting, an aluminum baseball bat in his hands. What was left of a crossbow rack—Brett's crossbow rack—lay in a pile of splinters at his feet.

It was cold in the barn but sweat streamed down Colt's face and steam rose from his spiky wet hair. He looked at the rubble, then started to look around in a way I really didn't like.

"Your lawyer's here," said Tyler. He snapped for Chet and the two walked to the door. He paused. "I better not get a flat from that glass." Then the two went inside.

Colt wrung his hands around the bat handle like ballplayers do to get a better grip. Then he threw the bat to the concrete with a metallic clang that echoed in the big barn.

"Do you want to tell me what's going on?" I said.

"My dad screwed me again." He kicked the wooden scrap pile.

"How?"

"He had a trail cam."

"Where?"

"By the stand."

I did not like where this conversation was going. "Why does that matter?"

"There's a picture of me."

"That night?"

"Yep."

"Where?"

"By the stand."

"No, where did you see it?"

"Online. Someone posted it."

I took a deep breath. I hadn't taken a position one way or the other yet on Colt going to the hunting platform, so our defense wasn't compromised, but this certainly made it harder. "You didn't tell me you went out there."

He shrugged. "I'm not going to testify. I didn't think it mattered."

"It matters."

"Then you're not going to like the rest."

"The rest?"

"Of the picture. I'm carrying my crossbow."

"There's a picture of you carrying the murder weapon?"

"That's bullshit, Nate. I didn't hit him!"

I went still. "What do you mean you didn't hit him?"

"I missed him by a mile."

I felt like I could use an aluminum bat about then, but before I could do anything, I heard the crunch of tires on the two-track. "That'll be your mom," I said. "Not a word, Colt, do you hear me?"

He shrugged. "It's all over Twitter."

"Twitter's not admissible against you! What you say is! Now listen to me and shut up!"

Colt nodded and kicked at the wood scraps again.

Sometimes, I don't know how my brother made a career out of coaching kids.

I heard a door slam. "Colt?! Colt!"

Rhonda.

"What in the...Colt!"

I had both hands up as I came out of the barn. "It's okay, Rhonda."

"Where is he, Nate? Did someone vandalize the house? Was Colt attacked?"

"He's fine. No one vandalized the house."

"What happened then?"

"Colt did this."

Rhonda's face flipped from worry to anger in a motherly flash as she pointed. "Is he in the barn?"

"I need to talk to him first."

"Why?"

"Something with the case."

"Bad?"

"Not good."

Her face twisted and she cut loose with a cursing streak that honestly put me to shame for its depth and creativity. With a final yell at the barn about outstanding truck loans and deductibles, Rhonda collected Rob and the two went into the house.

As I watched them go, I realized they'd gotten out of a brand new truck, or at least it looked like one to me. It seemed as if there was a lot of black and chrome with an extended cab and running lights. Honestly though, I'd had about enough of trucks that night so I ignored it and went back to the barn to find out what Colt was doing with a crossbow at the hunting stand on the night his dad was killed.

~

COLT HAD TAKEN a seat in one of those woven plastic lawn chairs with a metal frame. His forearms were resting on his knees, steam rising from his head. I grabbed another one of the light chairs and sat beside him.

"Show me the picture."

Colt pulled out his phone, swiped a few times, and handed it to me.

There was Colt in a hooded sweatshirt walking right toward the camera. The picture was clear, his face was visible, and best of all, he was carrying a crossbow in front of him. I magnified it.

The crossbow was loaded.

"Where did you find this?"

"I couldn't stream the game, our Internet sucks, so I was following the scores on Twitter. Someone loaded it into the comments after Tyler's last score."

"Who?"

"No idea. Some egg."

I handed him back his phone. "You told me you didn't see your dad after he came home."

"I didn't know he had a trail cam out there."

"Is that what this is from?"

"Must have been." Colt took his phone back and ducked his head. Drops of sweat fell from his hair to the gray concrete.

I stared at him. "What happened that night? The truth."

Colt kept his eyes on the growing puddle between his boots as he said, "The season was almost over. The playoffs were coming up. This was Tyler's last chance to win a state championship and get a big scholarship. Brett was bearing down way too hard on him. He needed to back off."

"So?"

"So I went out to talk to him about it."

"With a crossbow?"

"Hell yes with a crossbow."

"Why?"

"Because he had one."

"So what?"

"You have heard the story about him putting my head through a video game, haven't you?"

I thought. "Why didn't you talk to him in the house?"

Colt looked away and shook his head. "Tyler was in there. He'd just tell me he was fine."

"Was he fine?"

"He shouldn't have to be."

"What happened next?"

"I picked up my crossbow and went out to the stand"—he waved his phone—"apparently right past the trail cam and told Brett I wanted to talk."

"What did he say?"

"He said to hurry up, I was scaring the coyotes."

"Then?"

"I told him to back off Tyler."

"And?"

"He said, 'What I do works.' And I said, 'You're going to mess him up.'"

Colt stopped.

"And then?"

"And then my dad laughed and said, 'Don't worry. Tyler's tougher than you.' So I shot at him."

I didn't say anything.

"I just wanted him to jump, you know? To scare him."

"Did you?"

Colt shook his head. "Bastard didn't even twitch. He just said, 'You shoot as good as you throw,' and went back to looking through his night scope for eye flashes."

"Colt, look at me."

He did. His hair was still wet, but the steam had stopped rising. "Did you hit him?"

"I wasn't even close."

"Are you sure?"

"Missed him completely. Lost a good arrow." He gave a quick laugh. "Or thought I did."

"You're sure you didn't hit him?"

"No way. It went a couple of feet over his head."

I pointed at the phone. "This is a big problem."

"It seems like it."

I waved at the wreckage. "Why all this?"

Colt pressed his lips together. "Because he screwed me

again."

"How?"

"If he hadn't set up the trail camera, no one ever would have known I was out there."

I ignored the implication of that and said, "Well, they do. So you need to tell me the truth, about everything, from now on."

"Yeah."

"If this had come out for the first time at trial, you'd be on your way to Jackson."

His face brightened. "You can keep it out of the trial?"

"Hell, no! But I can prepare for it. So is there anything else?"

"That's all."

I thought the odds of that were slim but also that I wouldn't get more tonight. "You better go inside. I have the impression that your mom might want to have a discussion with you about the resale value of trucks."

Colt winced. "Probably."

∼

AS WE LEFT THE BARN, I saw Rhonda on the back concrete landing, smoking. I walked over to her. I was halfway there before I realized that Colt had skittered around to the front door, avoiding his mom. I couldn't say I blamed him.

"That all secret lawyer shit?" she said and blew smoke into the air.

"Mostly."

"Wanna tell me what it was about?"

I thought. "An incriminating picture was posted tonight." I told her about it.

"What was he thinking? What did he do?"

"Rhonda, this is going to be really hard, but please, don't ask him about that."

I watched the ember consume a third of the cigarette in one draw before she said, "What?"

"If he tells you, you can be called to testify to what he said."

That led to a new round of cursing and a quick accumulation of ash at the end of her dart.

As she lit another, I said, "This isn't my place, but I think you and Rob should stay here with Colt until the trial is over."

Rhonda winced. "Do you know how long it took me to get out of this place?"

"I know."

Rhonda shook her head. "I am not sleeping in that bed again."

"No one would expect you to."

She thought. "We could take turns staying here. Rob won't mind. I just really didn't want to come back here."

"It's only for a little while."

Rhonda scowled and folded into herself before she burst out, "I'm tired of that man screwing up my life!"

I nodded then pointed at the truck. "So is Colt. That's what this was about."

"That's something we have in common then." She nodded. "We'll do it. And you're going to find out where that picture came from?"

"If it can be traced, yes."

"He didn't do it."

"I know."

"You need to prove it, Shepherd."

"I'm working on it."

"We need more than that."

The glowing ember was reflected in her eyes. "I know that too," I said.

I stuck my head in the door and shouted goodbye to Colt and Rob. I said goodbye to Rhonda then I walked back to the drive. I had to walk around their new truck and noticed that the passenger door was still cracked open. I went around and saw that it was a fully loaded, brand-new F150 before I shut it. Then I got in my Jeep and drove home to see if I could figure out who posted the photo.

31

I'll spare you the mystery—we never did find out who leaked the picture. That night when I went home, I hopped on Twitter and found the entrance to the rabbit hole on the Panthers' Football Twitter account where someone had posted the picture of Colt with his crossbow in the replies. I followed a few threads, including one that led to @AlexisFury and another that led to a video of coyotes eating in the wild and felt scummier for it. Some would argue that if Colt really did murder his father, then he had every bit of this coming, which I suppose was true in an abstract, cosmic vengeance sense. But these pictures and gifs and memes were being posted on a high school football team's page, not in a court pleading, so it seemed to me that seeking justice had very little to do with it.

Every rabbit hole I followed ended in a troll's egg. I found nothing I could use, no identity of someone I could enforce the Court's gag order against, and no one I had helping me found anything later either. Instead, the only thing I gained that night was the knowledge that everyone who followed the team's page, and more, saw the picture of Colt and his crossbow.

Eventually, I just turned off my phone and went to bed.

~

THE NEXT DAY was Saturday so I waited until noon to call Olivia, not because she was sleeping but because Saturday was one of her busiest class days.

"This is Olivia," she said.

"Just lazing about? How do you live with yourself?"

"By helping those less fortunate than me. Speaking of which, you weren't here."

"I did a very special home workout today. It was invented by the great Emperor, Couchus Maximus."

"Hmph. What's up?"

I told her about the picture and what had happened with Colt the night before. "I don't think you're going to have any luck finding where the picture originated but could you check anyway?"

"Sure. My guess is that it's going to be like the @AlexisFury account—too many sources and layers to get to the real troll."

"Thanks. In the meantime, I think I have something that's more significant."

"Shoot."

"Remember that research I had you do on Steve Mathison?"

"Our everyman? Yes."

"I saw him at the football game last night hanging around Rhonda Mazur and Rob Preston. Thirties, blonde hair, well-dressed."

"That's still a pretty labor-intensive search."

"I also got the Illinois license plate number to his black Audi."

"Why didn't you say that in the first place?"

"Because then I wouldn't have had the pleasure of this conversation with you."

"Fair. Send me the license plate and I'll get a search done."

"Thanks. It's on its way."

We hung up and I ate a quick lunch before heading out to rake the front yard. Yes, I'm very aware of how late in the fall this was and you can be sure that Mrs. Nykerk and her husband Jerry were very aware of it too since, from what I could see, they raked their yard next door every day and gave my property the stink-eye any time there was a west wind. I can only offer in my defense that it is utterly unfair to compare the yard of a retired person to the yard of a lawyer since everyone knows that a lawyer's hands spontaneously blister when he (or she) even looks at a rake.

I was about a third of the way done when my phone buzzed. When I saw it was Olivia, I took the call and walked inside. I'd be lying if I said I didn't feel a perverse satisfaction in knowing that Mrs. Nykerk would even now be wondering if her lazy neighbor had any sense of decency at all.

"I didn't expect to hear from you today, Liv," I said.

"I didn't expect to be calling you, but with the license plate, it was easy. I thought you might want to know right away."

"Have I mentioned that you're extraordinary?"

"Not often enough." She paused.

"You're extraordinary."

"Thank you. Steve Mathison, Northwestern grad, majored in journalism and sports marketing. Lives in Chicago. The car is registered in his name. Apartment in a high-rent district downtown. Did one internship with an athletic shoe company and another with one of the major sports agencies. He's been out on his own for the last six years. He has a list of companies on his website that's a sports who's who but they're too big for him to be doing their traditional advertising and marketing. By all accounts, he's living well and working, somehow, in sports marketing consulting."

"Carrefour is not that far from Chicago, but it's a different world."

"That was my thought exactly," said Olivia. "If you saw him with Rhonda and Rob, I'd guess that Mathison had never been here before Tyler started taking snaps."

"Sounds right."

"He has an Instagram that I want to take a deep dive into. It looks like he's in a lot of different places with a lot of different athletes, most of whom I don't recognize so I'm going to do some crosschecking."

"Thanks, Liv. That's definitely something."

"An extra-something?"

"An extraordinary result by an extraordinary investigator."

"Flatterer. Talk to you later, Shep."

I thought about what Olivia had found for a moment, then grabbed my rake and went back outside to end the suspense for Mrs. Nykerk.

32

The next day was Sunday, so I decided to do what folks all over southeast Michigan did on a Sunday in November at the height of hunting season.

I went to Cabela's.

There was one of the great outdoors stores not too far from us over in Dundee and, once I told Cade Brickson I was going, I had instant company. We caught up on his bail bonds business (going well) and the gym (always good) and the recovery of his knee (also good, but no thanks to me). We had moved on to my yard (newly raked) when we pulled into the parking lot marked by a huge statue of two rearing bears, fighting.

Cade cocked his head as we parked. "What are you here for anyway?"

"A crash course in trail cameras."

"Ahh."

As we walked to the entrance, two little boys with floppy-eared hats and popcorn balls spilled out of the doorway and ran squealing right into Cade's legs. They both stopped and looked up, their faces a sticky mess.

"Yikes," one of them said.

Cade looked down behind his black wraparound glasses. "Where's my popcorn?" he said.

The boys squealed and ran back in through the doors.

Cade's mouth twitched. "I'll be in firearms when you're done."

We went in the entrance and Cade headed back to the far corner for firearms. I headed toward trail cameras, then took a detour down the archery aisle.

I found the crossbows. They had a good-sized collection, obviously, but it didn't take long to find the brand that Colt owned. I pulled one off the rack that matched Colt's and hefted it, thinking about carrying it through the woods in the dark. I absently picked up a field point arrow, thinking I could buy one to give to Dr. Gerchuk, and slid it into the crossbow's groove to see if it was the right size.

"Excuse me, I'm sorry, sir? Sir! You can't load that in here."

It took me a moment to realize that the man hustling down the aisle was talking to me.

"What's that?"

A tall, heavy young man with floppy blonde hair in a green Cabela's shirt jogged toward me, one hand half-extended. "You can't load that in here, sir."

I suddenly realized how what I was doing could make people jumpy. "Oh geez, I'm sorry," I said putting the arrow back. "That was stupid of me."

"No problem, no problem at all, sir." He came to a halt, breathing hard. "We just ask that you hold one item or the other when you're inside the store. We have a wonderful range out back where you are more than welcome to test any of the equipment."

I handed him the crossbow and felt bad about the relief that crossed his face. "I really am sorry."

"Not at all. Can I show you another one?"

"Actually, I need some advice on trail cameras."

"Excellent! They're right over here."

He led me a couple of aisles over to a wall of devices and asked a flurry of questions.

"Hunting or surveillance?"

"Hunting."

"Big game, small, or bird?"

"Deer and coyote."

"Night vision?"

"Please."

"Pictures, video, or both?"

"Both."

"Wi-Fi, Bluetooth, or cell data? And don't say Bluetooth unless you're going to be within one hundred feet of it when you're taking the pictures."

I thought about Colt's comments on the poor quality of Internet and streaming at the house. "Cell data."

"Perfect. So here are a few." He brought me three. "All of them will take good pictures. These two will take video and this last one is the most expensive because it has the most storage." He looked over his shoulder. "That's really not necessary though."

"Why's that?"

"Because this middle one will send it right to your phone or computer. You're already paying for storage in those. Why pay twice?"

"Why indeed? Do they all date stamp the photos?"

"Absolutely. It wouldn't do much good if you didn't know when deer were going by. Or predators."

"That's the truth."

He spent another few minutes showing me the ins and outs of how you attach the camera to a tree and where the best places to use them are, but he'd already told me the most important things—the pictures were date stamped and could be sent to other devices. I'd taken a lot of his time and I didn't know if he was on commission or not so, as he wound down, I picked the middle model and thanked him for his help. Then, I went back to find Cade.

Of course, you can't go to Cabela's without passing the mountain with all of the animals on it that was the centerpiece of the store. I walked around, past buffalo and moose, a black bear and a lynx, until I came to a display where coyotes were posed along with a rabbit. Coyotes aren't nearly as big as wolves, but they aren't dogs either and, as I stared at the small pack contemplating a rabbit lunch, I decided that it took a certain kind of man to go out alone at night to hunt them with a weapon that took a while to reload.

I also decided that I wouldn't want to be wounded when I was attacked by one. Or three. Or seven.

I left the mountain and found Cade who, true to his word, was still shopping. When he saw I was ready to go, he stopped looking at a clearance rack of canvas tactical jackets, bent over, and picked up three bulk boxes of ammunition—I think I saw .40 and 9 mm in there but I couldn't be sure—along with some gun oil. Of course, Cade being Cade, he carried them over to the cashier's line under one arm instead of using a cart.

I didn't offer to help since he was doing it on purpose. Standing there, surrounded by guns and ammunition, it occurred to me. "Why a crossbow?"

Cade stared at me, holding the bulk ammunition like it was nothing. "Are you going to tell me the rest of the question?"

"To kill someone. Why use a crossbow? When you've got all..." I trailed away and waved at everything around us.

"Probably because that's what was available."

"Seems overly complicated."

Cade reached the register and set his boxes down. As the

cashier rang them up, he said, "There are all sorts of things I can do when I fight. Sometimes the guy's open to a jab, sometimes a hook, and, every once in a while, he's open to a spinning back fist. It's more complicated, unless it's what's there."

The cashier told Cade he owed Cabela's a small fortune. Cade paid cash.

She handed him a receipt. "Would you like a cart, sir?"

"No, thanks. If you could just put the paid sticker on it, I'd appreciate it."

She did and, if her eyes were on Cade more than the barcode for my trail cam, well, who could blame her.

33

After I dropped off Cade and his munitions dump, I drove to my parents' house to watch the Detroit Lions. Although the weather was now cold and my dad had long since brought his dock in from the lake, the Sunday cookouts continued. The eating had just shifted inside.

With the run to Cabela's, it was just a few minutes before kickoff when I arrived. The driveway was full of cars and I noticed both Tom's and Kate's. I parked behind Kate, grabbed the tubs of potato salad that were my contribution, and hustled up the driveway to the house.

Tom opened the door right as I reached it. He had his coat on and a paper bag in his hand.

"Not staying?" I said.

He shook his head. "Still have film to break down before the staff meeting tonight. Edwardsburg runs the wing T."

The wing T is a running offense that is based on deception and can confuse the hell out of a high school defense. "I heard."

"They've got four kids who are all averaging over eight yards a carry."

"You'll want to stop that."

"Thanks."

"Good luck if I don't see you before then."

Tom nodded and started to leave.

"Tommy, a question." Tom stopped and I could practically hear the clock ticking in his head. "A quick one," I added. I reached in and shut the door so that it was only the two of us. I could feel the coil of Tom's impatience. "You've known Colt a long time. Is he capable of something like this?"

Tom raised his sharp jaw and surveyed me with his coach's eye. "Lawyers don't usually ask that kind of thing, do they?"

"No. And if they did, it would only be to someone they trust."

"Does it matter?"

"I think it might. I'm going to have to run things out there pretty far to defend him and I don't want to get my legs cut out from under me at the wrong time."

Tom looked at his car, jingling his keys, then said, "Do you remember Colt as a player?"

"Some."

"He was great in high school. If it wasn't for his brother, he'd be the best quarterback I've had in the last ten years. He doesn't have his brother's size or arm or playmaking ability, but he's every bit the leader Tyler is."

Tom shook his head. "That's not true—he's more. Tyler is cool-headed, never gets ruffled, and pulls people along with his talent. Colt is fiery and out there and did the extra things to bring the team together. He's one of the only captains I've ever had who absolutely would not tolerate one player picking on someone else within the team. Not only did he stop it, but he also made it so the guys didn't even *want* to do it. This one time, we had a linebacker who was picking on a new kid who just couldn't figure out how to..." Tom caught himself and waved a hand. "It's a long story, but the fact is Colt stopped what was going on and by the end of the season, that same linebacker was picking up the new kid for school every morning so he didn't have to take the bus. If Colt hadn't blown out a shoulder his senior year, we'd be playing for our second state championship this week instead of our first. Colt and Tyler are good boys, two of the best I've ever coached. And I mean as people, not just players."

Tom stopped.

"I'm sensing a 'but,'" I said.

"But Colt has a temper."

"I've seen it."

"If you're not part of his team, if you're coming at his people from the outside, he's ferocious. And he can lose track of his 'off' switch."

With that, I could see Tom's internal clock start ticking again, even more loudly for having been paused. He'd given me exactly what he was good at, an accurate concise assessment of his player that both reassured and concerned me.

Tom looked over his shoulder. "I really have to—"

"Go." I handed him one of the tubs of potato salad.

"Thanks," he said and was already halfway to his car.

I popped in the door at which point my nephew Justin yelled, "Pops said you're five minutes late so the Lions are already down 0–7."

I went in to see how the rest of the game would go and came to a decision about something to do later in the week.

34

I was in my office Monday morning when Olivia called.

"What's up, Liv?"

"I've been doing a deeper dive on Mathison. Remember that I said he's in sports marketing and represents a lot of manufacturers?"

"I do."

"I'm still not sure exactly what he does, but I know where he does it."

"I'm not following."

"So I dug into his social media posts, especially the pictures. Turns out most of them are at elite basketball camps and AAU tournaments."

"Okay."

"It looks like he's been around them a lot for the last five years. Plenty of pictures with big-name players and shout outs and whatnot."

"Is he an agent?"

"Not that I can tell. He's not registered with any organization and he's never posting that he got so-and-so a good deal or anything like that. Instead, it seems like he's just taking a lot of pictures."

I wasn't making the connection. "Still not seeing it."

"I don't know what his exact association is, but you name any big-name basketball event for high school kids in the last five years and he's there. Until last year."

"What happened last year?"

"Last year, he also started showing up at every elite quarterback camp in the country."

Now she had my attention. "Really?"

"Yup."

There is a circuit of camps, passing clinics, and all-star games that the top high school quarterbacks go to before they go to college. Quarterback is the highest profile position in football so the quarterback clinics are the highest profile events for high school football players.

"There was one out west last summer," Olivia said. "Tyler went."

"I see. And Mathison?"

"Was there too."

"Any pictures together?"

"No. And Mathison took plenty. I counted at least eight players from all over the country. But none with Tyler."

"Still."

"Exactly."

I thought. "Could he be a booster?"

"It doesn't seem like it. The kids he's taking pictures with are going to schools all over the country. There doesn't seem to be a pattern there."

"Okay. Is there still more to look for there or are you at a dead end?"

"I think there's more. I still don't know exactly what he does."

"Can you keep looking?"

"Can I? I *have* to. Now I want to know."

I smiled. "Excellent. Anything else?"

"One thing."

There was silence at the other end of the line. It took me a moment, and then I said, "You're extraordinary, Liv."

"Thank you. Talk to you later, Shep."

Olivia hadn't made a connection between the Daniels family and Mathison, but she had them in the same area code. It occurred to me that that must be what Megan Dira had too: the same area code, but no direct connection or she would have come straight at us harder. The thing I couldn't figure out is why in the world the State Public Integrity Unit would even care? Despite my curiosity, the problem still didn't seem directly related to Colt's case or the Daniels, so I set it aside for the moment.

An email from Ray Gerchuk had come in while I was on the phone with Olivia, telling me to call him when I had a chance. I did.

"Harassing me first thing on Monday?"

"I got called in this weekend and as long as I was here, I thought I'd work on our case," said Dr. Gerchuk.

"Great, what did you find?"

"How are they saying Colt shot his dad?"

"With a crossbow."

"No, not *what* are they saying he shot him with, *how* are they saying he did it?"

"They haven't had to describe the act yet. Why?"

"Because the wound angle is pretty pronounced."

"In what way?"

"It's at a pretty steep upward angle."

"What does that mean?"

"Well, if they were standing at the same level, the wound

would be pretty straight. This angle indicates the shooter was below the victim."

I thought about the picture. "Like the shooter was on the ground and the victim was on a platform."

"Exactly like that."

Some Mondays it just doesn't pay to get out of bed.

"That would be consistent with what we know so far. Can you extrapolate the height difference?"

"That would take an analysis of geometry and angles and shooting distance. I just examine the bodies, man."

"Right."

"That's why I wanted to talk to you right away, though. In case you wanted someone to check that end of it."

"Thanks. Any thoughts on cause of death?"

"So far everything is consistent with bleeding to death from the thigh wound as opposed to something else."

"Okay. Is there anything else you need?"

"I wouldn't mind looking at tissue slides. Right now, though, I don't think I add much."

"That's what it sounds like."

"How does it look against Edwardsburg this weekend?"

"Tommy says they're tough and well-coached and have four backs no one's been able to corral yet this year."

"Exciting. You're going, right?"

"I'm not sure yet."

"You've got to be kidding me!"

"I know, I know. Hopefully, but we'll see."

"Turns out you don't have to worry about this case anymore then."

"Why's that?"

"Because your dad's going to have your ass if you stay home."

"Talk to you soon, Ray."

We hung up.

Both of those conversations led to one more I needed to have. I dialed Rhonda Mazur.

"Yeah?"

"Rhonda, it's Nate Shepherd."

"Oh, hang on." I heard Rhonda yell that she was taking a break. "Just a sec. I have to get out of here so I can hear you."

I heard the echoes of rustling and bumping and the rush of wind on the speaker before it became quiet. Then I heard a rasping click-click-click and an inhale before Rhonda said, "What is it, Shepherd?"

"I've been contacted by a state attorney from Lansing again about whether Colt's had any dealings with a guy named Steve Mathison."

"Who's that?"

"You tell me."

There was an inhale and an exhale. "Not a big fan of lawyer shit, Shepherd."

"You saw him at the game Friday. Young guy, blond hair, fancy clothes, fancy car. Gave you a big hug in the parking lot."

I heard another inhale and then a chuckle. "Do you have any kids, Shepherd?"

"I don't."

"Let me explain how it works then. Before one of my boys goes out on a field where eleven maniacs are going to try to knock his head off his shoulders, I drink. And when I drink, I really don't remember a lot of details."

"So you don't remember him?"

"If he's who you say he was then of course, I remember him. He was damn handsome, and he hugged me. But a lot of people hug the quarterback's mom."

"You don't know why the state would want to know about him?"

"Not at all."

"He goes to a lot of camps. Could he have met Tyler at the quarterback camp out west?"

"Camps were always Brett's area, Nate. I'm not involved in any of that."

"Well, I'm pretty sure this state attorney, Megan Dira, is going to be contacting you about it. If she does, you'll need an attorney. Let me know and I'll get a couple of names for you."

"That sounds like money."

"You need to protect yourself. And Colt."

"We'll see. Anything else?"

"Are you and Rob going to the game Friday?"

This exhale was long. "Probably, but with what happened with Colt last game, we're still figuring it out."

"What if I stayed with him while you're gone?"

There was a pause, then, "Are you serious?"

"Yes. You don't get many chances to see your boy do something like this."

"Don't you want to watch your brother?"

"Coaches' careers are long, Rhonda. Your son's a senior. And the finals are on Detroit TV so Colt and I can watch it."

She cleared her throat once and then again. "That would be a big weight off our minds, Shepherd. I really do have to get back now though."

"All right. Talk to you Friday."

We hung up. Truth be told, I did feel a little bad about missing Tom's game, but I also knew that Tom didn't need me there. Judging from what happened last Friday night, though, Colt was in need of a teammate. And for now that was me.

35

I'm embarrassed to say it took me two full days to figure out another angle to pursue the Mathison connection from. Mathison was involved in big-time sports and was nosing around Carrefour and nobody knew more about what was happening in and around Carrefour North sports than Kenny Kaminski. So that Wednesday night, I decided dinner at Borderlands was in order.

The place was packed again. Waitresses were scurrying back and forth with buckets of beer and mountains of onion rings—one of Borderlands' specialties—and there was a modest wait at the door. I put my name in and said I did not mind waiting for a table instead of eating at the bar.

Kenny Kaminski came around and greeted the two families in front of me by name before shaking my hand. "Nate, it's good to see you. Are you here for dinner?"

"I am. And a word with you."

"Outstanding. I'll stop by after you're seated and ordered."

"Perfect."

Kenny said hello to the family who'd come in behind me and asked how the fifth grade girls' basketball team had fared that night. At news of the win, Kenny high-fived a grinning girl and slapped the shoulder of a beaming dad before making his way back to the dining room where he somehow knew that one table was short a place setting and another out of hot sauce.

It wasn't more than five minutes before I was seated and another five minutes after that before I had ordered—the Diablo Chicken sandwich, in case you're wondering.

The waitress had no sooner left than Kenny appeared and sat down across from me.

"Kenny, this place is packed every time I've been over here."

He smiled and nodded. "Things have been humming, for sure. We're just finishing our second location on the Ohio side and are about to start building a third over in Indiana."

I looked around at the crowd of families eating and friends meeting. "You certainly seem to have figured it out."

Kenny shrugged. "Every community needs a place for people to go. You just have to make it easy for them and give them the things they want. So what did you want to talk to me about?"

"The local sports scene. And it seems to me that no one knows it better than you."

Kenny smiled and shrugged again. "It's easy to know when you're interested. What's up?"

"Do you know a guy name Steve Mathison?"

Kenny frowned. "Not offhand, but I haven't really looked at the spring sports line-ups yet. Is he a transfer or something?"

"No, no, he's not a high school player. He's an adult. Young guy, thirties."

When Kenny's face still looked blank, I paused, then said, "Been around Rhonda Mazur and Rob Preston at some of the games."

Kenny's face cleared. "Fancy car, nice clothes?"

"Yeah! You know him?"

Kenny smiled and shook his head. "No. But I know the type. You're a little young, but do you remember Jackson Wheaton?"

"Sure. My dad took me and my brothers to see him play."

Kenny nodded. "Wheaton was the best running back to ever come out of Carrefour, North or South, and if North had had any kind of offensive line at all that year, the team would've gone a lot farther than it did. Anyway, there were a lot of guys like Steve Mathison hanging around Jackson Wheaton and my guess is that, when you find a quarterback as good as Tyler is, you're going to find a lot of Steve Mathisons, too."

As I digested all that, Kenny cocked his head. "Is this related to Colt's case somehow?"

"No, no, I just got an inquiry from somebody who thought I might be representing the family asking if I had any information about this Mathison and I had no idea who he is."

"Colt doesn't know him?"

I shook my head. "Not at all."

Kenny sat back. "You know, Rhonda and Brett and I go back a long way. I saw her more when she and Brett were together, but I've spent a fair bit of time with her. She's not very...sophisticated. You tell her to be careful of the Steve Mathisons who come around. Are you representing her?"

"No."

"Too bad. She could use it." Kenny frowned again. "How's Colt holding up?"

"About as you'd imagine."

He shook his head. "I can't imagine it at all. If you need anything for him, you be sure to let me know, okay?"

"I will. Thanks."

Kenny shrugged. "Brett would do the same for me. Here we go!"

The waitress arrived with dinner.

Kenny stood. "The Diablo Chicken again! You like it, eh?"

We paused as the waitress delivered the plate, silverware, and a smile before moving on.

"It's delicious, Kenny. You really do know what you're doing."

"Thanks. It's the pickles that make all the difference."

Kenny started to leave and then turned back and tapped the table. "Tell Rhonda to be careful, okay? I'd hate to see Tyler get taken advantage of."

"Thanks, Kenny. I will."

"And go Panthers."

I smiled. "Go Panthers."

I ate my dinner. And I'll be damned if the snap of the pickles didn't cut the heat of the Diablo Chicken just right.

36

The Thursday before the state championship game, I was working at the office. It was almost noon and Danny had left his lunch at home so I had offered to pay for a couple of grinders if he picked them up. He'd only been gone a few minutes when I heard the outer office door open. "That was quick."

A woman's voice said, "Nate?"

I stood and went out to the lobby where Jenny Reddy stood, holding a paper bag. Jenny was a little taller and a little thinner than average and her blonde hair was pulled back into a ponytail. She was wearing yoga pants and a zip-up hooded sweatshirt that hung a little loose. She smiled when she saw me, and she was one of those people who, when she did, made you feel entirely better about yourself.

"Hi, Nate," she said again and held up the bag. "Dan forgot his lunch."

"He did at that. He just...went to run an errand for me. Was he expecting you?"

"No. I'm sure he didn't want to bother me. I thought I'd bring it over to surprise him."

For the record, I'm pretty sure that the only person I've ever met who is nicer than Danny is Jenny. I smiled. "Good. I'd hate to think he forgot you were coming, too."

Jenny smiled and shook her head. "The closer you two are to trial, the more absent-minded he gets. Do you know that the week before the Braggi trial, he left the car running in the driveway when he came home? Didn't realize it until he took the garbage cans out before bed."

"Somehow he forgot to mention that to me."

"Yes, these trials..." She shook her head. "Well, he gets very focused."

"He's amazing at it. Danny is a fantastic attorney. I could never do this without him."

It was a compliment and I said it because it was true and because I wanted her to know that her husband was very good at his job.

Jenny Reddy didn't smile though. She winced.

That wince hurt more than a screaming fit.

It was gone in an instant, replaced by her warm smile. "Well, I'll leave this for him."

"You're welcome to stay. He'll want to see you."

"No, no, the baby is at my mom's while I run a few errands. I just had time to drop this off."

"It was good to see you."

"You too, Nate." Jenny went into Danny's office, wrote him a note to go with his lunch, then waved as she left.

That was the second time I'd heard from them about the type of cases we were handling. I should have seen it for the warning it was, but I didn't. Instead, I went right back to worrying about how I was going to defend Colt Daniels.

37

When I arrived at the Daniels' house on Friday afternoon, Colt opened the back door and Chet barreled out to say hello. After a sniff from him and a scratch from me, Chet took off toward the woods. I tried to grab him but Colt said, "That's alright, let him go. He stays in the yard."

I was an hour early. The house didn't have cable, so we had to make sure we could stream the game on Fox Sports Detroit. It only took one HDMI cable, two remotes, and five curses before we had the online broadcast up and running. By that time, the previous game had ended so that warm-ups for the Carrefour North versus Edwardsburg game had begun.

About then Chet scratched the back door and Colt let him in. Chet and I got reacquainted and then the yellow lab flopped into a corner.

I've described the Sunday outings at my parents' house to watch the Detroit Lions. It's a common experience, where a group of people get together to eat, drink, talk, and enjoy watching a game together.

This was nothing like that. Our brothers were about to play for a state championship.

Neither of us wanted to eat anything. Colt nursed a pop and I sipped a coffee and the two of us watched every bit of warm-ups that the broadcast showed. When we did talk, it was only during the commercials and mostly about the difficulties of defending Edwardsburg's deceptive wing-T offense. I won't spend much time on it, but basically the wing-T features three guys in the backfield and, when it's run really well, it's almost impossible to know who has the ball.

Edwardsburg ran it really well.

"We only need to stop them once," said Colt.

"Why's that?"

"Because Tyler is going to cram it down their throats every time."

I smiled. "I hope so."

"You watch."

We were silent until the next commercial. "How was Tyler doing this week?" I asked.

"Pretty good. He doesn't get rattled. He was treating all of it like it was just another game." Chet scratched at the back door. Colt got up and let him out as he continued, "That's why he's so good. He just keeps calm, sees what the defense is doing, and capitalizes on every mistake. Brett never really understood that."

That was the first time Colt had ever casually mentioned his dad to me.

"What do you mean?"

Colt shrugged and sat back down. "I'm pretty easy to get. I'm a traditional, rah-rah, let's-go-kick-some-ass-kinda guy. Tyler's not. He's so calm that it's easy to think he doesn't care because he never really says anything that makes you think he does. But he's always studying, always absorbing, taking in every little thing until he goes out there and slices the other team apart."

Colt shook his head. "Brett could never get a rise out of Tyler. So he'd nit-pick his technique instead."

"That's why you fought?"

"I kept telling Brett that his extra crap didn't make a gnat's ass of difference."

"What did your dad say to that?"

"He'd always say, 'Why do you think Tyler's so good?' It was infuriating." Colt shrugged. "That's why I was so mad at him when I came home."

"Why?"

"Brett didn't like the way Tyler had played the week before. Didn't think his footwork was 'crisp' enough. Thought he'd bobbled a snap. Of course, we'd won, and Tyler had thrown for four touchdowns, but Brett made him do footwork drills and throw a hundred balls through the tire anyway."

"The next day?"

Colt pointed. "That night. Right out back."

I glanced out the storm door. "Could he even see?"

"There's a spotlight on the barn that lights up the tree. And Brett had Tyler pull his truck around into the yard with its lights on so he could watch his footwork."

I was no Tyler Daniels, but I still remembered how sore I was on a Friday night after a game.

Colt shook his head. "Brett made him drill until the battery in Tyler's truck died and his lights went out. Then Brett said Tyler should've thrown faster or turned on his engine and wouldn't help him get his truck started. Tyler wound up calling Rob to give his truck a jump. That's how I heard about it. Rob was completely pissed, and he never gets mad about anything."

"Rob came up here?"

"The very next day. Fortunately, Brett was working that Saturday." Colt took a sip of his pop. "Rob's a good guy."

"Yeah?"

There was a scratch at the door. Colt stood up as he said, "He's great. Treats my mom good and, since he's been around, he's always been there for Tyler and me when we needed something."

Colt opened the door. Chet barreled back in and went straight to slurping up water from his bowl.

"What do you mean?"

Colt thought for a moment, then said, "Brett would help us if *he* thought it was important. So a football camp, a workout, someone to catch balls with, he was there any time. But if he didn't think it was necessary or thought you'd screwed it up in the first place? Forget it. Rob always helped us with that sort of stuff. Like after the battery died? It wouldn't hold a charge so Rob spent the afternoon with Tyler replacing it while Brett was off drywalling. Finally!" Colt pointed at the TV. "They're ready to start."

Chet took that as a signal to go outside. He scratched at the back storm door and Colt, without taking his eyes off the TV, opened it, letting Chet scurry off to do retriever things. I re-filled my coffee which, given the extent to which I was already wired, was likely a huge mistake.

The game got underway.

∾

BY HALFTIME, the score was tied 28–28. As we predicted, Carrefour couldn't stop the deceptive rushing attack of Edwardsburg and Edwardsburg couldn't stop Tyler from throwing the ball all over the field. Every possession had ended in a score.

"That has to be just killing my brother," I said.

"What?"

"Not stopping Edwardsburg's offense."

Colt chuckled which made Chet scramble to his feet and go to the back storm door. As Colt let the dog out, he said, "It's funny because Coach Shepherd is usually a pretty calm guy.

Intense but calm. He never really lit us up on offense the way he did with the defense."

I nodded. "He believes you need to keep your mind clear and calm on offense, exactly like you said with Tyler. On defense, he favors the crazed dog mentality. Speaking of which."

Chet was scratching from the outside. Colt went right back and opened the door, allowing the yellow lab to scramble back in and flop down next to the couch with abandon.

I chuckled. "Is he always like this?"

"Only every night."

"I wasn't sure if it was because I'm here."

"No. What Chet lacks in intelligence he makes up for in enthusiasm. It makes him a great bird dog though." Colt reached over and rubbed Chet's belly. "Doesn't it, Chet?"

Chet thumped his tail in agreement.

"Do you hunt him?"

"We do." His face darkened. "Or we did. My dad took us pheasant and grouse hunting a lot."

The lawyer part of me flashed. "Hey, you don't have any rifles in the house, do you? It would violate the terms of your bond."

"Don't worry. They're at my mom's."

I felt a wave of relief. "Good."

"Rob has a big safe so I just store them there."

The TV flashed stats from the first half of the screen, interposing them over a student section wearing black and waving red flags.

"Seems like we have a good crowd there," I said.

"I think Rhonda and Rob caravanned up with about five hundred cars."

"Yeah?"

"She texted me a picture." He smiled. "Along with a 'Miss you. Screw Edwardsburg!'"

It wasn't hard to hear her voice in what Colt said. Then the second half started and the two of us were completely absorbed. The only time either of us moved was when Colt let Chet in. And out.

~

I COULD GIVE you a play-by-play of the second half, but I imagine that's not why you're reading this. It turns out, though, that both the Edwardsburg coach and my brother were defensive geniuses who were insulted by what had happened in the first half and made adjustments that shut down each other's offense. If I hadn't been so invested, I would've enjoyed the entertaining camera shots of the two of them getting after their defenses for the next two quarters.

Late in the fourth quarter, Edwardsburg broke through first. The quarterback made a run fake then rolled out to his left and lobbed a little pass to a receiver who turned and ran fifty-three yards untouched for a touchdown. The extra point was good, giving Edwardsburg the lead, 35-28. Carrefour got the ball back down seven with one minute and fifteen seconds left.

What Tyler did then was masterful. He threw a series of short passes and marched the Panthers right down the field until, with eight seconds left, he faked a pass, then ran it in himself for a touchdown, which meant that an extra point would tie the game and force overtime.

Colt and I watched as Carrefour lined up to go for two points. They had one play. If they scored, we'd win. If they didn't, we'd lose. I leaned forward in my chair, gripping the arms.

As Tyler lined up behind center to start the play, Chet scratched at the back storm door.

"Goddammit, Chet!" said Colt.

"Stay there," I said. "I've got him."

Chet had no objection to me opening the door and Chet shot outside as I kept my eyes on the screen. Tyler took the snap, dropped back, and zipped a pass that bounced right off the receiver's hands, incomplete. We both cursed as the Edwardsburg players celebrated.

Colt saw it first. He jumped out of his chair and yelled, "Flag!"

There was a penalty on Edwardsburg for pass interference. It was a bad call and the Edwardsburg coach wasn't having any of the referee's explanation. I didn't blame him. The referee moved the ball closer and Carrefour tried again.

As the Carrefour offense went back to the line, the camera zoomed in on Tyler's face. There wasn't a flicker of emotion on it. He stood there until the referee spotted the ball, then directed two receivers from one side of the formation to the other. Tyler took the snap, dropped back, and lofted a high-arching pass to the back of the end zone. The receiver leapt up over the defensive back, snatched it out of the air, and got one foot down in bounds before he fell to the ground. The referee raised both hands in the air. Colt and I yelled, smacked hands, and generally carried on.

Carrefour North 36–Edwardsburg 35.

As the team streamed onto the field, I looked out the back door and saw Chet nosing around by the woods.

"Chet's getting a little far," I said.

"Just call him," Colt said without taking his eyes off the screen. "He'll come."

I opened the white storm door and yelled, "Chet!"

Chet straightened, looked back, and sprinted straight to me.

Right past the place where they had found Brett Daniels' body the day after he died.

Chet greeted me with an exuberance I no longer felt. I let him in, gave him a pat, and turned back to the TV to watch the trophy presentation. They called the name of each of the Carrefour North players to give them a state championship medal, then called Tom's name and handed him the team state championship trophy. But as Tom held up the trophy and the team swamped him, I couldn't get my mind off what I had just seen.

I decided it was time to go. There wasn't much to clean up, but I helped and half-listened as Colt talked about how well Tyler had played and how great Tom had coached. I nodded and I was polite and I'm pretty sure that Colt was involved enough with his brother's game that he didn't notice my distraction. Chet certainly didn't as I scratched his ears goodbye.

Colt walked me to the door. When we got there, he shook my hand and said, "I really appreciate this, Nate. Thank you."

"No problem, Colt. But stay off social media tonight. You'll be able to talk to Tyler and your mom when they get home."

"Don't worry, I learned my lesson on that."

I left. As I drove, I couldn't stop thinking about Chet. I had watched the yellow lab go in and out a dozen times that night, but it wasn't until I stood at the door that I'd realized that he'd been running right by where Brett Daniels' body had been found. But Brett hadn't been found until Friday night, close to twenty-four hours after he died. And since I knew that Colt was in the house Thursday night and Friday morning that meant one of two things.

Either Colt hadn't let Chet out into the backyard for twenty-four hours, which wasn't at all likely.

Or Chet had discovered something that Colt already knew was there.

38

I drove for a while and picked up something to eat, killing time. All I could think about was Chet, that big, bounding, cheerful yellow lab who couldn't stay in the house to save his life.

The working theory was that Brett Daniels had died on Thursday night. I supposed that it was possible that Brett had died after the boys had gone to bed and Chet was down for the evening. But Colt still would've had to let Chet out on Friday morning to do his business so the dog would've found Brett then. I supposed that it also was possible that Colt had been in a hurry that morning to get to Grand Valley and he'd kept a tight rein on Chet so he could get on the road, but I hadn't seen anyone put Chet on a rein yet, let alone a tight one.

No, something seemed very wrong and it didn't seem at all likely that it had taken Chet twenty-four hours to discover the body. I was pretty sure that Tiffany Erin didn't know about how Chet behaved so I didn't think that Colt faced jeopardy from that angle, but if there was a hole in Colt's story, then there was a hole in my case, and a hole is always more dangerous when it's hidden.

I chewed on it like a dog with a, well, you know, until I arrived at my destination.

In the past, I had made a very serious mistake, the worst one of my life, by letting work consume all of my attention to the exclusion of my loved ones. Actually, to the exclusion of my most loved one, at great cost. I had resolved not to let that happen again and so, despite my preoccupation with Colt's case, I made this last stop.

I parked at the end of the line of cars, got out of my Jeep, and grabbed the case of beer from the back seat. I went up to the front door of the modest ranch house and knocked. It took a moment but then it opened.

"You made it!" said Kate and gave me a big, joyful hug. She squeezed, kissed my cheek, then pulled back and grinned. "We're in the garage."

It took me a while to get there. Two nephews and a niece needed to be caught when they leapt in ambush from a couch, and then my mom, after she hugged me, needed to be assured that I had not, in fact, lost weight and that I was working a perfectly normal amount of hours.

"You're not coming back?" I said.

"I've already had Tommy time today." My mom smiled. "It's grandkid time."

I left her to it and followed Kate into the garage.

The furniture had been shifted from coach's office formation to big game formation. Mark and Izzy gave a little cheer as I entered although I'm not sure if it was for me or the case of beer, which Izzy promptly relieved me of. Once my hands were free, my dad hugged me.

I grinned. "How about that?"

His teeth flashed in return. "How about that?"

My dad smacked my shoulder as I made my way to Tom, who just stood there in his Panthers gear, his face cracked in a rare grin. I was surprised when he grabbed me in a hug and even more when he pushed me back and shook my shoulders around.

"I laughed and grabbed him again. "You did it, man."

"The kids played a great game." Tom's voice was raw and gravelly. Screaming signals over a cheering crowd will do that.

"They sure did. And you coached one."

"Couldn't stop them in the first half."

"Not even a little. But you adjusted."

"So did they. Edwardsburg has a great coach with a young team."

I smiled. "Then it's a good thing you got them when you did."

Tom stood there, grinning.

"Let's kick-off!" said Izzy. She tossed a beer over her head from the couch at me while Kate pitched one at Tom.

We caught them and grinned. Yes, I know I keep saying that, but that's what was happening; we were grinning until our faces about broke.

Tom pointed at his computer. "Want to watch a game?"

I cracked the beer. "If there's nothing better on, I guess."

Tom hit play.

READ

39

You wouldn't think that it would take two weeks to get an appointment with a Michigan DNR officer, but then again, late fall in Michigan is one of their busiest times. It used to be said that there were more armed men in Michigan on opening day than were mobilized for the Vietnam War. I don't know if that was true or not, but there were certainly a lot of deer tags and licenses to manage.

Two weeks after Carrefour North won the state championship, Michigan Department of Natural Resources Officer Samson Wald had time to see me. I made the drive over to the Unadilla State Wildlife Area in Grass Lake, Michigan, which is a small town just northeast of Jackson. Because wildlife and hunting appeared to be involved in Brett Daniels' death, Officer Wald had been called in to investigate.

I turned at the brown sign that marked the Unadilla Wildlife Field Office onto the gravel two-track that led me back to the small brown and white building. It looked like a long ranch house with a flagpole and an overly large garage. I pulled off to the side so that I wouldn't block the three garage ports and headed up to the door.

A man was standing in front of it. He was wearing a dark ball cap, a heavily insulated dark green shirt set off by a gold badge on his chest, and dark pants tucked into black boots. He looked like he was in his late forties, with a thick brown mustache and a ruddy face with crinkles at the corners of his eyes that spoke to a lot of time in the summer sun and the winter wind. One hand rested on his black gun belt while the other held a Yeti thermal cup with the Michigan DNR insignia on it. He sipped as he watched me make my way up the walk.

"Officer Wald?"

"Call me Sam," he said.

"Nate Shepherd," I said as I extended my hand. "Here to talk to you about the Daniels case."

His mouth twitched. "Didn't exactly think you were here for a hunting tag." He shook my hand anyway. "Come on in."

He took me back to a small office that had boards with maps and official notices and what looked to me like a blow up of the Waterloo recreation area that this office serviced.

"Thanks for seeing me. I know how busy it is this time of year."

He nodded. "The wasting disease outbreak hasn't made it any easier."

"Still not allowing baiting?"

Officer Wald raised an eyebrow.

"A suit and a bow aren't mutually exclusive."

Officer Wald didn't look impressed. "You know, the only reason I agreed to see you is because of what your wife did for the department on the emerald ash borer problem."

"I understand that."

"A lot of people around here remember how hard she worked."

"She certainly did."

"The department misses her."

I nodded. "We all do."

"So what do you need, Nate?"

"I understand you were called in to investigate the wildlife aspects of Brett Daniels' death over in Carrefour."

Officer Wald nodded. "I was."

"I have questions about two things, if you don't mind."

He stared at me, his ruddy face blank. "You represent the son who killed him?"

"Who's accused of it, yes."

He sipped. "Go ahead."

"First thing—are you allowed to hunt coyotes with a crossbow at night?"

Officer Wald nodded. "Yes, although people don't usually do it with a crossbow. It's hard enough to get them with a rifle."

"And night's okay too?"

"The state allows night hunting for coyotes. That's one of the reasons we eventually allowed those arrows with the lights on the nocks, so that people could find them in the dark."

"I'd always heard that coyotes are pretty hard to hunt."

"They are. But it's one of those things that some people have a knack for. This Daniels fella certainly did."

"Oh?"

Officer Wald nodded. "He always reported, and he bagged a good number of them every year. It takes a lot of skill to bring in as many as he did."

I nodded. "Second thing—did you get there in time to investigate his body?"

"I did."

"Do you know why the sheriff's office called you?"

"Once they found the victim, it was pretty clear that there was a wildlife aspect to the death, so they wanted me to take a look."

"What did you think when you saw him? The body, I mean."

"I could tell right away that coyotes had gotten into it."

"How? Tracks?"

"No, by the time I got there everything was trampled up pretty good. It was the feeding pattern."

"What pattern is that?"

"Whatever had eaten him had gone through the abdominal cavity. The kidney and liver and lungs were gone and the stomach and intestines were scattered about. There was some gnawing on the rib cage." He sipped, then shrugged. "That's how coyotes eat."

"Isn't it unusual for coyotes to attack a man like that?"

"It is. That's why it didn't make any sense to me when I first saw it. Coyotes had clearly fed on him, but you're not going to see a straight-up attack like that, especially against someone who was armed. They'd normally be scared right off. It made more sense later once I heard that your client,"—he raised a hand—"or *someone*, shot the victim with a crossbow first."

"As opposed to the coyotes taking down a healthy man?"

"Exactly."

"No chance the coyotes attacked and killed Mr. Daniels?"

"None."

I thought. "Do you have any sense as to how long it would have taken the coyotes to feed that much?"

"It depends on how many there were, I suppose." Officer Wald tapped the top of his thermal cup. "My thought was that it was consistent with him dying on Thursday night. I would say that it looked like a day's worth of feeding."

"And if there were more?"

"Then I would have expected more of the carcass, excuse me, the body, to be eaten."

Something occurred to me and before I thought about whether I should ask it, I said, "Do coyotes make a lot of noise when they eat?"

Officer Wald's mustache twitched. "They don't cover their mouths and use napkins."

"No, I mean, do they howl like when they bring something down?"

"It depends on how many there are. If it's a group, you're going to hear a lot of yipping and barking and fighting."

"Even if there are just a few?"

"They're coyotes, Nate."

I caught myself then. Officer Wald was going to be speaking to Tiffany Erin too so I couldn't afford to ask him whether that yipping and barking and fighting would be loud enough for someone in the house to hear.

Instead, I asked, "Could it have been a dog? I know there are feral packs up that way."

Officer Wald shook his head. "Dogs have a totally different feeding pattern."

"What's that?"

"If a dog had brought Mr. Daniels down, there would have been a lot more lacerations on his limbs and around his body and more wounds to his buttocks and thighs. This was classic coyote."

I asked my real question. "And the same would be true if a dog came upon the corpse?"

Officer Wald nodded. "A dog would worry at the carcass, the body, in a totally different way. They tend to feed from different access points." He paused. "Does that matter to you?"

"No. I just wanted to make sure I understand the wildlife end of this."

I stood before he could make any other connections to what I was asking. "I appreciate your time, Officer Wald. Thank you."

He stood with me. "Will there be a trial?"

"Unless the prosecutor dismisses."

"No plea?"

"Even if one's offered, we're not interested. My client didn't do it."

"That's not what I hear."

"'One hundred suspicions don't make a proof.'"

"Maybe. But then again, Dostoevsky didn't spend much time in Michigan."

I raised an eyebrow.

Officer Wald smiled. "A gun belt and books aren't mutually exclusive."

He walked me to the door. "I expect I'll be seeing you at trial in a couple of months then."

He shut the door without waiting for a reply.

40

I came back to the office after my visit with Officer Wald to find Danny standing by the printer, muttering.

"What are the voices telling you today?" I said.

"That I need to re-examine my life choices."

"I could've told you that. Why now?"

"Two things." He handed me a sheaf of papers. "Erin has updated her witness list. She's going to call Kenny Kaminski about the fight Colt had with his dad."

"We knew that."

Danny shook his head. "Check what she wrote on the topics for his testimony."

I scanned the disclosure. Under "Kenny Kaminski" was written "physical altercation between defendant and victim at Borderlands and other threats of violence and altercations between the two." I raised an eyebrow. "Other threats?"

"Exactly. Do you know of any?"

"No. Looks like I need to have another conversation with Kenny. What's the second thing?"

Danny pressed a button on the copier and a series of papers came shooting out, face down. "Know how they have the picture of Colt with a loaded crossbow but no evidence that he fired it that night?"

I nodded. I hadn't told Danny about Colt's admission to me that he'd shot at his father and missed that night because I'm just that paranoid. "It's a hole in their case."

"Consider it filled."

I watched with a sudden dread as the last piece of paper came out of the printer, which Danny then handed to me.

"Let me introduce you to the items associated with newly discovered State Exhibit Number 74."

I leafed through a series of crystal clear black and white photos that I assumed were the result of a night vision lens. The first seven showed Colt crossing the screen from right to left. He wore a hood, but he was looking up and his face was clearly visible. I recognized the third one as the picture that had been leaked on social media two weeks ago.

In all seven, he was holding a crossbow at waist height with both hands.

I nodded. "We've seen these. It's from the series she disclosed right after the one hit Twitter."

Danny shook his head. "You've seen those seven. You haven't seen these five."

He handed me another stack. I spread them out. The five pictures showed Colt moving from left to right. His head was down, his arms hung at his sides, and the crossbow dangled from his right hand so that it barely cleared the ground.

I didn't need Danny to tell me, but I looked closer. The five pictures showed the silhouette of the crossbow from behind. The string ran straight across at the T.

It had been fired.

I'd been planning on poking at this issue as a failure of proof. It wasn't.

"How could they have just found these?" I said.

"They claim that these trail cam pictures were on Brett's phone in a separate file that they only recently unlocked and found."

"That's some grade-A bullshit, Danny."

"It is, but she's technically still producing it within the court's time frame. I don't see a way to keep them out."

I shook my head. "No, the pictures are coming in. It's the delay that ticks me off." I went back to the witness disclosure. "Let's file a motion to exclude these alleged confrontations and threats Kaminksi supposedly knows about and force Erin to disclose what they are to try to get them in."

"Will that work?"

"We'll see."

"Don't they go to motive though?"

"Whose side are you on?"

"The winning side, I hope."

"Good man. Yes, it does, but I think she'll have to disclose what they are to do it. Maybe."

"Stop encouraging me with all that confidence."

We went to our separate offices. I thought of an issue with the trail cam and decided Olivia was the one to ask.

I called and she picked up right away. "Hey, Shep. I didn't see you this morning."

I instinctively looked at my calendar. "Were we supposed to meet?"

"The Panther scholarship dinner is tonight, isn't it?"

"It is."

"So you won't be able to get your evening lift in?"

"I suppose not."

"So I expected to see you this morning."

"I had another meeting."

"At five o'clock this morning?"

"Why would I have had a meeting at five o'clock this morning?"

"Because I was teaching a class then that was available for you if you couldn't motivate your sorry ass to lift on your own."

"See, I figured that class was so much fun that it was full."

"The only thing worse than a sloth is a liar."

"Perhaps. Hey, how hard is it to break into a smart phone?"

There was silence for a time, and then, "I don't know how to do such a thing, Shep."

I smiled. "Of course not. No, the prosecution in Daniels is saying it took them weeks to get into Brett Daniels' phone to obtain evidence." I told her the situation.

"Oh." I could hear the weight lift from the other end of the line. "It's possible if they didn't have the lock code. They may have had to send it out, which can take a while. That delay is a little on the outside but not unreasonable. I don't know that I can find out much about how this phone in particular was processed though."

"No, I don't want you to. Just wanted to see if you thought it passed the smell test."

"It's fragrant but not rotten."

"Got it. So are you going to the dinner tonight? Cade said you might come."

"I got a better offer."

"Impossible."

"But true. You and my brother will have to relive high school glory without me."

"Let me see, the glass blower/triathlete was a little artsy so I'm going to guess you're rebounding with a nurse/crossfitter."

"I will have you know that he is a physical therapist who's new to the area and joining a well-respected practice."

"And?"

"You're a jerk."

"Yes. And?"

"He's a crossfitter."

I chuckled as she punctuated my comment with a further characterization of the intelligence residing in my derriere before I said, "It won't be the same without you."

"I know. Have fun."

"You, too."

With that, I went back to looking at Tiffany Erin's most recent filings and kept myself occupied until the end of the day.

41

That Friday night, the Panthers' boosters club held its annual scholarship fundraiser at the Carrefour VFW hall. Fifty dollars a person or one hundred dollars a couple bought you a buffet-style chicken dinner, pitchers of beer and soft drinks, and the knowledge that most of your money was going toward the scholarship fund. The old hall was set up with long rows of tables that held twenty or so to a side with the table at the front of the hall reserved for silent auction items. Cade Brickson had won a scholarship back in the day and so had my brother Mark so they always supported it. Cade had convinced me to join them with promise of buying some drinks after, and it was always good to see Mark and Izzy, so I'd agreed.

I checked in, was issued my green dinner ticket, my two orange drink tickets, and my five blue door prize raffle tickets, and made my way through the crowded hall. I spotted Mark and Izzy at a table in the back. As I joined them, Izzy patted the table across from her and said, "Plant those sweet buns right here, Nate."

"Can't you control your woman?" I said to Mark as I sat.

"Nope," said Mark and sipped his beer.

Izzy batted her eyes at him. "Why darling, that's the nicest thing you've ever said to me."

Mark winked and took another sip.

Cade Brickson came in a moment later. Cade was dressed in his usual black t-shirt, jeans, and boots with his only concession to night being that his sunglasses were pushed up into his short dark hair. As he grabbed a chair, Izzy shook her head and said, "Good Lord, Cade, look at you. You're making me reconsider my life choices."

Cade smiled and nodded in a gesture that acknowledged that he could see how she felt that way.

Izzy leaned in. "Cade, don't you know any women taking your sister's classes that would be interested in a semi-surly, moderately attractive lawyer with a wonderful family?"

Cade looked thoughtful. "I'm not sure I'd want to do that to them, Iz. Most of them are friends."

"Well, I wish you'd try because he keeps ducking me."

"Seems rude."

"I know, right? Like tomorrow, a group of us are going to—"

"I'm working tomorrow," I said. "Big trial coming up."

"Liar," said Izzy.

"Convenient," said Cade.

"A little help?" I said to Mark.

Mark shook his head. "The more you struggle, the faster you sink."

"State champs, sons of bitches!" came a woman's yell from the door.

Cheers erupted from the other side of the room as Rhonda Mazur and Rob Preston walked through the door and joined a group of parents who lined a table on the other side of the hall.

"She seems to have a head start," said Izzy.

"That's the Daniels' mom," said Mark.

"Oh." Izzy looked at me. "Then I suppose she should let off some steam."

I was spared the trouble of deflecting questions about Colt's case when two women who looked to be in their mid-thirties walked up, one holding a roll of tickets (these were red) and a plastic bucket, and the other a wad of bills. "50/50 ticket?" said the woman with the roll.

"Ten for five dollars or nose to toes for twenty," said the woman with the cash. Neither took their eyes off Cade.

"Nose to toes?" said Cade.

The ticket woman pulled out some of the roll. "You get a string of tickets that goes from nose to toes."

"Mine or yours?"

"Mine," she said.

"I'll take that then."

The ticket woman flushed and unrolled the tickets, the cash woman fumbled to take Cade's twenty, and Izzy and I hid our smiles behind cups of beer. When both ladies made a point of saying they were here for family because they certainly weren't old enough to have high school children, Izzy choked mid-sip and Mark gently patted her back.

They delivered the tickets to Cade, thanked him, and moved on to the next table without asking if the rest of us wanted to buy. Cade smiled and laid the tickets out in the center of the table as if he were presenting a bolt of silk to a king. The rest of us laughed and let it pass because, honestly, it didn't do to encourage Cade on that score. Instead, we got up, took our turn in the buffet line, and returned to our spot to eat our chicken as Izzy grilled Cade about his dating life and I questioned Mark about my three nephews.

It wasn't too long before we'd finished our food and decided that we had done our duty for the Panthers. Mark and Izzy had to get home to relieve the babysitter so the four of us went up to check our door prize tickets and the silent auction items on the way out.

This being a fundraiser, I had half-expected a speech that people would ignore or talk over, but they did something more creative. They had two TVs, one on either side of the auction table, running a video for the Panther scholarship fund. It was a little hard to hear, but it was close-captioned so we could read what Melanie Stanshaw, president of the Panthers' Booster Club, had to say about dedication and opportunity and scholarships and Panther pride. It then cut to some entertaining clips of past winners, including one of a high school-era Cade Brickson throwing a man through the air. That was followed by other Panthers making a three-point shot, leaning at the finish line, and leaping for a magnificent spike. The last clip was of the final play at Ford Field as the Panthers won their first football state championship and the team rushed the field. Then the video ended with a shot of my brother Tom asking everyone to please support the scholarship fund.

I smiled, collected my door prize (a Panther ball cap) and followed Cade to the exit.

We were on our way to the door when I saw a wave. Kenny Kaminski was behind the check-in table, gesturing me over. I said goodbye to Mark and Izzy, told Cade I'd catch up to him, and ducked over to Kenny.

He was organizing cash in the cash box with the dark-haired woman I'd just seen on the video, Melanie Stanshaw. Kenny looked a little flushed and sweaty, which wasn't a surprise given how fast he was moving and the fact that he was still wearing his canvas coat, but he smiled. "Give me half a sec." Kenny banded two more stacks of bills, put them in the box, then tapped the top and said, "I'll count the rest in just a second" to Melanie, who nodded.

As we walked a little ways away from everyone, I said, "Are you at everything?"

"Oh, I just try to help out here and there. Melanie knew they'd be dealing with a lot of cash tonight so she asked if I'd help count and get it to the drop box."

"I'd say the event was a hit. You're going to need a Brinks truck."

Kenny grinned and straightened his canvas coat. "Kaminski security will have to do. Hey, I won't keep you but a minute. There was something I wanted to tell you about."

"No problem, Kenny. I needed to catch up with you, too."

Kenny cocked his head. "About what?"

"You showed up on the prosecutor's witness list today."

"I did?"

"You did. Have you talked to them?"

"No. Why would they want me to testify?"

"They listed altercations between Colt and Brett."

Kenny's face fell. "Oh. That damn video game fight?"

"Probably. But they listed 'altercations,' as in more than one. Do you know of any others?"

"You mean besides the scrap at my place?"

"Yes."

Kenny's frown deepened. "That's the only one that I know about."

"Are you sure?"

"Pretty sure."

"And you haven't talked to anybody about it?"

"No. And certainly not to anybody from the prosecutor's office."

"Hmm. Well, I guess you'll hear from them eventually. I just wanted to touch base with you, make sure I wasn't missing something."

"They're not going to get anything out of me that would hurt Colt, I can tell you that right now."

I shook my head. "Don't think about it that way, Kenny. If the prosecutor calls you, just tell her the truth."

"Well, the truth is I don't know anything that would hurt Colt."

"Good." I started to say goodbye then realized Kenny was the one who had called me over. "What did you need to see me about?"

"Oh, right. Well, it's sort of related. To helping the boys, I mean."

"What's that?"

"Brett was working the drywall at our two new locations I was telling you about."

"Okay."

"I've still been issuing payments for the work he did. I'm not sure how the boys are doing for money, but I wanted to make sure they knew the money was going into their dad's account. I think Rhonda's in charge of it, but I don't know and…" He looked away.

"What?" I said.

Kenny appeared to think before he said, "Rhonda and Rob are good people, really good people, and they love those boys but, well, I never got the impression that numbers were their calling, if you take my meaning."

"I think so."

"And one of the jobs was in Ohio and the other was in Indiana and Brett was an independent contractor so I know there will be different tax things and…" He held up his hands and you could see all sorts of words trying to tumble out.

I nodded. "I'm self-employed. I get it."

Kenny took a deep breath. "I just want to make sure the boys get what's theirs. And that they don't have any tax trouble or anything along the way."

"I understand, Kenny, thanks for letting me know. I'm not sure who's handling the estate, but I'll make sure they know about the payments."

Kenny looked relieved. "That's a weight off, Nate, it truly is. You can tell them, or the executor or whoever, that we're wrapping up each job in the next few weeks so there'll be a couple or three more payments each coming in."

"Got it." I gestured at the hall. "Great job tonight."

Kenny grinned. "We raised a lot of money for our Panthers. Thanks for your contribution. And you tell your brother we're saving room on our wall for another championship picture next year."

I smiled. "I'm pretty sure he's already at work on it."

Kenny shook my hand. "That's why I love that man. See you around."

"Sure thing."

I headed out to my car to find Cade in the parking lot talking to the 50/50 ticket women. He introduced me, we talked, and they politely invited me to join a group of their friends that were apparently meeting at the Turntable. I made a few excuses saying—well, you've heard them by now—and headed home.

42

It snowed Saturday morning. A lot. And it wasn't one of those big flakes drifting to the ground in a gentle tableau snowfall either; it was a wet snow with an edge of ice accompanied by a fifteen-mile-an-hour wind that drove little needles at an unpleasant diagonal right into your face. Visibility wasn't terrible, but enough snow had fallen, three or four inches at least, so that there were sections of M-339 where the only thing that marked the road was the deep ditch that fell away on either side.

I parked in the Daniels' drive behind Colt's truck. I flipped up the hood to my Carhartt coat and made my way to the front walk, which was shoveled, with high, exaggerated steps. As I did, Chet skidded around the corner of the house to give me a tail-wagging greeting. I took a moment to scratch his ears—both of them, of course, because you can't leave those kinds of things unbalanced—then climbed the steps to the front door. Chet seemed uninterested in joining me and scampered around again to the back.

Colt answered the door and was polite enough to hustle me right in out of the snow. "Do you want some coffee?" he said.

"Please." I stomped my boots to get the snow out of the treads before I joined him in the kitchen.

Colt handed me a steaming cup, and I took a grateful sip. "You didn't have to do this. Thanks."

He waved a hand. "No problem. I like to have a pot on when Mom wakes up."

"Has she?"

Colt gave a quick exhale through his nose. "No. It's just us."

"Good. There are a couple of things I need to talk to you about with the case."

Colt waved a hand at the battered table and we sat. "Shoot."

"The prosecutor gave us some new information yesterday."

"Like what?"

"Kenny Kaminski for one. They disclosed him as a witness."

Colt looked confused. "That's good, isn't it? He's a friend."

"They're going to ask him about the fight you and your dad had at Borderlands."

"Oh. But everybody knows about that. It's probably best coming from him."

"And they're going to ask him about other incidents between you and your dad."

"What other incidents?"

"That's what I'm here to ask you about."

"What?"

"What other incidents could they be calling Kenny to talk about?"

Colt's low brow got even lower as he scowled. Finally, he shook his head. "I can't think of any."

I leaned forward. "Colt. This is really important. The prosecutor wouldn't disclose this unless she had something. What incidents could Kenny testify about?"

Colt thought hard, or acted like it, before he shook his head and said, "I'm sorry, Nate, I just can't think of anything. You should ask Kenny, I bet he'd tell you."

"I did. He said he can't think of anything either."

Colt held out his hands. "There you go."

I thought there was more there but now I had both Kenny and Colt telling me there wasn't so I decided to leave it for the moment. "We have another problem."

It's rare to see a twenty-year-old look weary. Colt did. "What?"

"Remember the trail cam photo?"

Colt's brow furrowed. "Hard to forget. Mom says I'm going to be paying for that truck damage for a while."

"There are more." I tossed him the manila folder. "The first series was taken at 6:34. Those are the ones we've seen before."

"I remember."

"The second series was at 6:46. Those are new."

Colt opened the folder and leafed through the pictures. I watched Colt's face as it went from surprise to assessment to a stony mask. "So that shows I was out there, just like the other ones, right?"

"It does more than that."

"What?"

"Look at the crossbow in the second set."

His brow furrowed deeper, and then, "It's empty."

"Right."

He tossed the pictures on the table and shrugged. "I already told you I shot the crossbow. I missed."

"You told *me*, Colt. Your lawyer. No one else knew."

"Oh."

"Now they have proof."

"That's bad, right?"

"Yes, Colt. That's bad."

Colt cursed his father as a fornicator.

"I was planning on arguing that the prosecutor couldn't prove you shot the crossbow that night. I have to address it more now."

"How?"

"I'm not sure yet, but you have to give me a good reason why you went out there."

"I gave you a good reason."

"That your dad was training Tyler too hard? That's pretty thin, Colt."

Colt stared at me for a moment, then stood up and motioned for me to follow him. He opened the back door so we could look out the window of the white storm door. The snow was still coming down and the small flecks of ice pinged against the metal and glass. There was easily five inches on the ground now with the promise of more. "Okay," I said.

"Look over by the willow tree."

There was Tyler. As I watched, he bent over and pulled a football out of a wire mesh basket. He crouched down, held the ball in front of him, then ran back five steps, straightened, and rifled the ball twenty yards right through the tire that hung from the willow tree. Then he went back to the wire basket and did it again.

"What do you notice about the snow?"

It took me a moment to see it. "He's worn paths in it."

"Where?"

"Three steps left, three steps straight back, three steps right; five steps left, five-steps straight back."

Colt nodded. "That basket holds twenty balls. When he's done with this basket full, he'll gather them up and do five steps to the right."

"Then he'll be done?"

"No. Then he'll do that same progression with a seven-step drop. Then he'll be done. Do you know why?"

"Why?"

"Because it's Saturday. And dad says that's the workout that has to be done on Saturday."

"In this weather?"

"'Football is an outdoor sport, son.' Yes, that's a quote."

I watched Tyler sprint back and zip another ball through the tire. Then he picked up the basket, made his way over to the tree, and gathered footballs. Chet helped by nosing balls through the snow toward the basket.

Colt smiled. "He punctured three before we could train him not to pick them up with his mouth."

Tyler's black sweats and black stocking cap stood out against the white snow. He gathered the balls and brought the basket back to the spot. He pulled one out crouched, sprinted five steps back to his right, and launched the ball through the tire. Chet lay down next to the basket and watched.

The cold permeated through the thin metal of the storm door. Colt stepped back and closed the battered wooden main door, then looked at me. "Brett's dead, Nate. He's been dead for weeks and Tyler hasn't even thought about not going out there. He's thrown one hundred and eighty balls every Saturday because Brett drilled it into him that it had to be done. So, yes, I thought Brett was being too hard on him."

"And that made you mad enough to shoot at him?"

Colt's eyes lit up like the kid who'd taken a baseball bat to his father's truck. "No, the bullshit superior way he talked to me made me mad enough to shoot at him."

The anger in Colt's eyes had my attention. "What did he say exactly?"

And just like that, the anger was doused. "I told you before, he said Tyler could take it."

"What else?"

Colt shook his head. "He told me to go in the house and look at the stack of letters from the Big Ten, the SEC, and the ACC then come back and tell him just how wrong he was."

"What else?"

Colt stared. "Then he said that I didn't have to squeal like a dying rabbit. He had a coyote call for that. And that's when I left."

"That's when you shot the crossbow and left."

"Whatever."

There was a scratch at the door. Colt opened it and Chet bounded in, shook himself, then threw himself down and rubbed his back on the carpet.

It was too cold out for the dog.

I checked the window and saw that Tyler had started his seven step drops. I also realized that I hadn't seen him miss the tire.

"All right," I said. "I'll get going. I don't think that the prosecutor is calling Kenny for nothing. I need you to think about any other time you and your dad fought in public, okay?"

Colt nodded.

"The more I know, the more I can be prepared, and the more I can help you."

"I got it, I got it."

"You need to trust me."

"I do."

I decided to test that. "I mean it, Colt. I'm fighting with you. Back to back. Us v. all."

Colt's right hand twitched, then he stopped.

I nodded. "You know. You took the War Oath too."

Colt paused a beat, his face stony, then said, "What are you talking about?"

I stared at him. Then I left.

As I tramped through what was now five inches of snow to my covered Jeep, I had no idea whether Colt was telling me the truth. About anything. He wasn't, of course, but I wouldn't find that out for a while.

43

The following Monday, I arrived at the office to find more filings from Tiffany Erin on Colt's case. Before I could go through them though, another pleading popped into my inbox. A courtesy copy of a subpoena from Megan Dira.

I cursed and opened it. She was serving it on Colt today. She expected a response within fourteen days detailing all of the information he had regarding his family's contact with Steve Mathison.

I had to be honest, I wanted more information about what Steve Mathison was doing lurking around the Daniels family too. But from what I could see, Colt didn't know anything about it and, even if he did, two weeks before a murder trial wasn't the time to be talking to anyone. I was pretty sure I could quash it—yes, quash is actually the legal term and it does conveniently mean the same thing as squash—but it was going to take precious time to write the motion, time which was beginning to run short. I quashed a sigh and set the subpoena aside for now.

My phone buzzed. Olivia. "Hey, Liv."

"Shep. Have you still been following the Alexis Fury account?"

"Not much since I asked you to keep an eye on it. Why?"

"It started tweeting over the weekend that the prosecutor has evidence of a history of conflicts between Colt and his dad."

"That jibes with the prosecution's witness disclosure last week."

"Violent conflicts."

Dammit. "Got it."

"You don't sound very surprised."

"It's clear Erin has something, but I haven't been able to get to what it is. Does the account give any source for the info?"

"Of course not. It's Twitter."

I thought. "Why would this Alexis Fury focus on us?"

"She, it, is not, not exactly."

"What does that mean?"

"It means @AlexisFury is tweeting things about cases all over the country like this one."

"There are cases like this all over the country?"

"Let's just say there are more than enough high-profile murder cases to keep a troll busy these days."

"Lucky us. Let me know if anything else happens, okay?"

"Of course."

"That it?"

"That seems like a lot."

"It is. Thanks for all the work. You're extraordinary."

"It also seems like I need to buy you a thesaurus."

"I meant magnificent."

"Hmph. Better. See you."

"Bye."

I was still thinking about the cottage industry that was @AlexisFury when I got a text from Ray Gerchuk asking if I had time for a call. That was unusual, so I called back right away. "Hey, Ray," I said.

"Can you come over to my office?"

"Sure, what's up?"

"Brett Daniels might not have been shot with a crossbow."

"I'll be right there."

∽

TWENTY MINUTES LATER, I was sitting in Ray Gerchuk's office.

"How can that be?" I said.

Ray Gerchuk was always smiling. Now, he grinned. "It's an easy assumption to make. You have a through and through wound, the police tell you they found a crossbow arrow nearby, and it seems like a fair assumption."

"Don't bullets and crossbow arrows leave different wounds?"

"A broadhead arrow would for sure—the razored edges leave a much bigger hole than a small caliber bullet. But an arrow with a field point? If the coroner doesn't do a thorough examination, the wound from a field point looks almost identical to a bullet wound. It even has some black markings that look like bullet wipe if you don't do chemical testing to verify it."

"Did they do the chemical testing here?"

Ray's grin broadened. "Nope."

I was skeptical. "C'mon Ray, can you really confuse these two?"

"I did some research. I found a couple of articles documenting this happening, where the investigator couldn't determine whether it was a crossbow arrow or a bullet without the advanced testing on the bullet wipe."

That was the second time he'd used that phrase. "What's bullet wipe?"

"It's the residue from the bullet that's left behind in the wound. It usually leaves a black ring around the entrance. The thing is, an arrow shot from a crossbow can leave a similar ring."

"How do you tell the difference?"

"By performing very particular chemical tests on the residue."

"Which weren't done?"

"Which weren't done."

"That seems like something."

Dr. Gerchuk nodded. "That's why I called."

I thought. "It's still pretty thin, Ray."

"The science is there, Nate. The speed of the arrow causes a transfer of carbon material onto the skin that looks like bullet wipe unless you do the proper tests."

It hit me. "Say that again?"

"The speed of the arrow causes a transfer—"

I didn't wait. "That's it."

"What's it?"

"The other evidence I need to show it wasn't the crossbow arrow that caused the wound."

"Care to share?"

I shook my head. "Not 'til I'm sure. I don't want to corrupt your findings if I'm wrong." I thought it through. It made sense, but I was going to have to check it out. "Ray, this gives me a lot to work with. Thank you."

Dr. Gerchuk shrugged good-naturedly. "For a chance to stick it to Archuleta, I'd almost do it for free." He held up a hand. "Almost."

I stood. "Send me the bill."

"I can wait. You *are* going to want me to testify, aren't you?"

"You bet your ass."

"Then I can bill you when it's over."

My head was swimming as I left Dr. Gerchuk's office. If I could establish a failure of proof that Colt's crossbow arrow killed Brett Daniels, then I could raise doubt about one of the key links in the prosecution's case.

Of course, it also raised the question, if not Colt, then who? I didn't know. But I didn't have to prove who did it. I just had to raise a reasonable doubt that Colt had.

Dr. Gerchuk brought us closer.

44

I was on the way back to the office when I received a call from Megan Dira. "We served our subpoena today, Nate."

"Being under electronic monitoring does make that easier."

"I'm calling to tell you that if you need a little more than fourteen days, I can work with you."

"I appreciate that, Megan, but I just can't let Colt talk to anyone before his trial."

"When is that scheduled?"

"The second week of February."

There was a pause. "I need it by February 6th."

I smiled. "Interesting. Now why would you need information from the Daniels family by National Signing Day?"

"I didn't say that."

National Signing Day is the first day a high schooler can sign a commitment to play college football. "I can save you some trouble, Megan. Colt is returning to Grand Valley in the fall."

Megan Dira didn't laugh. Or speak.

"So does Mathison recruit for a college or something?"

"Or something. When can I expect your response?"

"My response will be a motion to quash."

"I'll oppose it."

"I expect you will. And it will certainly take time for the Court to consider the matter."

"I'm going to get this information."

"Maybe. But not from Colt."

She hung up. I didn't mind.

Her tone didn't sound good for the Daniels family but, again, that wasn't my concern right then. My concern was defending Colt from a murder charge.

I took the maximum amount of time allowed to respond before filing the motion to quash. I argued that forcing testimony from an accused, for any purpose, on the eve of his murder trial was all sorts of unconstitutional and unfair besides. Megan Dira's response was interesting—she still wouldn't disclose why her February 6th deadline was so important, I assume so she didn't publicly tip people off to what she was doing. That meant though, because it was a generic response, that she couldn't make a compelling argument for why the production had to occur right then. I followed up by arguing that any response from Colt could be delayed until after the trial, essentially daring her to declare that production by National Signing Day was a priority.

Megan Dira didn't take the bait. She simply said that the state had a compelling interest in obtaining the information right away.

The subpoena had been issued out of a court in the state capital of Lansing, and I had to burn a morning going there for a hearing. Fortunately, the judge saw things my way. He stated that no interest was more compelling than determining whether one citizen of the State had murdered another and ordered that any production from Colt on this collateral matter would be delayed until twenty-eight days after the murder trial.

As an added bonus, the judge also prohibited the state from

subpoenaing Colt's family members until the trial was over too, stating he didn't want any basis for a claim that the murder trial had been contaminated. It might have been a stretch but, from my perspective, it was totally reasonable. I'm sure Megan Dira didn't feel the same, but I didn't know because I didn't hear from her for a while.

The order about the family members reminded me about Kenny Kaminski's statement that he would be issuing payments for Brett's last drywall jobs. There are rules about payments to estates and rules about conflicts for lawyers and more rules about whether an accused can receive a benefit from the death of the one he's accused of killing and neither Danny nor I had time to learn about all that right then. I put Tyler in touch with an estate attorney in Dellville, Marv Lindhoffer, to help him sort through Brett's affairs and forgot about it.

As the trial approached, Tiffany Erin played the big city prosecutor game. She fought every point, made everything difficult, and made us expend as much time and energy as possible. She launched a flurry of motions that had Danny responding late into the night so that he was exhausted by the time we were a week out from trial. I helped as much as I could, but I was spending just as much time outlining my examinations of the witnesses and organizing our evidence. Neither of us took a day off in January as we prepared.

After his truck-smashing incident, I was able to keep Colt off social media, which was just as well because it seemed like @AlexisFury posted at least four times a day about the case. Shares and memes, news reports and rumors, pleadings updates and theories—they all flowed from the account, generating comments and likes and retweets and damn near every other thing that turned a trickle of information into a torrent. I made the mistake of checking once to make sure there wasn't anything too damaging or surprising and lost a swift hour to an endless stream of theories and random vitriol. I went back to relying completely on Olivia to monitor that account and trusted her to let me know if anything popped up that seemed important. She was happy to help and I immediately felt relief at not being pounded by that constant waterfall of malice.

Colt only freaked out one more time, which was pretty good, all things considered. On the weekend before the trial, I spent some time with him getting him prepared for what he was going to hear and see so that it wouldn't be a shock to him in the courtroom. He made it through the pictures of his dad's body, even the gruesome ones where the coyotes had pulled his intestines out. It was a punt, pass, and kick picture that did it. Tyler and Colt were standing on the Carrefour football field, each holding a trophy. They couldn't have been more than eight and six. Brett Daniels was down on one knee between them with an arm around each, smiling.

Colt lost it. He knocked over his chair and threw a Coke bottle at the wall and cursed his father for being a miserable prick before he slammed his way to the other room for a few minutes.

I didn't mind. That had been the point.

When he returned, he cleaned up the Coke-spattered mess and we made it through the rest of the materials. By the time I left, I thought I had inoculated him to most of the things that he was going to hear.

I still felt that way when we showed up the first morning of trial.

RUN

45

Trial lawyers build a profile of their ideal juror before they try a case. Sometimes, it's the result of focus groups and research and mock trials and sometimes, it's the result of stereotypical thinking about what aspects of the case will resonate with a particular person. We spend hours deciding what factors could predispose a juror to look favorably on our case—man or woman, young or old, black or white, kids or no kids, blue-collar or white-collar, religious or not religious, you name it. Once we know what we want, we try to find jurors with as many of those factors as we can. We're not always right, but our hope is that we can get our case headed in the right direction or, at least, keep it from sinking completely.

Judge LaPlante had us in the courtroom at 8:30 Monday morning and had seated a pool of potential jurors by 8:45. Judge LaPlante liked to question the jurors himself, and he made it clear to us that we were not to repeat anything he asked.

He was on the first juror—honest to God, it was the very first juror—and he was running down the usual basics: how old are you, are you married or single, do you work outside the home, have you been involved in any lawsuits, questions like that.

Then he asked, "Do you know any of the parties?"

The juror was a woman in her forties with curly brown hair and clear-framed glasses. "No, Judge."

"Do you know anything about the case?"

"No, not really. Only what I read from Alexis Fury."

I stood. "Your Honor, may we approach?"

Judge LaPlante has thick black eyebrows and intent black eyes. The moment I stood, he turned them both on me, the eyebrows expressing surprise and the eyes irritation. "Mr. Shepherd, are you objecting to my question?"

"No, Your Honor. I'd simply like to approach to address an issue with the Court."

Judge LaPlante pressed his lips together and waved us up. Danny slipped me the folder we'd prepared just in case and here I was having to use it on the very first juror.

Tiffany Erin and I stood in front of the bench as the Judge covered his microphone with one hand, leaned over, and said, "Why don't you tell me why you're interrupting my question, Mr. Shepherd."

"Your Honor, this juror just mentioned a social media account that has been publishing misinformation about this case for weeks. Here's a sample." I handed him the folder and gave a copy to Erin. I noted that she didn't feel the need to open it.

Judge LaPlante looked annoyed as he took the folder, but he opened it. The look on his face changed from annoyance to interest to concern as he flipped through the pages.

"Mr. Shepherd is certainly welcome to question any of the jurors about whether they've read this Alexis Fury person," said Tiffany Erin.

"Which will just emphasize the account and send every juror off to look at it."

Judge LaPlante looked at me. "Are you suggesting that we interview each juror in chambers?"

"That would take days," said Tiffany Erin.

"No, Your Honor. I'm suggesting, respectfully, that you ask the jurors whether they have read or seen anything about the case on social media. If they have, then we could do an individual examination if necessary."

"That's an awful lot of time, Your Honor," said Tiffany Erin.

Judge LaPlante held up his hand. "I am going to ask each juror whether they've learned anything about the case from the newspaper, TV, or social media. I will remind them that nothing they've seen or heard outside the courtroom is evidence and ask if anything they have seen or read will affect their ability to hear the case fairly based on the evidence you present. We are not going to open a Pandora's box of asking each juror for each and every account that they have reviewed. However, I agree with Mr. Shepherd that interjecting any of this material into the trial will interfere with Mr. Daniels obtaining a fair trial. As a result, no one will mention this account in open court, am I understood?"

We both nodded.

He looked back at the folder. "If either of you wish to remove a juror based on what they've seen or heard, it will be subject to the usual for cause and peremptory challenge procedure, which will be done outside the presence of the jury. If you want to question a juror further regarding outside sources they've reviewed, you will approach and give me the subject area first. Is that understood?"

"Yes, Your Honor," we both said. He waved and we went back to our seats.

Judge LaPlante asked a few more questions of Juror Number One then moved on to the next. He did exactly what he said. He asked each one if they'd heard or read anything about the case.

Most had, of course, because Ash County isn't that big a place, but they all said that nothing they'd read or seen or heard would interfere with their ability to decide the case fairly based on the evidence put before them. No one else mentioned @AlexisFury.

But I knew it was out there.

We picked a jury and, for all my fancy talk a little bit ago about the details of jury selection, there was no mystery to what Tiffany Erin and I were looking for—we both wanted to know what the jurors thought about football.

The jury ended up being evenly split. Six of the jurors didn't know football at all and couldn't have told you the difference between a touchback and safety. Of those, two were adamantly anti-football and thought it was a barbaric practice that was causing brain injury and siphoning valuable resources away from other, far more societally beneficial, activities.

The other six jurors were fans of some local high school, college, or pro team. Two of those were super fans, one with season tickets to the Michigan State Spartans, the other with tickets to the Detroit Lions, and both of whom were painfully optimistic about the next season. In the end, though, all twelve jurors said that they would be able to put any knowledge—or lack thereof—of the local football scene aside and base their decision in Colt's case solely on the facts presented to them in court.

We finished by noon. When we were done, the judge broke for lunch and told us we would give opening statements when we returned.

After Judge LaPlante and the jury had left, I turned to Colt. His low brow was furrowed. "What's going on?" he said.

I put a hand on his shoulder. "The trial will get started after lunch."

Colt was wearing a blocky blue suit that was a little baggy at the waist and a little long in the sleeves. It only added to his look of discomfort. "Everything takes so long," he said.

"Things will pick up this afternoon. Remember, just keep a straight face no matter what the prosecutor says. And keep your cool."

Colt nodded but, if his current expression was any indication, that was going to be difficult.

"Tell you what, why don't you go with your mom and Rob to get something to eat."

Rhonda and Rob were seated directly behind us in the gallery. I motioned and they came up. Rob wore a button-down shirt with a leather coat and appeared to have trimmed his beard. Rhonda had kept her black wool coat on and held a black purse with both hands. The lines around her eyes were more pronounced in the harsh fluorescent lighting of the courtroom.

"Think you guys could find Colt something to eat?"

Rhonda reached out and straightened Colt's suit coat then looked at Rob. "I need a smoke first."

Rob's red beard jutted out fiercely, but his eyes were kind. "Go ahead, honey. You can meet us over at Manny's deli. I'll get you a bagel."

"Cinnamon raisin?"

"You betcha."

Rhonda gripped her purse with both hands and left.

"Have him back by ten 'til," I said.

Rob nodded and led Colt away. I glanced over to Danny who was scrolling through his laptop. "We all set to go?" I asked.

Danny nodded. "Everything is loaded into the trial software and the projector is set."

"Go ahead and grab something then."

He reached into his briefcase and pulled out a paper bag.

"Look at you," I said. "Did you pack that yourself?"

He smiled and I swear to you he looked a little embarrassed. "Jenny did it."

"Then I'm sure it's better than what's in mine. I'll see you back here in twenty."

He nodded. I glanced over at the prosecutor's table. Tiffany Erin was standing there, removing documents from a black leather brief case that had a patterned, shiny finish that was almost reptilian. She wore a dark blue suit that contrasted sharply with her short, light hair. Her pale eyes clicked from exhibit to exhibit as her associate, a young woman also dressed in blue who appeared to be emulating her boss, whispered and handed her another. They didn't look over. They gave me the impression of two people pulling the tension back on a weapon, on a bow or a ballista or a catapult, loading it, and getting ready to fire.

I shook my head. Projecting images of my opponent preparing to launch her case like a cockable missile weapon didn't seem particularly subtle or bright on my part. I grabbed my lunch and my trial notebook and went to find a quiet place to go over my opening one more time.

46

When I went back into the courtroom, two things happened that surprised me. They shouldn't have, but they did.

The first was Rhonda. She and Rob had brought Colt back from lunch and Colt was sitting at the counsel table with Rob on the aisle, arms crossed, as if he were standing guard. Rhonda stood behind Colt, both hands on his shoulders.

As I approached, I could hear her as she leaned close and said, "You just sit there with a straight-face like Shepherd said. That woman's not going to hit you or hurt you. She only has words. They only hurt if you let them, you hear me?"

Colt jerked his head in a nod.

"Your dad was a son of a bitch, but he was right about one thing—you nut up and buckle down, understand?"

When Colt put a hand on hers, she gave him a quick kiss on the top of his head. Then she turned to me, her face dead serious, and said, "You too, Shepherd."

"On it," I said.

With that, Rhonda and Rob walked back through the swinging gate to the first row of the gallery behind us. They both sat there for a moment before Rob took Rhonda's hand.

False Oath

Then I got a second surprise. My brother Tom walked through the courtroom door.

It took me a second to realize it was him. Instead of his black and red coaching togs, he was wearing a dark blue suit with a white shirt and no tie. His short blonde hair was neatly combed; I don't think I'd seen him look like that since the last time we'd been at a wedding.

He walked down the aisle between the benches, through the swinging gate where he nodded to me and walked straight over to Colt.

Colt scrambled to his feet. "Hi, Coach."

Tom nodded and shook Colt's hand. "We're with you, son," he said.

Colt looked a little overwhelmed.

"Focus," said Tom.

Colt's face snapped back to true. "Yes, sir."

Tom looked at him for a moment then nodded and turned away. As he passed me, he gave me the same encouragement he'd given me since our childhood, his "3F mantra." He tapped me on the chest with the bottom of his fist and said, "Play fast, play free, don't f—"

He broke off and looked around the courtroom.

I grinned. "Yes?"

He gave me a wry smile. "Don't screw it up."

I smiled. "Thanks."

A moment later, Tiffany Erin and her associate walked in and a moment after that, court bailiff Patricia Weathers softly said that the Judge would be out presently.

Then the trial of Colt Daniels for the murder of his father got underway.

~

AFTER THE JURY WAS SEATED, Judge LaPlante said, "Ms. Erin, are you ready to proceed?"

"The State is, Your Honor."

"You may give your opening statement."

Tiffany Erin stood, her perpetual aloofness gone. Now, she exuded a bridled energy, as if she could barely contain a well of conviction. She took concise strides to the lectern and looked at the jury as if they should be convincing her of their worthiness to hear the case. She stood there a good ten seconds, inviting their attention, until everyone, including me, was waiting to hear what she had to say.

"Colton Daniels murdered his father. And that's not even the worst of it."

She paused for a moment, then said, "Colton Daniels is the oldest son of Brett Daniels. Colton lived with his father, along with his younger brother, Tyler, over on M-339 in a house on ten acres that abuts state land."

Tiffany Erin moved out from behind the lectern, utterly at ease. "You're going to hear testimony that Brett Daniels was a hard man, that he lived in a hard way, and that he was hard in the way he raised his two boys. Not abusive. Hard. Strict. Determined. You're going to hear that Colton's brother Tyler might be one of the best high school quarterbacks in the country. And that Brett Daniels did a lot of hard things to make him that way."

Tiffany Erin shook her head. "You're going to hear that Colton Daniels didn't like his father's methods much. You see, Colton was a quarterback too, not nearly as good as his brother, but he'd been trained by his father in the same way. You're going to hear that Colton argued with his father about the way he was training Tyler. You're going to hear that these arguments escalated until Colton attacked his father at Borderlands, in public, causing thousands of dollars of damage to the place. And you're going to hear that Brett got the better of Colton in that fight and that this made Colton awfully mad."

Tiffany Erin nodded sternly. "We talked about football a little earlier this morning. I know some of you don't follow it much and others of you live and breathe it. What we'll show you for purposes of this trial is that Tyler's team, the Carrefour North Panthers, were getting ready for the playoffs and, as they made that last push toward the end of the season, Colton finally reached his breaking point and decided to make his dad stop."

Tiffany Erin clicked the PowerPoint remote, and a picture of the hunting platform appeared on the screen. "You're going to hear evidence that on a Thursday night this past fall, Brett Daniels went out to hunt with his crossbow on this platform at the back of his property. We are going to show you that Colton Daniels went out there, too."

I knew the trail cam picture was about to go up. I stood. "Your Honor, I'm very sorry to interrupt counsel's opening statement, but I believe Local Rule 34 prohibits use of exhibits until they are actually entered into evidence at trial."

"These are demonstrative, Your Honor," said Tiffany Erin.

Judge LaPlante looked at her. "Those pictures are exhibits, are they not, Ms. Erin?"

"Yes, Your Honor."

"Then they will not be used until entered. You certainly may show any outlines or truly demonstrative exhibits on the screen at this time."

"Yes, Your Honor," she said, and turned off the projector.

As I sat down, Tiffany Erin turned back to the jury without missing a beat. "We will show you photographic evidence that Colton Daniels went out to that hunting platform at 6:34 that night carrying a loaded crossbow. We will show you photographic evidence that when Colton Daniels left the platform area twelve minutes later, he had fired that crossbow. And we will present you with medical evidence that proves Colton Daniels shot and killed his father, and that his arrow lacerated the main artery in his father's thigh so that his father bled to death when he tried to run back home."

Tiffany Erin took her position back squarely in front of the jury and crossed her arms. She bowed her head for a moment and waited. Then she looked up and said, "I told you that the murder wasn't the worst. No, the worst thing was the way Colton Daniels tried to cover up his crime. It wasn't enough that Colton Daniels left his father to bleed and die in his backyard. No, when he was done, Colton let the coyotes come in hopes they would hide what he did."

I made a conscious effort to not look at Colt. I had to trust that he could keep a straight face.

"How could coyotes cover up a crime?" said Tiffany Erin. "By eating the evidence. Colton Daniels left his father on the ground, in sight of his house, to be eaten by coyotes for more than a day. From Thursday night until Friday night, the body of Brett Daniels lay in his backyard and Colton Daniels ignored it. It wasn't until after the football game the next night, Friday night, that Tyler Daniels found the body. And by that time, there wasn't much left."

Tiffany Erin's eyes were bright. "There was enough though. The medical examiner will tell you that, incredibly, the wound that killed Brett Daniels was undisturbed, so that he could still determine how Brett Daniels had died. Even though Colton had tried to use coyotes to cover up his crime."

Tiffany Erin flipped a hand and gave me the barest of glances. "I don't know how Mr. Shepherd is going to try to justify this to you. Murder is bad enough. Using wild animals to eat your victim and cover up your crime is worse. Doing all that to your father...." Tiffany Erin trailed off and shrugged. "That's why, when we're done with the evidence, we will ask you to find

Colton Daniels guilty of the first-degree murder of his father, Brett Daniels. Thank you."

Tiffany Erin practically glided back to her seat. When she was done, Judge LaPlante said, "Mr. Shepherd?"

"Thank you, Your Honor."

I stole a glance at Colt as I stood. He had his game face on, stoic, hard, staring straight ahead despite the fact that he'd just been called a murderer who was depraved enough to call wild animals down on his father.

Good man.

I walked up to the lectern and said, "Colt Daniels has lost his father. And he didn't just lose him; he lost him in a horrible, horrible way. And as if that trauma weren't enough, the State is now accusing him of his father's murder."

I shook my head. "You'd think that if the State were going to accuse a son of killing his father, it would be extra careful, extra certain, so that it didn't inflict needless pain on a grieving family. Instead, you're going to hear the opposite. You're going to see photos of Colt going out to see his father. You're going to see photos that show there wasn't an arrow in his crossbow when he came home. The State is asking you to leap to a conclusion about what happened in between. The State will ask you to assume that this proves Colt killed his dad. It doesn't. And we're going to show you why."

"First, to be clear, there's no direct evidence that Colt shot his dad. There are no pictures that show that, no eye witness who saw such a thing, nothing like that."

"You're also not going to hear any direct evidence linking the arrow to the fatal wound. You're not going to hear about any DNA on the arrow, and you're not going to hear about any evidence of residue from the arrow in the wound."

"No, the State is resting their case on the testimony of a medical examiner who says the fatal wound was caused by an arrow that Colt shot. But we'll show that his examination was sloppy, that in a case where he should have been extra diligent, he didn't perform the most basic tests to confirm the type of wound he was examining. Further, we'll show you that the prosecution's theory violates fundamental laws of science, that Colt's arrow couldn't have hit his father as they claim. After we show you that evidence, you'll see that the most important part of the State's case, the part where it claims that Colt's arrow caused his dad's death, is based on an unproven, impossible, assumption."

"And these other awful allegations? About the coyotes?" I shook my head. "You're going to see some horrific pictures of what happened to Mr. Daniels after he died, of what he looked like when his sons found him. They're terrible. But the prosecution isn't going to present you with any evidence that Colt knew his father was back there. Instead, the only evidence they'll give you is that as soon as Tyler found the body, he called Colt and the two of them called the rescue squad and the police. That's the evidence. The prosecution's theory that Brett Daniels was somehow left out there is the worst kind of speculation."

I looked at them. "Brett Daniels is dead. The prosecution has accused his son of murder and hasn't taken the time or trouble to actually look at the evidence before accusing him. It's outrageous. We're asking you to do what the State should have done—we're asking you to look closely at all of the evidence, to not just skim the surface but to dig deep and pay attention and review every single bit of real, physical evidence. And when you take that time and make that effort, we think it will be clear that you should return a verdict of not guilty in favor of Colt Daniels. Thank you."

As I went back to my seat, Tiffany Erin was sitting there coolly, legs crossed, not taking a note and giving off the faintest aura of disdain for what she was hearing.

I put a hand on Colt's shoulder and sat down.

The jury went from staring at me to looking at the judge.

Judge LaPlante nodded. "Ms. Erin, are you ready to proceed?"

"Yes, Your Honor. The State calls Tri-County coroner, Dr. Warren Archuleta."

47

Dr. Warren Archuleta walked in, paused and raised his nose slightly, then moved on to the witness chair. He wore a patterned, brown wool suit with a solid brown vest and a red bow tie. He had brown hair swept straight back but dry, like he'd used a blow dryer and hairspray rather than product. He wore gold-rimmed glasses and had a neatly trimmed brown beard and mustache, which showed only the faintest sprinkle of white. He surveyed the room and sat down as if the witness chair were a throne.

Tiffany Erin rose to her feet. "Good morning, Dr. Archuleta."

"Good morning, Ms. Erin."

"Would you introduce yourself to the jury, please?"

"I am Dr. Warren Archuleta."

"And what sort of doctor are you?"

"I am a forensic pathologist and medical examiner."

"Perhaps you could describe your educational background to the jury?"

"Certainly. I obtained my undergraduate degree in biology from Dartmouth College after which I obtained my medical degree from Columbia University."

"That's very impressive, Doctor. Are you from the East Coast?"

"No, I was raised here in Michigan, in Bloomfield Hills. I went to Dartmouth and Columbia because I received academic scholarships after testing in the top one half of one percent on the college admission exams."

"I see. And did you pursue professional training after medical school?"

"I did indeed. After graduating, I completed both a residency and fellowship at Johns Hopkins University where I received specialty training in pathology and forensic pathology."

"And what brought you back to Michigan?"

Dr. Archuleta smiled faintly. "My wife's parents are elderly. They are very close."

"Well, that's fortunate for us."

Dr. Archuleta shrugged slightly in acknowledgment.

"You have been kind enough to provide us with a copy of your CV, your resume. Is this a true and accurate copy of it?"

Tiffany Erin placed a stack of papers that was easily one hundred pages in front of Dr. Archuleta. He leaned over and peered through his glasses. "It is."

"You research and publish?"

"I do."

"I see from your CV that you have published over six hundred and ninety-four articles and have spoken, I don't know, it looks like over nine hundred times?"

Dr. Archuleta gave a little smile. "I provided this to you about four months ago, Ms. Erin, so it's probably closer to seven hundred and three and nine hundred and twenty-four." A little smile. "Give or take."

"Thank you, Doctor. And you are now the coroner for the Tri-County area?"

"I have that privilege, yes."

"How long have you served in that capacity?"

"Approximately thirty-two years."

"In that time, how many autopsies have you performed?"

"I have performed or supervised over twenty thousand autopsies since I have been back here in Michigan."

"Goodness."

"That includes partial reviews, where for example a practitioner in an outlying area might have a question about one of his or her findings and sends it to me to get an opinion on an issue that might exceed their capabilities or their facilities."

"Sort of a reviewing role?"

That little smile. "I like to call it being an expert for the experts."

As she spoke, Tiffany Erin picked up the CV and put it on the evidence table. Actually, she dropped it with a pronounced thump, which seemed like overkill to me. "We'll send this back to the jury as an exhibit so that they can look at all of your publications and qualifications if they'd like but let me bring you back around to this case specifically."

"Certainly."

"Did you have the opportunity to examine the body of the victim in this case, Brett Daniels?"

Dr. Archuleta's face became grave. "Indeed, I did. What was left of it."

"What do you mean, Doctor?"

"I mean that by the time the body was recovered and given to me, it had been partially devoured."

"And did you take pictures as part of your examination?"

"That is a standard part of our procedure." He turned and spoke directly to the jury for the first time. "The pictures are graphic and upsetting. But they are also a very necessary part of recording my examination."

"I see," said Tiffany Erin as if this wasn't exactly what they had rehearsed. "May I show you some now?"

"If you have questions about what I found, I think that would be best."

A picture of Brett Daniels' body went up on the screen. His face was covered and his shoulders and chest were bare but, where his stomach should've been, there was nothing but space so that you could see straight back to his spine and ribs. Below the space where his stomach had been, his pelvis was intact.

There was a gasp. Several actually. I glanced over my shoulder and saw Rhonda Mazur's hand go to her mouth. Colt stiffened next to me. I put one hand on his back.

Tiffany Erin circled with her laser pointer. "Is this what you were talking about, Doctor? Where the abdomen is gone?"

"It is. That area appeared to have been devoured."

"I have more questions, but let's take this down first." Tiffany Erin clicked and the screen went blank, which was smart. Better to give the jury one horrifying glance that would stick with them rather than leave the image up and let them get used to it. "What area of Mr. Daniels' body was devoured, Doctor?"

"It was primarily the abdomen. There were some teeth marks on the throat and cheeks but for the most part, they ate the abdominal area and the adjacent ribs and spine."

"How did you know the area was eaten?"

"There were clear teeth marks and the bones, especially the ribs, had been gnawed upon."

A juror coughed. One of the season ticket holders.

"And did the devouring and gnawing you just described affect your ability to determine the cause of death in this case?"

"I thought it would, but it did not."

"How so?"

"I was able to find the wound which killed Mr. Daniels as that area was uncontaminated by whatever fed on his organs."

"And where was that wound, Doctor?"

"The wound was to Mr. Daniels' right thigh."

"Can you describe it for the jury, please?"

"I'm very sorry, Ms. Erin, but it would be easier to do so if I could utilize two of my pictures." He turned to the jury. "They are close-ups of the wound itself and not of Mr. Daniels' whole body."

The relief from the jury was palpable.

"Certainly, Dr. Archuleta, if you believe that would help the jury understand your findings."

"I believe it would help the jury see the truth of it, yes."

"Which two pictures would be most helpful, Doctor?"

"Autopsy exam Pictures 14 and 15, please."

Tiffany Erin clicked and the two pictures appeared on a split screen. "Could you tell the jury what these pictures are please, Doctor?"

"Certainly, Ms. Erin. The picture on the left, Autopsy Picture Number 14, is an entrance wound into Mr. Daniels' right thigh. The picture on the right, Autopsy Picture Number 15, is an exit wound out the back of Mr. Daniels' right thigh."

"What does that mean, an entrance wound and an exit wound?"

"It means that Picture 14 shows where something went into Mr. Daniels' thigh and Picture 15 shows where that same thing came out his thigh."

"And do you have an opinion as to what that thing was?"

"I do."

"And what is that opinion?"

"My opinion is that this wound was caused by a crossbow bolt. Excuse me, a crossbow arrow." He straightened his gold-rimmed glasses. "I'm afraid I'm used to using the literary term."

Tiffany Erin smiled, walked over to the evidence table, and picked up an arrow. It was metal and its shaft was red with two green plastic feathers and one white at one end and a field point at the other. "Dr. Archuleta, I'm going to hand you what's been marked as State's Exhibit 23. That is an arrow, correct?"

"Indeed, it is."

"Do you have an opinion as to whether this arrow caused the wound found in Mr. Daniels' leg?"

Dr. Archuleta tilted the arrow back and forth in his hands before he peered over his glasses at Tiffany Erin. "Well, to be precise, Ms. Erin, I cannot say that this particular arrow caused the wound in Mr. Daniels' leg. I can say, however, to a reasonable degree of medical certainty, that an arrow of the same size and shape as the arrow I am holding caused the wound in Mr. Daniels' thigh."

"I see. Can you explain?"

"Certainly. Often times, arrows have broad heads with razors that fan out like a triangle from the point to maximize tissue damage. This particular arrow has a straight point or a field point that does not maximize tissue damage but instead creates a through and through wound like the one found in Mr. Daniels' leg."

"So the wound is consistent with being caused by an arrow like the one you're holding."

"That is correct."

"Why can't you say that this particular arrow caused the wound?"

Dr. Archuleta gave that little smile. "I am not a detective, Ms. Erin. I have not conducted an investigation to link this arrow to the crime."

"Of course, Dr. Archuleta. The jury is going to hear testimony that this arrow was found—"

I stood. "Objection, Your Honor. Facts not in evidence."

Judge LaPlante looked at Tiffany Erin.

"I'll rephrase as a hypothetical, Your Honor," she said.

Judge LaPlante nodded. "Sustained."

"Dr. Archuleta, I want you to assume that witnesses will testify that this arrow was found at the location of Mr. Daniels' murder. Assuming those facts are placed into evidence, would you have an opinion as to whether this arrow caused the wound you found in Mr. Daniels' leg?"

"I would."

"And what is that opinion?"

"Assuming this arrow was found at the site, it would be my opinion to a reasonable degree of medical certainty that this arrow caused the wound in Mr. Daniels' leg. More specifically, the wound is consistent in size, shape, and form with having been caused by an arrow of this size, shape, and form passing through Mr. Daniels' leg."

Tiffany Erin smoothly took the arrow from Dr. Archuleta and held it up as she walked back to the evidence table. "Dr. Archuleta, how did the wound caused by the arrow kill Mr. Daniels?"

Dr. Archuleta turned to the jury. "There is a large artery that runs down the inside of the thigh called the femoral artery. It's the main artery that delivers blood to your leg. The arrow lacerated, or cut, the femoral artery causing Mr. Daniels to exsanguinate."

"What does exsanguinate mean, Doctor?"

"It means to bleed to death."

"So the arrow wound caused Mr. Daniels to bleed to death?"

"Indeed, it did."

"How long does that take?"

"It varies depending upon the size of the laceration to the artery. Here, the laceration caused by the arrow was significant. It would have killed him within minutes."

"Is that painful?"

"Of course. But the panic and shock of dying in that manner would have been worse."

"Dr. Archuleta, just so the jury is clear, it's your opinion that Mr. Daniels bled to death?"

"That is indeed my opinion."

"And he bled to death because of the wound in his thigh?"

"That's right."

She held up the arrow again. "A wound caused by an arrow?"

"An arrow of the same shape and size as the one you're holding, yes."

"And after he bled to death, his body was partially eaten by some animal or animals?"

"Sadly, yes."

"And fortunately, for the purposes of your investigation, those animals feeding on Mr. Daniels' body did not disguise the cause of death."

"Thankfully, they did not. The cause is quite clear."

"Thank you, Dr. Archuleta. That's all I have."

Tiffany Erin prowled back to her seat as I stood.

"Good morning, Dr. Archuleta."

Dr. Archuleta lifted his nose slightly. "Good morning, Counselor."

"You mentioned a moment ago that you have authored more articles and given more presentations in just the few months since this case began?"

"That's correct, I have."

"It sounded to me like you had authored another nine articles and given another twenty-four or so speeches, is that right?"

"Excellent math, Counselor. Yes."

"In just four months?"

Dr. Archuleta gave that little smile. "I have staff that assists me in developing the research for the articles and the graphics for the presentations, but yes."

"That's on top of doing around two hundred and eight autopsies during that time?"

Dr. Archuleta nodded. "If one divided twenty thousand autopsies by thirty-two years and divided that yearly number by twelve and then multiplied that monthly number by four to account for the four months that have ensued between when I was contacted and us speaking here today, then yes. Two hundred eight point three three autopsies is a good approximation of the number of autopsies I've performed in that time. Again, my compliments on your math skills."

I smiled. "Thank Apple for my iPhone calculator, Doctor. I'm not nearly smart enough to do that in my head."

Dr. Archuleta nodded in agreement. "Of course, examining the actual records of what I've done in that four months would be more accurate, but if you'd like to use a seat of your pants calculation instead, that's as good as any."

"So, Doctor, using a seat of my pants estimation, between the day Mr. Daniels died and today, you've performed two hundred and eight autopsies, written nine articles, and given about twenty-four speeches?"

Dr. Archuleta's small smile was accompanied by an adjustment of his gold-rimmed glasses. "Your summary skills equal your math skills, Counselor."

"So that's a yes?"

He paused. "Yes."

"How do you keep track of all that?"

"I find it to be within my capabilities to do so."

"I see. And you have staff that helps you?"

"I mentioned that."

"To research the articles?"

"The preliminary research, yes."

"To put together the PowerPoints for your speeches?"

"Which I revise, yes."

"To perform your preliminary examinations on autopsies?"

"I review all of the findings."

"But your staff performs some of the preliminary testing, doesn't it?"

"In some cases. Not all."

"That's a lot to keep track of, isn't it?"

"As I mentioned, Counsel, I find that I can. And ultimately the decision and findings in an autopsy that I sign off on are mine."

"You took time out of your busy practice to handle the autopsy of Brett Daniels personally?"

"In a case as important as this, I absolutely did."

"By important, you mean a possible murder case?"

"Yes."

"It's important to be careful and thorough in a murder case?"

"It's important to be careful and thorough in all cases."

"Great, so as part of your careful and thorough investigation in this case, what were the results of your sodium rhodizonate test?"

Dr. Archuleta blinked. "The sodium rhodizonate test?"

"Yes. I've studied your autopsy and I can't find...well, here, Doctor, here's a copy of your autopsy report. Could you show me where the results of your sodium rhodizonate test are listed?"

Dr. Archuleta left the autopsy report right where I put it. "Why would I do a sodium rhodizonate test?"

"I didn't ask that question, Doctor. I asked where the results of that test were listed."

"It wasn't necessary."

"See, that's not the question I asked either. Let's make this easier—is it fair for me to assume that you did not do a sodium rhodizonate test in the case of Brett Daniels?"

"I did not. It wasn't necessary."

"Doctor, let's explain this a little to the jury. Wounds like those suffered by Brett Daniels often have a little black ring around them, right?"

"They do."

I motioned to Danny who popped Autopsy Picture Number 14 onto the screen. "This is the picture you took of Mr. Daniels' entrance wound, correct?"

"It is."

"There is a small black ring around the wound, right?"

Dr. Archuleta would be the first to tell you that he was not stupid. He saw where this was going. He peered and said, "I don't know that I see one on that photo."

I didn't even have to motion for Danny to blow it up so that the circular wound was five feet tall. A black ring was clearly visible around the edge. "My apologies, Doctor, that was a small picture. You can see it now, can't you?"

"Yes."

"Now, Doctor, it's your opinion that this black ring was left by the passage of an arrow through Mr. Daniels' thigh, right?"

"That's right."

"A black ring like this can also be left by the passage of a bullet, true?"

"It was left by an arrow here."

"That wasn't my question, Doctor. A black ring like this can be left by the passage of a bullet, right?"

"In cases where a wound is actually caused by a bullet, yes."

"And when a bullet passes through a body, it can leave lead residue at the entrance wound, true?"

"True."

"A carbon arrow will not leave lead residue at an entrance wound, right?"

"It will if the arrow had a lead component."

"Doctor, I want you to assume that crossbow arrows in

general, and State's Exhibit 23 in particular do not have a lead component. Can you do that?"

"I can."

"The sodium rhodizonate test detects the presence of lead, doesn't it?"

"It does."

"It's often used to determine whether a wound was caused by a bullet, isn't it?"

"It is, but as I've said, Counselor, that test wasn't necessary here."

"You've mentioned that a few times, Doctor. You were told about the crossbow arrow by law enforcement, weren't you?"

"I was."

"You were told about the arrow before you conducted the autopsy, right?"

"I don't see how that has any relevance."

"That's clear. You were told about the crossbow arrow before the autopsy was performed, weren't you?"

"Again, I don't see how that matters."

"Do I have to ask a third time, Dr. Archuleta?"

Dr. Archuleta pulled his vest straight. "Yes."

"And you were given the arrow, true?"

"Yes, but only after I had completed my examination."

"But before you issued your report, right?"

"Why would that—"

"Doctor. Please."

"Yes. But I still don't see how that's relevant."

"That's fine. Do you hunt, Doctor?"

"Of course not. I mean, no."

"That's all I have, Doctor. Thank you."

Tiffany Erin was standing by the time I turned around. "Dr. Archuleta, was there any need to perform the sodium rhodizonate test in this case?"

Dr. Archuleta looked side to side for a moment before he straightened his vest, lifted his chin, and said, "Absolutely not."

"Why not?"

"Because this wound was completely consistent with being caused by a crossbow arrow of the same shape and size as that which was found at the scene in this case."

"And did knowing that a crossbow arrow was found at the scene prevent you from doing a complete and thorough exam?"

"It did not."

"Did having the arrow help you conduct a complete and thorough exam?"

"Of course. It would be ridiculous to ignore evidence at the scene related to the cause of death. That's what we're trained to do. In such a circumstance, one should think horses, not zebras. In other words, the most obvious solution is usually the correct one. I conducted a complete and thorough examination of Mr. Daniels and my conclusion regarding the cause of his death is to a reasonable degree of medical certainty, not probability, *certainty*."

Tiffany Erin nodded. "Thank you, Doctor."

I stood. "Doctor, the sodium rhodizonate test is commonly used in your profession to determine whether there is lead residue in a wound, isn't it?"

"Only when it is appropriate, which it was not in this case."

"You've done the sodium rhodizonate test before, right?"

"When it was appropriate, yes."

"In hundreds of cases? Thousands?"

"Hundreds certainly. But as I've mentioned—"

"Yes, Doctor, you certainly have. Let's make this absolutely clear for the jury—you didn't perform a test to determine if there was lead residue in Brett Daniels' leg wound, right?"

"It was not appropriate to do so."

"Are you having trouble keeping track of my question, Doctor?"

He shifted and straightened his vest. "No."

"So?"

"I did not test for lead."

"No further questions, Your Honor."

48

At the end of the day, Rhonda and Rob were waiting outside the courthouse with Colt as Danny and I caught up to them. Rhonda was holding a mitten in one hand and smoking barehanded with the other.

As we approached, Rhonda blew a cloud of smoke into the air and said, "So will it be like this all week?"

"Pretty much," I said. "And maybe into next."

"Should we be here?"

"If you can."

Rhonda and Rob exchanged a look.

"Don't worry about it, Mom," said Colt.

"What's up?" I said.

"National Signing Day is Wednesday afternoon," said Rhonda. "They're having a big ceremony for Tyler."

"We tried to get them to change it, but everyone said there's no way we can wait," said Rob. "They're sending a camera crew out so that he can be part of the Pigskin Top 20 Package."

"You should be there for him, Mom," said Colt.

"That's no problem at all, Rhonda," I said. "You can miss one afternoon. And it sounds like a great event."

The ember fired as Rhonda inhaled. She crossed her arms and tapped the filter with her thumb before she exhaled, "Are you sure?"

"I am. Go."

"What kind of mom—"

"The kind who loves both of her sons," said Colt.

Rhonda rubbed her lip with a thumb, then nodded.

"Has Tyler made up his mind?" I asked.

"He's got it narrowed down to five schools, but he's keeping everyone guessing," said Rob.

Rhonda burned down the last bit of ash. "Including us, the little shit."

I smiled. "Danny and I have to get ready for tomorrow. I'll see you here at 8:30." I put a hand on Colt's shoulder. "You did a good job today, which is more tiring than you think. Make sure you get a good meal and some sleep. And stay off your phone."

Colt gave a brusque nod.

"All right, I'll see you all tomorrow."

The three of them piled into Rob's new F150 truck and Danny and I went to our cars. As we walked, Danny smiled. "A good meal *and* some sleep?"

I smiled. "We can get the meal anyway. Black Boar Cubans?"

"I pick up, you pay?"

"Done."

~

THE NEXT MORNING, Tiffany Erin decided to call two investigating officers. The first was Sheriff's Deputy Randy Pavlich. Deputy Pavlich was in his early thirties with short blonde hair and the slightly stiff manner of a police officer who hadn't testified much yet. After leading him through his credentials as an eight-year member of the department, Tiffany Erin said, "Deputy Pavlich, were you called to the Daniels' home on the Friday evening in question?"

"Yes, ma'am. I had just finished a domestic disturbance call when I received a dispatch of a body found out on M-339. It turned out to be the Daniels' home."

"And who made that call?"

"I don't know who made the call, that went to the dispatcher. The defendant, Colton Daniels and his brother Tyler were there when I arrived."

"And were you the first law enforcement officer on the scene?"

"I was."

"Were you aware that it was Brett Daniels' body at the time?"

"I didn't know Mr. Daniels so I couldn't have said who he was but the boys, they knew it was their dad even though...well, the boys were able to say it was their dad."

"Why did you hesitate there, Deputy Pavlich?"

"Because, although there had been some damage, the decedent's face was still intact."

Tiffany Erin crossed her arms. "Meaning other parts of him were not?"

"No, ma'am, they weren't. The coyotes had gotten after him pretty good."

"What do you mean 'gotten after him,' Deputy?"

Deputy Pavlich shifted in his seat and looked from Tiffany Erin to the jury. "Meaning a portion of the body had been eaten and some of the entrails scattered."

"I see. And did the defendant or his brother say how the body had been found?"

"Yes, ma'am. They said that when Tyler had gotten home from the game, his dog Chet, a big yellow lab, had found the body."

"And did either of them give you an indication of how long it had been since they'd seen their father?"

"They each said that they'd seen him the night before, after the two of them had eaten dinner."

"They both said they had seen him that Thursday night in the house?"

"Yes, ma'am."

"Did the defendant Colton Daniels ever indicate to you that he had gone out to see his father while he was hunting?"

"No, ma'am, he did not."

"What did you do then, Deputy?"

"I called for more deputies to come out. The boys had already called the rescue squad."

"Why was that necessary?"

"We're not that big an outfit so the rescue squad takes the body to the coroner's office if there's going to be an investigation."

"And did you investigate the scene that night?"

"As much as we could in the dark and then again as soon as it was light the next morning."

"Did your investigation reveal anything about the cause of death?"

"Yes, ma'am. At first, I assumed that it was a hunting accident and that the coyotes had just fussed after the body some."

"And when did that theory change?"

"The next morning."

"Why?"

"That was the first chance we had to go out and take a really good look at the hunting platform. We found a couple of things that didn't make sense."

Tiffany Erin put a picture of the hunting platform up on the screen. "Is this the platform you're referring to?"

"Yes, ma'am."

"And what didn't make sense?"

"First off, there was blood on the platform and on the ladder leading down."

"Brett Daniels' blood?"

"It turned out to be, yes ma'am. Then there was Mr. Daniels' crossbow."

"You're talking about Brett Daniels' crossbow?"

"Yes, ma'am. According to his sons, he had gone out that night to hunt coyotes. We found that Brett Daniels' crossbow had been discharged and tossed aside."

"Can you explain what you mean please, Deputy?"

"Yes, ma'am. We found an arrow that matched others in Brett Daniels' quiver stuck straight into the ground approximately 12 feet from the platform."

"What did that lead you to conclude?"

"That Brett Daniels had shot the crossbow almost straight down from the platform and had missed whatever it was that he was shooting at."

"And why did you conclude that his crossbow was thrown aside?"

"Because it was lying on the ground ten to twelve feet away on the other side of the platform. If it had been dropped, it would have been directly below it."

"I see. What did you do next?"

"That all seemed unusual to me so I went back up to the property, to the barn."

"And why did you do that?"

"Because that's where I had been told that Mr. Daniels kept his hunting equipment."

"I see. And what did you find in the barn?"

"I found several racks that were used to hold crossbows."

"Was there anything significant about those racks?"

"Yes, ma'am. At one end was a rack marked 'Brett' that was empty."

"I see."

"At the other end was a rack labeled 'TD' that held a crossbow and ten arrows lined up in a row of holes in the bottom."

"Okay."

"And in the middle was a rack with 'Colt' burned into the top."

Tiffany Erin put up a picture of Colt's crossbow rack. "Is this a true and accurate picture of the rack you're referring to?"

"Yes, ma'am."

"And what was significant about it?"

"The crossbow was there. But one of the arrows was gone."

She pointed at the picture. "You're referring to this empty hole here?"

"Yes, ma'am."

"Why was that significant?"

"Because the whole scene was just...well, it was strange."

"What did you do next?"

"I grabbed two other deputies, went back out to the platform, and broadened the search area."

"What were you looking for?"

"If I'm being honest, ma'am, I wasn't really sure."

"We appreciate that, Deputy. Did you find something?"

"Yes, ma'am, I did."

"What was it?"

"First, I found an arrow."

Tiffany Erin picked up the arrow from the evidence table and handed it to Deputy Pavlich. "Can you identify this for the jury, please?"

"Yes, ma'am. This is the arrow that I found."

"Okay, Deputy. A couple of things. Where did you find it?"

"A couple hundred yards away from the platform."

"On the same side of the platform or the opposite side of where you found Brett Daniels' arrow."

"On the opposite side."

"And were you able to identify the owner of the arrow?"

"Yes, ma'am. The arrow matched the other arrows that were in Colton Daniels' crossbow rack."

"Deputy Pavlich, did you seek to arrest Colton Daniels at that time?"

"No, ma'am. Although we were interested in him, we did not feel there was enough evidence and…"

"Yes, Deputy?"

Deputy Pavlich glanced over at Colt. "Seeing as how he had lost his father, we wanted to be sure before we did anything."

Tiffany Erin nodded. "So did you continue your investigation?"

"We did."

"What did you do?"

"First, we investigated whether there was a history of conflict between the defendant and his father."

"And what did you learn?"

I stood. "Objection, Your Honor. Hearsay."

"Sustained," said Judge LaPlante. "The witness will limit his answers to matters and events within his personal knowledge."

Tiffany Erin didn't miss a beat. She produced a piece of paper and handed it to Deputy Pavlich. "Deputy, can you identify this document?"

"I can. It is a copy of the police report of an encounter between the defendant and his father at the Borderlands restaurant."

I stood. "For the reasons stated in our motion *in limine* Your Honor, we object to the introduction of this exhibit."

Judge LaPlante nodded. "And for the reasons set forth in our ruling, we find that this document is admissible as a business record and that its relevance outweighs its potential prejudicial effect. Ms. Erin, you are reminded that the testimony of this witness will be limited to the fact that this report exists and the role it played in his investigation. He may not testify as to the underlying incident within it."

"Understood, Your Honor," said Tiffany Erin. "Deputy Pavlich you mentioned that you found this police report in the business records of the Ash County Sheriff's Department, is that right?

"It is."

"And what impact did this report have on your investigation?"

"We learned that there was a report of at least one claimed public altercation between the defendant and his father, which in turn caused us to further examine the events surrounding Brett Daniels' death."

"What did you do?"

"Over the next several days, we continued to search the area surrounding the platform and the barn."

"And what did that search reveal?"

"It revealed fingerprints on the crossbow that were eventually matched to Colton Daniels."

"What else?"

"We found a coyote call at the scene."

"What is a coyote call?"

"It is a small device that attracts coyotes by mimicking the sound of a wounded rabbit."

"Where did you find the call?"

"Over in the weeds behind the barn. That's why we didn't find it at first."

"Why is that?"

"Because it wasn't near the platform or Mr. Daniels' body, which were the two primary areas we searched."

"How far from Brett Daniels' body was it?"

"Approximately fifty yards."

"And was this location where it was found on the route between the platform and where Brett Daniels died?"

"It was not."

"What did that mean to you?"

"It meant that the call was not placed there by Mr. Daniels. He wouldn't have been able to throw it that far if he'd wanted to."

"I see. And in the ensuing days of your investigation after Mr. Daniels' death, did you find anything else of significance?"

"Yes, ma'am."

"And what was that?"

"We found the trail cam near the platform."

"I see. And did Colton Daniels tell you that the trail cam was there?"

"No, he did not."

"How did you find it?"

"Because wildlife of some sort was involved, we brought in Michigan DNR officer Sam Wald to take a look. Knowing that Mr. Daniels was hunting coyotes, Sam wondered if there was a trail cam out there somewhere and sure enough he found one."

Tiffany Erin raised a hand. "I don't want you to tell me about what Officer Wald did."

"Oh, right, I'm sorry."

"No problem. It is fair to say, though, that Officer Wald gave you the trail cam?"

"Yes. Yes, he did."

"And did you find pictures from it that were relevant to your investigation?"

"Eventually, yes, ma'am."

Tiffany Erin ran him through the process of identifying the photos of Colt walking toward the platform before she blew up the last one on the screen and said, "And were you able to identify the man in this picture?"

"Yes, ma'am. It's the defendant Colton Daniels."

"And is he carrying something?"

"Yes, ma'am, two items."

"What are they?"

"He is holding a flashlight, which is on, alongside a crossbow."

"I see. And was there anything significant about the crossbow in your opinion?"

"Yes, ma'am. It was loaded."

"How can you tell that, Deputy?"

"If you zoom in a bit, yes, thank you, you can see that the string is drawn back, there, the fletching of the arrow, there, and the point of the arrow, there." On each use of the word "there," he circled with the laser pointer.

"Did you find any other pictures from the trail cam that were relevant to your investigation?"

"Yes, ma'am. We found five more that were time stamped approximately twelve minutes later."

Two pictures appeared on the screen. "What are we looking at now, Deputy?"

"Those are pictures of the same person, Colton Daniels, walking away from the platform area."

"Was there anything significant about these photos to your investigation?"

"Yes, ma'am. You can see that now, instead of holding the crossbow with both hands, he is holding the flashlight in one hand and the crossbow is hanging down at his side in the other."

"And why is that significant?"

"Could you blow up the photo please, ma'am? Of the crossbow?"

"Certainly." She did.

"In this picture, ma'am, you can see that the crossbow has been discharged."

"Deputy, we're looking at this from the back. How can you tell?"

"Do you see the position of the string, ma'am? How it's going straight across like a 'T' instead of being pulled back like a 'V'?"

"Ah, yes, I see it now."

"That's because it's been fired."

"So what did you do next?"

"We provided this information to the coroner, Dr. Archuleta. Shortly thereafter, he confirmed that the cause of Mr. Daniels' death was exsanguination due to an arrow wound."

"And then what did you do?"

"I consulted with Sheriff Dushane, my superior officer, and then assisted with issuing a warrant for Colton Daniels' arrest."

"Thank you, Deputy Pavlich. Those are all the questions I have for now. Mr. Shepherd might have a few."

I stood. "Good morning, Deputy Pavlich."

"Good morning, sir."

"Let's start with the trail cam pictures, Deputy. You have gone through the pictures for the entire night Mr. Daniels is believed to have died, is that right?"

"That's right."

"There are no photos of my client shooting the crossbow are there?"

"No, but we know that he did, sir."

"I know you think so. But there are no photos of him actually shooting it, are there?"

"There are not."

"There are no photos showing him aiming it, right?"

"I suppose not."

"And there are certainly no photos of his arrow in Brett Daniels, are there?"

"Well, no, but—"

I waved. "I understand you have a picture of my client with a loaded crossbow and a picture of him with an empty crossbow. My point is you don't have any pictures of what happened in between, do you?"

"Well, no sir, but...may I explain?"

"Sure."

"Mr. Daniels, Brett Daniels, did have an arrow wound in his leg."

I nodded. "Let's be a little more specific. Brett Daniels had a wound in his leg that Dr. Warren Archuleta said was an arrow wound, right?"

"That's right."

"You didn't find an arrow in Brett Daniels' leg, did you?"

"No, no sir."

"Instead, that is the assumption you're making based on your interpretation of the evidence you found, is that fair?"

"That's fair."

"Now you eventually found the arrow you identified a moment ago, is that correct?"

"It is."

"It's the arrow you believe wounded Brett Daniels, right?"

"That's right."

"You did not find any blood on the arrow, did you?"

"We did not."

"You did not find any blood on the ground around where the arrow landed, did you?"

"We did not."

"The arrow was not broken, was it?"

"No, sir."

"It was not bent?"

"No, sir."

"There was nothing on the arrow itself to indicate that it had passed through Brett Daniels' leg, was there?"

"Well, there was the wound in Mr. Daniels' leg."

"I didn't ask about the leg, Deputy Pavlich, I asked about the arrow. The arrow itself did not have any blood on it, right?"

"I acknowledged that, sir."

"There was no skin or flesh or hair on it, was there?"

"There was not."

"There was no fabric or cloth material?"

"No, sir."

"So I will ask you again, Deputy—there was nothing on the arrow itself that indicated it had passed through Brett Daniels' leg, was there?"

Deputy Pavlich shifted in his seat. "I suppose not."

"You mentioned that the fingerprints on the crossbow matched my client's, do you remember that?"

"I do."

"That was not a surprise since it was his crossbow, true?"

"I suppose that's true, sir."

"You also mentioned that you found a coyote call behind the barn approximately fifty yards away from where Brett Daniels' body was found?"

"Yes, sir."

"You did not find my client's fingerprints on that coyote call, did you?"

"No. We did not find any fingerprints on the coyote call."

"Deputy Pavlich, the coroner, Dr. Archuleta, has already testified in this case. He told the jury yesterday that Brett Daniels would have died within minutes of being wounded."

Deputy Pavlich nodded. "That's consistent with what he has told me."

"You have traveled the distance between the platform and where Brett Daniels was found, haven't you?"

"I have, sir."

"To get there in a few minutes, he would've had to have moved at a fairly fast pace, true?"

Deputy Pavlich thought. "He would have had to move briskly, yes, sir."

"Especially if he were slowing down towards the end from losing blood, right?"

"That's right."

"My client doesn't appear to be running in those trail cam pictures you found, does he?"

"No, sir."

"He appears to be walking slowly, doesn't he?"

"The time stamp would seem to indicate that, yes sir."

"There is no picture of Brett Daniels following my client, is there?"

"There is not."

"In fact, there's no picture of Brett Daniels on the trail cam at all, is there?"

"No, sir."

"So Brett Daniels couldn't have walked away from the platform by the same route as my client, could he?"

Deputy Pavlich frowned. "I guess not. But the ladder is on the other side of the platform, away from the game trail that was being photographed."

I went over to the evidence table and picked up Colt's red arrow. "This is the arrow that you identified as being shot from Colt Daniels' crossbow, true?"

"It is."

"And it was found 230 yards from the platform, wasn't it?"

"Oh, I don't know as I could say that."

I gestured and Danny put a picture up on the screen. "You planted a flag where you found the arrow, right?"

"That's right."

"Is this a picture of that flag and that area?"

"It is."

"You have no reason to disagree with a measurement that put that flag 230 yards from the platform, do you?"

"No, that sounds about right."

"Incidentally, you didn't do a trajectory analysis of the arrow's flight, did you?"

Deputy Pavlich looked confused. "Sir?"

"You didn't do a mathematical analysis to figure out the angle at which the arrow was shot and how far it traveled, did you?"

"No, sir, I mean, we know how far it traveled. Why would we?"

"That's fine, Deputy. I just wanted to know the answer. You showed pictures of Colt Daniels' crossbow rack earlier, do you recall that?"

"I do."

"That rack had spaces for ten arrows, one of which was empty, right?"

"That's right."

"Of the arrows remaining, four were field points and five were broad heads, correct?"

"Yes, sir."

"Do you hunt, Deputy Pavlich?"

"Yes, sir."

"You would agree with me that if one was going to use an arrow to kill an animal over fifty pounds, the broadhead arrow would be the better choice, wouldn't it?"

Deputy Pavlich thought for a moment before he said, "Yes, sir, it would."

"That's all I have right now. Thank you, Deputy."

Tiffany Erin stood. "Deputy Pavlich, can a field point kill a person?"

"I think we know that, ma'am."

"In reviewing the time stamps on the photos, there's no question that Colton Daniels discharged his crossbow between 6:34 and 6:46 p.m., is there?"

"No, ma'am."

"Mr. Shepherd made a point of saying that there was no blood or other material on the arrow. Does that mean that it did not pass through Brett Daniels' leg?"

"No, ma'am. Between the flight and being outside in the weather, we weren't surprised that there was no material on the arrow. And pulling it out of the ground would sort of naturally wipe off the point, too."

"Arrows pass through animals all the time when hunting, do they not?"

"Yes, ma'am, they do."

"Without breaking?"

"Yes, ma'am. Hunters reuse their arrows all the time even after they've been used to harvest a deer or a moose."

"Mr. Shepherd also asked you whether his client's fingerprints were found on the coyote call. Do you remember that?"

"I do."

"And you said they were not?"

"That's right."

"Why was that significant to you?"

"What was significant was that no fingerprints were found on it. It's true Colt Daniels' fingerprints were not on the coyote call but neither were Brett Daniels' or anyone else's."

"And why did that matter?"

"Because it indicated a strong possibility that the device had been wiped down."

"Thank you, Deputy. That's all I have."

I stood. "Deputy Pavlich, it was cold that Thursday night, wasn't it?"

He thought. "Well, it was November in Michigan, sir."

"Brett Daniels was wearing gloves when you found him, wasn't he?"

"Yes, sir."

"If he was wearing gloves, he wouldn't leave fingerprints on the coyote call, would he?"

"No sir, but it was too far away to have been from him."

"Isn't it most likely that the person hunting the coyotes had the coyote call?"

He opened his mouth, then shook his head. "I, I just didn't think it made sense."

"You agree though that might be why there weren't any fingerprints on it?"

"Maybe. But it still doesn't explain how it got there."

"And you don't have any evidence, at all, that my client put it there, do you?"

"No, sir, I don't."

"Thank you, Deputy. That's all I have."

Judge LaPlante looked back and forth between us then said, "Deputy Pavlich, you may step down. Counsel, members of the jury, why don't we take our morning break now. Please be back at 10:15."

The judge hit the gavel and we stood as the jury exited the room.

None of them were looking at us.

"Those pictures are really bad," whispered Colt.

"It's what we expected," I said.

"I'd find me guilty."

I smiled and put a hand on his shoulder. "Well, it's a good thing you're not on the jury."

49

I once knew an attorney back in my law firm days that called certain evidence "accelerants." What he meant was testimony or conduct that inflamed the jury and drove it to a result in the case that it might not otherwise reach. The next witness that morning was Michigan DNR officer Samson Ezekiel Wald and, by the time he was done, I was pretty sure that was why Tiffany Erin had called him.

It started out simply enough. Officer Sam Wald took the stand after the break and he looked pretty much how I remembered him—ruddy skin, reddish-brown hair, and a thick brown mustache that covered most of his upper lip. Rather than his dark green field uniform, he was wearing his dress uniform of dark green pants and matching tie with a gray shirt that prominently displayed his badge on his chest. He smiled at the jury and, if he didn't look completely comfortable, he didn't look uncomfortable either.

Tiffany Erin smiled at him as he sat. "Could you state your name please, Officer?"

"Samson Ezekiel Wald. But that's a bit of a mouthful so most people call me Sam."

"And what do you do for a living, Officer Wald?"

"I'm an officer for the Michigan Department of Natural Resources. I work out of our office in Grass Lake that is part of the Waterloo Recreation Area."

"And what do you do as a Michigan DNR officer?"

"We have a variety of responsibilities. The Department of Natural Resources manages all of the natural resources in Michigan, which can range from water to minerals to plant and animal life. I serve in the Wildlife Management Section."

"And what do you do in the Wildlife Management Section?"

"Lots of different things. I enforce hunting and fishing licenses so I spot-check folks to make sure they have a permit to take any animals in their possession. I also investigate poaching or excess-catch activity."

"And is the DNR involved directly in wildlife management, too?"

Officer Wald nodded. "We are. We monitor animal activity, so in northern Michigan that might include following up on bear or cougar sightings. Here in the southern, lower Peninsula, a lot of what I do is deer management. Besides checking on tags, I inspect hunting sites to make sure no one is using bait piles, and I help monitor the deer population for signs of wasting disease or other illnesses."

"It sounds like a very broad range of responsibilities."

Officer Wald shrugged humbly. "It keeps me out of trouble."

"And is coyote management a part of your responsibilities too?"

Officer Wald smiled. "I don't know that anyone can 'manage' coyotes. But yes, if there is an issue with the coyote population, that comes under our jurisdiction, too."

"And in your capacity as a wildlife management officer for the State of Michigan, have you dealt with and studied coyotes?"

"I have."

"How so?"

"I've studied their life-cycle and breeding habits, their range and hunting habits, and of course, I'm familiar with the Michigan rules governing hunting and trapping them. Like anyone who's hunted around here, I've run them off a deer I've harvested and I've been called out to scenes to determine if they were the culprits in attacks on domestic animals."

"Domestic animals?"

"Pets or farm animals mostly."

"I see. And do you occasionally cooperate with the investigations of sheriff's departments or the state police?"

"It's rare, but the odd thing will come up where we have reason to work together."

"And were you asked by the Ash County Sheriff's Department to assist in the investigation of the death of Brett Daniels?"

"I was. Deputy Pavlich called and asked if I could help him out."

"In what respect?"

"Deputy Pavlich told me that he had a case where coyotes had either killed a man or fed on his body."

"And did you then take part in the investigation?

"I did. I went over to the property out on M-339 and investigated the scene. I started with Mr. Daniels' body."

"And what did you find?"

"Now mind you I was there to assess the involvement of wildlife with the death."

"I understand."

"The first thing I found was that coyotes likely had fed on Mr. Daniels."

"What led to that conclusion?"

"The feeding pattern was consistent with coyote behavior. Coyotes typically go through the abdomen and eat the lungs and liver and kidneys but remove the intestines. That's what had occurred in this case."

Tiffany Erin put on a questioning look. It was fake as hell, but I didn't blame her for that. "What do you mean?" she said.

"I mean that Mr. Daniels' lungs, liver, heart, and kidneys were gone and that his intestines were strewn about the yard."

"Could it have been some other animal?"

"That's possible but not likely. There were other signs that this was coyote activity."

"What were those?"

"There was some gnawing on the ribs. There were also teeth marks on the throat."

"What's the significance of that?"

"When a coyote kills its prey, it typically suffocates it by crushing its windpipe."

"And you state that those marks were present here?"

"Some, yes."

Tiffany Erin crossed her arms and walked away from the jury. "Officer Wald, can you estimate how many coyotes fed on Mr. Daniels' body?"

"You know, I can't, Ms. Erin. By the time I got there, most of the signs had been trampled, although in fairness the grass and ground there was pretty hard, and I don't know that I would have been able to see anything anyway."

Tiffany Erin turned. "Officer Wald, what is a coyote call?"

"It's a call used to attract coyotes. It mimics the sound of a wounded rabbit. The coyote comes closer when it hears the sound, giving the hunter a shot at it."

"Why does it come?"

"Because it believes there's an opportunity for easy prey."

"I see. A coyote call was found at the scene here, wasn't it?"

"It was."

"Was it near Mr. Daniels' body?"

"No, it was a ways off. Fifty yards or so I'd guess."

"Officer Wald, will a coyote attack a healthy man?"

Officer Wald shook his head. "Almost never. Normally, coyotes are afraid of people. They're in every county in the state, and even most cities, and you almost never see them."

"What about a wounded or dying man?"

"That would be different."

"How so?"

"A man who was dying or bleeding severely would be an attractive target, especially if he couldn't fight back or was unconscious." He paused, then said, "Easy prey is easy prey."

Tiffany Erin nodded. "Officer Wald, as an expert who is familiar with coyote behavior, do you have an opinion as to whether Mr. Daniels was alive or dead when the coyotes began to eat him?"

"You know, I honestly can't say, Ms. Erin. My suspicion is that he was dead but given the marks on his throat, it's possible that he was in the last moments of his life."

"Oh, my goodness."

Officer Wald nodded solemnly. "Not the way you'd want to go, no."

"Officer Wald, I want you to assume hypothetically that Mr. Daniels was bleeding to death on the property in back of his home."

"Okay."

"I also want you to assume that while that was happening a coyote call was sounded."

"Fine."

"Would that have a good chance of summoning the coyotes?"

"If they were in the area, sure."

"And would a dead or dying man attract their attention?"

"Certainly. They'd be cautious at first, but sure."

Tiffany Erin nodded and walked a few steps away again, her arms crossed, one hand on her chin as if thinking. "Officer Wald, are coyotes loud when they eat?"

"If there is more than one of them, yes, ma'am."

"Are coyote calls loud?"

"Certainly. They have to be loud enough to get the coyotes' attention."

"Is it audible from one hundred yards away?"

"And then some."

"And the coyotes, are they audible from one hundred yards away when they're eating?"

"If they're agitated, sure."

Tiffany Erin moved a little closer to the jury. "Officer Wald, Deputy Pavlich testified earlier today that you found a trail camera, is that true?"

"It is."

"Tell us about that."

"I was looking around the platform, and I got a pretty good line on where I thought the game trails were and which direction a coyote might approach from. After that, it was just a matter of checking sight lines."

"And did the camera have pictures on it?"

"Not exactly. This particular model was set to forward pictures to a phone. I helped the deputies unwind all that."

"The trail camera didn't take any pictures of Brett Daniels?"

"No, from the blood trail it looked like he would not have crossed the camera's field."

"The blood from his leg wound, you mean?"

"Yes."

"Officer Wald, if Brett Daniels had been wounded in the abdomen, we wouldn't know it today, would we?"

"No, ma'am."

"Why not?"

"Because all of the wound evidence in the abdomen is gone."

"Consumed?"

"Or removed, yes."

"But the thigh where Mr. Daniels had been wounded was intact here, wasn't it?"

"It was. Unlike other animals, coyotes typically do not feed on the thighs and buttocks."

"So, we were just lucky here?"

"Well, I don't think Brett Daniels was lucky, but the investigating officers were fortunate that there was still physical evidence of Mr. Daniels' wound."

"The coyotes almost concealed the cause of Mr. Daniels' death, didn't they?"

"Almost. But not quite."

"Thank you, Officer Wald."

I looked at the jury. They were uniformly sickened. I was going to have to be careful and quick.

"Good morning, Officer Wald."

"Good morning, Mr. Shepherd."

"As Ms. Erin mentioned, Dr. Archuleta testified regarding the cause of death yesterday."

"So I understand."

"He testified that Brett Daniels bled to death."

"That's what I hear."

"He did not testify that Mr. Daniels' larynx was crushed or that he was suffocated by a coyote."

"I see."

"Would you defer to Dr. Archuleta's testimony regarding the cause of death?"

"Sure."

"You also mentioned that a coyote call was found in the backyard, right?"

"That's right."

"You didn't find anything that linked my client, Colt Daniels, to that device, did you?"

"No."

"And you don't have any evidence that he sounded that call, true?"

"True."

"You mentioned that the call is loud?"

"It is."

"If someone was wearing headphones in the house they might not hear the call even if it was being sounded in the backyard, right?"

Tiffany Erin stood. "Objection. Facts not in evidence."

"Your Honor, I'm merely establishing that a variety of indoor household activities could prevent the call from being heard."

Judge LaPlante thought for a moment before he said, "Overruled."

"Do you remember the question, Officer Wald?" I said.

"I do. Yes, if someone had headphones on it, it would be hard to hear the call."

"The same would be true for a variety of activities whether it was watching TV or listening to the radio or even being asleep, true?"

"Yes, that's true. It's not so loud that you couldn't cover up the noise from a distance."

"The same would be true of coyotes feeding, correct?"

"How do you mean?"

"I mean that someone in the house could be doing things that made it so they didn't hear a coyote feeding."

"That would be true. Although if the coyotes got wound up, the howling would cut through just about anything."

"But they don't always get wound up, do they?"

"They don't."

"Sometimes they eat silently, right?"

"Right."

"And you don't know if they howled here or not, do you?"

"No."

"So, it's entirely possible that Colt and his brother Tyler could have slept through the tragedy that was unfolding in the backyard without hearing a thing."

"Yes."

"Mr. Daniels left a pronounced blood trail from the platform to where he passed away, right?"

"He did."

"Do you hunt deer, Officer Wald?"

"I do."

"Have you ever shot a deer and had to track it down?"

"I have."

"Can you tell from its blood trail whether it's running and when it slows down?"

Officer Wald nodded. "Yes."

"How?"

"When the deer is running, the blood is farther apart and as it slows, the blood becomes heavier."

"Did you notice anything like that here?"

Officer Wald thought. "I did."

"You would agree with me that it appears Brett Daniels was running when he first left the platform, wasn't he?"

"I would say the blood trail looks that way."

"And then he slowed down?"

"The blood trail looks that way."

"Did you review the pictures from the trail cam?"

"I did."

"There are pictures of my client walking away from the platform, is that right?"

"That's right."

"There are no pictures of Mr. Daniels running into the camera frame, are there?"

"No."

"There is no picture of Brett Daniels pursuing my client, are there?"

"No."

"Now, about Mr. Daniels' blood trail, a coyote could have found that blood trail on its own, right?"

"That's right."

"That happens all the time in the wild, doesn't it?"

"Yes."

"Hunters often have to drive coyotes off from a deer they've harvested, right?"

"They do."

"In fact, there are a lot of parts of the state where, if you don't find your deer before sunset, you probably won't find much of it the next day because of the coyotes."

"That's true."

I thought. There was no question that the coyotes got to Brett Daniels so all I could do was show that Colt hadn't summoned them or ignored their noise. "That's all for me, Officer Wald. Thank you."

"Sure thing."

Tiffany Erin stood. "Officer Wald, you mentioned that it would be possible for a person in the house to not hear the coyote call or the noise of feeding in the backyard, is that right?"

"That's possible, right."

"You don't know one way or the other what people in the house heard, true?"

"That's true."

Tiffany Erin acted as if she were about to sit down when she turned back and said, "Dogs are pretty sensitive to coyotes, aren't they?"

"Usually."

"I imagine that a dog, like say a yellow lab, would tear out after a group of coyotes in its yard—"

I stood. "Objection, Your Honor. Speculation. Facts not in evidence."

"Sustained."

"Officer Wald, it appears that Brett Daniels died on Thursday night, are you aware of that?"

"I am."

"And he was found on Friday night, is that right?"

"That's my understanding."

"How was he found Officer Wald?"

"It's my understanding that the boys' dog found the body."

"Does that surprise you?"

"No. In my experience, a dog would go right for it. Especially if the dog knew the person."

"But it was not reported on Thursday night, was it?"

"Not as far as I know."

"And it was not reported on Friday morning, was it?"

"Not to my knowledge."

"Officer Wald, I want you to assume that both Colton Daniels and his brother Tyler advised the police that they were in the house studying and sleeping on Thursday night and that they both awoke on Friday morning and left to go to school, Tyler first, Colton second."

"Okay."

"I want you to assume that their dog Chet, a yellow lab, was with them."

"Fine."

"Dogs need to go outside to urinate within a twenty-four-hour period, don't they?"

"Unless they go in the house, yes."

"So we really only have two options, don't we? Either the

boys kept Chet in the house for twenty-four hours from Thursday night to Friday night, or Chet went outside and Colton did not report what the dog found."

I stood. "Objection. Speculation."

Judge LaPlante thought. "Overruled. You'll be allowed to follow-up, Mr. Shepherd."

We all looked back to Officer Wald. He smoothed his mustache with a thumb and forefinger, thinking, then said, "Both of those are true. Another option would be that the dog was taken out in a place where he was not near the body, like the front yard."

"We can agree that if the dog was let out in the backyard, he would've found the body?"

"I think that's fairly certain given the location of the body." He thought. "Yes, I think that's true."

"No further questions."

I stood. "Officer Wald, you don't have any idea why Chet didn't find the body until Friday night, do you?"

"I don't. I can't even say for sure that he did or didn't find it before that. I'm just taking the boys' word for it."

"And Chet certainly could have been let out in an area or taken for a walk or urinated somewhere else that would explain why he wasn't in the backyard before Friday night, right?"

"Right."

"You have no idea."

"None."

"You and Ms. Erin are guessing what might have happened if Chet went into the backyard."

"No, to be fair, Mr. Shepherd, I'm pretty certain what would have happened if Chet went into the backyard." He paused. "What Ms. Erin and I are guessing about is whether Chet did."

"And you don't know that at all."

"I believe I already said that."

Officer Wald was deepening a hole in my case. I decided to follow those immortal words of wisdom and stop digging.

"No further questions, Your Honor. Thank you, Officer Wald."

Michigan DNR Officer Samson Ezekiel Wald nodded and slowly made his way out of the courtroom as the judge dismissed us for lunch.

50

In a criminal case, the State has to prove the chain of custody of the evidence—it has to show how the evidence was found, who took it, where it was stored, and how it arrived in court to eliminate any doubt that it had been tampered with along the way. On Tuesday afternoon, Tiffany Erin put up one chain of custody witness after another—the person who took possession of the arrows, the person who fingerprinted the crossbow and the coyote call, and the person who had stored them all in the evidence locker. She called the deputy who took pictures of the hunting platform and the body, then called the technician who had downloaded the pictures from the trail cam.

In doing all this, Tiffany Erin was like an undertaker in an old western nailing the lid on a casket, slowly placing a nail on the wood, tapping it with the hammer to line it up, then methodically hitting the head of the nail squarely so that it went in perfectly straight before moving six inches to the right and doing it again, and again, and again, until the lid fit squarely on the box without a bit of overhang and everything was sealed tight inside.

By the time she was done that afternoon, Tiffany Erin had

laid the groundwork for all of her evidence—she had established that it was Colt's arrow that was found at the scene, that it was his crossbow with his fingerprints on it that was found in the barn, and that the pictures showing him go to the hunting platform with a loaded crossbow and departing with an empty one were true, accurate, and accounted for.

Oh, and she finished exactly at 4:29 p.m., which I thought was just showing off.

When she was done, the judge dismissed us for the day. It was none too soon.

None of that testimony was dramatic, but it was devastating. It linked Colt bit by bit, piece by piece, to the death of his father. More importantly, Tiffany Erin didn't screw it up. All of the evidence she needed came in without error and without fail.

As people filed out of the courtroom, Rhonda and Rob came up to the rail. "That seemed better than this morning," said Rhonda.

There was no reason to worry her about something she couldn't control. "There were no surprises," I said.

"They still don't have any direct evidence that Colt shot the bastard."

I didn't mention the picture of him with the alleged discharged murder weapon. Instead, I said, "Right."

"You have to point that out to them."

Rob touched her elbow. "Rhonda."

Rhonda crinkled her eyes and waved a hand. "I'm sorry, Shepherd, a whole afternoon without a smoke is making me cranky."

"We just wanted to remind you that we'll be here in the morning tomorrow but not in the afternoon," said Rob.

I nodded. "The signing day ceremony?"

Rhonda nodded. "Over at the school. We didn't have a choice on the time, the local news is gonna be feeding it to ESPN."

It made me queasy. "Rhonda, remember those reporters aren't your friends. If they can get you to say something about Colt's trial, they'll run with it."

"I know, I know, I know. We'll stay in the background. It's Tyler's moment."

"Nothing is off the record, no matter what they say."

"I've got it, Shepherd!" Rhonda raised a hand again. "Sorry."

"No, I'm sorry, too."

"I'm gonna go get that smoke. I'll meet you out there, baby," she said to Rob and left.

"I wish I could be there," said Colt.

"We know," said Rob. "You're a big part of this, too. We'll be thinking about you."

Colt shook his head. "I don't want Tyler thinking about this at all. He should enjoy tomorrow."

"He will," said Rob.

"Has he said where's he's going yet?" I asked.

Colt smiled. "Not my brother. Nothing but cool nods and 'I'll let you knows.'"

Rob looked at me. "Are you done with him?"

"Yeah, you can take him. 8:30 tomorrow morning. Danny or I can bring him home."

"That would be great, thanks."

Rob put his arm around Colt and the two of them walked out.

Danny and I got our things and went to our cars. "What did you think of the dog evidence?" I said on the way.

"I think you can probably explain away Thursday evening and say that, if our case is true, then Brett's body wasn't there yet when they let Chet out for the night." Danny shook his head. "I don't know how you're going to explain Friday morning though. They had to have let the dog out and he should've found the body."

I nodded. "Unless he did find it and Colt didn't report it."

"Or Colt steered him away from it."

"Both of which are bad."

"Right." We were quiet until we arrived at our cars, then Danny said, "You did get Wald to admit that Brett wasn't chasing Colt. That was helpful to our timeline."

I smiled at him. "Do you really think the jury heard anything Wald said after he explained how a coyote eats a man?"

Danny smiled and gave me a finger-gun. "Remind them, Boss. That's why they pay you the big bucks."

"I have to find a new line of work."

"That's what I keep telling you. See you at the office."

∾

THE ASH COUNTY court isn't usually very busy, but there was still a line at the metal detector every morning at eight o'clock. The building held most of the county offices so there was always a rush of people arriving to contest traffic tickets or file deeds or pay property taxes. I was a couple minutes late Wednesday morning so I was caught in the line when I heard a "Hey, Nate," and felt a tap on my shoulder.

I turned to find Kenny Kaminski, smiling and wearing a tie with his ever-present canvas coat. I smiled back. "A suit and everything, Kenny?"

He held the bulky coat out to each side, showing the suit beneath. "I can't remember the last time I wore this thing. Probably my brother's wedding."

"Looks good.

As we inched forward, he said "Yeah, I'll have to change back into my North colors for this afternoon."

My mind was already in court. "Why's that?"

"Tyler's signing, of course. Big day for the family."

I nodded. "Right. Sorry, a little distracted."

Kenny's eyes got big. "Oh, hey, am I allowed to be talking to you?"

"Sure, Kenny. You're just a witness. Are you going on first?"

"I think so."

"That's fine. We won't talk about it."

Kenny looked relieved.

To take his mind off it, I said, "That'll be exciting this afternoon, for sure."

Kenny's eyes lit up. "It sure will. Cameras and all those fans watching...I don't suppose Colt knows what school Tyler's going to pick?"

"Not a clue."

Kenny shook his head. "I tell you that kid is as cool as they come. That's why he's going to be a great quarterback. Well, that and the cannon on his right shoulder."

We got to the table with the plastic baskets and I started emptying my pockets of keys, wallet, and phone and was about to put my briefcase on the conveyor for the x-ray when Kenny said, "Oh, shoot."

"What's wrong?" I said as I fished two quarters out of my pocket.

Kenny had one hand in his pocket and one hand on his back in the typical motion you make when you're preparing to empty your pockets.

"I left my phone in the car charger. I'll see you in there." Then Kenny got out of line and went back out the doorway.

I walked through the metal detector, put the things in the basket back in my pockets, and grabbed my briefcase off the conveyor belt before heading up to Judge LaPlante's courtroom.

∼

Tiffany Erin stood. "Your Honor, the prosecution calls Kenneth Kaminski."

Kenny set his canvas coat on the bench in the gallery and made his way to the front. He must have hustled to his car and back because his face was red and he was sweating a little even though it was the middle of winter. I glanced at Rob and Rhonda as he passed. Rob's face was neutral, but Rhonda wasn't as successful hiding her feelings. She was clearly agitated with Kenny as he walked by and, considering that he was about to testify against her son, I couldn't really blame her.

Kenny sat down, straightened his suit coat, and nodded. Tiffany Erin waited, arms crossed, for him to get settled, then after he'd been sworn in and given his name and address, said, "What do you do, Mr. Kaminski?"

"I own Borderlands bar and restaurant. Actually, soon to be the chain of Borderlands bar and restaurants."

"Oh?"

"Yes. We're opening new locations in Ohio and Indiana."

"Congratulations."

"Thank you. We're pretty excited about it."

"Mr. Kaminski, have you known, excuse me, I should say *did* you know Brett Daniels for very long?"

"I sure did. Brett and I went back to high school. We knew each other, gosh, some twenty-five odd years."

"Does that mean that you know his boys, too?"

"Well, sure, Ms. Erin. I've been around Colt and Tyler since they were born."

"So I suppose we should explain a couple of things to the jury. You did not want to be here today, did you?"

"No offense to you, Ms. Erin, but I sure didn't."

"You refused to come voluntarily, is that right?"

"This isn't something I would volunteer to do, no."

"We subpoenaed you to come here, right?"

"If by subpoena me you mean you had the sheriff's department show up at 6:15 during a dinner rush and hand me a piece of paper ordering me to be here, then yes, Ms. Erin, you subpoenaed the heck out of me."

Tiffany Erin walked away from him, arms crossed, long fingers drumming in the crooks of her elbows. "Mr. Kaminski, I'm going to ask you an unusual question, but I think it's important for the jury to hear the answer."

Kenny cocked his head. "Shoot."

"You don't think Colton killed his dad, do you?"

"I sure don't, Ms. Erin. Colt would never do such a thing, and I don't think anyone who knows him thinks he would either."

"This is uncomfortable for you today, Mr. Kaminski?"

Kenny looked up and everything he was feeling was right there in the front of his eyes. "Yes, Ms. Erin. Yes, it sure is."

"We won't keep you long then. You mentioned you own the Borderlands Bar and Restaurant in Carrefour, Michigan, is that right?"

"Yes, it sure is."

"Colt Daniels and his father Brett had an altercation in your restaurant, didn't they?"

I stood. "Objection. Leading."

Judge LaPlante turned to Tiffany Erin. "You're entitled to a little leeway, Ms. Erin, but I think that's about all of it. See that you don't lead on the remainder of this topic."

Tiffany Erin nodded and said, "Do you remember my question?"

"I do. I don't know if I'd call it an altercation so much as a disagreement."

"I see. How long ago was this?"

"I don't remember exactly, almost two years ago, give or take."

"And what happened?"

"Well, Colt and his dad got in an argument after a game."

"Can you give us any more detail than that?"

Kenny looked from Erin to the judge then over to the jury before he said, "I'm afraid I really don't remember much more than that, Ms. Erin. It was a long time ago and I had a pretty full place that night."

"That's certainly understandable, Mr. Kaminski. I'm handing you what's been marked as State's Exhibit 51."

I stood. "Your Honor, we object on the basis of both hearsay and relevance of this incident."

"Your Honor," said Tiffany Erin, "we're referring the witness to his statement to refresh his recollection and do not intend to offer the document itself into evidence."

"Overruled. You may proceed, Ms. Erin."

Tiffany Erin stood a little closer to Kenny and pointed. "Is that your signature at the bottom of the page, Mr. Kaminski?"

"It is."

"Is that your handwriting here in this section?"

"It looks that way."

"Would you take a moment to read your description of the incident?"

"I sure will."

The clocks in the courtroom were digital so you couldn't hear the ticking of the secondhand, but you could hear every rustle and every shift and every movement as Kenny spent a minute reading over his statement. Eventually, he raised his head and said, "Okay."

"Mr. Kaminski, what did you see happen that night between Brett Daniels and his son Colton?"

"Well, it seems I saw them have a bit of a tussle."

"Mr. Kaminski, a tussle to me means a little pushing and shoving. You reported more than that to the officer, didn't you?"

"A bit."

"Were any punches thrown?"

"I don't believe any landed."

"That's not what I asked, Mr. Kaminski. I asked if any punches were thrown."

Kenny looked down. "Yes. Yes, there sure were."

"By whom?"

"By Colt."

"At whom?"

"At his dad."

"Did you know why?"

"I was just trying to break things up."

"And did you?"

"Eventually."

"What happened before you broke things up?"

"Well, the table got pushed to the side and the two of them sort of slammed against the wall on the way over…Well, before it broke up."

"Did they slam into something after the wall?"

Kenny looked down at the paper before he nodded and said, "Yes. Yes, they sure did."

"What?"

"One of our video games."

"What happened to the video game?"

Kenny looked at the jury before he looked back down the paper. "It got a bit nicked up."

Tiffany Erin turned to him and crossed her arms. Those long fingers began to drum again. "Mr. Kaminski, I am very aware that Brett Daniels was a friend of yours and that you've known Colton since he was a baby. But you are required to tell the truth. What happened to the video game?"

Kenny paused before he said, "It was broken."

"What was broken?"

"The glass screen and the components behind it."

"And what broke the glass screen and the components behind it?"

"Well, that would have been Colt's head."

"What happened?"

Kenny shifted in his seat. "Colt charged Brett and Brett took him by the shoulder and spun him around and put his head through a video game screen."

"Was Colton hurt?"

"No, he was fine."

"But it was serious enough that you called the police?"

"Well, I didn't. One of my girls did. I don't know that I would've since neither Colt nor Brett were hurt and boys will be boys and all."

"But you completed this report?"

"That's kind of embarrassing, Ms. Erin, but I knew the insurance company was going to require a police report to cover the damage to the video game, and I didn't want Brett to pay for it." He stared at the report. "I wish I hadn't now."

Tiffany Erin walked a little closer, fingers drumming. "Mr. Kaminski, I asked you what started the fight and you didn't really answer. Do you know?"

"I still think it was more of a scuffle than a fight."

"What started the scuffle, Mr. Kaminski?"

"Colt thought that Brett was being too hard on Tyler about how he'd played that night."

"You were a little more specific than that in your statement, weren't you?"

Kenny opened his mouth, closed it, then said, "See, me and Deputy Cordell thought it was funny. That's the only reason we put it in there, so we could bust Brett's chops about it."

Tiffany Erin's pale eyes didn't blink. "I like funny things, Mr. Kaminski. What did you report?"

Kenny looked at Erin, then at me, then the judge. He got

three blank stares in return before he said, "Colt told him that he—meaning Brett—couldn't throw a football fifty yards through a tire, let alone pick up a blitzing linebacker when he did it, so he could take his extra footwork drills and shove them up his, um, rear end."

"I see why you might think that's humorous, Mr. Kaminski. And did insurance cover the damage to the video game?"

"Mostly. Brett paid the difference. I told him how that wasn't necessary, but he insisted."

"Your friend Brett was a hard man, wasn't he?"

"He had his own way of looking at things."

"Was he hard on his boys?"

"He loved those boys more than anything. And he did what he thought was necessary to make them successful."

"Even though it was a little extreme?"

"I don't know that any real football family would think that, Ms. Erin."

Tiffany Erin nodded, arms still crossed, and wandered away from the jury. Then she went completely still. Her fingers stopped drumming, she stopped pacing, and she looked down at the floor in the middle of the courtroom. "That's not the only time you saw Colton and Brett fight, is it, Mr. Kaminski?"

I kept my face straight. I didn't know what she was talking about. I looked at Kenny and he didn't seem to know either. He shifted, looked around, and said, "Well, I sure can't think of another time, Ms. Erin."

"Are you certain?"

"Yes, ma'am. If they had another scuffle, I sure didn't see it."

Tiffany Erin raised her head and looked straight at Kenny. "What about after the Hamilton game last year?"

Kenny scowled for a moment. And then his face went white. He didn't speak.

"Were you at the Hamilton game last year, Mr. Kaminski?"

"I was." His voice barely registered on the microphone.

"Were you standing with Brett next to the visitors' locker room after the game?"

"I was."

"Did Brett talk to Tyler as he was coming off the field that night?"

"He did."

"What happened?"

Kenny glanced at the jury. "Tyler had a bad game. Brett talked to him about it."

"What did he say?"

"I don't know exactly. I was giving them some space."

"How long did they talk?"

"A while."

"How did it end?"

"When Coach Shepherd, Coach Tom Shepherd, came out of the locker room and told Tyler to join his team."

"Coach Tom Shepherd. Is that Nate Shepherd's brother?"

"It sure is."

I felt a momentary shift of the jury's attention to me and then back to Kenny.

"What happened once coach Tom Shepherd and Tyler went into the locker room?"

Kenny stared at her. "There was barely anyone at that game."

Tiffany Erin didn't blink. "What happened once coach Tom Shepherd and Tyler went back into the locker room?"

Kenny opened his mouth, closed it, then said, "Colt charged his dad."

"From behind?"

"Yes."

"He hit him with both forearms in the middle of his back?"

"Yes."

"Then what happened?"

"Brett spun him around a bit."

"He slammed Colton up against the cinderblock wall, didn't he?"

Kenny stared at her. Tiffany Erin stood there like a pale statue, waiting.

"Yes," Kenny said.

"Brett put his forearm against Colton's throat, didn't he?"

Kenny didn't say anything.

"Mr. Kaminski, Brett Daniels put his forearm against Colt Daniels' throat and pressed it against the wall, didn't he?"

"Yes, he did."

"What did Colton say?"

Kenny looked from Colt to Erin and back to Colt before he said, "He told Brett to back the 'f' off."

"And what did Brett say?"

"Brett said, 'Tyler isn't soft like you, he can take it.'"

"And then what did Brett say?"

Kenny cocked his head. Then his face went even whiter and this time he looked sick. He shook his head. "I don't remember."

Tiffany Erin stepped closer, her pale eyes implacable. "Brett Daniels dug his forearm into Colton's throat and said, 'the next time you come after me...'"

I stood. "Objection, Your Honor. Leading and prejudicial."

Tiffany Erin didn't take her eyes off Kenny. "Your Honor, this witness is a longtime family friend. He is clearly hostile. I'm entitled to a little latitude. I'm entitled to put this statement in front of him, and he can admit it or deny it before the Court on penalty of perjury."

Judge LaPlante looked at both of us, his black eyes intent. Finally, he said, "Given Mr. Kaminski's relationship, I will allow a leading question on this statement. But then the answer is the answer, Ms. Erin."

Tiffany Erin stepped closer until she stood directly in front of Kenny. "Mr. Kaminski, after Colton pushed him, Brett Daniels spun Colton into the locker room wall and put his forearm across Colton's throat, Colton told Brett to back the 'f' off and Brett said, 'he's not soft like you, he can take it.' Do we agree that is your testimony?"

"It is."

"And do you remember what Brett Daniels said next?"

"I do not."

Tiffany Erin didn't take her eyes off Kenny. "Brett Daniels then said to Colton, 'You're 0 for 2. The next time you come after me, you better bring a gun.' That's what he said, isn't it?"

Kenny stared at her. "How do you know this?"

"That's not an answer, Mr. Kaminski. Did Brett Daniels say to Colt that 'The next time you come after me, you better bring a gun'?"

There was a long pause and for a moment I thought that Kenny wasn't going to answer. Then he said, "Yes." Kenny lowered his head and whispered. "Yes, he sure did."

51

I leaned over next to Colt so that I blocked the jury's view of him. He was shaking. I put one hand on the back of his chair and said, "Don't move your head. Is that true?"

To his credit, Colt stared straight ahead and, without moving his lips, said, "Yes."

I stood. I passed Tiffany Erin who kept a perfectly straight face as if she hadn't just knifed my case like an assassin.

Kenny had testified about two incidents where he'd seen Colt attack his dad, both of which appeared to be true. It didn't leave me much to work with.

"Mr. Kaminski, you said at the very beginning of your testimony that you didn't believe Colt Daniels killed his father. Do you still believe that?"

"Yes, yes I sure do. Colt's a good boy. There's no way he did it."

"From your perspective, did Brett and Colt have a good relationship?"

"They had a great relationship. They hunted, fished, worked out together, well, I can't tell you how many times. Brett loved those boys."

False Oath

"What about those scuffles you witnessed? Don't they change your opinion?"

"No, no they sure don't. I've seen a lot worse than that between fathers or brothers at my bar, where they scrap a bit and then buy each other beers after."

"Ms. Erin asked you about two incidents between Colt and his dad. Were you worried for the safety of either of them at any time?"

Kenny smiled. "No. I really don't think that either of those 'incidents,' like you called them, mattered at all. In my experience, boys will be boys and this kind of thing just comes with the territory, especially with football types."

"You didn't see anything in either of those encounters that concerned you?"

"No, Mr. Shepherd, I really didn't."

"Even when they broke your video game screen?"

Kenny smiled and waved. "Like I said, insurance covered all of that. I run a cash business that closes at two in the morning so I have bigger worries than a couple of guys roughhousing, believe me."

"And when they were roughhousing, Brett got the better of Colt both times, didn't he?"

"He sure did. It was more like a pup barking at the big dog, you know?"

"Do you know, Mr. Kaminski, that Ms. Erin has shown the jury pictures of Colt going to and from the hunting platform that night with a crossbow?"

"Yes, I sure do."

"That doesn't change your mind about Colt?"

"Of course not."

"Why?"

"What else would you take to a hunting platform except something to hunt with? Besides, you'd have to be pretty stupid to waltz right by a camera on your way to kill someone."

And that was it. I didn't have anything else. Tiffany Erin had called Kenny to testify about two incidents where Colt had attacked his father, both of which were true. He couldn't offer any more than general platitudes that he didn't believe that his best friend's boy had killed his best friend, and I'd pushed that about as far as I could, which meant I needed to get Kenny off the stand and not give Erin too much to rehash.

"That's all I have, Mr. Kaminski. Thank you."

Tiffany Erin stood. "Mr. Kaminski, you filed a claim for a little over three thousand dollars to have the screen replaced on that video game, didn't you?"

"I did."

"That's more than just a little damage, isn't it?"

Kenny waved. "Those screens are special glass. They know they have you by the bal—well, they have you in a tight spot, so they charge the heck out of you. It was just a two-by-two piece of glass. If it had been in a door, it would have cost fifty bucks."

"Mr. Kaminski, you did not see Colton and Brett Daniels the night that Brett Daniels was killed, did you?"

"No, no I sure didn't."

"So you didn't see what happened between Colton and his dad that night, did you?"

"I didn't have to see it. I know that Colt would not hurt his dad." Kenny nodded his head for emphasis.

"That's not true, Mr. Kaminski. You've seen Colton attack his dad twice."

"Like I said, Ms. Erin, I view that more as horseplay than attacking."

"Does horseplay usually end with someone telling a person to bring a gun next time?"

"People say all sorts of things when they're mad, Ms. Erin."

"The fact remains that Brett Daniels challenged his son to bring a gun if he was going to attack him again, didn't he?"

"That is what he said."

"Brett Daniels is dead, isn't he?"

Kenny looked around. "Do I really have to answer that?"

"Yes, you really do."

"Yes. My best friend, Brett Daniels is dead. And I don't think his son killed him."

"That's all I have Mr. Kaminski. Thank you."

I was not to get a better answer than the last one he gave. I stood and said, "No further questions, Your Honor."

Judge LaPlante nodded and dismissed Kenny. As he walked off the stand, Kenny swerved at the last moment and, before Tiffany Erin could say anything, put his hand on Colt's shoulder and squeezed. Colt looked up at him and nodded and then Kenny hustled out the door.

I wasn't sure if that helped or hurt.

"Members of the jury," said Judge LaPlante, "that concludes our proceedings this morning. Every week I have to spend an afternoon on criminal matters and Wednesday afternoons are my time to do that, so I will be dismissing you early today. You are reminded not to discuss this case with anyone else and not to begin deliberations with each other until all the evidence has been submitted. I also remind you to stay off social media and not to read anything that you find there, none of which is evidence that can form the basis of your decision. I will see you tomorrow morning at 8:30."

After the jury filed out, Judge LaPlante said, "How far are you from being finished, Ms. Erin?"

"I think I'll need a little part of Thursday morning, Your Honor, and then we should be done."

"And how about you, Mr. Shepherd?"

"Depending on what the State does, I may be done by midday Friday, Your Honor."

"All right. Let's see if we can get this done this week. I'll see you both Thursday morning."

Judge LaPlante rose and left.

Tiffany Erin turned towards me. Normally, there's a lot of conversation between the lawyers in between sessions, but she had kept it to a bare minimum, so this caught my attention.

"He didn't tell you about the other fight, did he?"

I shrugged. "It didn't sound like a fight."

Tiffany Erin's pale eyes were focused on me, which hadn't happened more than a handful of times. "Describe it however you want. Brett Daniels invited exactly what happened. And the jury could see it."

"Yeah, it sounds like Brett was a real prince."

This was normally where the prosecutor would offer some kind of deal. Not a great one, but a deal nonetheless. Instead though, Tiffany Erin just turned back to her table and collected her things.

Turns out, she was just gloating.

"Let's head on back," I said to Danny. I realized Colt was still standing there. "That's right, you need a ride back to your place, don't you?"

Colt nodded. "The signing is this afternoon."

"I can take him," said Danny.

"No, I'll do it. Colt and I can talk a little, and I want to clear my head before we get back to work."

Danny nodded, the two of us divvied up our stuff to take home, and we left.

∽

COLT WAS quiet for the first part of the ride before he said, "Did we just lose?"

"No. But it definitely made it harder."

"I didn't even think of it, Nate."

I wanted to rail at him, to scold him, to tell him that he might've screwed himself more thoroughly than Tiffany Erin ever could have but that wouldn't help. And the fact is, there was plenty of blame to go around—if Tiffany Erin had found it, I should've too.

"All we can do is move forward, Colt. First, were there any other fights between you and your dad? Any at all?"

Colt shook his head. "That's it."

"And Erin was right? Your dad really said, 'The next time you come after me you better bring a gun?'"

"Pretty much."

I had planned on ignoring whatever had happened back at the house the rest of Thursday night because it seemed like there was more risk than reward there. Now though, I felt like I might need any evidence I could pull together.

"So after you went back to the house that night, you went to your room and worked on your paper?"

"That's right."

"And you didn't hear anything? No coyotes, no calls, no gunshots?"

"No."

"Nothing?"

"I had earbuds in most of the time."

As I turned down M-339, I thought about the picture I could paint of that night. There was no way I could put Colt on the stand—the best case scenario was that he would admit that he had shot the crossbow at his dad and missed. Tiffany Erin would destroy him. But if I had someone else confirm that they didn't hear anything that night, or that they saw Colt a few times when they got a pop or went to the bathroom or let the dog out, or even that he seemed calm and wasn't upset, that would be something."

"I'm going to have to call Tyler."

Colt's head whipped around. "Why would you do that?"

I shrugged. "I have to have someone testify that you were acting normally in the house that night. And that he didn't hear anything unusual either."

"But Tyler's signing his letter of intent today! Don't pull him into this."

"He's already in it."

"They took our statements. Can't you just read those?"

"Not exactly. Besides, it will be more effective coming directly from him."

"Nate, we—he—has been working for this since we were kids. You're going to screw it up."

"Colt, if he doesn't testify, you might go to jail for the rest of your life."

"If he does testify, I might go to jail for the rest of my life, right? Right?"

"Of course, but it's about doing all we can to stop that."

"So stop it! Get your evidence some other way besides Tyler."

"There isn't another way. You and Tyler were the only ones there."

"So find one! I thought you're supposed to be some great lawyer."

That about tore it for me. "I'm the one who has your back, Colt. Me. It's us, you and me, v. all. You need to listen to me."

"Us v. all, my ass, Nate, I'm the one with my hand in the wolf's mouth, not you!"

I whipped into his driveway and slammed on the brakes. "Tell me you're not that stupid."

"What?"

"Tell me you're not trying to keep Tyler from testifying because of some stupid high school tradition."

Colt's eyes were focused and angry. "I don't know what you're talking about."

"I played for Carrefour North, Colt! I know the War Oath. I took it before it was illegal. Tell me that's not why you're trying to keep Tyler off the stand."

Colt still looked furious but backed off a notch. "No. That's not it."

Another thought hit me. "Jesus, don't tell me that my brother had you do it."

"No, no, Coach Shepherd had no idea." Colt stopped.

"So, you *did* do it."

Colt looked away.

"How long? How long has this been going on again?"

Colt shrugged. "Some of the upperclassman had heard about it from their dads my sophomore year."

"Five years? You guys have been doing this again for five years?"

Colt shrugged again.

I put aside my fear for my brother's job and focused on the problem in front of me. "That tradition has nothing to do with your current problem, which is going to jail for the rest of your life for killing your dad."

"I didn't kill my dad."

"I have twelve jurors right now that aren't so sure. I need to put your brother on the stand to show you were acting normally at home the night your dad was killed. We're not keeping Tyler off the stand because you made a high school promise to have his back."

Colt turned back to the two-track drive. "I didn't see Tyler that night after I came back to the house."

"Oh, come on."

He shrugged. "I already told you, we were both studying in our rooms."

"You had to have gone to the bathroom or gotten something to eat or grabbed a drink."

"We did not see each other."

"Who let the dog out?"

"What?"

"Chet. He had to have gone out to pee. Who let him out?"

Colt paused before he said, "I did."

"Bullshit."

"I did."

"Convenient."

"It's the truth."

I stared at him for a moment then idled my Jeep up the two-track driveway to the old metal-roofed house. I put it in park, reined in my temper, and said, "Why are you fighting this? Tyler will want to help you."

Colt shook his head. "My father was a prick, Nate. But all of that is about to pay off for Tyler. We can't screw it up."

"How could Tyler testifying for his brother screw it up?"

"It's the wrong kind of attention. If pictures go out of him in court, then he's always the guy on the stand at his father's murder trial."

"And if his brother is acquitted, that's a lot better, isn't it?"

Colt shook his head. "No one wants to be associated with that. You just can't do it."

"Colt, I have to protect you from—"

Colt's eyes flared. "Us v. all isn't you and me, Nate. It's me and Tyler. We don't have anyone else. And you're not pulling him down with me!"

I stared at him and saw the guy who smashed the truck. Who charged his dad. Who shot the crossbow. I decided there was no reasoning with that man. "Get out, Colt. I have work to do."

Just like that, the anger was gone. Colt leaned away, then popped the door. He didn't look back as he climbed the two concrete stairs and opened the white metal storm door. Chet came barreling out, ran a quick circle, then presented himself for an ear scratching. Colt obliged then went inside. Chet followed.

I left.

∼

DECADES AGO, hazing was part of football. Every program had something, some tradition that the upperclassmen kept secret from the underclassmen that usually involved fear and a joke. If you ask enough people who played in a certain era, you'll hear stories about senior hit days or flame jumps or some such thing that involved scaring the bejesus out of the freshmen and then joking with them afterwards.

At Carrefour North, that tradition had been the War Oath.

On the last night of training camp, all the freshmen were taken to an upperclassman's house, preferably a farm. There was always a dog—a Pit Bull or a German Shepherd or a Doberman, chained outside frothing and barking like a lunatic. After a cookout to celebrate the end of summer practice and the beginning of the season, the senior captains, in suitably solemn tones, told the freshmen the story of Tyr, the Norse God of War, who helped the gods trap Fenris Wolf. The story goes that the gods wanted to put a chain around Fenris Wolf's neck. Fenris Wolf was understandably skeptical so Tyr volunteered to put his hand in the wolf's mouth as security for the gods taking the chain back off again. So Tyr put his hand in the wolf's mouth, the wolf let the gods put the chain around his neck, and the gods decided that Tyr's hand was a small price to pay for keeping the monstrous wolf chained until the end of time. The now one-handed god of war became a symbol of courage, self-sacrifice for the greater good, and keeping your word.

About that time, a dog would start barking and everyone would remember the fearsome dog chained out front. Then the seniors would say that it was time for the freshmen to take the War Oath, the oath all North football players shared, to guard each other's backs, to always stand together against everyone for each other. And, in the tradition of Tyr, they'd do it with their hand in the wolf's mouth, so to speak.

The freshmen were then taken, one by one, into the barn to stick their hand through the hole in the wall into the dog's mouth as they recited a simple oath, the War Oath: "Back-to-back. Us v. all. Or the wolf take my hand."

You can imagine the reactions—fear, nonchalance, crying, cursing—you name it. As a freshman, you knew they were joking, you were pretty sure they were joking, but man, they seemed awfully serious, but I'll be damned if I'm going to punk out so my hand is going through the hole and holy shit I feel breath and teeth and a tongue and the wolf has my hand, no it's not a wolf it's that crazy ass dog so I better get through this oath —there, it's done, my hand is out and everyone is laughing and some other senior comes around with some little ass chihuahua or a bichon or a lab that's been trained to hold birds gently in its mouth from the time he was a pup. And everyone laughs and you curse them out, but you laugh too and sometimes the seniors will encourage you to scream as loud as you can just to screw with the next guy waiting outside.

Tom was older than me when I did it. He never spilled a word about what was going to happen.

It sounds corny, and it is, from the outside. But those kinds of things went on for decades in high school and college programs.

A few years after I graduated, a kid got really upset and I couldn't blame him. This was right around the time that hazing was being outlawed in high schools and, when the War Oath tradition came to light, it was outlawed too. I know Tom gave a speech every year forbidding hazing, talked to the kids about taking care of their teammates instead, about protecting each other, about all of the sentiments of the War Oath without the dog-induced fear and abuse. I thought he'd been successful in eradicating it.

Apparently not.

As I drove back, I didn't think that Colt was letting the Oath affect his thinking with Tyler, but the words had flowed out so easily, so reflexively, that it sure seemed like it. And with two boys who had been so thoroughly inculcated in football from the time they were small, I couldn't discount the fact that this silly revived tradition might be skewing Colt's thinking.

But the more I thought about it, the more I thought that there was no reason why Tyler shouldn't be called to the stand. The headlines were already out there. No one could be surprised if Tyler was called, especially if his testimony was harmless alibi testimony that showed his brother was in the house, studying.

Tyler had told the police that, after dinner, he'd gone to his room to watch film and that, as far as he knew, Colt had gone to his room to finish his paper. He didn't report seeing or hearing anything unusual that night in his room or when he'd left the next morning to go to school.

I didn't see how I could get that evidence in any other way. Which meant I had no choice.

I would have to put Tyler on the stand regardless of what Colt thought.

52

As I walked into the office, I saw that I'd missed a call from Olivia. I redialed her.

"Eventful day, huh?" she said.

"I've had better. How do you know?"

"You haven't checked Alexis Fury, have you?"

"I've been a little busy."

"Let's just say there's been a lot of retweeting of a meme that says, 'Next time you better bring a gun,' then a picture of Colt holding the crossbow and the words 'Will this do?'"

I swore. A lot.

"So, how is it going?" she said.

"About that good."

"Do you need anything?"

"Not at the moment. I'll text you if something comes up."

"I'm here. Keep fighting."

"Thanks, Liv."

Danny waited by the door until I was done, then came in and sat down. "That was bad today."

"It was. I want you to write a limiting instruction for the

judge to read to the jury, the one about not considering evidence of past acts."

"Doesn't it go to motive?"

"That's what Erin will argue, but let's give it a try."

"Done. Anything else?"

"Just go through the testimony from yesterday and make sure Erin established a chain of custody for everything. I think she did, but let's double check against the transcript."

"Okay."

"What do you think about putting Tyler on the stand?"

Danny cocked his head. "To establish that Colt was in the house and that it was quiet?"

I nodded.

"He didn't see much. I suppose it might help a little."

"I'm trying to think of the downside."

"It would let Erin go through the prior incidents with his dad and Colt again. And I suppose we'd both bring up testimony about his dad being hard on him."

I nodded. "I'm not sure which way that cuts, whether it will create sympathy for Colt or a motive."

"And of course we could have the same problem we had today."

"What's that?"

"He might say something we don't expect that makes things a lot worse."

I sighed. "We're on the same page. We may have to do it, but let's see how Gerchuk and the trajectory expert do first."

"To see if they get your point across?"

"I see what you did there."

"Thought it was worth a shot."

"Go away."

Danny and I got back to work.

∽

THERE ARE ALWAYS MORE things to do than time to do them during a trial. An afternoon off like this was a gift, so I spent most of it working on my examinations of the witnesses I was going to call the next day. It barely registered with me that it was 5:30 p.m. when my phone buzzed from a Lansing number. I didn't recognize it so I turfed it. The voicemail popped up a minute later, so I listened.

"Nate, this is Megan Dira from the Public Integrity Unit. I'm calling to let you know that we will be reissuing our subpoena for Colton. We will still be looking for information on Steve Mathison, but we've added another name and want to know about Jimmy Benoit, too. I know you're in trial right now so we are requesting the information by the end of next week. Thank you."

The woman never stopped. I would have to move to quash the subpoena just like the last one, but later. I shot a quick text to Olivia asking her to research Jimmy Benoit the same way she had looked up Mathison, so I knew what we were dealing with and then went back to work.

∽

IT WAS ten o'clock that night when my phone buzzed. Olivia.

"Are you still at the office?"

"I am."

"Good. I'm sending you something." I heard a couple of clicks in the background. "There, you should have it in a second."

"What's up?"

"Jimmy Benoit is another marketing guy with murky responsibilities."

"What do you mean?"

The email from Olivia came in and I opened the attachment, which was a series of screenshots showing Jimmy Benoit's social media pages.

"Do you have it?"

"Just opened it. So, he's a one-man marketing firm with a supposed client list involving massive companies that use international firms for their marketing campaigns?"

"Bingo. Does he look like anyone to you?"

Jimmy Benoit looked to be in his early forties with square black glasses and overly moussed hair. "I don't think I've seen him before, no."

"No, not what he physically looks like. What he does."

My mind was on leg wounds and arrow trajectory so it took me longer than it should have to make the connection. "He looks like he's in the same business as Steve Mathison."

"Exactly."

"Whatever the hell that is."

"Right. And I'll save you the trouble of figuring out the next one."

"I'm hurt."

"I can hear the mush sloshing around in your head from here. Benoit has the same kinds of clients as Mathison but not the same clients."

"What do you mean?"

"It's pretty heavy on apparel, shoes, and sports drinks."

"But different brands?"

"Exactly."

"So they're competitors?"

"They certainly seem to work for competing companies."

"But competitors for what?"

"His social media looks a lot like Mathison's. Mostly pictures at events with recruits but not linked to any particular school."

"And Megan Dira wants information about whether the Daniels family has any connection with either of them. So it's got to be related to Tyler right?"

"Which brings me to my last bit. Scroll all the way to the bottom."

I did. "What am I looking for?"

"The likes on Jimmy Benoit's Twitter feed from this afternoon."

Jimmy Benoit had liked a bunch of signing day tweets—tweets of players announcing their choice of schools, of universities welcoming players, of parents humbly thankful for blessings, and of coaches ready to get things rolling. Right in the middle of them was a cluster related to Tyler—one from his own account announcing his decision, one from the school he'd picked, and then a whole series of congratulations from Carrefour North High School, the Panther athletic department, the boosters club, and all sorts of friends and family and organizations, including the Borderlands bar and restaurant account.

"Sure looks like he was tapped into Tyler's announcement today," I said.

"It sure does."

"So why would the Michigan Public Integrity Unit care? Tyler didn't pick a Michigan school."

"That's why they pay you the big bucks. I just deliver the information."

"Thanks, Liv. Have I mentioned you're extraordinary?

"Not often enough. Get some sleep."

After we hung up, I went back to leg wounds and arrow trajectories and didn't think about Megan Dira for another day.

53

Tiffany Erin finished her case on the morning of the fourth day of trial. She put on two more witnesses to establish the evidentiary foundation of the pictures and the arrow, giving her one more chance to show both things to the jury. Then she rested.

I moved to dismiss the case and to his credit, Judge LaPlante actually seemed attentive as he listened. The moment I finished though, without even taking any comment from Tiffany Erin, he denied my motion and asked if I was ready to proceed with my first witness. I said I was and called Dr. Ray Gerchuk.

Even on a dreary winter day, Dr. Gerchuk had a spring in his step as he made his way to the stand. His blond hair was freshly cut, his skin had a hint of tan that suggested a holiday vacation, and he smiled as he sat.

"Dr. Gerchuk, could you tell the jury what you do please?"

"I am a forensic pathologist. I'm the coroner for Carrefour, Ohio."

"I see. And have you performed autopsies?"

"Thousands, yes."

"Dr. Warren Archuleta performed the autopsy in this case. Do you know him?"

"I do."

"What is his reputation as a coroner?"

"That he is very well educated and maintains a busy practice."

"Did you review his autopsy report in this case? "

"I did."

"What is your understanding of Dr. Archuleta's findings?"

"Dr. Archuleta described a lacerated femoral artery that resulted in Mr. Daniels bleeding to death."

"Do you agree with that finding?

"I agree that there was a lacerated femoral artery, yes. I also agree that a laceration of the size Dr. Archuleta described in the location he described would have caused Mr. Daniels' death."

"Were there findings you disagreed with? "

"Yes."

"What were those?"

"It was one primarily. I disagree with Dr. Archuleta's opinion on the mechanism that caused the laceration. According to Dr. Archuleta, it was a crossbow arrow."

"And you disagree with that opinion?"

"I think the more accurate way to say it is that I don't believe there was any evidence to support Dr. Archuleta's conclusion."

"I am afraid that I don't understand the distinction, Doctor."

Dr. Gerchuk smiled and looked at the jury. "Dr. Archuleta's report conclusively established that there was a laceration of the femoral artery. He described it, he measured it, and he documented the basis for his conclusion that Mr. Daniels bled to death from that wound. However, there was no scientific basis in his report for his conclusion that the laceration was caused by a crossbow arrow."

"But Doctor, they found a crossbow arrow near the hunting platform, didn't they?"

"Yes. But that doesn't mean the arrow caused the injury.

What I'm saying is that there was nothing done in the autopsy itself that demonstrated that the wound was inflicted by the arrow."

"Well, let's start with the obvious question then—can something besides an arrow cause a wound like the one in Brett Daniels' leg?"

"Absolutely. The entry and exit wounds such as the one Mr. Daniels sustained here can be caused by a variety of projectiles including an arrow, a bullet, or a pellet. All of these things can cause similar wounds."

"Of the same size and shape?"

"Yes. And with the same markings."

"So the wound alone does not support a finding that the injury was caused by an arrow?"

"The wound itself just indicates that it could have been caused by several things, one of which was a field point arrow."

"Doctor, are you suggesting that a pathologist can mistake a bullet wound for an arrow wound? Those seem awfully different."

"A broad point arrow makes a very different wound than a bullet. However, a field point arrow, like the one supposedly used here, creates a bore that is very similar to a bullet hole. To the naked eye, they can be very difficult to tell apart."

"Really, Dr. Gerchuk? Could a pathologist really mistake a bullet wound for an arrow wound?"

Dr. Gerchuk nodded. "It's documented in the literature. There have been several studies where people or animals were killed and law enforcement was unable to tell if it was a bullet wound or a crossbow wound. It was only through a microscopic examination and additional testing that the distinction was made."

"So there are tests that can narrow this down?"

"Yes. And Dr. Archuleta didn't perform any of them."

"Could you give me an example, please?"

"Sure. If you're going to eliminate a bullet as the cause of a wound, you need to perform a sodium rhodizonate test on the tissue."

"What is the sodium rhodizonate test?"

"The sodium rhodizonate test detects the presence of lead residue in the wound that is left by a bullet."

"Does an arrow leave this residue?"

"No. Arrows like the one found at the site here are made of carbon. The results of a sodium rhodizonate test would have given Dr. Archuleta, and us, a good indication whether it was one or the other."

"You also mentioned a microscopic investigation?"

"Yes. The pathologist looks for barreling or striations in the wound microscopically that would indicate to you that it came from a bullet as opposed to the smooth puncturing of a field point arrow."

"Dr. Gerchuk, are you suggesting that Dr. Archuleta wasn't able to tell the difference between the two when he performed his microscopic examination?"

"No. I'm certain he could have *if* he had done it. However, there was no indication in his autopsy that he examined the wound striations microscopically or that he performed the test I described."

"Why do you think that is, Doctor?"

Tiffany Erin stood. "Objection. Dr. Gerchuk does not know what Dr. Archuleta was thinking."

"Sustained," said Judge LaPlante.

"Dr. Gerchuk, as a forensic pathologist, do you sometimes get information from the police department regarding the manner in which a body was found before you perform the autopsy?"

Tiffany Erin stood. "Objection. Relevance."

"Sustained," said Judge LaPlante.

"Dr. Gerchuk, did the autopsy report indicate that the crossbow arrow was provided to Dr. Archuleta prior to his examination?"

"Yes."

"Dr. Gerchuk, in your experience as a forensic pathologist, can having a proposed murder weapon influence an investigation?"

Tiffany Erin stood. "Objection."

Judge LaPlante thought. "Overruled."

"Certainly," said Dr. Gerchuk. "We often are asked to attempt to match wounds to weapons."

"So here we know that Dr. Archuleta was provided with the arrow prior to his examination, true?"

"That's true."

"And you can find no evidence that Dr. Archuleta performed any testing, at all, to determine whether the wound was made by a bullet?"

"No such test was performed."

"As a result, can a bullet be eliminated as the cause of Brett Daniels' death?"

"No, it cannot."

"So do you have an opinion as to what caused the laceration of Mr. Daniels' femoral artery?"

"It's my opinion that the wound was caused by a bullet or an arrow. And that no one can have an opinion to a reasonable degree of medical certainty which one it was."

"Why is that?"

"Because no testing was performed to determine whether it was one or the other. Therefore, anyone who says they know what caused the wound is guessing."

"Dr. Gerchuk, I'd like to switch gears for a moment to one other issue."

"Sure."

"You've read the description of the size of the laceration in Mr. Daniels' femoral artery?"

"I did."

"Do you agree that this laceration caused him to bleed to death?"

"I do. It was sizable."

"Doctor, given the size of the laceration, is it possible for you to estimate the amount of time it would've taken Mr. Daniels to bleed to death?"

"Within a broad range, yes."

"And what is that estimate, Doctor?"

"I would estimate that with a laceration of the size described, Mr. Daniels would have bled to death in four to ten minutes."

"Doctor, with a wound of that sort, would Mr. Daniels have been able to climb down the platform ladder?"

"It appears that he did and that is not surprising. There was very little muscle damage that would have prevented him from walking."

"And would he have been able to run?"

"At the beginning. Until he was overcome from blood loss."

"But the wound itself would not have prevented him from running?"

"No. It would've been the blood loss which did that eventually."

"Doctor, I want you to assume that Mr. Daniels was about a quarter of a mile from the platform when he passed. Would he have been able to cover that distance with his wound?"

"It sounds to me as if he did. That does not surprise me."

"That's all the questions I have, Doctor. Thank you."

Tiffany Erin was on her feet and visibly reining herself in as she waited for me to pass by her table. As soon as I did, she strode forward and said, "Dr. Gerchuk, are you seriously asking the jury to believe that a bullet killed Brett Daniels?"

"That's not what I said, Ms. Erin. I said that no one can say whether a bullet or an arrow killed Mr. Daniels, including your expert."

"Dr. Archuleta is a county employee, not my expert."

"I apologize, Ms. Erin. I thought you called him as a witness to support your case."

"I did. As an independent examiner."

"I see. Then what I'm saying is that no one, including the independent examiner you called to support your case, can say whether a bullet or an arrow killed Mr. Daniels because the proper testing wasn't done to determine that fact."

"Dr. Gerchuk, you're aware that an arrow was found at the scene, aren't you?"

"I am."

"A bullet wasn't found at the scene, was it?"

"I don't believe anyone looked for one, Ms. Erin."

"No bullet was found, was it?"

"To my knowledge, there wasn't a bullet lying there in plain view of the investigating officers to see the same way the arrow was, no."

"That's right. But an arrow was found at the scene that Dr. Archuleta, the examining pathologist, determined was the cause of Brett Daniels' wound."

"An arrow was found at the scene, which Dr. Archuleta speculated was the cause of Brett Daniels' wound."

"Dr. Gerchuk, you didn't examine Brett Daniels' body in this case, did you?"

"I did not."

"You would agree with me that, as the examining pathologist, Dr. Archuleta was in the best position to inspect Mr. Daniels wound, wasn't he?"

"He was. I wish he had."

"He certainly had a better view of the wound than someone like yourself who examined his report later, true?"

"That's true."

"So Dr. Archuleta was in the best position to determine the cause of that wound, wasn't he?"

"He would've been if he'd performed the sodium rhodizonate test. But since he didn't, he's guessing."

"He's not guessing. Dr. Archuleta examined the wound and made a determination."

"Without doing the proper tests, he can't eliminate any cause of the wound, so he is guessing."

"And his 'guess'"—she gestured the air quotes—"correlates with the arrow that was found on the scene, doesn't it?"

Dr. Gerchuk smiled. "Correlation doesn't equal causation, Ms. Erin. You know that."

Tiffany Erin smiled tightly. "We can agree though that whatever caused the wound caused Mr. Daniels' death, right?"

Dr. Gerchuk nodded. "That's right."

"Are you aware that there is a picture of Colton Daniels carrying a crossbow out to the platform on the night Mr. Daniels died?"

"I am."

She popped the picture up on the screen of Colt walking with the crossbow in front of him, took a laser pointer, and circled the portion of the arrow that was visible. "Dr. Gerchuk, do you see this arrow that was in Colton Daniels' crossbow the night of the killing?"

"I do."

"As you sit here today, you can't state that this arrow did *not* cause Mr. Daniels' death, can you?"

"No, Ms. Erin, as I mentioned, no one can say whether that arrow or a bullet caused Mr. Daniels' wound."

"Dr. Gerchuk, are you aware of any pictures of a gun from that night?"

"I am not."

"Are you aware of any pictures of a bullet from that night?"

"I am not but, as I mentioned, that's not relevant to the physical findings."

"Right. You don't believe it's relevant that this arrow that was fired by Colton Daniels was found in the area surrounding the platform, do you?"

"No, I do not. That chance recovery doesn't establish the cause of the wound."

"I see. You mentioned that Dr. Archuleta was my expert, do you remember that?"

"I do."

"I didn't pay Dr. Archuleta to testify at this trial. You're being paid aren't you, Dr. Gerchuk?"

"I am."

"Mr. Shepherd's firm is paying you to testify today?"

"He is."

"He's paying you five thousand dollars for half a day of testimony, isn't he?"

"That's my rate. Would you like to know where it goes?"

"It's enough to know that it goes to you, Doctor, thank you. No further questions, Your Honor."

Tiffany Erin had remained cool and professional throughout her exam but, having seen her the previous weeks, I could tell she was angry. I let her pass, picked up Colt's arrow, and stood in front of the jury.

"Dr. Gerchuk, you mentioned that you don't think it's relevant that this arrow was found in the area surrounding the platform, do you remember that?"

"I do."

"Why not?"

"The fact that the arrow, the one you're holding, was found in the woods that night doesn't mean that it was shot through Brett Daniels' thigh."

"But it makes it more likely, doesn't it?"

"No."

"How can you say that?"

"Well, for one, a second arrow was found out there, too."

I went over to the evidence table and picked up the broadhead that Brett Daniels had shot into the ground that night. "You mean this one?"

"Yes. And that arrow was right next to the platform. Using the prosecution's logic, we could conclude that this arrow was used to kill Brett Daniels because it was nearby. But we know that's not true because the physical facts say otherwise, the broadhead would have caused a different kind of injury. The fact that it was near the platform means nothing."

I held up Colt's arrow. "But this arrow could have caused the wound."

"Yes, it could have. And so could a bullet. And because no one did a proper test, we can't know which. Again, I'm not saying that the arrow didn't cause the wound. I'm saying that no one can say definitively that it did. And certainly not because it was found in the area."

"Thank you, Doctor." I put the two arrows down on the evidence table and was walking back to my seat when I stopped and said, "I did pay you for your professional time to be here today, Dr. Gerchuk. Ms. Erin wasn't interested in hearing where that money goes. Would you like to mention it?"

Dr. Gerchuk smiled. "I would. My wife and I set up an endowment some years ago for a summer science camp program at LGL University. It's a weeklong program for kids who don't have access to certain advanced science programs in their schools. Any money that I make from testifying as an expert goes to that."

"So that's why the check is made out to the Summer Learning Fund?"

"That's right."

"Thanks, Dr. Gerchuk."

Tiffany Erin stood. "There are two arrows on that table, right, Dr. Gerchuk?"

"There are."

"There are no bullets there?"

"I don't believe law enforcement found one, no."

"There is a picture of Colt Daniels holding his crossbow near the platform, right?"

"That's what you showed me."

"There is no picture of anyone with a gun, is there?"

"Not that I'm aware of."

"And an arrow that could have caused the wound was found at the scene, right?"

"Yes, the arrow found farthest away from the platform could have caused Mr. Daniels' wound but we'll never know if it did."

"No bullet was found at the scene?"

"No."

"Or gun?"

"That's right."

Tiffany Erin crossed her arms and drummed her fingers. "You mentioned the saying a little bit ago that correlation does not equal causation. Do you remember that?"

"I do."

"Have you ever heard the saying 'if you hear hoof beats think horses not zebras?'"

Dr. Gerchuk smiled. "I have."

"It means the simplest solution is usually the best one, doesn't it?"

"It does. But, if you're in the middle of the Serengeti, you should at least look for stripes."

Tiffany Erin went over and picked up the arrow. "This is the simplest answer, isn't it?"

"It would've been a simple yes or no. If Dr. Archuleta had done his job."

Tiffany Erin paused, and she could see the same thing I did: the jury was getting tired of this circular argument. To her credit, she set the arrow down, and nodded and said, "No further questions, Your Honor."

Judge LaPlante dismissed Dr. Gerchuk, who nodded to me as he left. I didn't have much time to think about it as the judge said, "Will you be calling another witness, Mr. Shepherd?"

"Yes, Your Honor. The defense calls Mr. Edgar Spright."

54

Edgar Spright was a small, spare man in his early sixties whose brisk, clipped steps made it look like he was race-walking to the stand. He had white hair loosely combed over to the side and energetic blue eyes that lit up as he sat down and leaned forward to grab the rail in front of the witness chair with clear eagerness to get things rolling.

"Could you state your name for the jury please, sir?"

"Certainly. My name is Edgar Spright."

"And what do you do for a living, Mr. Spright?"

"I began my career as a mechanical engineer, but I've always been fascinated by mathematical and mechanical problems, especially those that aren't entirely clear and require some investigation, so I eventually branched out from my day job as an auto design engineer into an accident reconstructionist."

"What is an accident reconstructionist?"

"It's someone who goes in after the fact and determines how an accident happened based on factors and variables that are known from the evidence."

"Do you recreate auto accidents?"

"That's certainly the most common use for my services. In

those circumstances, we evaluate things like angles, lengths of the skid marks, rates of speed, and impact evidence to determine the order of events leading up to the accident. However, our discipline can be applied to any number of situations. All that's required are some landmarks or known variables and then the math does the rest of the work."

"Are there certifications involved in order to become an accident reconstructionist?"

"For the reputable ones there certainly are. It requires an underlying background, through education or experience, in working with the mathematical formulas that allow someone to reconstruct an accident. There are two national organizations that certify you after you pass their test."

"And have you done all that, Mr. Spright?"

"I certainly have. As I mentioned, my underlying degree is in mechanical engineering, I have thirty years of experience in the engine industry, I have been doing accident reconstruction for twenty years, and I have been certified by both major organizations which do so."

"Really? Do you need to be certified by both?"

Mr. Spright waved his hand. "No. I just enjoy the tests. I like to see what kind of problems they come up with."

"Now, Mr. Spright, this case does not involve an auto accident."

"No, Mr. Shepherd, it most certainly does not."

"So how is it that you can add to the jury's knowledge in this case?"

Edgar Spright's face lit up with enthusiasm that beamed around the room. "Math can shed light on any situation, Mr. Shepherd. That's the beauty of it. Math rules are math rules and we can apply them to all sorts of situations to find out what actually happened when we weren't there. I think I can do that for the jury in this case."

"You know that, in this case, Colt Daniels is accused of killing his father."

"I do, I do. It's most serious."

"Before we get into the facts of this case, let me ask you first—have you ever been engaged to render opinions regarding the facts surrounding a murder or a shooting?"

"Yes, I most certainly have. The same principles apply in those types of cases only, instead of deciding when a driver hit his brakes or where a car swerved, I determine the flight path of a bullet or use mathematical principles to determine where a person likely shot from."

"Mr. Spright, have you been given the opportunity to review this case?"

"I have. I reviewed the State's exhibits and evidence, reviewed witness statements, and I made a visit to the site of the alleged crime and took some measurements there."

"And based on that investigation, do you have an opinion in this case?"

"I do indeed."

"And what is that opinion?"

"It is my opinion, to a reasonable degree of scientific certainty, that the arrow belonging to Colt Daniels that was found at the scene did not cause the wound that killed Brett Daniels."

"Mr. Spright, how in the world can you say that to the jury?"

"I'm not saying it, the math is."

"What do you mean?"

"It's mathematically impossible for Colt's arrow to have hit Brett Daniels." He leaned forward, eyes alight. "May I show you?"

"I wish you would."

Mr. Spright bounded out of his seat and scampered around the rail to a large whiteboard that had been set up in front of the jury. He took the cap off of his marker and said, "We're going to have to use two equations. Based on the blood and the evidence at the scene, we know that Mr. Daniels was shot while he was standing on his hunting platform. So our first equation is going to essentially be a right triangle formed by Mr. Daniels standing on top of his hunting platform, a point on the ground, and the point where Colt was standing with his crossbow. Now first, we know that the hunting platform is 10 feet off the ground." He drew a horizontal line across the whiteboard to show the platform.

"And how do we know that, Mr. Spright?"

"Because I measured it, of course. Now we also know that Brett Daniels was shot in the upper thigh, which was another 30 inches above the base of the platform. As a result, the top point of our triangle is 12.5 feet above the ground." He made a dot then drew a vertical line straight down and wrote "12.5 ft." next to it. He made a second dot on the bottom of that line. "This second point is a spot on the ground directly below Mr. Daniels. The last point of our triangle is going to be determined by where Colt Daniels was standing on the ground. Now we know he couldn't have been right under the platform or too close to it, or he wouldn't have been able to shoot up there. And we also know that he wasn't in the view of the trail camera, which was set about 30 feet from the platform. So let's put him between 20 and 25 feet from the platform. We'll start with 25 feet." Mr. Spright drew a straight line to the left from the second dot representing the ground and wrote "25 ft." underneath it. "So we have a right triangle that goes from Brett Daniels on top of the platform, straight down 12.5 feet to the ground, and over 25 feet to the left where Colt Daniels was standing. We also know that the angle for this corner of the triangle on the ground below the platform is 90 degrees. And once we know these three things, 12.5 feet off the ground, a 90-degree angle, and 25 feet away, we have the firing angle that would be required for Colt to hit a target 12.5 feet above the ground."

"How do we know this, Mr. Spright?"

He grinned. "Why math, of course! We can thank the Greeks for getting us started with these triangle equations."

I walked around so I could look at the board along with the jury. "So, Mr. Spright, if Colt Daniels were standing 25 feet away and shooting at a target 12.5 feet in the air, what would his firing angle be?"

Edgar Spright scribbled some numbers on the board before he said, "His firing angle would have to be 26.56 degrees. Would you like me to take you through the math to get there?"

"We can come back to that if we need to. First, tell us why that's important?"

Mr. Spright practically jumped out of his suit. "Because once we know his firing angle, we can calculate how far Colt's arrow would fly."

"And how do we do that?"

"With the second equation!" Mr. Spright turned back to the board. "We have the advantage of knowing exactly how fast Colt Daniels' arrow flew."

"We do?"

"Yes. His crossbow shoots exactly 150 feet per second."

"And how do we know that?"

"First, because the manufacturer certified that's how fast Colt's crossbow shoots arrows. And second, I independently tested the crossbow at a firing range and found that it does, in fact, shoot at a rate of 150 feet per second."

"I see. So what is this second equation, Mr. Spright?"

"It's both simpler and more complicated than the first one. But basically, if we know the launch angle of an arrow and the speed at which it traveled, we can mathematically calculate how far the arrow will fly."

"Really?"

Edgar Spright shot both hands out. "It's math!" He turned back to the board. "We know that an arrow that is shot at 150 feet per second with a 26.56-degree launch angle will travel 186.5 yards before it lands. He drew an arc on the whiteboard and wrote "150 ft. per sec." along the arc and "186.5 yards" in a straight line along the ground.

When he was done, Edgar Spright said, "Now as I mentioned, this calculation assumed that Colt was standing 25 feet from the platform when he shot the crossbow. Let's bring him in to about 20 feet which, when I was looking at it, was about as close as you could get and still have a shot at a target standing in the middle of the platform. From 20 feet, his launch angle is 32.005 degrees, which—when the arrow was shot at 150 feet per second at a target 12.5 feet in the air—means the arrow would travel 209.5 yards."

Mr. Spright was a whirling dervish of math at the board and his enthusiasm was contagious. But even with the visual aids, I was barely hanging onto the math and I thought that might be true for the jury too, so I said, "So Mr. Spright, can you summarize your calculations without giving all the math steps?"

He smiled. "That's a lot less fun, but sure. What all this means is that, if Colt shot his crossbow so that his arrow hit his dad's thigh, you would expect to find that arrow between 186 and 209.5 yards away. And as a practical matter, I would expect the arrow to be even closer than 186.5 yards since, if it had actually gone through Brett Daniels' thigh, that would've slowed the arrow down. But let's just assume that it didn't slow the arrow down at all. Then, through simple math, we know that the absolute farthest away that the arrow could have been found was 209.5 yards. And, if the prosecution's case were true and the arrow actually passed through Brett Daniels, I would expect the arrow to be significantly closer, certainly closer than 186.5 yards away."

"So why is all that significant?"

"Because the arrow was found 230 yards away! And, you see, once we know that—"

"Hang on a minute, Mr. Spright, how do we know that?"

"Because I measured it, of course! The police marked where they found the arrow, and I measured that distance from the platform!"

"You were able to measure that distance accurately?"

"Of course. Lasers are amazing! So anyway, we know, according to the police, that the arrow was found 230 yards away."

"And what does that tell us?"

"That's the fun part!" The smile on Edgar Spright's face vanished, and he looked first at the jury and then at the judge. "I'm sorry, Your Honor, I don't mean that the subject of this trial is fun."

Judge LaPlante's mouth twitched. "We understand what you meant, Mr. Spright. Please continue."

"Thank you, Judge." Edgar Spright brought his enthusiasm down a notch as he said, "We now just run the equations in reverse. We know that the arrow traveled for 230 yards at a speed of 150 feet per second. To travel that distance at that speed, the math tells us that the arrow had to have been shot at a 40.36-degree launch angle. And if we know that angle, we can plug it into our first equation and know how high the arrow was when it went over the middle of the platform." Edgar Spright's eyes shone.

"How high was it?" I said.

"17 feet!"

"And the platform was how high?"

"10 feet."

"And Mr. Daniels was how tall?"

"According to the autopsy, 6 feet, 1 inch."

"So the arrow traveled—"

"One foot over Mr. Daniels' head!"

I glanced at the whiteboard, which was now a riot of scribbles and numbers. "Mr. Spright, because we're in court, we have to say some of this in certain legal terms."

"Absolutely."

"Mr. Spright, in your capacity as an accident reconstructionist and using the math you've just described to the jury, did you reach an opinion in this case?"

"Yes, I did."

"And what is that opinion?"

"That there is no way, to a reasonable degree of scientific probability, that Colt Daniels' arrow hit his father Brett Daniels in the leg."

"Do you have an opinion as to what the actual flight of that arrow was?"

"I do."

"And what is that opinion?"

"It is my opinion, to a reasonable degree of scientific probability, that the arrow was shot one foot over Brett Daniels' head."

"Mr. Spright, what is the basis for that opinion?"

Mr. Spright jerked his head a little. "Why the math, of course. Given the strength of this crossbow, the only way that the arrow could've been found where it was is if it had been shot at an angle that made it pass the platform on a flight path one foot over Mr. Daniels' head."

"Do you have any doubt about this, Mr. Spright?"

"None at all."

"But Mr. Spright, they have a picture of Colt Daniels with the crossbow, with the arrow."

"Do they have a picture of Colt Daniels suspending the laws of math and physics?"

"No."

"Then it doesn't matter. If the arrow had been shot at an angle to hit Brett Daniels, it would have been found dozens of yards closer to the platform. The only way it could have traveled to the spot where it was found was if it had been shot in the way I described. The arrow did not hit Brett Daniels."

"Thank you, Mr. Spright. No more questions at this time."

Tiffany Erin stood and, for the first time, I saw her take a notepad with her to the lectern. As she passed, I saw that it was covered with neat rows and columns of numbers. She tossed the notepad onto the lectern and said, "Mr. Spright, an equation is only as good as its variables, right?"

"Sure. Whatever you put in affects what you get out."

"So if any of your variables are incorrect, say like the distance you estimate that Colton Daniels was standing from the platform, it would alter your calculation, wouldn't it?"

"It would, but that's why I've selected the range of 20 to 25 feet bounded on one end by the trail cam and on the other by how close you could get and still have a shot at the platform."

"True, but couldn't Colton Daniels have stood farther away from the platform without being in view of the trail camera?"

Mr. Spright shook his head. "No. In order to shoot the arrow in the direction it was found, he would have been in view of the trail camera if he backed up any farther."

Tiffany Erin crossed her arms. "You raise an interesting point, Mr. Spright. You are assuming that Colton Daniels shot the arrow, right?"

Mr. Spright's eyebrows scrunched. "We know he shot the arrow."

"We do, don't we?"

"Yes, based on both the picture and the fact that it was found 230 yards away."

"And there's no question from your calculation that he shot the arrow at the platform, is there?"

"Directly over it, yes."

"You just believe that, based on your calculations, Colt Daniels shot the arrow one foot over his father's head, right?"

"I don't believe that, the math proves that."

"The math proves that Colton Daniels shot the arrow directly at the platform, right?"

"Directly over top of it, that's right."

"And you can't say whether Colton Daniels was angry or mad or arguing with his father when he shot that arrow, can you?"

Mr. Spright smiled and shook his head. "I'm afraid that math has its limits, Ms. Erin."

"So that's a 'no?'"

"That's a 'no.'"

Tiffany Erin walked a few steps away and drummed her fingers on her arms. "Other things besides launch angles and crossbow strength affect how far an arrow travels, don't they?"

"What do you mean?"

"Wind, for example, could cause an arrow to travel farther?"

"The wind that day was at 5 mph out of the southeast so I think it unlikely that it affected the distance the arrow traveled but rather would only have caused a potential drift in direction."

"But it's possible that wind could've affected the arrow's flight?"

"I don't think anyone can testify to a reasonable degree of scientific probability that it did that night."

"But it's possible?"

"I would say it's not impossible, but that it is unlikely. Regardless, I would expect that, if the arrow had actually hit

Brett Daniels, then it would have been found dozens of yards short of where it was."

"So if the arrow didn't cause the wound in Brett Daniels' leg, what did?"

"Excuse me?"

Tiffany Erin walked over to the whiteboard and threw a hand at it. "You've given the jury this dazzling array of math to support your opinion that this arrow did not cause the arrow-like wound in Brett Daniels leg. So what did?"

"Oh, I have no idea. I wasn't asked to look at that."

"It's been suggested that the wound could've been made by a bullet."

Mr. Spright nodded. "That would be a whole different set of calculations to determine where the bullet eventually fell to—"

"Thank you, Mr. Spright, I'm not asking you about the supposed trajectory of this theoretical bullet because I don't think it exists. Instead, I have a different question. Sound travels at a known rate, doesn't it?"

"It certainly does."

"And decibels are a known, mathematical quantity, right?"

"They are."

"And you have been to the scene where Brett Daniels was killed and observed the distance from the platform to his home, haven't you?"

"I did not measure it, but I have a rough estimate of the distance."

"That's great. Do you have an opinion as to whether the sound of a gunshot in the area of the platform would have been audible at the house?"

"What type of gun?"

"Well, since its theoretical, let's just call it a typical handgun or rifle."

Mr. Spright thought for a moment. "Yes, a shot should be audible from that distance."

"And, of course, that's assuming that one's hearing wasn't being interfered with by something else, like headphones or a TV."

"A shot at that distance would likely be audible even with some interference."

"And it would be audible to both a human and a dog?"

I stood. "Objection, Your Honor."

Tiffany Erin shrugged. "Mr. Shepherd put this theory out there, Your Honor. I think I'm entitled to some latitude to explore it."

Judge LaPlante thought. "Subject to the limits of Mr. Spright's knowledge of human and canine perception, I'll allow it."

Mr. Spright smiled. "I live in the country, Ms. Erin. My dog and I can hear gunshots from some distance."

"That's all I have Mr. Spright. Thank you."

I stood. "Mr. Spright, did Colt's arrow hit Brett Daniels?"

"Absolutely not. The laws of math say it's impossible."

"Thank you."

Tiffany Erin never sat down. "Mr. Spright, you're just as certain that Colton Daniels shot his arrow, aren't you?"

"I am."

"Right at his dad's hunting platform?"

"Right over it, yes."

"We know that as a matter of math too, don't we?"

"We do."

"Thank you, Mr. Spright."

Then the judge dismissed him and Edgar Spright bounded out of the courtroom.

55

Danny and I were just sitting down at the conference table that night with our Black Boar sandwiches when Olivia called. I put her on speaker. "Hey, Liv."
"Tough day, huh?"
I froze mid-unwrapping. "I didn't think so. Do you?"
"I don't. But @AlexisFury does."
I cracked my neck. "What's being posted now?"
"'Defense expert admits that defendant shot at father.' Then side-by-side pictures of Colt with the crossbow and your expert making a goofy face with his hands out to both sides. Did he really do that?"
"Yes to both, but he was proving that Colt didn't hit his dad and the goofy look was endearing." I looked at Danny. "Wasn't it?"
Danny took a bite and nodded. "The jury loved him."
"How did it really go then?" she asked.
"I thought it went well. What did you think, Danny?"
Danny took another bite before he answered. "Gerchuk and Spright were great witnesses. Everything they said—Gerchuk pointing out that the wound could have been from a few things

and Spright proving that the arrow couldn't have hit Brett—was solid." He took another bite.

"I'm sensing a 'but.'"

Danny chewed and nodded. "But it seems a little far-fetched once the charm wears off. And we haven't given them an alternative explanation."

"We're not obligated to."

Danny shrugged. "You asked."

"There you have it, Liv."

"All right," she said. "Do you need any more research from me tonight?"

"No. Thanks though."

"I'll leave you to it then." She hung up.

I unwrapped the rest of my sandwich. "So do you think we have reasonable doubt?"

Danny chewed thoughtfully, if that's possible. "I meant what I said, those witnesses were really good, but those pictures of Colt going out there and back are awfully damning. And knowing that he shot at his dad…" Danny shook his head. "I know we can't afford to put Colt on, but without being able to give the jury an explanation of why Colt shot at his own dad, it looks pretty bad."

I took my own turn chewing with thought and added a side of worry.

Danny pointed around his hoagie bun. "And you know what I think was surprisingly effective?"

"What?"

"Erin's questions about the gunshot making noise. I mean think about it, whoever you believe, there would have been a lot going on—a gunshot or a coyote call, and in either circumstance Brett running down off the stand, dying in the backyard, and attracting coyotes. And Colt doesn't hear any of it? It's hard to believe. And if he heard it and didn't do anything?" He shrugged.

"Then the jury could assume that Colt knew what was happening." I replayed the day's testimony. "Erin hasn't made a point of that yet. Do you think the jury has noticed it?"

"I think it's more of an undercurrent right now, but I'd be willing to bet that she's going to hammer on it at closing."

"Would you say we're winning or losing right now?"

Danny chewed on his thought sandwich before he said, "Losing. By more than a little."

I shook my head. "Dammit. I think so, too. And I agree with you, we have to give the jury more of an explanation for why Colt would've gone out there like that."

"By like that, you mean with a loaded crossbow?"

"Right." I crunched up my wrapper and stood.

Danny leaned back in his chair. "This looks like the time when you announce some grand strategic reason why you can't stay in the office and slog away."

"I would if I could, Danny, but I have to go convince the Daniels that Tyler has to testify."

"How are you going to do that?"

"With your help." I told him what I needed.

Danny sighed. "Give me ten minutes."

"Done." I went back into my office and packed up the things I would need to work on at home after I went to the Daniels' house. By the time I was done, Danny was finished and handed me what I had asked for. "Thanks."

Danny nodded. "I'll finish up the jury instructions. We're closing tomorrow, right?"

"Probably. We'll put Tyler on in the morning, and I'd imagine we close in the afternoon."

"Okay. Good luck."

"Thanks." I was at the door when I stopped and said, "You're doing a great job, Danny."

Danny waved. "You say that to all the associates."

"Turns out, I do."

"Bye."

I left.

∾

IT WASN'T a long trip to the Daniels' house, but I still had time to think. There was no question in my mind that I had to put Tyler on the stand. I had to explain the pressure that Brett was putting on Tyler and why Colt might want to stand up to that. I could also have Tyler testify that he didn't hear anything that night, which would explain Colt's failure to hear it, too. I didn't know if Tyler would be willing to do it, and I knew that the family, including Colt, didn't want him to, but I was becoming convinced that we'd lose if we didn't.

It was dark when I pulled into the two-track driveway. My lights flashed past the concrete porch and came to rest behind Tyler's old pickup and a silver F150. It took me a second to recognize it before I realized it was Rob Preston's old truck. I got out of my Jeep and went up to the back door. Chet's howl let me know he'd seen me coming. Rob Preston opened the door, his red beard jutting out fiercely in the dim light.

"Nate," he said in his gravelly voice. "Come on in. Did Colt know you were coming?"

I bent over and gave Chet a quick double scratch under the ears. His tail thumped the wall in appreciation.

"I don't think so. Is Tyler home, too?"

"He's here. Just doing some homework."

"Is that your old truck? I thought you turned it in for a new Ford?"

Rob frowned so that his mouth disappeared into his beard and nodded. "I did. Had to take it back though. Something was wrong with the transmission so I just turned it in and took the old one back while I figure out something else."

"Did they hassle you?"

Rob waved. "The dealer was pretty good about it since they still had my old truck. Did you eat yet?"

"I did, thanks."

"We did too, but we have some left if you want." He gnawed at his beard. "Colt's not eating a lot."

"That's not surprising, Rob."

"I suppose not. Come on back." Rob led me on the short trip to the dim kitchen. Colt was slouched on the couch in the small family room, watching TV. He glanced over, then sat up. "Nate? What's up?"

"We need to talk."

Colt turned off the TV and walked over. He was wearing sweats and a Panther Pride t-shirt and I could see that Rob was right, Colt had lost weight. His low brow scowled even lower as he said, "Is something wrong?"

"Not exactly. But we need to talk about tomorrow."

"Sure."

Just as Colt started to sit at the kitchen table, Chet scratched at the back door. Colt detoured and let Chet out, freeing the very good boy to sprint into the backyard.

"I'll let you two work," said Rob, and disappeared into the front room.

Colt sat down. "What is it?"

"Do you remember what I told you we had to do to win?"

"Yeah, you said we had to establish reasonable doubt."

"That's right. We have to convince the jury that you might not have done it."

Colt nodded. "And the engineer and the doctor helped with that today, right?"

"They did."

"I mean, I didn't understand all the math stuff but that engineer guy proved exactly what I told you."

"He did, but that's why I wanted to talk to you. I don't think it was enough."

"What do you mean? He said I didn't do it!"

"You just said you didn't understand the math stuff?"

"Not really but—"

"I don't know if the jury did either. I think we have to give them a little more."

"Okay. So what do we do?"

"Tyler has to testify."

Colt shook his head. "No. No way. We're not getting him involved in this."

"Colt, he *is* involved in this. Period. He's the reason you went out there to talk to your dad, right?"

"It doesn't matter. He's not going on."

"It *does* matter. Right now, all the jury knows is that you went out there with a crossbow and that you shot it. Even though physics say your arrow couldn't have hit your dad, all they know is that you went out there and shot it. We have to give them more, we have to tell them that your brother didn't hear or see anything unusual that night once you came back."

Chet scratched at the back metal door.

Colt got up. "What do you mean unusual?"

"He didn't see you acting frantic, you didn't take a long shower or throw away clothes, there were no howling coyotes, there was nothing that would have let either of you know that something had happened to your dad."

Colt opened the door, and Chet came barreling back in. "We can't do that to him. Besides, my mom would never go for it."

False Oath

"Colt, you could go to jail for the rest of your life. We have to do everything we can to stop that, including putting your brother on the stand so he can say that it was quiet in here and everything was normal and you didn't act like you'd just killed your dad!"

Colt shook his head. "Forget it, Nate. Tyler's not doing it."

"Not doing what?" said Tyler as he walked into the kitchen. He was decked out in orange gear from his new college commitment as he leaned over and ruffled Chet on the scruff of his neck.

"I need to call you as a witness tomorrow," I said.

"No, he doesn't," said Colt.

"For what?" Tyler straightened. I always forgot how tall he was until I saw him again.

"It doesn't matter," said Colt. "You're not doing it."

"To talk about why Colt was upset, about why he went out to talk to your dad."

"Because of the way he was treating me?" said Tyler.

"Yes."

"No," said Colt.

I kept my eyes on Tyler. "And to explain that you didn't hear or see anything unusual that night when Colt came back."

"Is it important?" There wasn't a flick of emotion on Tyler's face. Just cool calculation.

"No," said Colt.

I nodded. "It might keep your brother out of prison."

Tyler opened the door to what was really more of a small closet than a pantry and pulled out a bag of dog food. It rattled into the bottom of the clean metal bowl next to the kitchen cupboard and Chet nosed the bag aside and dug in. Tyler shook out the last of the bag and said, "We need more dog food." It was almost exactly like the first time I had met the two of them here. Almost.

I watched Chet wolf down his evening meal and lick his bowl sparkling clean, leaving a fine sheen of saliva, before he moved over and sloppily lapped up half a bowl of water. Colt was yelling something about Tyler ruining his life, while Tyler coolly replied that he could do whatever he wanted.

I just stared at the bowls.

When Chet was done with his drink, he went to the back door and scratched. Colt let him out. I stood. The boys fell silent.

I took out what Danny had given me before I left. "Here," I said to Tyler.

"What's this?"

"It's a subpoena. Be in court tomorrow at 8:30."

I should've expected it. Colt was young and I knew he had a bad temper, bad enough to shoot a crossbow at his dad. I saw him coming just a second before he smashed me into the fridge. I was too late to avoid it but, as my shoulder bounced off the metal, I was able to shift and lock him up in a cross-body tie so that he couldn't punch me with his near arm. He was spitting mad though and screaming that I wasn't going to wreck his brother's life.

Rob appeared out of nowhere. He put both arms around Colt and yanked him back, yelling, "Knock it off, Colt! Enough!"

Colt was kicking and struggling, his feet just off the ground, but Rob's grip was iron. Rob looked at me over Colt's shoulder and said, "Best go, Nate."

I started to step away, but I looked at Tyler first. He just nodded and said, "I'll be there."

"Thank you," I said and left.

As I went out the side door to my Jeep, Chet barreled around the corner to say goodbye. I gave him a quick pat. Then Tyler opened the back door and whistled and Chet bounded away.

I pulled out of the two-track and onto the asphalt of M-339. It was dark, with no light anywhere except from the metal-roofed house I was leaving.

I had an examination and a closing to prepare for tomorrow. I didn't have a lot of time. But I drove around anyway, for almost half an hour, I think. I wasn't going anywhere at first, just driving around in the dark country roads of Michigan, thinking, with no lights except my own. I drove as far away as Glass Lake, near my parents' house, before circling back slowly, subconsciously, toward my destination.

At one point, I pulled over and made a call. I was surprised the person answered. We talked for a good twenty minutes until we were both sure we were on the same page and on the way to an agreement of sorts. Then I continued to drive.

Eventually, by the most circuitous route possible, I pulled into the driveway of the person I now had to see. I had to make sure he heard it from me.

I turned off the car, took a deep breath, and walked up to the front door of the small ranch house. I knocked. My sister-in-law Kate answered the door.

"Nate? Is everyone okay?"

"Everyone's fine, Kate. I'm sorry to startle you. I know it's late."

"It's never too late, you know that." She opened the door and gave me a quick hug and a kiss on the cheek. "What is it?"

"I need to talk to Tom."

56

We sat in the garage that he had converted into his football office, in the place where he had spent countless hours in joyful, maniacal discipline devoting his life to a craft that paid pennies. I found myself staring at the state championship team picture, the same one that hung in Borderlands, the one with the kids all lying around the trophy in the middle of Ford Field, most of them holding up one finger.

The silence stretched out until Tom finally said, "Are you sure?"

"Almost certain. We'll know tomorrow."

"I have to call now. Tonight."

"Can you wait until after we're done?"

"Tomorrow? No. I have to act on it same as you."

I nodded.

Tom appeared to think. "You're concerned because it might affect Colt's defense? If the other side knows in advance?"

"Yes."

"I'll call tonight, but it's late. The office will be closed. I'll leave a message. Is he going on the stand right away in the morning?"

"Yes."

"Then the information should break at about the same time."

I don't know what I was expecting—an outburst, anger, disappointment? I'm not sure. It was none of that. Not even a clenched jaw. I didn't know what to make of it.

Tom stood. "Well, you have a case to win and I have a call to make."

"There's one more thing."

Tom's expression didn't change, but he rolled his head in a slow circle before he said, "What?"

"The kids are doing the War Oath."

Tom shook his head. "I stopped that. We don't allow it."

"They've been doing it for five years."

Tom stared.

"This one I'm sure about," I said. "It won't come out on the stand tomorrow, but I thought you needed to know."

Tom's jaw jutted forward. "Right. I need to call the superintendent now. About both things."

"Sure."

Tom shook my hand and gave me a one shoulder hug.

"Tommy, I—"

He pulled back. "Don't apologize for doing the right thing, Nate. And thanks for coming to me right away."

I pretended not to notice Kate's look of concern as I walked through her house to the front door and left.

The relationship between a little brother and a big brother can be a strange mix—part rivalry, part hero worship, part lifelong best friend. As I drove home that night, I felt grief for the pain I was going to cause my brother, and a deep admiration for the man he was.

I didn't sleep a lot that night, but there was only one day of trial left, so it didn't matter.

57

There was extra tension on my side of the courtroom the next morning as we waited for Judge LaPlante to get things started. Colt sat stiff and straight beside me, not meeting my eye. Rob brought Rhonda in seconds before 8:30; a move that I knew was on purpose to keep her away from me. I smelled the waft of cigarette smoke as the two of them sat down in the row directly behind us. I avoided Rhonda's glare and looked at the gallery. There were a few other people scattered about but not many, about the same amount as had been there all week, which was good, because it meant that word hadn't leaked out about who was testifying that morning.

Tiffany Erin sat at her table, legs crossed, an island of remorseless calm.

A moment later, Judge LaPlante came in and we all stood. "Good morning, everyone," he said. "Patricia, could you bring in the jury, please?"

Patricia Weathers went over to the jury room, opened the door, and whispered. The jury filed out and took their seats.

After greeting them, Judge LaPlante turned to me and said, "You may call your next witness, Mr. Shepherd."

"Thank you, Your Honor. The defense calls Tyler Daniels."

Tyler stood from his seat in the back row and came forward. As he did, a man ducked out of the gallery and into the hall. Word was about to spread.

Tyler wore a tailored suit that might have been more expensive than any that I owned. I was surprised and then I remembered that elite quarterbacks, even high school ones, go on elite interview circuits.

Tyler might as well have been walking to study hall. He was blonde and he was big and he smiled at his brother and nodded to the jury as he took his seat in the witness chair.

"Could you swear the witness, please," Judge LaPlante said to Patricia Weathers.

"Could you raise your right hand, please," Patricia Weathers said.

Tyler did.

"Do you swear to tell the truth, the whole truth, and nothing but the truth, so help you God?"

"I do."

I stood at the lectern. "Could you state your name please?"

"Tyler Daniels."

"Tyler, are you related to Colt?"

"I am. He's my older brother."

"Is he your only sibling?"

"Yes. It's just the two of us."

"The decedent, Brett Daniels, he was your father?"

"He was."

"I'm sorry for your loss."

"Thank you."

"And who is your mother?"

"Rhonda Daniels. Actually, Rhonda Mazur now."

"I see. Your mom and dad were divorced?"

"Yes."

"How long ago?"

"About five years now."

"I assume that when your mom and dad divorced, they separated?"

"They did."

"Your dad stayed in the family home in Carrefour, Michigan?"

"Yes, it belonged to his dad and he had hunted that property since he was a kid so my mom moved out."

"Where did she go?"

"To an apartment at first."

"Was that in Carrefour, Ohio?"

"It was. Then later she and her boyfriend bought a house together."

"Over on the Ohio side?"

"Yes."

"I see. And when your parents divorced, where did you and Colt live?"

"With my dad."

"Why?"

"Colt was halfway through high school at the time so he wanted to stay with dad and finish there."

"That's Carrefour North High School?"

"That's right."

"How about you? Where did you want to live?"

"I wanted to live with Colt."

"What about your dad?"

Tyler shrugged. "Him too. But I loved my mom and my dad so I didn't really want to pick between them. I just wanted to stay with Colt."

"Did your dad teach you how to play football, Tyler?"

He smiled. "From the time I was little."

"Colt too?"

"Colt first. Then me."

"Did he teach you things to become a better quarterback?"

"Since I can remember."

"Did he make you do drills after practice?"

"That's how you get better."

"Did he ever curse at you after football games when you played poorly?"

"When I needed it."

"Did he ever do things like take away the car keys or ground you from going out if you had a bad game?"

"If I needed to refocus, sure." He smiled. "It worked out."

"It certainly has. Tyler, I want to take you back to last year, your junior year, okay?"

"Sure."

"Colt had left home to go to Grand Valley State University, is that right?"

"That's right."

"So it was just you and your dad?"

Tyler smiled. "And Chet."

I smiled. "We should tell the jury, Chet is your yellow lab?"

"He is."

"So with Colt away at school, it was just you, your dad, and Chet?

"That's right."

"The Carrefour North football team had a pretty good run that year, didn't they?"

"Not great."

"Not great? You made it to the state finals, didn't you?"

"We did. But we lost."

"Still, second in the state is pretty good, isn't it?"

"*When* you lose doesn't matter."

"I see. How did your dad take it?"

Tiffany Erin stood. "Your Honor, I've given counsel an awful lot of leeway here since this is the accused's brother and the victim's son, but how is any of this relevant?"

Judge LaPlante looked at me. "Mr. Shepherd?"

"I believe this is all relevant to the circumstances surrounding the evidence that the State has put on, Your Honor, but I will move things along."

Judge LaPlante nodded. "Please do. Overruled."

"How did your dad take the loss, Tyler?"

"He helped me set up a training plan so that it wouldn't happen again."

"What wouldn't happen again?"

"Us losing the way we did."

"How did you lose?"

"I threw an interception."

"Didn't you throw for four touchdowns?"

"I threw an interception."

"I see. So your dad set up a training plan?"

"Yes. Drills, weights, film, all that stuff.

"I see. A couple of days a week?"

Tyler laughed then saw I was serious. "No. Every day."

"Rain or shine?"

"Rain or shine."

"Or snow?"

Tyler smiled. "Football is an outdoor sport."

"Or sleet?"

"We can't control the weather on game day."

"Did you tell your brother about this practice plan?"

"Of course. We texted or talked most days."

"Even after Colt was gone?"

"Yes."

"What did Colt think about this plan?"

Tiffany Erin stood. "Objection."

"Sustained."

"Did you ever witness your brother and father argue about your training?"

"Yes."

"At one point, they got in a fight at Borderlands?"

"They argued."

"That was over your dad's training plan for you?"

"Yes."

"You said that during your junior year Colt was living away, up at Grand Valley, right?"

"He was."

"He stayed up there most of the year?"

"He did."

"When he came home, did he normally stay with you?"

"Yes. We stuck together as much as we could."

"Was it harder to live with your dad once Colt went away to school?"

Tyler appeared to think for a moment, then said, "Yes."

"Your best friend was gone?"

"Yes."

"Now Tyler, the night your father died, that was, what, the eighth week of the season?"

"It was."

"And Colt had been away at school?"

"He had. That week though they had some sort of fall break, and he came home to see me play."

"And he stayed with you?"

"He did."

I had been very careful about everything I had asked Tyler so far. And so far, because of the way I had worded it, he had told the truth.

Now we would see.

"Tyler, the jury has seen pictures from a trail cam of Colt going out to see your dad on the night he died. Are you aware of that?"

"I am."

"Do you know why he did that?"

"He wanted to talk to Dad."

"About what?"

Tyler looked down. "About me."

"Why?"

"Because we were getting ready for the playoffs and we were ramping things up."

"We? Or he?"

Tyler raised his eyes. "Both."

"Colt wanted to talk to your dad about it?"

"Yes."

"So why didn't Colt just talk to him about it after dinner that night?"

Tyler cocked his head. "Excuse me?"

"You mentioned that Colt stayed with you that week? When he was on fall break?"

Football players are often accused of being stupid. Tyler was not. I could see him make the connection. He didn't answer me for a few seconds and I didn't prod him. Finally, he said, "Yes."

"So why did Colt go out to the woods to talk to your dad? Why didn't he just talk to him after dinner that night?"

"Because we didn't eat with him."

"Oh, right, because your dad got home late from work?"

To his credit, Tyler didn't hesitate. "No. Because we weren't staying with my dad. We were staying at my mother's. In Ohio."

I felt the rustle behind me. I ignored it and said, "Why is that?"

"Because that's where I lived."

"Since when?"

"Since last summer."

The rustle became a commotion. I wasn't surprised.

I turned to see Rob leading Rhonda out of the room. The two of them were whispering furiously. Judge LaPlante banged his gavel. "Quiet. Please."

The whispering continued until Rhonda and Rob reached the door. As he opened it, Rhonda turned and yelled, "You're supposed to be helping them! You're supposed to be helping my boys, not screwing them over, you son of a bitch!"

Judge LaPlante banged his gavel again as Rob guided her out.

Two other sets of eyes were boring into me. Colt's low brow was a storm cloud as he leaned forward, hands folded, jaw clenched. Tiffany Erin sat back in her chair, arms folded, long fingers drumming.

Both looked furious.

I turned back to Tyler. He took one glance at Colt and then trained his eyes on me, calm, cool.

"So you had moved into your mom's house last summer?"

"Yes."

"Why?"

"Colt was up at school most of that summer for a class. Without him here, and without having to go to school for eight hours a day..." He stopped and shrugged.

"Without having to go to school eight hours a day what?"

"It became a little much."

"What did?"

"My dad. All of it."

"Did Chet move out with you?"

"Yes. He's my dog."

"Did you tell anyone that you had moved?"

"No."

"Why not?"

"At first, it was because I was planning to move back when school started."

"Did you?"

"Move back?"

"Yes."

"No, I didn't."

"Why not?"

"Because I got used to living with my mom and Rob."

"Did you think about switching schools once you had moved?"

"Not really. We had almost won the state championship at North the year before. I knew we could do it this year. I didn't want to let my team down. And I wanted to win."

"Did your North teammates know that you were living in Ohio?"

"No. My dad's house is a little out of the way and my friends didn't really like coming over anyway so it wasn't hard."

"Did your coach know that you were living in Ohio?"

"No way. Coach Shepherd would have kicked me off the team."

"Are you sure?"

"Absolutely. He would have done anything he could for me personally, but I would have been gone."

"So the jury understands, why would you have been off the team?"

Tyler didn't blink. "Because I was living outside the school district in another state, so I wouldn't have been eligible to play for Carrefour North."

"Did anyone in the Carrefour North school administration know that you had moved to Ohio?"

"No. Just me and Colt and Mom and Rob."

"So did you and Colt have dinner with your dad at all the week that he died?"

"No. We were at my mom's."

"To your knowledge, had your brother Colt seen your dad at all that week?"

"Not that I know of."

"So the only time Colt would have had to talk to him was when he went out to see your dad the night he died?"

"That's the only time that I'm aware of."

"Tyler, you have not been here for the trial, but there has been a question raised several times by the prosecutor about why you and your brother wouldn't have heard certain things. I'm going to ask you about those, okay?"

"Sure."

"If there had been a gunshot at your dad's house on Thursday night, would you have heard it?"

"No."

"Why?"

"Because Colt and I were at my mother's house."

"If there had been a coyote howling near your dad's home on Thursday night, would you have heard it?"

"No."

"Why?"

"Because Colt and I were at my mother's house."

"Could Chet have found your dad's body on Thursday night or Friday morning?"

"No."

"Why?"

"Because Chet was with me at my mother's house."

"If there had been a commotion at all, from your father running or calling for help or fighting with someone on Thursday night, would you have heard it?"

"No."

"Why?"

"Because Colt and I were at my mother's house."

"Were you there at your mother's house Thursday night when Colt came back from visiting your dad?"

"I was."

"What time was that?"

"About 7:00, 7:15."

"Did he have blood on him?"

"No."

"Was he upset?"

"No."

"Did he say anything about your dad?"

"Yes."

"What?"

"He said Dad expected me to be there to watch film Friday night after the game, just like always."

"What happened next?"

"Mom and Rob weren't home so the two of us studied in our rooms until we went to bed."

I nodded. "You and Chet found your dad on Friday night, right?"

"We did."

"Was that the first time you had been to your dad's house that week?"

"Yes."

"Why did you go there?"

"Like I said, I usually watched film with my dad Friday night after games. I hadn't seen him at the game, which was unusual, but I knew he expected me. His truck was there when I pulled in so I didn't think anything of it until Chet found him."

"Chet found him right away?"

"He did."

"What did you do?"

"I called Colt. He told me to call the rescue squad. And they both arrived pretty quick."

"Tyler, you talked to the police that night, didn't you?"

"I did."

"Where did you tell them you lived?"

"At my dad's house."

"Why?"

"Because if I wasn't living there, I wouldn't be eligible and the playoffs were about to start. And..."

"And what?"

"And because we didn't think it mattered."

"We?"

"Me and Colt."

"Why didn't you change your statement?"

"They never talked to me again."

"The police?"

"Right. And, and we won."

"The state championship?"

"Right."

"So to make sure I understand this, whatever happened at your dad's house on Thursday night, you weren't there to see it?"

"I was not."

"And you weren't there to hear it?"

"I was not."

"And after 7:15 that night, Colt wasn't there either?"

"He was not."

"And how do you know that?"

"Because he was with me. At my mother's house in Ohio."

"No further questions. Thank you, Tyler."

As I passed Tiffany Erin on the way back to my table, her look of fury was gone. Instead, she had a look of intent predation.

As I sat down, Colt hissed into my ear. "What the hell are you doing?"

"Uncovering the truth."

"Do you have any idea what you've done? How much you've cost my family? You've—"

"Colt. I need to hear her questions."

Danny leaned in and tapped Colt to get his attention so that I could listen as Tiffany Erin stood there, arms folded, drumming her fingers like talons.

"Mr. Daniels, you are eighteen years old, aren't you?"

"I am."

"That means you're a legal adult in the state of Michigan."

"Okay."

"I feel compelled to ask you, you do realize that lying under oath is a crime, don't you?"

"I do."

"Do you know that lying to a police officer in the course of a murder investigation is also a crime in the State of Michigan?"

"I did not."

"Well, it is. So, my question to you is, which crime did you commit?"

I stood. "Objection, Your Honor."

"I'll rephrase, Judge."

Judge LaPlante nodded.

"Mr. Daniels, are you lying today about where you were on the night your father was killed?"

"No."

"Mr. Daniels, are you lying today about where your brother Colton was on the night your father was killed?"

"No."

"Mr. Daniels, did you lie to the police officers who questioned you on the night your father was found about where you lived?"

"Yes."

"Mr. Daniels, did you lie to police officers who questioned

you on the night your father was found about where your brother lived?"

"Yes."

"Mr. Daniels, were you present when your brother spoke to police officers on the night that your father was found?"

"Yes."

"Did your brother lie to police officers about where he was living?"

"Yes."

"That's a little convenient, isn't it?"

"Excuse me?"

"This case has been pending for months and in that time you never once came forward and told anyone about where you and your brother were living when it's clear that information would have helped him. And now, at the last minute, you show up and testify that you lied to the investigators?"

"I don't think that's convenient at all."

"Well, I do. Is it your testimony today that you have never told anyone about where you were living?"

"That's correct."

"Not school staff, not coaches, not friends?"

"That's right. No one."

Tiffany Erin pointed a long, accusatory finger at me. "But you told Mr. Shepherd, your brother's attorney?"

Tyler shook his head. "No. No, I didn't. I don't know how he figured it out."

"Oh, come on. Your brother told him, didn't he?"

"No. My brother's going to be pissed about this. Excuse me, mad."

"You would really have the jury believe that you and your brother maintained this lie so that you could play football?"

"So that I could get a scholarship to play football, which I did."

"Even if it meant your brother might go to jail?"

"My brother will not go to jail. Or at least he shouldn't."

"Why in the world would you say that?"

"Because he didn't kill my dad."

"Oh, who did?"

"I don't know. But it wasn't Colt."

"I see."

Tiffany Erin strode over to the evidence table. She picked up the crossbow. "This is your brother's crossbow?"

"It is."

"This is your brother's arrow?"

"It is."

She strode over to her computer and tapped a button. The picture of Colt walking toward the platform with the crossbow popped up. "Is this your brother with a loaded crossbow?"

"It is."

She clicked.

"Is this a picture of your brother with the same crossbow?"

"It is."

"Has it been fired?"

"Yes."

"And after this picture was taken, your brother came home —or I should say, came to your mother's home in Ohio?"

"Yes."

"About half an hour later?"

"If that time on the picture's right, a little less."

"Did Colton tell you that he'd shot your father?"

"No. He told me dad expected me Friday night to watch film."

"You had seen your dad and brother fight in the past?"

"I had."

"You had seen your dad put your brother's head through a video game screen?"

"Yes."

"You had seen your dad and brother argue about you and your training?"

"I had."

"Did you know that your brother was going out there that night with a loaded crossbow?"

"No."

"Is that a lie?"

"No."

"Are you sure?"

I stood. "Objection."

"Sustained," said Judge LaPlante without looking up.

Tiffany Erin turned her back on the jury and she stared at Colt and at me. It seemed like she was done but then she turned and said, "You love your brother, don't you, Tyler?"

"Of course."

"You would do anything for him?"

"Anything I could."

"Including lie?"

Tyler paused. "Not here."

"He lied for you though, right?"

"Not here in court, no."

"The night of the police investigation. He lied for you then, didn't he?"

Tyler paused. "Yes."

"You would do the same for him, wouldn't you?"

"Not here. Not now."

"So you say. No further questions."

There were some things I wanted to ask Tyler, but I didn't want to give Tiffany Erin another shot at him, so I stood and said, "No further questions, Your Honor."

"You may step down, Mr. Daniels."

Patricia Weathers walked around the bench and whispered

in Judge LaPlante's ear. Judge LaPlante nodded and said, "Mr. Daniels, please wait in the gallery and do not leave the courtroom yet."

"Yes, sir." Tyler stepped down and went to take a seat. He didn't look at Colt as he walked by.

"Members of the jury," said Judge LaPlante, "We're going to take a brief break. I'm going to ask that you stay in the jury room for the next five minutes or so and then I'll let you go so you can use the restroom and get a drink. Please wait until Ms. Weathers comes to get you."

We all stood as the jury filed out. When they were gone, Judge LaPlante said, "Counsel will see me in my chambers. Now."

Usually, I would have had Danny come with me. This time though I told him to stay and mind Colt and Tyler. I didn't want anyone to have access to them while I was gone.

Judge LaPlante had been a calm presence throughout the trial, but I could see the burn he had going as we filed into his office.

"Mr. Shepherd, did you have knowledge of this alibi evidence before this morning?"

"I did not, Your Honor."

Tiffany Erin snorted.

"I had suspicions, but Tyler had never told me what you heard today."

"You exposed that young man, you know."

"The truth did, yes sir."

"Which truth?" said Tiffany Erin.

Judge LaPlante shot her a look and Tiffany Erin raised one hand and nodded.

Then his black eyes came back to bear on me. "Do I have your representation as an officer of the court that you did not have knowledge of this evidence before this morning?"

"Your Honor, I developed suspicions about this last night. I took actions in case those suspicions turned out to be true. But no one told me that Tyler and Colt were living with their mother on the night of the incident until just now in this courtroom."

I felt the weight of Judge LaPlante's assessment. Then he nodded and said, "All right. We have another issue. Word of Tyler Daniels' testimony has leaked out, and there is a group of reporters gathered outside the courtroom. I will not have my court turned into a circus. Ms. Weathers is having them moved to a common area near the courthouse entrance. I cannot have them contaminating the jury when they go out to use the restroom and get water. We will wait for five minutes and then I will dismiss you."

The look Judge LaPlante gave me was hard. "Mr. Daniels, Tyler Daniels that is, is going to be hounded with inquiries. I'm going to issue an order that, to preserve the integrity of trial, no witness may comment to the press until after the jury has returned its verdict. It would be my personal suggestion that Mr. Daniels use that time to secure counsel and formulate a response to those inquiries. Am I clear?"

"Yes, Your Honor."

"Your Honor, this is outrageous," said Tiffany Erin. "My office will be moving for sanctions after the trial is complete."

"That is certainly within your prerogative, Ms. Erin. Of course, in analyzing the conduct in this case, I will have to analyze the conduct of the attorneys throughout the entire case, including things like compliance with, and subversion of, the Court's extradition process."

Tiffany Erin didn't look cowed in the least, but she also didn't say anything.

Judge LaPlante let the silence sit there for a few long moments before saying, "Do you have any more surprises for us this afternoon, Mr. Shepherd?"

"That's my last witness, Your Honor."

"Very well. We'll give the jury an extended break so that we can put together the jury instructions. Closing will be in an hour and a half. Go."

As we left, Tiffany Erin leaned close, "So your client is a murderer *and* a liar?"

"My client loves his brother," I said, and held the door open to let her pass.

58

Before I give a closing, I normally like a brief period of quiet so I can organize my thoughts about how the evidence has come out and mesh it with my theory of the case. I plan all that out ahead of time but, until the trial is actually done, you don't know for sure how the evidence is going to play out. Like with Tyler's testimony, for example. So that brief period, even if it's only ten minutes, is vital.

I did not have any quiet time before closing in this case.

As soon as I left Judge LaPlante's office, I got on the phone with Ronnie Hawkins to ask her to come right over so that she could represent Tyler. Ronnie was a local lawyer I'd worked with recently on the Archie Mack case and her most important attribute at the moment, besides being a talented lawyer, was that her office was right across the street. She told me she'd be there in five minutes.

While we waited, I explained to Tyler and Colt what was going on.

"What do you mean there are possible criminal charges for what he said?" said Colt. "He told the truth!"

"We'll go over the details later, Colt. This isn't the time to talk about it."

"This isn't the time to talk about it?! When the hell *should* we talk about it?"

Tyler reached out and touched Colt's elbow. "When your trial is done."

His brother's words or the touch doused the flames. The anger went out of Colt's eyes and he nodded.

A short time later, the jury was excused from the jury room to take a break, which I took to mean that the reporters had been cleared out front. As the last juror went out, Ronnie Hawkins came in and shook my hand. "Hi, Nate. Which one is Tyler?"

Tyler looked at me. "Ronnie's a woman?"

"Ronnie is an attorney," said Ronnie Hawkins. "Your brother and Nate have some other things to do. Why don't you come with me and I'll explain what's going on."

I thanked her, and then Ronnie Hawkins and Tyler left.

As the two of them went out, Rob Preston came in. I expected anger but, although his red beard jutted as fiercely as always, he was surprisingly calm as he said, "You know this ruined a lot of things."

"Maybe. Probably. I'm going to help you work through it. You and Rhonda shouldn't say anything to anyone."

"She won't. She's mad, but she's dialed in on the boys right now."

"Where is she?"

"She went with that new attorney and Tyler."

"Why aren't you with them?" said Colt.

Rob tilted his head. "Because I'm here for you."

Colt rocked backward at the words before he ducked his head and said, "Thanks."

Patricia Weathers waved to me and said, "The judge wants to go over the jury instructions now."

"Okay." I turned back to Rob and Colt. "We've got maybe half an hour. Are you two okay to stay here?"

"We'll be fine," said Rob, and the two of them sat down together.

With that, Danny and I went in to Judge LaPlante's office and went through the jury instructions with Tiffany Erin and her associate. When we were done, the judge sent us back to the courtroom and said we'd be closing in ten minutes.

I checked my email on my phone real quick to make sure Ronnie didn't need anything from me. She didn't, so I went out into the hallway, found a quiet corner with no one around and called Megan Dira. I told her what had happened in court that morning. She confirmed our discussion from the night before and said she'd be in touch soon. I hung up and as I put my phone away, Patricia Weathers came out and said in that soft voice of hers that the judge was ready for closing. I hurried in, motioning Colt back to the table on the way. Rob smiled at Colt, patted his back, and nodded to me. Then, after a period of scurrying where new people with notepads took seats in the gallery and Tiffany Erin made sure her projector was squared away, Judge LaPlante came in and the jury was seated. We were ready to close the case.

~

"Ms. Erin, are you prepared to present closing argument?"

"Yes, Your Honor."

"You may proceed."

"Thank you. "

Tiffany Erin glided up. "Colton Daniels killed his father." She stood there. "Colton Daniels killed his father and left him for the coyotes to eat. And he did it with premeditation when he loaded his crossbow, walked back to his father's hunting platform, and shot him with it."

"When you look at the evidence—not speculation about a mysterious gunman or elaborate equations or last-minute lies—when you look at the actual evidence, you'll see the same thing. Colton Daniels killed his father."

Tiffany Erin stepped back then, out of the way of the screen. "On that Thursday evening last fall, Brett Daniels went out to the platform on the back of his property to hunt. At 6:34 that evening, Colton Daniels went out to that same platform carrying a loaded crossbow. How do we know this? Because we have the trail camera footage."

The picture popped up on the screen.

"Here he is, Colton Daniels, walking toward the platform with a loaded crossbow raised in front of him. It's not resting on his shoulder, it's not hanging at his side. It's raised and it's loaded."

She went over to the evidence table. "It was loaded with this arrow." She held it up to the jury. "This *exact* arrow. Twelve minutes later, at 6:46, we *know* Colt Daniels left the scene of the killing." The picture popped up. "We don't know exactly what happened in those twelve minutes, whether there was an argument or a fight or a perfectly normal conversation. We don't know what happened in those twelve minutes except for one thing. We *know* that Colton Daniels fired his crossbow. Look." She used the laser pointer to circle the crossbow hanging at Colt's side. "We know the crossbow has been fired. We can see the arrow is gone, the same arrow that was found at the scene. And we know that Colton Daniels walked away after he shot it."

Tiffany Erin set the arrow down and stood back in front of the jury. "Let's keep focusing on what we know. We know that

Brett Daniels wasn't found that Thursday. We know that he was found on Friday night by Tyler Daniels and his dog."

Tiffany Erin put the picture up, the one of the partially eaten body. Most of the jury looked away. It was impossible not to. "We know that Mr. Daniels' body had been lying in his yard for a day and that coyotes had gotten to it. But fortunately for the investigation, the coyotes didn't eat the area where the wound was that caused his death. That wound was right on his upper thigh." She put the picture up of the entrance and exit wound. "You heard from Dr. Wayne Archuleta, an educated and experienced pathologist who has investigated tens of thousands of deaths and hundreds of murders. Dr. Archuleta is the only person you have heard from who actually examined Mr. Daniels' body, the only person who physically inspected the wound, the only person who measured the laceration in the femoral artery that caused Mr. Daniels to bleed to death. Let me say that again. Dr. Archuleta is the *only* person who physically saw and inspected this wound. And it's Dr. Archuleta's opinion that a crossbow arrow"—she walked back over to the table and picked it up—"*this* crossbow arrow, caused the wound that killed Mr. Daniels. This arrow which we *know* was shot by the defendant Colton Daniels."

Tiffany Erin paused and shook her head, her pale eyes intent. "Killings don't happen in a vacuum. You've heard evidence, not theories but actual evidence, about the bad blood between Colton Daniels and his father. You heard about the time two years ago when Colton argued with his father and his father put Colton's head through a video game screen. I want you to think back to Mr. Kaminski's testimony and remember that it was Colton Daniels who attacked his father that night after an argument about Tyler. Then a year ago, the same thing happened again—Colton attacked his father at a football game and his father stopped him, put him against a wall, and told him that the next time Colton attacked him, he'd better bring a gun."

She paused. "Colton didn't bring a gun. He brought a crossbow. But it accomplished the same thing."

Tiffany Erin crossed her arms in the way that we'd all become familiar with, bowed her head a little, and drummed those long fingers. "Incredibly, though, the killing isn't the worst part, isn't the most thoroughly evil part of this whole thing. No, the worst part is that, according to the statement Colton himself gave to the police, he went back into the house and worked on his paper while his father lay bleeding in the dirt. He stayed in his house all that night, knowing his dad was dead or dying outside, and then the next morning went to Grand Valley to turn in a paper, a very convenient paper, so that he was on the road all day and got back just in time for his brothers' game. And after that game, he let his own brother, his younger brother who he was supposedly trying to protect, find this." She put the picture of the entrail-strewn body back on the screen. "And that wasn't an accident either. Colton knew what the body was going to look like. Do you know how we know this?"

She went over to the evidence table and picked up the green metal box. "From this. This coyote call was found fifty yards from Mr. Daniels' body, too far away for him to have dropped it and outside of the path Mr. Daniels would've taken back to the platform. Now it's possible that the coyotes would've found Mr. Daniels anyway, because he was bleeding so much. But we found this coyote call just fifty yards away from his body so I think we know exactly how the coyotes found Mr. Daniels."

Tiffany Erin hit the switch. A rabbit began to scream.

Have you ever heard a rabbit scream? It's high-pitched and it's piercing and it's awful. After five seconds, between the sounds of the screaming rabbit and the picture of Brett Daniels' partially devoured body, the jury began to squirm in their seats.

Tiffany Erin let it run for fifteen.

When she turned off the call, the relief in the courtroom was palpable. "I'm sorry. I know that made you uncomfortable. It should. But Colton Daniels didn't sound that call in front of a picture. He sounded that call within fifty yards of his father's body."

Tiffany Erin set the coyote call back on the desk and came back to the jury.

"Fortunately for us, Colton didn't realize that coyotes feed on the belly first, didn't know that they would leave the site of the wound intact so that we would know how Mr. Daniels was killed. And we do. The evidence has shown us exactly how Colton Daniels killed his father."

Tiffany Erin had every juror's eyes on her. "Murder is a crime. Murdering your own father is even worse. And this,"— she gestured to the screen and then turned it off—"*this* is unspeakable. That's why we are asking you to convict Colton Daniels of murder in the first degree of his father Brett Daniels. When you look at the evidence, the actual evidence, the conclusion is inescapable. Colton Daniels must be found guilty of murdering his father. Justice demands it."

I waited until Tiffany Erin sat down before I stood and walked up to the jury. A few of them were still looking at her. A few were staring at the now blank screen. The rest looked up at me, waiting.

It took a few moments but soon, the others turned to me, too. When they did, I said, "When I was a teenager, we used to go to Cedar Point every summer. When the rollercoaster lines got too long, my friends and I would play the midway games. I always liked the one where you had a hundred shots from a pellet gun to try to shoot out the red star. Have you ever played it? There's a little red star hanging on a piece of paper and you only win if you shoot every bit of red off the paper. So you'd sit there and shoot pellet after pellet into the middle of the star until you knocked it all out and you'd think you'd won and then the vendor would bring the paper up and the two of you would check it real close and if there was any red, any red at all, left on the card, you lost. It didn't matter how much you shot out of the middle, if you didn't hit all the points of the star too, you didn't win."

"The same is true here. The State has to prove its case beyond a reasonable doubt. If there are any areas of doubt, if there are any points left on the star, they lose."

I had a couple of nods but not as many as I'd hoped. I did have their attention though as I continued.

"The State is trying to keep all your attention on the middle. It's highlighting certain bits of evidence and ignoring the parts of the star that are necessary to prove its case, hoping that you'll just assume they're true. But that's not what the law requires, the law requires you look at *all* of the evidence. And we think that when you do, you'll see that the prosecution hasn't come close to proving its case beyond a reasonable doubt."

"What do I mean?" I stepped back and popped the pictures of Colt going to and from the platform onto the screen. "How many times has the State shown you these pictures?" I went to the evidence table and picked up the arrow. "How many times has Ms. Erin held this arrow up to you? Listen, there's no question that Colt went out to the hunting platform between 6:34 and 6:46 that night and there's no question that he shot his arrow. But the prosecution wants you to make a leap; they want you to *assume* that Colt shot and killed his father in that twelve-minute window. But the State hasn't provided you with any evidence at all that the arrow actually hit Brett Daniels."

I shook my head. "Let's talk about the arrow itself. Surely if the arrow had ripped through Brett Daniels' leg, there would have been evidence left behind on the arrow. But was there any blood? No. Any skin? No. Any hair or even fabric from his jeans? No. Not one bit. There was not a single shred of evidence linking Brett Daniels' body to the arrow."

"So what about the other way around? Surely the State would be able to provide you with evidence from Brett Daniels' body linking his fatal wound to the arrow? But it didn't. Instead, the State gave you the opinion of Dr. Warren Archuleta. Dr. Archuleta came in here and gave his opinion that the arrow caused the wound in Brett Daniels' leg. But an opinion, even from an expert like Dr. Archuleta, has to be based on facts, and Dr. Archuleta didn't provide us with any facts to support his opinion. He didn't do a microscopic examination of the striations around the entry wound to determine if a high-velocity bullet or a low velocity arrow made them. He didn't provide us with any carbon fragments that matched the arrow. In fact, he didn't even perform the sodium rhodizonate test to find out if the wound was caused by an arrow or bullet, a test so simple that he's done it hundreds of times in hundreds of autopsies. If he'd just done that one test, that simple test, we might have a conclusive answer, an answer beyond a reasonable doubt. But he didn't do the test. Instead, he just wants us to believe his opinion because he said it."

I waved a hand. "I suppose it's understandable—you heard how busy Dr. Archuleta was; he had speeches to give, articles to write, and dozens, no *hundreds*, of autopsies to perform. And then the sheriff's department handed him an arrow. So Dr. Archuleta eyeballed it and decided the arrow must have caused the wound. And we know he just eyeballed it, just assumed it, because he didn't perform any of the tests that would have let us know for sure."

"The prosecution has scoffed at that, that an examiner could mistake an arrow wound for a bullet wound. But you heard from Dr. Ray Gerchuk, a coroner just as experienced and just as educated, tell us that there are documented cases of crossbow wounds being indistinguishable from bullet wounds, of cases where one was confused with the other." I held up my hands. "And the fact is, that confusion is easy to avoid. To figure out which one is true, the State just had to perform the sodium rhodizonate test. That's it-then we would have known, we would have known if there was lead from a bullet in the wound or not. But the State didn't do it."

"So, we have an arrow that's totally clean with no evidence to link it to the body"—I held the arrow up one last time before putting it back on the table and stepping closer—"and we have a wound with no evidence to link it to the arrow. That means the State hasn't provided you with any evidence to link Brett Daniels' wound to Colt's arrow. That's reasonable doubt right there. But there's an even bigger problem with the State's theory —*it's physically impossible.*"

"We brought in Edgar Spright. Mr. Spright has spent decades reconstructing accidents." I smiled. "Now, I know there was a lot of math in his testimony, and I'll be the first to admit that avoiding math was one of the reasons I went to law school in the first place. But that's what experts like Mr. Spright are for. He showed you mathematically, as a matter of physics, that if the arrow had actually hit Brett Daniels, it wouldn't have landed where it did. Remember that the arrow was found 230 yards away from the platform. And he showed you that, in order to travel 230 yards, the arrow would have had to have been fired at an angle that sent it over the platform at 17 feet above the ground, far above Brett Daniels' thigh. He also showed you that, if the arrow had been fired at an angle so that it could have actually hit Brett Daniels' leg, it would have traveled no farther than 186 to 209 yards. And if something slowed the arrow down, like say a man's leg, it would've been even closer."

I put both hands up. "I doubt any of us can match Mr.

Spright's enthusiasm for math. But using the math, he showed us, as a matter of science and trajectory and *evidence*, that this arrow could not have hit Mr. Daniels in the leg. It's mathematically impossible."

I shrugged. "Math is just as available to the State as it is to me. And yet the prosecution didn't call a witness to explain to you how their magic arrow theory could be mathematically true. Instead, they ignored the math completely and kept pointing at the middle of the star, at the evidence that doesn't prove the most important parts of their case. They kept telling you to look at the pictures. So let's do that, let's look at the pictures."

I put the pictures of Colt leaving the platform back up on the screen. "The pictures put Colt out there at the platform, sure. We've discussed that. But they don't prove their theory of how the killing occurred. In fact, when you really study the pictures, they aren't consistent with how Brett Daniels died at all."

"Both Dr. Gerchuk and Dr. Archuleta said that once Mr. Daniels was wounded, he would have bled to death in four to ten minutes. We also know that he ran almost a quarter of a mile, in boots, bleeding, before he came to the place where he died."

I blew up the picture of Colt walking away, head down, crossbow hanging at his side. "Does that look like someone running away after he shot someone? Does that look like someone who's being charged by an enraged, bleeding man? Or does it look like someone walking away, dejected, after another unsuccessful talk with his father? I invite you to study these pictures and decide for yourself."

I turned the screen off. "And don't stop there. Consider how those pictures fit with all the other evidence. We know that the last picture was taken of Colt at 6:46 p.m. and we know from Tyler's testimony that Colt returned to his mother's house a little after seven, not bloody, not winded, not dirty or upset. And the boys stayed there the rest of the night, working on their school assignments. We know something happened to Brett Daniels later that night. We know he died in a terrible way. But the boys weren't there to see and hear whatever it was."

I shook my head. "We know that Tyler and Colt both told the police that they were staying with their father that Thursday night and I'm not asking you to ignore that. I'm asking you to understand it. At the time, it was thought that Brett Daniels had died in a hunting accident so neither of them would've known that there was a murder investigation going on. And I know it seems silly to you and me, but to a high school kid and his older brother who have dedicated their young lives to football, winning a state championship and earning a college scholarship are a very big deal. And they're not alone—sports networks all over the country devote whole days of coverage to the games and to the kids' announcements of where they're going to school."

I raised a hand. "I'm not saying it was right that they lied to the police about where they lived. I'm saying it was understandable. It took a great deal of courage for Tyler to come forward today and tell you what actually happened. There's going to be a personal cost for him. It might cost him his scholarship. It will certainly cost him and his school and his teammates their state championship. But he told you what happened; he told you that he and Colt were at his mom's house Thursday night and Friday morning. Which is also the only explanation that makes any sense. Had they been there Thursday night and Friday morning, one of the boys and their dog would have discovered Mr. Daniels before Friday night. Instead, Tyler discovered him Friday night and immediately called the authorities."

"When Ms. Erin comes back up here, she'll probably question whether Tyler told the truth today, whether he was telling a lie now to save his brother. But you know what she didn't do?

She didn't put on any evidence to the contrary. She could have. She could have called Tyler's mom or her boyfriend or someone else around town to testify that the boys were actually staying at their dad's. But she didn't. So the testimony in this case, Tyler's testimony, establishes that he and Colt were at his mom's on Thursday night."

"All those gaps in the State's evidence are bad enough. Their last accusation is so baseless that I don't even want to mention it but so terrible that I feel like I have to. The prosecutor has suggested that Colt sounded a coyote call to summon those scavengers to hide his supposed crime. And what evidence has she given you to support this awful accusation? None. Not a thing. Ms. Erin hasn't produced a single bit of evidence to connect Colt to that coyote call. No pictures, no fingerprints, no witnesses. Not even a footprint. Instead, she just lobbed this baseless theory out there, hoping you'd believe it without thinking, without studying the evidence. She wants you so outraged that you'll just assume that Colt sounded the call, just like she wants you to assume that Colt shot his father."

I looked over at Tiffany Erin. Her legs were crossed, hands folded in her lap, regarding me with those pale eyes as if I were giving tomorrow's weather forecast. "Ms. Erin gets to come back up here and speak to you again. I challenge her to offer you a single shred of evidence that Colt sounded that call. She won't be able to. She'll justify it in some way, but the real reason is because she can't. And when she fails to give you that proof, I encourage you to disregard that part of her case completely and see it for what it is, an attempt to evoke a reaction in you that's so strong that you'll forget to study the evidence."

I was looking at the jurors the whole time, of course, from one to the other to the other. They were all paying attention, but I wasn't getting anything back from them. Just their attention. I kept going.

"Now I've told you that I want you to consider all of the evidence and that means we have to talk about one last thing. Ms. Erin has told you about two arguments between Colt and his dad. And I think those arguments, those fights, help us make sense of all this, too."

I raised my chin. "Brett Daniels was a hard man. The kind of man who hunts coyotes alone at night with a crossbow. The kind of man who was no-nonsense and tough and who exercised an unrelenting discipline to make a top quarterback. You've heard that Colt disagreed with how Brett applied those methods to Tyler. You heard that Brett put Colt's head through a video game during one of those disagreements and slammed Colt against a wall during another. And more importantly, you heard testimony that Brett told Colt that the next time they had one of those discussions, Colt had better bring a gun."

"Well, on that Thursday night, Colt felt he needed to have another one of those discussions with his dad. You heard Tyler testify that Brett was ramping things up as they got closer to the playoffs and you heard Tyler say that Colt thought it was too much. And we know that the three of them weren't living together so Colt had to make a special trip out to see his dad. And once he realized his dad was out hunting, Colt would've known that his dad was armed."

"We don't know the nature of that conversation between the two of them that night. The State hasn't proven it to you. But we do know that both of them fired their crossbows at some point. Colt's arrow went over his dad's head and ended up 230 yards away. And Brett's arrow was sticking out of the ground at the base of the platform. And as far as anyone can tell, as far as the *evidence* is concerned, no one was hit by an arrow that night."

The jurors' expressions stayed blank as I went on.

"We know that Brett Daniels was wounded later that Thursday night, wounded so that he bled to death. Unfortunately, the State didn't do a good enough investigation to tell us who shot him or what he was shot with. Instead of performing tests to figure out what happened, a busy coroner eyeballed a wound and an arrow that was found two football fields away and decided that was close enough."

"But close enough isn't the standard. Beyond reasonable doubt is. The State has to prove every part of its case, has to knock out every point on that red star. And they haven't done it. The State hasn't proved that Colt's arrow caused Brett's wound. In fact, they haven't even proved that Brett's wound was caused by an arrow at all. And when we dug into the evidence and the science and the math, really dug into it instead of eyeballed it, we discovered that Colt Daniels' arrow could not, by the laws of science, absolutely could not have caused the wound in his dad's thigh.

I shook my head. "Colt Daniels didn't kill his dad. The fact is I don't know who did. And neither does the State."

"When you study the evidence, you'll see that the State hasn't met its burden, it hasn't proven its case beyond a reasonable doubt. We think that when you look at all of the evidence, every single bit of it, you'll see that Brett Daniels couldn't have died the way the State says he did. And that's why we ask that, after you've considered all of the evidence, you return a verdict of not guilty in favor of Colt Daniels. Thank you."

As I sat, Tiffany Erin got up shaking her head. "Mr. Shepherd is a fine lawyer, and I expected all sorts of creative arguments from him, but I have to say that being accused of ignoring the evidence isn't one of them. I'm not even going to spend much time on it. Please, by all means, examine the evidence. Examine the pictures of Colton Daniels going to the scene of the murder with his loaded crossbow. Study the picture of him leaving the scene with the empty crossbow. Inspect the arrow, his arrow, which was found at the scene. Pull up the picture of the wound in Brett Daniels' thigh; a wound that the medical examiner, the only medical examiner who examined Brett Daniels' body, says was caused by that arrow. It's true that the fingerprints were all wiped from the coyote call so leave that out of it if you want as you consider the facts. Colt Daniels went to the hunting platform, fired his crossbow, left, and his father died of a crossbow arrow wound. No amount of lawyering or fancy experts can change those facts."

"The one other thing I want to talk about is Tyler Daniels. Mr. Shepherd admits that Tyler and the defendant lied to the police when they were first interviewed. He then paints a picture of Tyler Daniels making a great sacrifice to come forward to tell the truth now. I want you to consider two things about that. First, there is no question that Tyler Daniels lied. The only question is when. He was either lying to the police the night his dad was found or he's lying to you now."

"And despite what Mr. Shepherd says, I submit to you that it's more likely he's lying now than it is that he was lying then. Now, his brother is facing life in prison. Then, some football eligibility was at stake. Which one was most likely to evoke a lie? Which one makes it worth the risk? You know. Just like we know that the evidence puts Colton Daniels at his dad's house with the murder weapon on the night his father was killed. Tyler Daniels is lying. Don't believe him."

"Once you take out Tyler Daniels' lies, we're left with one conclusion—Colton Daniels killed his father. Don't let him get away with it. Thank you."

The jury stayed impassive. I couldn't get a read on them as Judge LaPlante said, "Members of the jury, the time has come for you to deliberate on the evidence. I will now read to you the instructions of law, which govern this case. It is important that you do not use your own interpretations of what the law is or should be. Instead, the law is encompassed by these instructions."

Judge LaPlante then spent the next forty-five minutes reading the jury instructions. I followed along on my own copy to make sure that he read them correctly so I couldn't pay much attention to how Colt was doing. I knew it probably wasn't great.

When the judge was done, he took a break to let either side object if we wanted to. Neither of us did, so the judge thanked the jury and instructed them to begin their deliberations. We stood as the jury filed out. Not one of them looked our way.

"How long will it be?" whispered Colt.

"There's no way to know," I said.

He scowled, then nodded.

Once the jury left, Judge LaPlante said, "Please make sure Patricia has your cell phone numbers. We have a few hours yet before the Court closes for the day so I suggest you stay nearby and we'll call you if the verdict comes back."

Judge LaPlante looked at both of us and it seemed significant, but I couldn't tell exactly what it meant as he said, "I am also advised that, due to the testimony this morning, there are still a number of reporters waiting outside the courthouse. You may want to take that into consideration when deciding where to wait."

Then Judge LaPlante left.

"So what are we going to do?" said Colt.

"Find a place to wait," I said.

59

We eventually found our way to Judge EJ Wesley's courtroom on the next floor up—me and Danny, Colt and Rob. I had spent a good amount of time with Judge Wesley's bailiff last fall when we had tried the Archie Mack case and, when I explained what was going on, he invited us to camp out in the jury room. When we were settled, I sent Danny to go get us some coffee since he was the least likely to be recognized.

"Have you heard from Rhonda and Tyler?" I asked Rob.

"Just texting them now." Rob's thumbs worked the phone. It wasn't too long before he said, "They're at the attorney's office across the street."

"Ronnie's? Tell them to sit tight there. We'll let them know when the jury comes back."

"Right." Rob gave one last thumb punch then set the phone on the table. We sat in silence for a moment before Colt said, "What do you think they're going to do?"

I shook my head. "I'm not sure, Colt. I think we gave them enough for reasonable doubt. But I'm just not sure."

Rob smiled at Colt and nodded. "That Spright guy was

pretty persuasive on the arrow. And Nate explained the pictures pretty good, too."

Colt looked unconvinced. "That Erin woman was right though."

"About what?" I said.

"We lied. Then or now."

"Hopefully they'll see why it makes more sense that Tyler is telling the truth now."

When Colt looked at me, he didn't seem mad. He seemed tired, curious. "How did you figure it out? That we were living with my mom?"

"It was a lot of little things, but it was mostly Chet. That night we watched the football game; he must've gone in and out to the backyard a dozen times. There's no way he wouldn't have found your dad Thursday night if he'd been there. I still hadn't put it together though until last night when I saw Tyler feed Chet, and I remembered what the house had looked like the first time I was there—Chet's food bowl was dusty, there were only crumbs in the bag, and Tyler filled a bone-dry water bowl. And I realized that Chet hadn't lived there in a long time."

"You shouldn't have done it, with Tyler."

I shrugged. "Ultimately, it was Tyler's choice. And he didn't want you to go to jail."

Colt looked away. "Tyler didn't know what he was choosing."

"I think he did."

My phone buzzed and I was so jumpy about it being a call from the bailiff that I answered without looking.

"Nate Shepherd."

"Nate, this is Megan Dira."

That'll teach me.

"Hi, Megan," I said. "I'm sorry, but this really isn't a good time. I thought you were the Court."

"Jury out?"

"Yes."

"I heard Tyler testified?"

"He did."

"I'll be in touch."

I hung up.

"Who was that?" said Rob. His voice really was a raspy rumble.

"The attorney from the State who wants to know about your dealings with Steve Mathison and Jimmy Benoit."

Rob scowled. "Jimmy who?"

"One thing at a time."

Danny returned with the coffees. As he handed them out, I asked, "Is there much of a crowd?"

"Not too many, but every one of them has a camera or a phone."

"Gotcha. How'd you avoid them?"

Danny smiled. "By not being newsworthy."

"Well done."

"How's Mom doing?" said Colt to Rob.

Rob smiled. "I wish I'd bought stock in Marlboro last week."

Colt laughed. "You're only her boyfriend. I'm her son, I should've told you."

Rob put a hand on Colt's shoulder, laughed, and squeezed. Then the laughter trailed away and their smiles drained from their faces and they stared at the table.

A few minutes later, Colt looked up at me. "Your brother didn't know. About Tyler."

"I didn't think so."

"I should tell him."

"He already knows."

Colt raised a thick eyebrow.

I thought about deflecting the unasked question, then decided Colt deserved the truth. "I told him about my suspicions last night. I wasn't going to have him blindsided by it this morning."

Colt winced. "What did he do?"

"He was going to talk to the state today."

"The state?"

"The athletic association. To alert it that he might have used an ineligible player."

"So we'll take second?"

I shook my head. "We used an ineligible player, Colt. The whole season's gone. Every game he played in will be forfeited."

Colt was quiet for a moment before he said, "Well, people will know who really won."

"No, Colt, they won't. Tyler should've been playing for Carrefour South."

That came out far harsher than I meant it, which was pretty small of me considering Colt was waiting for a verdict in his murder trial. "That was out of line. I'm sorry."

"Don't be." Colt looked away. "I'd want to defend my brother, too."

"Now that it's over, can I ask you about one thing that's really been bothering me?" said Rob.

"Shoot," I said.

"You put on all that evidence about how it couldn't have been Colt's arrow that killed Brett."

"Yes."

"You convinced me."

"Good."

Rob almost looked embarrassed as he looked at Danny, then at me, and tilted out his hands. "But then who did it?"

He'd hit the biggest hole in our strategy of course. "I don't know, Rob. My bet is that whoever it was shot him with a gun, but I really have no idea who it might've been. I just know it wasn't Colt."

"I'm not crazy about that."

"That it wasn't Colt?"

Rob looked grim. "No. That there's someone walking around out there who's meaner than Brett and cold enough to call coyotes on him."

That really wasn't something I could disagree with so I nodded and sipped my coffee.

Einstein has a whole relativity thing about how time is flexible and can have different speeds depending upon the observer. He supposedly once compared it to the difference in how a man would experience two hours with a beautiful woman or one minute with his hand on a hot stove. He didn't actually say that, but it proved his point then and it proves my point now. We spent the rest of that afternoon in the jury room with our hands on a hot stove, twisting in the wind, or whatever expression you'd use to explain that time crawled past, that each minute dragged on, and that the future stretched out before us to an infinitely receding horizon.

And then my phone buzzed, the bailiff let us know that a verdict was in, and time accelerated as the moment arrived when Colt would find out how he would spend the rest of his life.

Rob texted Rhonda and we headed back to the courtroom.

∽

When we walked through the doors to the courtroom, my brother Tom was standing there, waiting for us. Tom strode up, jaw jutting, his lean face looking like it was ready to spit nails.

Colt took a step back. "Coach, I—"

Tom grabbed his hand, and said, "Listen, Colt. Stand tall, chin up. No matter what. Do you hear me?"

Colt blinked. Then he said, "Coach, I'm so sorry—"

"Stop it!" The muscles in Tom's jaw rippled. "We'll be fine. You stand firm up there with Nate." He tapped Colt's chest with the bottom of his fist. "Back to back. Us v. all." Tom looked around the courtroom. "You shouldn't have said the words but since you did, this seems like the place to remember them."

Colt's mouth worked until he said, "Thank you."

I put a hand on Colt's back and guided him up to the table. I looked over his head and mouthed to Tom, "Thanks."

Tom gave me a brusque wave and took a seat near the back.

More people filed in. Tiffany Erin and her associate strode down the aisle and, even at this point, after a week of going at it, she made no effort to say hello or acknowledge my presence. Rhonda Mazur came next, blowing up the aisle with the overwhelming smell of cigarette smoke. She wouldn't look at me either. Instead, I heard her whisper to Rob, "I left Tyler at the lawyer's," then she came up to the gate, reached out, grabbed Colt's hand, and pulled him close. As she squeezed him, her eyes clenched closed. Then she pulled back and Rhonda's face went to stone as she gave Colt a kiss on the cheek and said, "Nut up, son."

Then she straightened, still not looking at me, and turned back to her seat.

She saw my brother at the back of the room and froze.

Tom stared at her, his look hard. Then he left his seat and walked down the aisle.

Rhonda watched him for a moment, then turned back around and faced the front of the courtroom.

I knew both of their tempers. I was concerned.

Tom came up and stood next to her, facing the front. Rhonda stared straight ahead. After a moment, Tom put his arm around her, leaned down, and whispered so that I could barely hear. "He's a good boy." Then he hugged her with one arm.

Rhonda bit her lip, nodded, and rubbed Tom's back quickly.

Then the two of them dropped their hands and stared straight ahead.

I didn't think much more of this was going to help Colt keep it together at all. Just as I was about to make up something to talk to him about, Patricia Weathers walked out of the judge's office and said, "All rise."

We were already standing as Judge LaPlante came in. He sat and said, "I understand we have a verdict?"

"We do, Your Honor," Patricia Weathers said in her usual soft voice.

"Let's bring the jury in then."

We all stood as Patricia went over to the jury room door, knocked, and ducked her head in. I heard voices cut abruptly short. A moment later, the jury filed in.

They were not looking at us.

When they were sorted and seated, Judge LaPlante said, "Members of the jury, have you reached a verdict?"

A woman stood. One of the non-football fans. "We have, Your Honor."

"Please hand the verdict form to Ms. Weathers."

She did. Patricia brought the papers over to Judge LaPlante, who looked at it, then handed it back. His face didn't twitch.

"Go ahead and give it back to the foreperson please, Ms. Weathers."

I could feel Colt twisting next to me. I put one hand between his shoulder blades and patted and hoped that I had done enough.

"Members of the jury, in the matter of the State of Michigan versus Colton Daniels, on the charge of murder in the first degree, how say you?"

The foreperson still wasn't looking at us as she said, "Your Honor, we the jury find the defendant not guilty."

There was a gasp behind me.

"And on the charge of murder in the second degree, how say you?"

"We the jury find the defendant not guilty."

The gasp behind me became a sob. I squeezed Colt's shoulder. He just looked stunned.

Judge LaPlante nodded. "Members of the jury, I wish to thank you for your service. What you have done is no easy task and yet it's foundational to our system of justice. You are now released from your duties and from your restriction not to discuss the case. People may ask you about your deliberations. You are free to speak to them about it, but you are in no way obligated to do so. Thank you for your time and attention."

"I'm free?" said Colt. "I'm really free?"

I smiled. "You're really free."

Colt turned around and grabbed Rhonda and Rob over the railing. As the three of them embraced, Tom caught my eye, reached over Colt's shoulder, and shook my hand. It was fierce. "Good work," he said.

I waved him off and smiled.

I turned back and found Tiffany Erin waiting patiently, her hands clasped in front of her. When she had my attention, she took a step forward and offered her hand. "Congratulations."

"Thanks. You try a great case."

She shrugged and, if the compliment meant anything to her, it didn't show on her face. "You will not be hearing from *my* office any further on this case."

There was something odd about her tone, but before I could put a finger on it, she turned away and went back to her table to collect her things.

Danny was doing the same at our table. I leaned over and shook his hand. "Nice job."

"You, too."

"Sure you don't want to keep doing this?"

"Certain."

"Had to try. We'll talk."

Danny nodded.

I saw that Judge LaPlante was still sitting behind the bench so I went up to see him. His dark eyes held a little light as he said, "Congratulations, Mr. Shepherd."

He extended his hand over the bench and I took it. "Thanks, Judge. Could you tell?"

He smiled for one of the first times during trial. "Not at all. My opinion changed from day to day. You both did a fine job."

"Thank you, Judge."

Tiffany Erin was standing back a little ways so that it was clear she didn't want to talk to the judge along with me so I nodded my thanks again and went back to the table. I watched out of the corner of my eye, curious. Tiffany Erin stayed up there a little longer than I did but not by much. She went back to her table and never really looked my way as she and her associate packed up.

Finally, I decided she was a riddle I wasn't going to solve, stopped not-watching her, and gathered my things.

PITCH

60

People used to ask if I was happy after winning a trial. Back when I practiced civil law, when the primary stakes were money, I felt more embarrassed by a loss than excited by a win. Now though, when the stakes were a person's life that was not my own, I felt nothing but an overwhelming sense of relief that someone wasn't going to be locked up for the rest of their life because I should have done a better job.

Rhonda, Colt, and Rob were a different matter. Their joy was palpable, their victory was new, and I'm pretty sure that it was only the presence of the judge that kept Rhonda from yelling "Screw the State!" as we walked out the courtroom doors.

Right into Megan Dira.

Megan Dira was waiting in the hall like a shadow, standing there in a black suit holding a black briefcase in front of her with both hands. "Nate," she said.

I stopped. "This really can't wait?"

"No. It really can't."

"Who is this person standing between me and a beer, Shepherd?" said Rhonda.

False Oath 435

"I'm the state attorney you've been ignoring, Ms. Mazur," said Megan Dira.

Rhonda looked at me and grinned. "We've been kind of busy kicking the State's ass."

"So I understand. Congratulations."

"So if you'll excuse us—"

"Rhonda, Rob," I said. "We have to talk to her."

Rhonda stopped mid-step. "What?"

"There are some things we need to discuss. I thought it could wait until Monday but..."

Megan Dira shook her head. "It can't."

Joy was replaced by confusion as Rhonda, Rob, and Colt looked at each other. Finally, Colt said, "What do you want us to do?"

"Follow me," I said, and led them away.

~

WE WENT BACK UPSTAIRS to Judge Wesley's empty jury room. Rob and Rhonda and Colt and Danny and I sat on one side of the table as Megan Dira sat down on the other and opened her black snakeskin briefcase.

"Ms. Mazur, Mr. Preston, I'm an attorney with the State's Public Integrity Unit. I need information about your dealings with Steve Mathison and Jimmy Benoit."

As Rhonda opened her mouth, Megan Dira raised a hand. "Please don't say anything to me, especially if it's untrue. Instead, let me remind you that your son Tyler just admitted on the stand that he and Colt lied to police officers about their whereabouts and where they lived on the night they found Brett Daniels' body. That is a crime."

"They weren't in court," said Rhonda.

"No, they weren't. So it's not perjury. But it is a crime to mislead a police officer in the State of Michigan during the course of his investigation."

Rhonda scoffed. "Since when?"

"Since five years ago. You should know that there are some other things we can add to that." She pulled out a folder. "Here is Colton's college application and tuition statement claiming in-state residency this year at Grand Valley." She pulled out another folder. "Here is Tyler's application to two in-state universities claiming to be a Michigan resident. And here are both of their FAFSA forms for financial aid and scholarships this year in which they declared, under penalty of law, that their residence is their father's house in the State of Michigan. You will see that all of these documents are dated after Tyler said that he had moved for the summer."

Rhonda started to talk and Megan raised her hand again. "Please, Ms. Mazur, don't respond to me now. I don't want your family to get into any more trouble. Because both boys were eighteen and applied to college on their own, I don't have any documents that are signed by you, Ms. Mazur. It is solely your sons who have either lied to police officers or lied on their forms. However, at least some of the information I'm requesting, maybe all of it, is going to come from you. I'm going to tell you what I'm looking for and I'm going to give you until Monday to provide it to me. My purpose today is just to lay out your options."

"Listen, if you think—"

"Rhonda." Rob had one hand on her arm. "We can talk after she leaves."

It appeared to take everything she had but Rhonda clenched her teeth, folded her hands, and waited.

"What I do as part of the Public Integrity Unit is investigate corruption by state officials. Let's say, hypothetically, that a state university had a sponsorship contract with an athletic apparel company. And let's say that this apparel company used recruiters to steer young athletes to the universities with whom it had sponsorship contracts."

Colt scowled. "Why would they do that?" I noticed that Colt was the one who asked the question. Rhonda and Rob glanced at each other.

"Hypothetically, athletic apparel companies put great value on having famous athletes wearing their products. And, when some of those athletes become pros, the competition for endorsements is fierce, especially at the premier positions—scoring guard, pitcher...quarterback."

The room became quiet.

Megan Dira continued, "And let's say, hypothetically, that there were folks at the state universities who knew this was going on and, in some cases, even helped. That would be something that the Public Integrity Unit would investigate."

"But your focus would be on the state university employees?" I said.

Megan Dira nodded. "That's correct. My interest would be the connections between the recruiters and the university, not the recruiters and the athlete. So, here's my proposal to you, Ms. Mazur. I want you to tell me everything your family has to do with Steve Mathison."

The research Olivia had done for me clicked into place—the camps, the athletes, the seemingly unconnected signings with universities across the country.

I'd been focused on the kids. I'd never noticed the brands that the universities' teams were wearing.

"And in exchange?" I said.

"In exchange, all of the college-related crimes and charges would go away."

"What about the charge for misleading the police officer?"

"That's not under my jurisdiction. Colt and Tyler will have to deal with whatever consequences there are for that. However, I can tell you that the penalty for that offense will be much more severe if it is part of a pattern of criminal deception rather than an isolated incident."

"What else?" I said.

"We also want to know anything you had to do with Jimmy Benoit."

"Who the hell is Jimmy Benoit?" said Rhonda.

I raised a hand. "We'll discuss it in a minute. Anything else?"

"That's it. Give me all of the details of your dealings with those two people by Monday and I will see to it that Tyler and Colt are not charged for all of their false filings with the state and federal government. We'll also give you Rhonda, and you, Rob, complete immunity from prosecution for anything you tell us. If you don't, or if we determine later that the disclosure was incomplete, we will withdraw that protection."

"End of day Monday?"

Megan Dira appeared to think. "5:00 p.m. But no later." She closed the briefcase but left the folders. "You still have my number?"

She'd contacted me often enough. "Yes."

"Then, I look forward to hearing from you." She snapped her briefcase shut and gave Colt an assessing look. "I'm sorry for your loss," she said, then she left.

Colt looked like he'd eaten a frog. "Nate, can she do that?"

"She can." I thought. "Colt, do you know anything about Steve Mathison?"

"I don't."

"Then go out into the courtroom, sit down, and don't talk to anybody."

"Really?"

"Really."

Colt walked out and as he did, it was clear that someone had placed the world back on his shoulders.

As the door clicked, I turned to Rhonda and Rob and said, "Tell me everything you know about Steve Mathison."

∼

BRETT DANIELS HAD BEEN the one who took Tyler to the elite quarterback camps. Except one time. That one time, Brett had been under the gun to finish the drywall on a commercial construction project so Rhonda had agreed to drive Tyler to Indianapolis for the weekend. Watching games was one thing but watching drills was quite another and Rhonda had been bored out of her tree. As she sat, half-watching in the mostly empty stands, a man had bummed a smoke and struck up a conversation. He turned out to be Steve Mathison.

"He was funny," said Rhonda, "and he was easy enough to look at and he never once mentioned a five-step drop or throwing on platform or any of that other bullshit-nonsense these football types are always spewing at these things. The boys were going to be staying in the dorm that night and he eventually invited me to dinner with some of the other parents."

"It was a fun group, there was a dad from Arkansas and a mom from Kentucky and a couple from Nebraska. The parents at these quarterback camps can be a real pain in the ass, with over-achieving, braggy types making sure their kids get all programmed up, but these were good people. So we drank too much, stayed up too late, and I overslept the next morning so that I barely made it back to the camp in time to pick Tyler up at the end of the morning session." Rhonda stopped and looked at the ceiling. "Can we smoke in here?"

"No," I said.

Rhonda squirmed in her chair, then said, "So a couple

weeks later, just as the summer 7-on-7 passing leagues were starting, I get a call from Stevie M. saying he is gonna be in the area and wanted directions to the stadium so he could watch. I tell Rob and he's suspicious, of course, so he comes with me and when he sees Stevie M. I think maybe Rob's going to pop him just on principle, but it turns out Stevie fishes almost as much as Rob and the two of them hit it right off. We're watching the game and Tyler just launches one down the field and Stevie claps and he asks where Tyler is planning on going to school, and we say we don't know and Stevie says well, he's certainly going to have a lot of options. Then I said I'm glad to hear it because that's the only way Tyler's going to afford it and I think he's talented but then every mom does."

Rhonda tapped her fingers on the table in a rapid beat. "So, Stevie comes to at least half of those 7-on-7s and he's always fun and he can't stop saying how talented Tyler is and how he's gonna light the world on fire. Then, at one point, he says that he knows the chief recruiters at some schools and he can make sure that they're paying attention to Tyler. I tell him I got a box full of letters back at the house that say they're already paying attention to him and Stevie nods and says he understands and says that he can make sure certain people pay *special* attention to him. And I say since Tyler's one of the best quarterbacks in the country he should be getting special attention. It wasn't too long after that that the real conversations started."

"What are the real conversations?"

Rhonda tapped faster and looked at Rob.

Rob nodded. "For the boys."

Rhonda turned back to me. "Stevie said it didn't make any sense for the coaches and the administrators and the schools and the apparel companies and the TV networks to make millions off Tyler and for him to make nothing. He gave me a list of schools and said if we picked any one of them, he would see to it that Tyler started getting benefits right away."

She looked down. "And he gave us some money up front, no strings attached he said, to show us he was serious."

"How serious?"

Rhonda shrugged. "To us? Very serious."

I had a suspicion about what was next but I asked anyway. "Could you tell what the schools on the list had in common?"

"Not at first. But the gear we started getting made it pretty clear."

"All the universities on the list had a contract with that apparel company?"

"Yep. And all we had to do was pick one of the schools on that list."

"All Tyler had to do," said Rob.

"Right," said Rhonda. "And we were happy because it wasn't limiting Tyler's decision at all. There was a school in every major conference in every part of the country and they were all good programs so we felt like Tyler could still go wherever he wanted. And we felt that since he was the one with the talent, since he'd be the one filling the stadium, it was only right that he get a little piece of what everyone else was making off of him."

I remembered something. "The new truck," I said to Rob.

Rob nodded. "I bought it with the first payment. Steve said that we'd have to be careful, that things being given directly to the player were too easy to spot but that a gift from your parents wouldn't look suspicious. So I bought the truck, and I was gonna drive it for the rest of the year and then give it to Tyler when he left for school." He smiled through his beard. "The running joke was that I was driving his truck."

"How much did Tyler know about this?"

"Nothing. Tyler doesn't know how much I make so I don't think he thought twice about it. And he was leaning toward the schools we wanted him to go to so we didn't have to say much. We would just encourage him about how this school was great or that program was really up and coming, stuff like that."

Something else occurred to me. "Wasn't Brett going to all the 7-on-7s?"

"Of course. But, us being us, we usually sat on opposite sides of the stadium. And by the time Tyler moved in with us the summer before his senior year, we figured we had the most influence on him."

"Was Brett part of this deal?"

Rhonda shook her head.

"Did you ever discuss it with him?"

"You mean share the money? Hell no."

"So then what happened?"

"So then Brett finds a way to screw things up right at the very end. He dies, Colt gets arrested, and all of us are focusing so much on making sure that Colt doesn't go to prison that no one notices that Tyler has decided he wants to wear creamsicle orange on Saturdays."

"And that school wasn't on the list?"

"That school was not on the list." Rhonda was tapping with both hands now.

"What happened?"

"Well, Stevie M. is about as pissed as he can get and I don't blame him because we'd told him more than once that we had it all squared away. He screams for his money back and I'm inclined to tell him to piss off, but Rob here is more honorable than me, so he sells the truck back and we give Stevie most of his money less the part that was just long gone."

"What did Mathison say?"

"He said he looked forward to Tyler never making the college playoff."

"Nice."

"And that's about it."

I thought. Everything Rhonda said made sense and it fit with the research that Olivia had done. I nodded and said, "Now what about Jimmy Benoit?"

Rhonda looked at Rob then looked at me and said, "We don't know any Jimmy Benoit."

"Are you sure? I think he's in the same racket as Mathison."

"I think we would know who's trying to pay us off to get our son to go to their school."

Rhonda had told me so much about Mathison that I was inclined to believe her about Benoit. I nodded and said, "All right, you can think about it over the weekend, but if you tell Megan Dira all of this—*all* of it—she'll prevent any college-related charges from being filed against the boys."

"What about this lying to the cops thing?"

"She's promised me that she'll recommend a reduced sentence for cooperation."

Rob's eyes got wide. "A reduced sentence?"

"They lied to a police officer about a murder, Rob. That's a crime."

Rhonda looked at me. "Is this what's best, Nate?"

"For the boys, yes."

She sat there a moment, tapping, then held out her hand. "Give me the bitch's card. We'll call Monday."

I slid it across the table. "Whatever you do, don't lie when you talk to her."

"We're learning that," she said and put the card in her pocket.

I stood. "All right, we're going to have to run the gauntlet. Let me handle the press and—"

There was a gravelly rasp, and I turned back to find Rob squeezing the table with both hands. His beard was quivering as he said, "So the boys still—" He broke off with a choke.

Rhonda put one arm around him and put her other hand on his. "They'll be alright."

Rob shook his head. "I'm not feeling like we won anymore."

She rubbed his back. "We did, baby. It's just a new game now."

His voice was a gravelly whisper. "They *have* to be okay."

"I know, baby. They will."

Rob's shoulders began to shake and he bowed his head.

Rhonda looked at me. "Hey Shepherd, Rob's lunch isn't agreeing with him too good. Could you give us a few minutes?"

"Of course," I said, and Rhonda rubbed Rob's shoulders and squeezed his hand and whispered to him as I left.

61

It was a mess getting out of the courthouse, but there's a difference between a New York City mess and a Carrefour, Michigan mess. There were maybe twelve reporters waiting for us outside. I gave them a short statement about being pleased that justice had prevailed and being thankful for such an attentive jury. Then I told them that, at the end of the day, we all had to remember that Colt had lost his father and asked them to please respect the family's privacy since that loss was still fresh. After, I put them all in my Jeep and we drove around the block a couple of times before pulling into the rear entrance of Ronnie Hawkins' office just across the street.

We put the family all in one room while Ronnie and I went to another and I filled her in on everything that Rhonda and Rob had told me. Then the two of us went back in and she said that she agreed that dealing with Megan Dira was the best thing for Tyler, too.

By that time, it was getting close to 7:30 at night. We had all just finished a trial and I could feel myself crashing. They stood and we all prepared to leave.

Colt looked at me. "Can I go wherever I want?"

"You can."

He looked at his mother. "Could you stay up at dad's house one more night?"

"Sure thing," Rhonda said. "We'll get some pizzas."

"Thanks."

They all began to file out the door of Ronnie's small conference room. Rob and Tyler and Rhonda passed me and Colt was about to when he suddenly grabbed me and gave me a fierce hug. I was surprised, but when he didn't let go I hugged him back.

"I didn't do it," he said.

"I know."

He squeezed. "Thank you."

"You're welcome."

Then Colt let go and followed his family out the door.

"It's nice when you get the innocent ones," said Ronnie as they left.

I nodded. "More nerve-racking. But nice."

Like I said before, I was crashing so I got in my car to go home. My plan was to have something to eat and a beer or three, but there was one more thing I needed to check so I made a call.

"Congratulations, Shep!" said Olivia.

"You heard already?"

"It's been posted all over."

"Yeah? What did Alexis Fury have to say about it?"

"You know, almost nothing."

"Really?"

"Yeah. There was a cryptic post about respecting juries then the account started in on a woman whose mom went missing on a family RV trip."

"Huh. Small favors, I guess."

"Going out to celebrate?"

"No, just going home. Can you look something up for me?"

"And you say I'm a slave-driver."
"Just one last thing on this case."
"Sure, but I'm on my way out."
"Off to see the physical therapist?"
"That's so last month."
I chuckled. "Tomorrow would be fine if you could fit in."
"What do you need?"
I told her.
"That's no problem. I have most of it done already."
"Great. Thanks, Liv."
"Hey, Shep?"
"Yeah?"
"You're extraordinary."
I smiled. "Must've rubbed off. Have a good night, Liv."
"You, too."

I went home, made it through one enchilada and two-and-a-half beers, and fell asleep.

Party, party.

∼

I SLEPT IN ON SATURDAY. Late. I was on my second coffee and leafing through the mail that had stacked up during the week when I noticed the electricity shut-off notice. I rifled through the bills to see if there was anything else I'd let slide during the trial, then hopped online to pay the bill and keep the lights on.

Those kinds of things had been a lot easier to manage with Sarah.

As long as I was on the computer, I figured I'd better do the same triage with work. I checked my emails for any other time bombs, but fortunately there were no emergencies. The only thing that was unexpected was an email from the probate attorney, Marv Lindhoffer. I'd put Tyler in touch with him to help with Brett's estate. Marv had emailed me thanking me for the referral, congratulating me on the verdict, and letting me know that, now that Colt had been acquitted, he had an interest in Brett's estate so Marv needed to speak with him.

Lawyers are a psychotic, work-a-holic bunch so I took a shot that Marv Lindhoffer was working on Saturday and, sure enough, he answered his office phone. After I gave him Colt's cell phone, Marv said, "I appreciate that, Nate. I've been sitting tight with the estate until the trial was over. Now that it is, we can get some things moving. There are some significant assets that will be passing to the boys, and I'd like to get the title squared away on the house."

"Sure."

"And of course, I'll authorize a distribution to Colt to pay your fee for the case."

"Those boys have a hard enough road ahead of them," I said. "I don't want them to use that money on me."

"I wouldn't worry about that, Nate. Brett had a very successful drywall business and this year was better than ever. The boys will still have plenty of money. Just tell me what your fees are and I'll see that you're paid."

I thought about the funding for Brett's business and how far that money would have to go for his sons. "I've already been paid, Marv. Thanks though. I'll let Colt know to expect your call."

"Okay. Oh, that's the other line. Take care, Nate."

I stared at the phone for a moment then decided I'd been sitting long enough. I went over to the Brickhouse, got a good workout in, and then talked to Olivia for quite a while. When we were done, I took the small folder she had for me and left.

I was feeling a lot more like myself by that evening so I went to Borderlands for dinner.

False Oath

∽

I'D FINISHED my appetizer and was waiting for my Diablo Chicken when Kenny Kaminski appeared. He was wearing his bulky canvas coat and his face was a little red. "Nate," he said. "I didn't know you were here. No, sit, sit. I was just outside. All this damn freeze and thaw is just destroying my asphalt." He shook my hand and slid into the seat on the other side of the booth. "I am so sorry," he said.

That caught me off guard. "For what?"

"The state championship. That's got to be just killing Tom."

"Oh. Right."

"Well, I for one believe him when he said he didn't know anything about Tyler and you can bet that I'm going to lead the drive for him to keep his job."

"That's not necessary, Kenny."

"Of course it is, Nate! You don't get coaches like Tom every day, no you surely don't. When you do, you have to keep them. Is it true that he called the state himself?"

"It is."

"Sterling, just sterling. You just can't find men with that kind of character in coaching. What a great example for our kids."

"I agree."

He pointed to the state championship team picture on the wall. "That picture's staying right there, let me tell you. They might take it away on paper, but we know those boys won it out there on the field."

"I don't know that Tom would count it either, Kenny."

"Well, I suppose we can just agree to disagree on that. But I'm forgetting myself, congratulations on the verdict!"

"Thanks, Kenny. It was a close thing."

"Now you remember what I said to you at the beginning of

this, I'll pay any part of your fee that Colt can't. The important thing is that Brett's boys are taken care of."

"There's no problem with my fees, Kenny."

Kenny cocked his head. "How did they manage that?"

"I don't delve too deeply into my client's finances."

"Of course not, of course not. But murder trials are expensive, aren't they?"

I shrugged.

"Well, remember, you just let me know if there's any difference that needs to be made up."

"There isn't. Speaking of the trial, though, it had me squirreled away for a few weeks."

"I bet."

"I was sorry I missed Tyler's signing day. It looked like a nice event."

Kenny smiled. "It sure was. Rhonda and your brother were there, all sorts of people. I was just dying to see which place Tyler was going to pick."

I nodded. "I'm sure a lot of people were."

"And when he put on that orange hat? Well, that was quite a sight."

"I imagine so."

"I just wish Brett had been there to see it. That's all he ever wanted for those boys and he worked so damn hard with Tyler to get him there."

I shook my head. "Just the time going to camps alone."

"Exactly. He took that boy everywhere, everywhere. I don't know where he found the energy."

"Tyler said you went once in a while?"

Kenny nodded. "There was one in Texas and one in Louisiana. Those were long hauls and Brett wanted company so we could take shifts driving through the night."

"It takes a team to raise a quarterback."

Kenny hit the table with the palm of his hand. "I like that. It surely does. I was just glad I could help." His face clouded over. "So, what's next with the case, anything?"

"The prosecutor can't appeal so that wraps up Colt's case. I don't know that they're investigating the death anymore."

Kenny's face became hard. "That means whoever did it is going to get away with it?"

I shrugged. "It would be hard to try somebody else after all the evidence the State put on. Seems like built-in reasonable doubt."

Kenny scowled as he shook his head. "That's not right."

"No, it's not."

"My friend deserved better than that."

"Yes, he did."

My Diablo Chicken came. As I thanked the waitress and picked up the sandwich, Kenny stood. "This is on me, by the way," he said.

"No, Kenny. I'll take care of it."

Kenny waved. "Your money is no good here, Nate. My thanks for taking care of Colt." He held out his hand.

As he did it, I took a bite of my Diablo Chicken and the hot sauce oozed all over the back of my hands. "Ah, sorry," I said with a muffled mouthful.

Kenny laughed. "I'll have her bring you more napkins," he said, and did just that as he left.

I ate my Diablo Chicken, taking my time, savoring the heat of the sauce and the cool snap of the pickles. When I was done, I actually sighed and stared at the plate for a moment before I asked the waitress for the bill. She smiled and said it was taken care of as she hustled off to the kitchen. Then I put fifty dollars on the table, took my last look at a few of the best pictures, and left.

62

The following Monday, all of us went to see Megan Dira. Me and Colt, Ronnie and Tyler, and Rhonda and Rob, who were now represented by their own lawyer. I wasn't in there for Rhonda and Rob's meeting. When they walked out of her office, Megan Dira asked if she could speak with me. Just me.

She leafed through papers as I sat. She told me that if what Rhonda and Rob had told her about Steve Mathison was true and if they continued to cooperate, she would hold up her end of the bargain and neither Colt nor Tyler would be the target of her investigation. Then she thanked me for my time and cooperation and encouraged me to call her later if I had any questions. When I told her that neither Rhonda nor Rob knew Jimmy Benoit, she put a manilla folder into a brown file and said that was the same story they'd told her. When I told her that there were pictures on Jimmy Benoit's social media showing him at quarterback camps in Texas and Louisiana last year, she put the brown file onto a shelf behind her desk and nodded. And when I said that Tyler had attended those same camps with his dad, she said that she was aware of that since she'd been investigating this case for quite some time and, if I would excuse her, she had several more meetings yet that morning.

Then I said that a man named Kenny Kaminski had attended the Texas and Louisiana camps with Tyler and Brett. I told her that Kenny Kaminski was an old, old friend of Brett Daniels and that Brett Daniels had been installing drywall on two of Kenny Kaminski's new restaurants in the months before he died. I mentioned that, if the books for Brett's business were to be believed, these two projects were huge and I suggested that it might be worthwhile to look into how much it actually cost to drywall a restaurant these days. Finally, I offered that Kenny ran a cash business, which meant that he had to protect large amounts of cash each night when he left his restaurant, which led me to guess that he had a concealed carry permit to match the concealed carry canvas coat he was always wearing. Then I apologized for taking so much of her time.

Megan Dira stared at me for a good long while. Then she thanked me and said she really did have to get to her next meeting.

I wasn't on the inside for a lot of what happened over the next few months so I can't tell you all of the details. Tiffany Erin brought charges against the boys right away. The penalty for misleading a police officer investigating a crime increases depending on how serious the crime is that they're investigating. As you might imagine, investigating a murder is about as serious as it gets so Colt and Tyler were both charged with felony misleading, which was punishable by up to four years in prison. Ronnie and I argued that their place of residence wasn't a material fact to the investigation, and Megan Dira did step in to say that the boys were cooperating with another investigation but, even with all that, Tiffany Erin believed that lying during a murder investigation had to be punished. Although she was willing to reduce it to a misdemeanor, she insisted that the boys needed to serve time to set an example. They were each sentenced to three days in the Dellville jail, which Ronnie and I thought was pretty good for a felony-level crime Tyler had admitted to on the stand. True to her word, Megan Dira made all of the other crimes of falsification on their various applications go away so that wound up being the last criminal punishment the boys faced from the circumstances surrounding their father's death.

When Tyler reported to jail late that spring, the college he'd committed to play for revoked his scholarship. By the time he got out, Rhonda and Rob, after burning all of their creamsicle orange sports gear, had called all of the coaches at all of the major programs who had shown interest in Tyler, but they all said that it was too late, that all of their scholarships were gone. That was a lie, of course; the fact was that no big institution wanted to take the chance on the bad publicity that would come with picking Tyler up.

A smaller Division II school in northern Michigan decided the gamble was worth it. The school brought Tyler on, and through the first half of their season, Tyler has lit up their league at a record-breaking pace. The school sits at the top of the national polls and Tyler is a candidate for the Harlon Hill trophy, the award that goes to the best player in Division II college football. The thought is that, if he wins it, he'll probably transfer up to the big boys in Division I. I hope he does.

Colt served his three days at the same time as Tyler, then went back to Grand Valley the following fall to continue his studies. It turned out that Brett had left the house to Colt and Tyler. With Tyler busy playing ball, Colt worked with Danny and Marv Lindhoffer to get his dad's estate settled. I know Danny asked Colt a few times if he wanted to sell the house, what with the memories and all, but Colt said he'd hang on to it for now since he and Tyler wanted to get their Michigan residency back and he'd never find cheaper land to hunt. It was a practical, pragmatic decision Brett would have approved of.

Chet, by all accounts, was doing just fine. He remains a very good boy.

After we wrapped things up with Colt, Danny told me that he was done with murder trials. I could tell he was nervous about telling me, but I said it was fine. It seemed to me that between our last two cases, he had enjoyed his exposure to real estate and estate planning law. I said I'd be happy to share an office with someone who was doing general business work like that and would even keep paying that person a salary if he could bring in some matters on his own. Danny was relieved and Jenny was happy and I didn't take it personally.

What unfolded with Kenny Kaminski took longer and I didn't know what was happening until I received a call one day from Megan Dira. The boys had already served their sentences by then so I was concerned when I picked up the phone and said, "Is there a problem, Megan?"

"Good morning to you too, Nate. And no. I just thought you might want to know how some things are progressing."

"Do I?"

"I think you do."

"Okay. Shoot."

"Rhonda Mazur and Rob Preston have played a key role in our investigation of Steve Mathison so I wanted to assure you that there will be no further action against Colt and Tyler on our part."

"I appreciate that. I'll let them know."

"Also, between this investigation and others, I was able to follow the chain from Jimmy Benoit up to an employee at a Michigan university. Both will be prosecuted."

"Congratulations."

"Thank you. More importantly, based on a tip I received

from a certain defense lawyer, I was also able to follow certain financial information down the chain from Jimmy Benoit to a man named Kenneth Kaminski."

"Interesting."

"It was. If we hadn't known where to look, I don't know that we would have found it. But once we did, we turned our forensic accountants loose. Basically, they found a large payment into Kaminski's company traceable to a shell corporation linked to Jimmy Benoit. There were more layers than that but our accountants are very good."

"It sounds like it."

"Then, when we dove into Kaminski's books, we discovered that the amount of money Kaminski was paying Brett Daniels to install drywall in his new restaurants was completely out of proportion to the work being performed."

"I see."

"And we found an interesting pattern to the payments."

"How so?"

"Each time Kaminski paid Daniels for the drywall work, he tacked on a portion of the Benoit money. After four payments, though, the Benoit payment, the extra part, was cut in half so that only seventy-five percent of the Benoit money was ever paid out."

"Your accountants are that good?"

"I wasn't kidding. Any guesses on when that first reduction happened?"

I thought. "I don't know if it would have been before or after."

"Two days before Brett Daniels was killed."

"That *is* interesting." The second arrow, Brett's arrow, embedded in the ground at the foot of the hunting platform was beginning to make more sense.

"It was a smart system. If Brett hadn't been killed, I don't think anyone would have noticed. Along those lines, it turns out that Kaminski was carrying a .38 caliber pistol when we arrested him. He had a permit for it but fortunately we'd been warned about the tactical coat he carried it in."

"That *is* fortunate."

"It made us wonder how our tipster knew."

I sighed. "Your tipster saw a similar coat on a sales rack at an outdoor store and didn't make the connection until much, much later. So much later, that he felt downright stupid."

"He shouldn't. You take the breaks when you get them. Anyway, I discussed the matter with Tiffany Erin. As I'm sure you know, there's no way that we would be able to find the bullet to do a ballistics match."

"I said the same thing at trial."

"And without that definitive proof—a link to the murder weapon or an eyewitness—Ms. Erin believes that she can't prosecute anyone else for Brett Daniels' murder since the trial of your client would create reasonable doubt."

"Also my thought."

"But as you can imagine, paying someone an excess amount for work they're not doing to hide the source of the money amounts to RICO violations, money laundering, and all sorts of other interesting things."

"I imagine so."

"And of course, people who run a cash business can find themselves susceptible to cutting corners on their tax obligations."

"You don't say?"

"Ms. Erin is quite enthusiastic about working with me to assemble those charges."

"I get that impression of her."

"We'll probably have to get our federal counterparts involved, too."

"Only makes sense."

"You might not believe it, but the sentences for all of those state and federal charges can add up to a greater sentence than a murder charge."

"Oh, I believe it."

"Especially if the prosecutor is not inclined to make a deal."

"Or wants to make an example of someone?"

"Exactly. And you know what the craziest part of all this is?"

"I honestly can't imagine, Megan."

"If Mr. Daniels and Kaminski had just waited a year, none of this would even have been necessary."

"What do you mean?"

"The new NIL rules are coming down this summer."

"NIL rules?"

"'Name, Image, and Likeness.' College athletes will be allowed to endorse products directly. A good quarterback like Tyler at a well-known school would be positioned to make plenty of money."

I shook my head. "I guess patience is rare in murderers these days."

"Except the most dangerous ones."

I thought about my own recent case history and decided that sentiment was absolutely true.

"Well, I think that's all," she said.

"That's enough. Thanks for letting me know."

"Oh, and Ms. Erin would never say it, but she would want the boys to know that she's going to get the man who killed their father."

"Thank you."

She hung up. I had a lot to process, but I knew one thing for sure—I would not want Megan Dira and Tiffany Erin hounding me if I had done wrong.

There was one last bit of fallout from Colt's trial and it was resolved on that same day. I worked until seven, made a call, then left. I picked up some beer along the way.

∼

KATE GAVE me a hug as she opened the door. She looked at the beer, smiled, and said, "Not too late. The kids have baseball tomorrow."

"Wouldn't think of it. You joining us?"

"As soon as I get Charlie to bed."

"Excellent."

She didn't have to tell me where he was. I went out to the garage where Tom had his face in the computer.

"Jesus, do you ever stop breaking down film?" I said.

I walked around his desk and peeked. When I saw a Viking swinging an axe at a huge bear, I laughed. "Is that Assassin's Creed Valhalla?"

Tom looked embarrassed. "Don't tell Kate. It just came out."

I smiled, put a beer in his hand, took one myself, and put the rest in the fridge.

I clinked his can and said, "Congratulations on the board vote."

"Thanks."

"Was five to two what you expected?"

"I wasn't sure."

"They had to have realized that you didn't know about Tyler."

"They did. It was actually the War Oath that was the problem. The board was concerned that I didn't know that hazing activity was going on in my program. Some thought it showed a lack of control. When the investigation started, I was pretty sure I was gone."

"What changed their mind?"

"None of the players were hurt. None of them had told anyone about it, even their parents, so no complaints or information was being ignored, and they all agreed that I took a consistent, strong stance against hazing."

"Good."

"They said what tipped the scales, though, was that I called the school superintendent about the hazing and the state athletic association about Tyler's eligibility before the testimony came out at your trial. That convinced them that I didn't know. So they voted to let me stay on."

I raised my beer. "Smart choice."

"Do you know who called me after the vote?"

"Who?"

"The Edwardsburg coach."

"Really?"

Tom nodded. "He said congratulations." Tom broke into a rare grin. "And that he expected me to get our team back to the finals next year so he could beat us straight-up on the field."

I smiled. "Sounds like your kind of coach."

"He is."

We talked about Colt and Tyler then, about what had happened to them but more about their toughness, and about what we hoped their future might hold. We never questioned Tyler's decision to testify for Colt any more than we questioned why ice is cold or why wheels roll; some things just are. I almost told Tom about my call with Megan Dira but then decided that, given Colt's temper, and Tom's, I shouldn't tell anyone anything about Kenny Kaminski until he was locked up for good.

After a little while, I saw Tom getting twitchy, looking at the screen, fiddling with his mouse.

I pointed. "Want to watch some game film until Kate joins us?"

He grinned. "Sure. Which one?"

"I've never really broken down the state championship game with you."

Tom shook his head. "It turns out we shouldn't have been there. How about the state semi-final game the year before?"

"Perfect."

Then he hit the controls and the film of the game where Tom led Carrefour North to its best finish ever began to play.

THE NEXT NATE SHEPHERD BOOK

Just Plea is the next book in the Nate Shepherd Legal Thriller Series. Click here if you'd like to order it.

FREE SHORT STORY AND NEWSLETTER SIGN-UP

There was a time, when Nate Shepherd was a new prosecutor and Mitch Pearson was a young patrol officer, that they almost got along. Almost.

If you sign up for Michael Stagg's newsletter, you'll receive a free copy of *The Evidence,* a short story about the first case Nate Shepherd and Mitch Pearson ever worked on together. You'll also receive information about new releases from Michael Stagg, discounts, and other author news.

Click here to sign up for the Michael Stagg newsletter or go to https://michaelstagg.com/newsletter/

ABOUT THE AUTHOR

Michael Stagg has been a trial lawyer for more than twenty-five years. He has tried cases to juries and he's won and he's lost and he's argued about it in the court of appeals after. He still practices law so he's writing the Nate Shepherd series under a pen name.

Michael and his wife live in the Midwest. Their sons are grown so time that used to be spent at football games and band concerts now goes to writing. He enjoys sports of all sorts, reading, and grilling, with the order depending on the day.

You can contact him on Facebook or at mikestaggbooks@gmail.com.

ALSO BY MICHAEL STAGG

Lethal Defense

True Intent

Blind Conviction

False Oath

Just Plea

Made in the USA
Coppell, TX
06 January 2025